CURSED

A KINGDOMS OF EARTH & AIR NOVEL

KERI ARTHUR

KA PUBLISHING PTY LTD

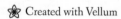 Created with Vellum

With thanks to:

The Lulus
Indigo Chick Designs
Hot Tree Editing
Robyn E.
The lovely ladies from Central Vic Writers
J Caleb Design for the amazing cover.

ONE

I raised my face to the storm-clad sky and let the rain wash the sweat and blood from my skin.

Some of that blood was mine.

Most of it was not.

I drew in a deep breath and savored the scent of pain, anger, and confusion that rode the air. This day—this moment—had been a long time coming, and I intended to enjoy every second of it.

If only because seconds were probably all I had left.

My gaze returned to my opponent. He was broad and thickset, a man-mountain whose long black hair was tied back in an ornate ponytail—a practice common amongst those of the high court. His almond-shaped eyes were dark gold and his skin brown.

He was my brother. My twin.

And heir to the ancient kingdom of Cannamore.

He knelt on the wet concrete, his expression a satisfying mix of horror and surprise, nursing an arm that ended in a bloody stump halfway between his elbow and his wrist.

Even though the blood had already begun to coagulate, the concrete around his knees remained slick and red.

I lowered my bloodied sword. Like the leather practice armor we both wore, it was an archaic choice in an age of guns and other technologies. But tradition stated all males of royal blood must be able to wield such a weapon, and it had become somewhat prestigious amongst the men of the court to be able to do so with precision and grace.

I wasn't male. And I could certainly never claim my sword use to be either graceful or precise. But then, I'd never been properly trained. I'd just learned to survive.

I took a step back, even though I wanted nothing more than to strike while he was down, to separate his head from his body and then claim what was rightfully mine. But I had no desire to court the agony that would hit if I in any way attempted to finish what I'd started. That I was standing here relatively unhurt and pain free was in itself a miracle.

"What have you done?"

His words were little more than a harsh whisper; I doubted anyone else in the yard heard them. As the king's official heir, Vin was always accompanied whenever he left the sanctity of his own quarters, but his entourage stood far enough away that they wouldn't hear our soft exchange. And they wouldn't move—either against me or to help my brother—until he so ordered it.

"I've done what I should have done twelve years ago." My voice was flat but filled with old rage and bitterness. Of course, what I *should* have done twelve years ago was kill the bastard, because I certainly wasn't capable of doing so now. In truth, it was surprising I'd even been able to maim him.

I motioned to the hand that lay between us—a hand that still gripped the rather plain-looking weapon known as the

King's Sword. With a blue-white glass blade, it was unlike any other sword in Cannamore and nigh on indestructible. In fact, there was only one other weapon like it, and neither my brother nor the king knew about it. I very much intended to keep it that way.

"I warned you both that your deception would bring nothing but sorrow and pain."

Even as I said that, jagged blue light flickered across the surface of the embellished silver bracelets adorning my wrists. It was a warning of the pain that would follow if I said anything more about either the sword or the lies that were now bound to it.

But I'd learned long ago just how far I could push the magic of the restraint bracelets. Until the king appeared and ordered me silent, I very much intended to grab this rare chance of unrestricted speech and give free rein to the anger and hatred that had burned in my gut and my heart ever since my brother had been given what was rightfully mine.

"Do you think you're above the will of this land?" I continued. "Do you think the king is?"

Footsteps echoed faintly, a harsh rhythm that spoke of anger and death. I glanced past Vin, but as yet there was no sign of the king or his guards. But he was coming. I could feel the ever-increasing vibration of his fury through the stones under my feet. I needed to hurry.

"The king's mind rots and his strength wanes. The Skaran have become emboldened and harry our forces at both the Karva Pass and Black Water Gateway," I continued. "This wrong *must* be righted if Cannamore is to maintain its freedom, and you both know it."

The light in Vin's eyes was murderous. "You're a *woman*."

And no woman had ever sat on the glass throne or ruled these lands.

But that was not what was written in the ancient text etched into the wall above the throne in the Hall of Kings. *Whomsoever draws the sword from the ancient seat of this land shall rule it, and they shall bring peace and prosperity to its people.*

For nearly a thousand years, it had been the firstborn son of every Cannamore king who'd drawn the sword, and the land and her people had indeed prospered.

Vin was firstborn, but it had not been his hand that had freed the blade from the glass throne.

It had been mine.

As a reward, I got not a kingdom, but rather a prison in the form of two beautiful but very magical bracelets.

"You will pay for this," Vin said. "Pay with your life."

I raised my eyebrows. "And how do you plan to do that, brother, given you fear the curse even more than you fear me taking back what *you* have stolen?"

His gaze narrowed, but whatever piece of poison he was about to spit died as the gates to the practice yards were flung open, and the king and his entourage stormed in.

For the briefest of moments, the spark of my defiance trembled and died. Like Vin, he was a big man with an even bigger temper. Years of anger and deceit might now be taking a toll on the inner workings of his body and mind, but outwardly, he hadn't changed. And while his physical strength might not be what it once was, none but those closest to him were aware of that.

I could certainly testify to the fact that his fists were still very dangerous.

Of course, there'd always been an edge of restraint in even the worst of his actions. But not, as Vin had so scathingly noted, because I was a woman. Rather, it was due to nothing more than the lightning bolt port-wine stain that decorated the lower half of my spine. It was the mark of a god and had been borne in the past by both our greatest warriors and by those who'd come close to utterly destroying this land.

It was both my curse and my savior.

The only reason I still lived.

Why he hadn't exercised his kingly right to offer me in treaty to the rulers of one of Cannamore's territories—or even one of her trading partners—I couldn't really say. But I rather suspected my brother had some hand in me remaining in this wretched place—though not because we were twins or in any way close.

I think he feared that if I were to become the queen or consort to the ruler of another territory or land, I might very well use my influence to start a war and reclaim what had been taken from me.

And I certainly couldn't deny it would be a rather sweet temptation.

The black cloud of fury that was the king—a man I'd stopped calling my father the day he'd not only denied me what was rightfully mine but also locked me into the hell of utter obedience via the bracelets—halted to one side of my brother. I stiffened my spine but knew such courage wouldn't last long. It never did.

His gaze swept Vin and then moved to the severed hand. After a moment, he dismissed my brother's entourage, ordered Vin—and his hand—to be taken to the court healers and medics, and then finally turned his attention to me.

"This time you have gone too far."

His voice, like his golden eyes, held none of the fury I could taste in the air or feel through the stones. The more sensible part of me quailed; fists I could handle, but this stillness was something I'd not seen before and, I suspected, was infinitely more dangerous than his blows ever could be.

"It was not my idea to practice with full blades," I said. "He's lucky all I removed was his hand."

Heat flared in the bracelets, a warning pulse of impending doom if I didn't watch my words. But I had no doubt that even if I *did*, doom would still arrive.

"I have been patient with you," he continued, as if I hadn't spoken. "I have given you the upbringing that befitted your station—"

"Befitted my station?" I broke in furiously. "I'm your *heir*—"

"Quiet," he said calmly. "You will say no more. And release that sword."

I did. I had no other choice. The minute I disobeyed, the minute I tried to say anything else after such an order, the bracelets would flare to life and burn the words from my mouth and my brain. And the near-vegetative state I'd lapsed into for several hours after my first—and only—attempt to do so was not an experience I ever wanted to repeat.

"You are a curse on our bloodline, Nyx. You bear the brand of Lokain, the god of war and the destroyer of houses, and you are a threat to both this house and to Cannamore itself. I should have banished you at birth as the priests begged me to."

Then why didn't you? I wanted to ask, even though I knew the answer. Mom had been one of the few able to manipulate my father's wishes to her own advantage, and I had no doubt it was through her strength and determination that I not only survived but had been educated in a manner befitting a princess of the royal line.

All that had ended on the day she died—which had been precisely one hour *after* I'd drawn the sword from the throne. According to the king, she'd taken her life to avoid the shame of a daughter who'd so flouted tradition and expectation. Whether that was true or not, I'd never really know, but her death was a weight I would bear through eternity.

And yet, at the same time, my actions had come not from rebelliousness, but rather the belief *she'd* instilled in me that—marked by the god or not—I was every bit as worthy and capable as my brother.

A point I'd proven by claiming the King's Sword.

I continued to meet his gaze, defiant to the last even if my insides quaked. The figurative axe didn't fall. Not immediately. Tension wound through me, though I knew it would only make the pain that was still to come far worse.

"You will scream, my child," he continued remotely. "As you have never screamed before. And if you beg your god hard enough, for long enough, then perhaps he will grant you death. And if he does not... I will find a way to be rid of you. Permanently. *That* I promise. Now burn, child. Burn."

With that simple command, he set the bracelets alight. But this was no ordinary fire—it was one born of magic and was as incandescent and powerful as the earth itself. It tore through every muscle, every cell, until it felt as if all the fibers of my being were becoming nothing more than molten ash.

I did scream.

Screamed until my throat was raw, until my vocal cords ruptured and my voice gave out.

And then I screamed on in silence.

But never once did I beg.

TWO

I have no idea how long it took to regain full consciousness. It could have been hours or it could have been days. I only know that I fought it with every ounce of strength I had left.

But as much as some part of me wanted to simply give up and slip away, I was nothing if not stubborn. There was absolutely no way I would give either the king or my brother the satisfaction of finally seeing me dead.

I opened my eyes, only to have utter darkness greet me.

The fear that I'd been blinded surged but just as quickly subsided as I caught a glimmer of brightness from beyond the barred window high above me. A star. It was dark because it was *night*.

The relief that hit was so fierce that tears stung my eyes and trickled down my cheeks. I didn't wipe them away. I couldn't. Not immediately. Every part of me felt weak and washed out, to the point where even breathing hurt.

That I was no longer in my castle quarters was obvious. Not just because of the bars on that small window, but also because of the rough straw scratching my spine and the cold caress of sea air against my skin. It didn't take much brainpower to realize where I was as there was only one place in Divona—Cannamore's capital and home of the glass throne—where the "accommodation" was so austere and the waves so close. I'd been thrown into the cells of the eighth tower. Or, as it was more commonly known, the Hangman's Keep. In centuries long past, it had been in this place where those who'd been sentenced to death by rope were held the night before their execution. And while hanging might have been banned long ago, it wasn't like anyone would or could gainsay the king if he ordered it done.

He wouldn't, though. I bore Lokain's mark, and he could neither kill me by his hand *or* by his order. The god of war didn't take kindly to those who shed the blood of his favorites beyond the boundaries of battle, and his retribution—in the form of the destruction of any who so dared—was the stuff of legends. *That* was the sole reason behind me being ordered into the training yards with Vin. They'd hoped to take my life in battle—even if only in practice—and avoid the god's fury.

They should have known I would not go down without a fight. I'd not only survived that very first day but every day since, and while my fighting style was far from pretty, I'd become proficient enough to hold my own against all comers.

But to win—and sever Vin's arm in the process....

The ashes of true fear stirred. The king might not kill me outright, but it was very possible he'd leave me to rot in this place. Or maybe even sell me into slavery. While it, like hanging, might long be banned in Cannamore, the trade ships often brought tales of fiery lands with less-refined ideals.

I took a deep breath in an effort to remain calm and, in that moment, realized something else.

I was not alone in this cell.

The raw smell of unwashed masculinity stung the air, but from where I lay, I couldn't see him. Nor could I hear the soft whisper of breath. But he was watching me—judging me. I might not be able to see him, but that instinctive part within—the same part that had finally broken through the restrictions of the bracelets and given me the strength to harm Vin—could sense it.

I did a quick mental check of the weakness and the hurt that assailed every part of my body. None of it spoke of violation. Whoever this man was, he hadn't yet touched me.

That didn't mean he *wouldn't*.

I thrust my fingers down into the straw—straw that felt as foul as the stranger smelled—until I met stone. It might be cold and hard, but it held a pulse few in Divona would hear. That pulse was angry.

Deeply, murderously angry.

I'd only felt such fury twice before—once when the king had denied my claim to the throne and set these bracelets on me, and the other a year later when, before the full assembly, he'd ordered Vin to draw the sword from a replica throne—a throne that had been made in secret and which only a handful of the king's most trusted staff knew about.

That was not only the day the king's strength had began to wane, but also the day the earth magic—a magic that countless numbers of Cannamore rulers had used to keep these lands whole and free—had stopped answering his call.

Whether it still answered Vin's I couldn't say. I knew he was aware of it, just as I was. Knew that he, like I, had at the age of fifteen undertaken the initiation ceremony to bind our energy to the earth, a process that stopped accidental or uncontrolled usage. But I had no idea if these days he could mold earth, stone, or metal to his will, or draw on the earth's energy as a weapon. I doubted it, if only because he wasn't known for his self-control; curse or not, he *would* have lashed out with that power if it had been his to call. Of course, I'd spent many a long year hoping he *could* at least hear the earth's voice, and that she endlessly vented her fury over him taking what was mine.

Not that the earth could actually talk. Rather, it was the souls of all those who'd come before us—not just past kings, but earth witches who could hear and control the earth. It's said that on death, such souls became a part of the collective consciousness that inhabits the deep recesses of the ground. It's these voices that offer wisdom, opinions, and, sometimes, even rebukes to the next generation of those born with the ability to hear and control.

I'd heard them once, but they had long since fallen silent.

I took a deep breath and pushed upright. Every part of my body protested the movement, but I bit my lip against the scream that stormed my burning throat and fought on. I might be naked and weak, but I wasn't about to face whatever might come lying down.

The effort left my head spinning and my body bathed in sweat. I ignored it as best I could, and pushed back on my butt until my spine pressed against the wall. The surface was cold and slimy, but it had little to do with the chill that raced across my skin. I dragged my knees closer to my chest and wrapped my arms around them. It made me feel less exposed, if nothing else.

"If I wanted to fuck you, Princess, I would have done so by now," he said. "It's not as if you could have in any way resisted me."

His voice was deep, smooth, and held the slightest hint of brogue that spoke of the highland tribes inhabiting the wilder regions of the Westal Ranges.

"Such restraint from a highlander is beyond imagining." The words came out as little more than a harsh rasp, but it was a serious gift to have *any* vocal ability left. "Has our dear king perhaps robbed you of the capacity to plunder?"

He laughed, a sharp sound devoid of warmth. "Indeed he has not. But we men of Westal have an innate desire to do the exact opposite of what the king obviously wants, so your maidenhood remains intact."

"My maidenhood was lost *long* ago."

Sexual naivety had *never* been valued here in Cannamore's court. Which was why at the age of fifteen—the legal age of consent—I'd undergone not only the Earth initiation but also the Ceremony of Eisha. Within the Golden Temple, and under the guidance of the goddess's priests and priestesses, I'd been introduced to sensuality and the art of both giving and obtaining pleasure.

Of course, when I'd drawn the sword only a few weeks later, the king had used that knowledge to the full, regularly offering my services to emissaries from the territories and neighboring courts—even occasionally to traders from overseas lands such as Gallion and the smiths of Salysis—in order to gain a negotiating advantage.

And it wasn't like I could gainsay him. Not with these bracelets on.

I scrubbed a hand across gritty eyes and then studied the darkness to my right. My cellmate was little more than a shadow. A thickset, wild-haired, foul-smelling shadow.

Which was odd. My eyes should have adjusted to the darkness by now, and *that* meant there was something else at play here, even if I had no sense of magic being used.

"What brings a man from Westal to a place like this?"

The bitter taste of blood began to taint my saliva. I swallowed heavily, but it did little to ease the heated soreness in my throat. I probably shouldn't be speaking, but I had little other choice. Not if I wanted to understand the situation and survive.

"I not only had the temerity to fuck the wrong person, but I got into a fight about it afterward—a fight I won." His voice held little emotion—he might as well have been speaking about the weather. "What brings a princess?"

"Removing the hand of the king's heir."

"Did you now?" Despite the darkness, I felt his gaze skim me, but its touch was cold. Disparaging. "Forgive my disbelief, but you are half your brother's size—how did you manage such a feat?"

"I may be half his size, but I'm still a daughter of the ancient Bel-Hannon line of kings. The Sifft heritage runs true in us."

"Meaning you can attain wildcat form at will?" He sounded amused rather than impressed by the thought.

"No."

Which in itself was nothing but the truth. Centuries of interbreeding with other races *had* erased the ability to shift into wildcat form from the blood of those who could claim Sifft heritage. But many did at least get some of their other capabilities—be it greater strength, extraordinary night vision, sharper senses, some degree of telepathy with others of our kind, a high tolerance of pain, or the ability to heal faster than normal.

Both Vin and I had inherited *all* the DNA adaptions. It was the reason Vin hadn't bled out in the practice yard, and why—if the medics successfully reconnected his hand—its viability and strength would be reinstated.

"But size isn't always an advantage," I continued. "Especially if your opponent is light on their feet and therefore has speed on their side."

His teeth flashed, white in the darkness. I wasn't sure if it was a smile or a snarl.

"That is indeed true." He paused. "Is it not unusual for the females of the Bel-Hannon line to be taught the art of the sword?"

"Yes." And like so many other actions that had been forced on me since the bracelets had locked me into the prison of the king's bidding, I'd had no choice. "Although no one would ever call my use of it art."

"Is that why you bear so many scars?"

If he could see the scars in this darkness, he had better sight than me. "Yes."

"And are not such things considered distasteful to those of this court?"

"Again, yes." Especially when they weren't just on my body but also my face. It might be only one, but it was a somewhat ragged line that stretched from my left temple to my cheek. I'd been damned lucky not to lose my eye in that particular fight.

But disfigurement and distaste was the whole point of the scars—they made me the object of much scorn but also the recipient of much curiosity.

And while it might not be unusual to see Cannamore's women holding positions in the military—be it as a ground force fighter or as a divisional leader—to my knowledge, I was the first highborn female to ever pick up a weapon. Of course, there *were* territories in which it was commonplace —the Mauvaissians, for instance, had a long history of fighting female queens. In fact, their leaders were chosen in a duel to the death, and a woman known as the Red Queen currently ruled there. I knew from experience she was as fierce and as strong as any of the men who'd shared my bed.

The highlander continued to study me, and it rather felt like he was determining what he should do with me—whether he should use or maybe even kill me.

The king had undoubtedly tossed me here in the hope that he would do the latter. And given the highlanders had neither forgotten nor forgiven the forcible annexing of the Westal Mountains into the Cannamore territories—even if it *had* happened well over a thousand years ago—the fact that I still breathed was rather surprising. Especially as, even today, the wise didn't dare transgress into Westal region without prior approval, as the highlanders' response was swift and very often brutal.

That he was even in this city was something of a puzzle. Divona, with its soaring stone and steel castle, the beautiful but austere metal constructs of many of its residences, and wide but treeless streets, was not a city in which mountain men such as he would ever be comfortable. Indeed, I could only remember seeing one emissary from the Westal region in the last twelve years, and the only reason I remembered *him* was because he'd politely refused the offer of my services.

"Does the fact you're here mean you're going to be shipped to the Karva Pass?" I asked.

Part of the treaty conditions with the Mauvaissians was providing a two-hundred-and-fifty-strong fighting force on a six-month rotating basis. The Mauvaissians were the fiercest of fighters, but they were also nomadic. While they no more wanted the Skaran in their lands than we did, staying bound to one place for too long was not in their nature.

Of course, the king honored the agreement in numbers

but not intent. Instead of sending two hundred and fifty trained soldiers, he offered criminals the choice of doing time at the border and then having the rest of their sentence terminated.

It was rather unusual for those who'd chosen border service to be kept here in the eighth tower, however. They were normally taken to a secure area in the military district and given some basic training.

The highlander shrugged, the movement nonchalant. "Who knows? I rather suspect we've put your father in a somewhat difficult position."

I frowned. "We? Unless you've an invisible friend, we're alone in this cell."

His teeth flashed again. "Indeed we are. My brother rots in a cell one floor down. Apparently we were making too much noise, so they separated us."

"So who did you and your brother seduce and then fight?"

My voice was harsher than it had been only moments ago, and that band of red-hot iron was growing tighter. I had no doubt a sensible person would have stopped talking, but, unfortunately, no one had ever ascribed *that* particular quality to me.

"If I tell all my secrets now, what will we have to discuss in the long nights to come?"

What indeed. "Is there water here?"

"In the hangman's cells?" He laughed again. "Food comes but once a day—if we're lucky—and is accompanied by a small flask that is removed along with the bowl ten minutes later. A last feast for the damned, I'm afraid, is nothing but a myth."

I grunted. Though my last meal had been a very long time ago, I wasn't really hungry. Perhaps it was the uncertainty of the situation, or perhaps it was merely a bit of self-preservation kicking in. After all, it wasn't practical to hunger for something I wasn't likely to get.

And maybe if I'd applied *that* reasoning to the heritage stolen from me, I would not now be wearing restraint bracelets or be locked in a cell with a Wildman.

"What fate do you think your father intends you, Princess?"

"I dare say only the gods could tell me that, and they haven't talked to me of late."

"A statement that suggests you and they have had conversations in the past."

"Doesn't everyone in need ask for help from their god of choice?" A somewhat bitter smile touched my lips. "Of course, the conversations do tend to be rather one-sided."

"That's because any god or goddess worth their salt would have forsaken this wretched city long ago."

"In that, I believe you're right."

In fact, I rather suspected the gods had fled around the same time as the earth magic. But the people of Cannamore —a province rich with both fertile pastoral lands and mineral wealth—didn't seem to have noticed or cared. After long years of peace, her people had grown fat and lazy. It was only thanks to forced alliances—such as the one with the Westal Wildmen—that we hadn't yet been invaded. But not only was there great restlessness along those borders of late, some of the old alliances were under pressure. Right now, the king was holding everything together; he might be a fading force, but few were aware of that, and his grip on these lands was still tight.

But my brother?

His arrogance was more likely to alienate than bind.

Of course, there was no saying *I* would have coped any

better given the chance. The king wasn't alone in his thinking that no woman would ever sit on the glass throne.

After a moment, I asked, "How long have you been in this place?"

"Three weeks, near as I can figure." It was dispassionately said, and yet I could taste the anger in him. Blue ice glittered briefly in the shadows that still surrounded him. "I will have my revenge for this treatment of us, of that you should have no doubt."

"A promise I'll hold you to if you get out of here and I don't, highlander."

"There's a whole lot of repressed fury evident in that simple statement, Princess. It would be easy to think you hate your father."

"Are all Wildmen as perceptive as you?" I ground out. "Or is it just your special—"

My voice died before I could finish. Completely and utterly. I couldn't even dredge up a squeak. I swallowed heavily, trying to ease the raw burn, but it didn't help. Nothing would, I suspected, except utter silence on my part. While my vocal cords *would* heal, I still had to give them time.

"Talent?" he finished for me. "Oh, I have plenty of those, dear woman, as you'll undoubtedly find out as the days and nights drag on."

If *that* was a threat, then it was at least a pleasantly said one. A vast improvement over the many Vin had flung my way over the years.

I closed my eyes and tried to rest. The highlander made no further attempt at conversation, but he continued to watch me. I gained a sudden sympathy for caged animals.

The night crept by, but dawn brought no relief in the form of food or water. Wan beams of light speared into the cell, finally revealing not only its tiny dimensions but also my companion.

He was a big man—perhaps even as big as my brother—with shaggy, matted brown hair, a thick if tangled brown beard, and eyes that were as blue as the summer skies but as cold as the deepest winter night. He was bare-chested and wearing a ragged kilt so stained with dirt and gods knew what else it was impossible to tell which of the five tribes he might have come from. He wore no boots, and the soles of his feet were thick and calloused, suggesting that even before he'd been thrown into this cell, he'd spent a lot of his time barefoot.

"Like what you see?" The amusement in his tone touched neither his expression nor his eyes.

I shrugged. He certainly wasn't the worst specimen of manhood ever placed in front of me, but he *was* the foulest smelling. If there was one good thing to be said about the many courtiers and emissaries who'd graced my bed over the years, it was that they were all fastidious when it came to their appearance and personal hygiene.

"I'll take that as a yes." The amusement in his tone was deeper, but his gaze remained coldly accessing. "I've been thinking, Princess—"

"Always dangerous—" I managed to say before my throat shut down again.

"Considering it was *not* thinking that got my brother and me into this mess, I'll respectfully disagree." He paused. "What would you do to get out of this cell?"

Whatever I needed to, I wanted to say, but the words remained locked inside. I raised an eyebrow in silent question.

"If that freedom also included getting away from both

this city and your father," he continued, "what price would you pay?"

I hesitated. While I had no desire to either spend the rest of my days in this cell or to suffer whatever new indignity the king and my sibling might currently be planning, this man was an unknown. I certainly had no desire to step from one disastrous situation into another.

"Why?" I croaked.

He raised an eyebrow. "This is my game, Princess. Answer the question."

"Would depend—" I swallowed against the growing bitterness of blood. I really had to stop talking soon.

"On remuneration?" He finished for me.

I nodded.

"What if the price was a kingdom? Or the life of everyone you care about?"

I'd already lost my kingdom and, since my mother's suicide, had no champions within the high court. But there were those within the servant class who, while not exactly friends, shouldn't pay a price for either my freedom *or* my revenge.

"Would depend," I managed. "Why ask?"

"Because the winds of change whisper to me this morning, and she has bloodshed on her mind. I'm in the mood to appease her."

I raised my eyebrows. While the energy of the earth, air, and sun had been harnessed to power everything from transport systems to lighting, the use of wind as a *weapon* was a gift very few in Cannamore could claim. There was a smattering of weather witches who were in constant demand to control our oft-unpredictable climate, especially during cropping season. But the ability to commune with the wind—to not only hear her whispers of what happens and her warnings of the future but to draw down on her fury and use it against others—was rare.

I *had* heard rumors of Westal mages who could do both, but I'd never really believed it. After all, if such mages *did* exist, surely the Westal Ranges would have retained their independence rather than being annexed into Cannamore.

Besides, if this man was a mage, then how had he come to be here? And why wouldn't he have used his mistress to escape this place?

I opened my mouth to ask, and then closed it again. As much as I might want to question him, if I wanted to keep some semblance of voice, I *had* to rest my vocal cords as much as possible. I made a motion for him to go on.

"There is really nothing more to say." He raised a grimy hand and rather elegantly motioned to the cell around us. "Either you stay here, or you pay the price for your freedom."

Without knowing what the cost? I didn't want to die in this place—or any other, for that matter—but accepting such an offer without knowing either the details or even anything of the man making it would be nothing short of insane.

"Are you planning an escape?" I asked hoarsely.

"No." His eyes glittered with a light that oddly spoke of wind and rain and things no one such as I could see or hear. "I'm about to be released."

"That's not what you implied—"

"The wind wasn't speaking to me last night. She is now." That odd light faded from his eyes, but his gaze remained compelling. "Think on it, Princess, and let me know. In the meantime, I suggest you stop talking."

I scowled at him, and he laughed. It was a sound as harsh as my voice and one that held little merriment. "You'll

21

have to do better than that if you want to intimidate me. I've seen fiercer looks on groaner piglets."

Groaner was the inappropriate nickname of the large and rather savage husked black boars that had once roamed freely across the Sundar flatlands but these days—thanks to their being hunted to near extinction—were generally only found near the Kannel Mountains.

I leaned my head back against the stone and watched the flickering rays of sunlight. Time crept by. Insects crawled across my legs, vermin rustled through the straw, and the distant sounds of everyday life beyond our prison drifted in through the window high above. The Hangman's Keep was one of sixteen towers that had once protected Old Divona. It teetered on a finger of land that thrust out into what was now known as Belrain Bay, which had formed after the massive landslip that had happened over a thousand years ago. It had resulted in not only a huge chunk of Cannamore's coastline breaking away but had also created the ring of islands that now helped protect the two main ports from sea attack. To this day, no one knew what lay behind the massive line of destruction, though some journals from that time had noted the epicenter seemed to be far offshore—from the lands we now knew as Gallion—and that it wasn't a tremor, but rather the earth being drained of so much energy that it could no longer hold its substance.

New Divona, born after much of the old city had ended up at the bottom of the newly created bay, was perched high on the cliff's edge and was not only the home of the king, but where the high council—which consisted of the ruling lords and ladies of the twelve lands that made up the whole that was Cannamore—met. The rest of the city was divided into distinct districts that swept down the hill toward the Merrigold River. The first district was the military zone, the second belonged to the merchants, trades, and the danseuse, and the final to the lower classes—servants and the like. Eisha's golden temples weren't situated within the city, but rather on the largest of the islands that had broken away from the mainland. In the best of my dreams, I found myself back there, taking my place amongst the red-clad priests and priestesses, welcoming initiates and teaching them the pleasures of life.

But it was a dream I would never claim in reality. I might not know what path the god of war intended for me, but I doubted it involved such happiness or peace. Not when I bore his mark.

As the afternoon sunshine faded and the chill of early evening crept into the air, a door slammed and footsteps echoed through the gathering shadows, drawing ever nearer.

"It seems we have visitors," the highlander noted.

"It could be a food delivery."

"That's not the steps of our keepers, but rather someone more refined."

Meaning the king, perhaps. Even if Vin *had* recovered enough to come here, he'd have considered the smell and dour conditions an assault on his sensibilities.

As the steps grew closer, I resisted the instinctive urge to straighten and simply kept my arms locked around my knees. Electronic beeps ran across the silence as someone accessed the lock pad, and then the door slid to one side and the king stepped into the cell.

Hate rose in a wave so thick and fierce that it was all I could do to stop myself from rising up and striking the bastard. My muscles quivered with energy, but I tightened my grip on my knees and kept still. It wasn't as if I'd get anywhere near him.

His gaze swept from the highlander to me and a cold

smile touched his lips. "I do hope you've been suitably accommodating to our guest, Nyx. I'd hate for him to return home with tales of our inhospitality."

I didn't say anything. I wasn't about to waste precious words on the man.

"Her hospitality is not in question," the highlander growled. "Yours, dear Rainer, shall be discussed long in the war rooms of my people."

I glanced sharply at him. The only people who dared use the king's first name were the rulers of the other eleven territories—but how could he be a ruler and yet be in here? Such an action could very well lead to unrest and with raiders testing our borders, that was surely the last thing my father would want.

"Come now, Donal, you can hardly waltz into Divona, seduce the wife of a high-ranking lord, subsequently beat said lord to a pulp when he confronts you on the matter, and expect to walk away without penalty."

"I was not the initiator of that seduction." Only the slightest edge in the highlander's voice gave away the anger I sensed in him. "And perhaps if Lord Brannon tried harder to satisfy his lady, she would not seek it elsewhere."

Cool amusement briefly flirted with the king's lips but, as ever, failed to touch his eyes. "Be that as it may, you and your brother maimed Lord Brannon and killed seven of his men. That is not something I can simply brush away."

Donal didn't reply, but contempt joined the anger.

"Anyway," the king continued. "I have finally reached an agreement that both your father and Lord Brannon can live with. In return for your brother's freedom, you shall do six months service at the Mauvaisse border."

"My father would not agree to such a thing," Donal

replied evenly. "He would not risk the life of one son to save the other."

"He would if the only other choice was the loss of both."

"Are you insane?" I ground out. "Why would you even contemplate such a—"

"Quiet," the king said, without even bothering to look at me.

Fury rose, but it was impotent in the face of his order. All I could do was clench my fingers and dream of a day when it would not be so.

He half turned and clicked his fingers. The man who immediately stepped into the cell was tall and thin and wore the blue uniform of a communicator—a rare group of people who had the ability to speak mind to mind, and who were used in every court when instant communication was required. The silver circlet around his head mechanically enhanced the range of his ability, but it came at the cost of slowly frying his brain. Communicators rarely lived past the age of forty, but both they and their families were so well compensated that few ever walked away from the position.

"Contact Lord O'Raen's communicator, Huron."

The O'Raens held the bleak lands to the east of the Black Water Gateway, which included much of the Black Mountains themselves. They were also one of the biggest and most powerful tribes in the entire Westal region, so it was a dangerous step to be alienating them in this way.

The communicator closed his eyes and, after a moment, the circlet began to shine.

"Alja, I am in the company of your younger son," my father said. "Please proceed."

The circlet shone brighter, its cool blue light banishing the shadows as the communicator dutifully—but silently—relayed the message.

After a few seconds, the reply came—one the communicator gave voice to.

"I have reluctantly agreed to the king's terms," he said, in a tone not dissimilar to Donal's, "and have given my word that you will honor them. The situation as it now stands is completely unacceptable. The wind continues to agree that good shall come of this. Just survive, Donal, no matter what."

Survive no matter what. It was an odd thing to say. The Skaran might be hazing our border forces, but they'd yet to mount a full attack and—from the snippets I'd gleaned from the various emissaries—there was no sign of a military buildup to suggest *that* was their immediate plan.

As the circlet's power died and the communicator opened his eyes, the king looked at Donal and said, "Do you agree to the terms set?"

"My father has given his word. I have no other choice but to honor it." The light in Donal's eyes was hard—cold—and yet oddly satisfied. It made me suspect this outcome was not unexpected. That it was, perhaps, even desired. "I wish to see my brother before I am sent to Mauvaisse, however."

"That can be arranged."

"And I wish to take the woman with me to the border."

Surprise and instant denial leapt to my lips, but I clamped down on both and met Donal's gaze. He raised an eyebrow, challenging me.

The time of choosing had come.

The king glanced my way, amusement once more evident. "What say you to that, daughter?"

"I say the gods have taken whatever sanity either of you might have had."

"A simple yes or no, Nyx."

I continued to stare at Donal, weighing the king's stated desire to be rid of me against the unknown that was the highlander. When it came down to it, it wasn't a really hard decision.

"No," I said.

The king laughed and clapped Donal on the shoulder. "So be it then. She is yours."

I couldn't help the somewhat bitter smile that briefly touched my lips. Sometimes the king was all too predictable.

His gaze returned to mine. "You will obey Donal as you have obeyed me. Once the two of you are beyond the walls of this city, I cede my rights and my power to his will and his word."

As he spoke, light flared across the bracelets, a flash of blue that briefly lit the shadowed confines of the cell. Donal's gaze narrowed, but he didn't say anything.

"The relief squad leaves for Karva Fortress on the morn. You'll both join them." The king paused, his gaze sweeping Donal somewhat critically. "But not before we clean you up, I think. You, highlander, reek."

Donal snorted—a sound of contempt if ever I'd heard one. "Sorry to offend your sensibilities, Rainer, but bathing facilities were a little hard to come by in this cesspit."

"Ruffians are not generally given such comforts." He stepped to one side of the door. "Morton, Banks, escort the two of them to the princess's quarters. If the highlander makes any attempt to escape, shoot him."

"And my brother?" Donal said. "When do I get to see him?"

"Before you both depart tomorrow."

Donal nodded. "I would ask one more thing, Rainer."

"You push your luck, highlander."

Another of those uncaring smiles touched Donal's lips. "A blanket for the princess. It is unseemly for royalty to be paraded naked through the streets."

The king raised an eyebrow and looked at me. I returned his gaze evenly. We both knew what the answer to Donal's request would be, so I had no idea why he was even pretending to consider it.

After a few seconds, amusement twitched at his lips and he said, "No."

"Well, then." Donal began unlashing the waist bindings on his kilt. For one horrible moment, I thought he was going to offer me the wretched thing, but he simply dropped it to the straw and added, "What is good for one is good for the other."

The king laughed. "This is *one* procession that is certainly going to attract attention."

He stepped back and waved Donal forward. The highlander glanced at me. "Are you coming willingly, or shall I throw you over my shoulder?"

"Try it," I growled, "and my foot will bury itself in your balls."

Amusement creased the corners of his blue eyes. "I do so like a challenge, Princess. Perhaps we should see who is faster implementing their threat."

I scrambled to my feet. Walking naked through the streets of Divona would be bad enough, but at least I wasn't alone in that—and he, with his size and muscular if filthy body, would draw far more attention than me. But *that* would certainly change if I were thrown over his shoulder like so much naked rubbish.

The court considered me enough of a joke. I didn't need to add anything else to it.

I followed him out into the corridor, the soft sounds of

my footfalls lost not only to the noise being made by the king and his entourage but also the fury that continued to beat through the cold stone under my feet. I wondered if the king felt it. Wondered if he even cared.

The front guard paused to code open the final door and then led us out into the old tower's courtyard. This place had once housed the soldiers whose job it was to defend a one-mile portion of the wall. That wall—like much of the eastern side of the tower—was long gone, but the halls, kitchen, and the western portion of the barracks still remained, though the latter was only used when prisoners were being housed within the tower. The rest of the time the place belonged to spiders, vermin, and seabirds.

Three short-range carriages were waiting in the court-yard. Unlike many other passenger and haulage vehicles—which used a form of electromagnetic repulsion technology to move once beyond city limits—these were powered by the sun. All three bore the sword and cat crest of the Bel-Hannon kings, but one was far more ornate. The king was not one to forgo his comforts, even if only for the few minutes it would have taken to get from the castle to here.

Our guard led us away from the vehicles and toward the tower's exit on the far side of the courtyard. Though the gate was open, there was little evidence of movement or noise coming from the roadway beyond. Which wasn't surprising given this tower—positioned as it was on a crum-bling finger of rock that jutted out into violent seas—was no longer used defensively. Newer towers had been built on more stable ground along the coastline, forming a new defense system that combined neatly with the towers that already lined the length of the Merrigold River. These were all manned twenty-four seven even though it had been a long time since our borders had been seriously tested. Not since the Mauvaissens had been annexed into Cannamore, in fact.

A gentle breeze stirred around me, thick with the raw saltiness of the sea. I drew it in deeply, trying to erase the scent of fouled straw and unwashed man from my nostrils. It didn't help with the latter, but mainly because Donal walked so close that our arms occasionally brushed.

I wondered if it was a deliberate reminder that I now belonged to him. Wondered if sex on order was to be part of the price of freedom.

My lips twisted. After twelve years of being so used, I should be well resigned to such a fate. But I wasn't, and never would be. My time in the temple might have been years ago now, but it had given me not only Eisha's gift of sexual empowerment but also the belief in freedom of choice. That every man and every woman had the right to desire and to love whomsoever they pleased, however they pleased, as long as it was consensual.

It was that *last* part that had run like poison through my veins in the many long nights I'd faced since the bracelets had been placed on me.

One day, I would find a way out of them.

One day, I would have my revenge.

On the king, on my brother, and on all the men and women who had so ill-used me over the years.

Of course, the latter was hardly practical given I'd be all but declaring war on ten of the twelve ruling families, but it was nevertheless a dream that had sustained me through the worst of my nights.

Behind us, the carriages powered up, the soft hum of their engines almost lost in the angrier cry of the crashing waves.

"You're seriously going through with this madness?" the king said. "And all for the sake of one worthless woman."

"It is not my madness." Donal neither stopped nor glanced back at the king. "And that woman is a princess and should be treated as such."

My gaze shot toward his, but all I saw was dry amusement. He was baiting the king; the words themselves meant little.

"Care to wager that you won't feel the same after a few weeks spent in her company?" the king said. "She's cursed, Donal, and no good will ever come of her or from her."

"I am not the one who brings ill-fortune to Cannamore," I said. "Your lies—"

"I did not ask for your opinion, Nyx," he cut in, "so be silent."

I clenched my fists, but the fury that burned within remained impotent. Silent.

Donal stopped and turned around. I had no choice but to do the same, given our guards also stopped.

"What lies does she speak of, Rainer?"

The king's smile was as cool as his expression. "Did you not hear me? Her tongue is as poisonous as her mind, but I'm more than willing to take her off your hands if you've changed your mind—"

"Oh, you can be sure I've not changed my mind." *About anything.* He didn't say that last bit out loud, but the words seemed to hover in the air regardless, holding a deep and very dark threat.

"Good." The king's golden gaze was cold when it came to mine. "But you should be aware that she's no longer welcome here. If you ever return to Divona, she's not to accompany you."

"Or what?" Donal replied contemptuously. "You'll lock us up with the rats again?"

My father merely smiled. "You and she had best make use of a guard's carriage. I imagine your father would not appreciate you walking through the streets like a common trull advertising his wares."

"And here I was thinking the streets of mighty Divona were above such an age-old profession."

"Indeed we are, in that trulling is as regulated and as taxed as the more respected danseuse. And the company of either, I might suggest, would have been a better choice than the wife of a high court lord."

Donal didn't reply, but I nevertheless felt the quick stab of his anger. Sensitivity to emotions wasn't something I'd been overly prone to in recent years—probably because shutting that part of me down had been a necessary part of survival—but it was a gift that often came with being Sifft.

The guard behind me poked me in the back with the point of his sword. I clenched my fists and half swung around, but it was another impotent gesture, and we both knew it. He laughed and prodded me again, this time with enough force that it pierced my skin.

"Your day will come," I murmured, as blood began to dribble. "Trust me on that, soldier."

"Good," he replied, his tone mocking. "Because your reputation certainly precedes you, Princess."

I didn't reply. What was the point? This man, like most of those who were either a part of the royal court or whose job it was to support and protect them, only knew what the king wanted known. They didn't know the real me; to be honest, I wasn't even sure that I knew the real me anymore. Certainly Mom wouldn't have recognized me if she'd walked through the gates right now. The bright days of my childhood were long gone, buried under layers of not only cold hatred but also the determination to survive no matter what the abuse. I rather suspected those layers had taken something very important from me.

As Donal neared the carriage, one of the guards stepped forward and opened the door. The highlander nodded but didn't immediately enter. Instead, he stood to one side and offered me his hand. I hesitated, and then placed my fingers on his and tried to ignore the warm, grimy roughness of his palm as I stepped into the confines of the carriage. It held none of the plush comforts of the one the king—or, indeed, any of the other court members— used on a daily basis. The seats on either side of the cabin were plain wood and there was no padding to cushion the ride.

I sat down on the side facing the driver's cabin, my back stiff and my arms and legs crossed. Donal sat opposite. He didn't say anything. He simply watched me.

It was rather unnerving, if only because his expression gave no hint as to what he was thinking. And though I'd felt his anger only moments ago, that nebulous empathy seemed to have flickered out as quickly as it had arrived.

The door closed and the carriage dipped as the guard climbed into the driver's cabin. Almost immediately, we were on the move, the vehicle emitting little more than a barely audible whine as the batteries engaged. I stared out the window as we drove through the gate and onto the strip of land that connected this outcrop to the mainland. The waves on either side reached toward us, the droplets of water glittering silver in the dusk's fading light.

Divona's formidable metal curtain wall soon came into sight, her rusting sides gleaming orange and silver. The lights atop the nearest tower were already alight, their fierce beams sweeping the cliffs and pinning the carriages in brief but blinding brightness before moving on.

In very little time, we were back in Divona and moving toward the castle. Though the previous incarnation had been a true fortress, the impassable nature of the cliffs had afforded its replacement a bit more flexibility. While her outer walls were made of a no-nonsense metal that was considered impregnable to all known weaponry, the buildings within played with space and structure. In some ways, they reminded me of a child's game of shapes, in that there was a rectangular base made of thick bluestone blocks—the remnants of the old great hall—onto which a variety of different shapes seemed to have fallen. My quarters were within what was known as the triangle wing—a red metal construct that was generally used to house emissaries and visiting dignitaries. The king and my brother lived in the hexagon quarter, and it was a place of white marble, rich tapestries, and gold fittings. It was also the most secure building within the castle grounds and had an exit into an underground tunnel that led to the white cliffs and safety in times of attack.

As the carriage came to a halt outside the guarded entrance into the triangle wing, Donal reached back and knocked on the wall. "I require two blankets to protect the modesty of myself and the princess."

The guards didn't immediately answer, but I could hear the murmur of conversation as they cleared the order with their superiors. It was obviously approved, because a few minutes later, the door opened and two blankets were handed in.

I nodded my thanks at Donal and wrapped the thick woolen blanket around my body. No doubt the method of my arrival and my nakedness would soon be the subject of all manner of court gossip, but if the king were true to his word, then I would be gone from this wretched place on the morrow. Gossip would no longer be my problem.

I wasn't entirely sure the highlander and his unknown intentions were a grand improvement, however.

I headed through the metal and glass entrance and strode down the wide hallway to my room at the rear of the building. The guards and Donal followed, the heavy footsteps of the former echoing on the cool red flooring. Despite all the metal surrounding us, there was an airy grandeur to these halls, in part due to the triangle of heavy glass that ran the entire length of the building's roofline, and in part due to the myriad of tiny lights. In the darkest hours of night, they made it appear as if thousands of fireflies had been trapped within the walls.

Two guards waited either side of the door into my quarters. Neither greeted me—they simply opened the wide doors and stepped back.

My room was as airy as the rest of the building. Sheer pale pink curtains covered the metal walls, and the plush sofas and cloudsaks that defined the center of the room were a mix of that same pale pink, deeper maroons, and silver. The bedding platform sat at the far end of the room and was partially hidden by a metal screen of entwining silvery branches and leaves. There was an ablutions area—again partially screened—to the right of this.

"The king has ordered replacement clothes for you, Lord Donal," one of the guards said. "But neither of you are to leave this room until collected in the morning."

"So I believe." Donal's tone was curt. "You are dismissed."

The door closed. Holding the blanket a little tighter around my body, even though I was sure he had no intention of forcing his will upon me just yet, I turned around and said, "Why did you ask the king for me?"

He raised an eyebrow, his expression mocking. "You didn't want to remain in that place, did you?"

"Just answer the question, highlander."

"Donal, if you'd please. And perhaps I will. But only after we both shower. I'm sure my aroma is as unpleasant on your nostrils as it is on mine."

"*That* is a certainty." It came out little more than a husky whisper. My voice was giving out again, damn it.

His grin flashed. "Then I shall take first honors in the bathing area." He paused. "Unless, of course, you'd like to share."

I snorted and shook my head.

"Your loss," he said amicably, and continued on.

I frowned after him. The man was an enigma—a dangerous unknown who was plotting with his mistress for who knew what gain. And for good or for ill, I was now a pawn in those plans.

I walked across to the small desk situated under one of the windows, picked up the scribe quill, and swiftly placed an order for food, coffee, and a healing tonic. While quills didn't have the immediacy of halos—which were basically Q-shaped versions of the communicator circlets that hooked around the ear and came without the same brain-frying tendencies—they did at least offer a secondary means of fast communications. Every quill was magically paired with another, and what one wrote the other echoed. In this case, the quill's pair was in my maid's quarters, and was far easier —and quicker—to use than a bell. The king, it seemed, didn't trust me with a halo, though why I had no idea. It wasn't like I could broadcast my situation to those in the court.

Although up until yesterday, I hadn't thought it possible to hurt my brother, either.

Donal hadn't surfaced by the time the refreshments had arrived, so I poured myself a tonic and then filled my plate with meats, sweetbreads, cheese, and a thick slice of warm brioche. My appetite, it appeared, had returned full force.

He came out just as I was reaching for another slice of bread. He not only looked cleaner, but his wild hair had been tamed into some semblance of order by one of my silver clasps, and his beard—newly trimmed—enhanced his strong features rather than hid them. A pink towel was wrapped around his hips and oddly added to the overall impression of virility.

"I must say, Princess, I didn't think pink would be your color of choice."

"It's not." My voice was still scratchy, but the tonic had at least eased some of the burning. "But it's the color the king thinks those he sends to my bed will expect."

He raised that eyebrow again. "So you really do bed emissaries on your father's orders? I had not in truth believed the rumors."

"Oh, they're all too true, but it's not like I had any other choice—"

"You're of royal blood—"

"Who is nothing but a slave to the king's wishes." I threw the brioche onto the plate and thrust up. "If you'll excuse me, I need a shower."

He let me pass without saying anything, but his disbelief harried my heels as I stepped into the bathing area. I dropped the blanket, slapped the auto heat button, and then stepped into the shower. The water was hot—not quite scalding but not far from it—and, as I had done more times than I cared to remember over the last twelve years, I raised my face and allowed the water to sluice over my face and body. It helped erase my memories no more now than it had all those other times, but it did at least wash the sweat, blood, and grime from my skin.

When I finally stepped free of the water, I quickly finger-combed my hair. It was cut unfashionably close to my neck and had elicited many comments about how much prettier I'd be if I only grew it out, but hair length was one of the few things in my life I *could* control. Besides, very short hair was impossible to grab during battle.

I pulled one the gowns from the hooks on the wall to the side of the mirror and wrapped it around my body as I returned to the living area.

Donal had finished the rest of the meat plate and was pouring himself a cup of coffee. "Would you like one?"

"No, thanks."

I filled my cup with the rest of the tonic and then perched on a cloudsak opposite him. "Are you going to answer my question now, or is this some game you play?"

He regarded me evenly over the rim of his cup for several seconds, and then said, "I rarely play games, but I begin to believe you're well versed in such things."

"All courts have their intrigues," I replied. "If you do not learn the rules quick enough, you die."

"Indeed, but if your earlier comment is anything to go by, I think there is far more behind your artifices than mere courtly machinations."

I didn't bother replying. I simply sipped my drink and waited for him to continue.

"That being the case," he said eventually, "I suggest we attempt what is undoubtedly a rarity in this place."

"Restraint?" I replied, voice bland.

He laughed, and for the first time, there was a hint of

real warmth in the sound. "No, honesty. And I have to admit, I find your sharp tongue rather refreshing after the polite formality of Cannamore's lords and the teasing sweetness of her ladies."

"And yet it was this very sweetness you sought when you decided to take your ease in this place."

That brief flash of warmth faded. "She said she was free. If I'm guilty of anything, it's trusting the word of a woman." He drained his cup and thrust to his feet. "Do you have ale in this place?"

"Use the scribe pen on the desk to order what you wish and a maidservant will bring it up."

"Ah, good."

I watched him walk across to the unit, and then said, "What is it you truly wish of me, highlander?"

"Honesty, as I said," he replied evenly. "But I also offer a deal—one that has benefits for both of us."

"Such as?"

He didn't reply immediately, and when he finally did, it was with another question. "How safe is it in this place?"

My eyebrows rose. "That depends on what you mean by safe."

"Do the walls have ears?

"No, but they quite often have eyes." Though I doubted anyone would be watching us now, given the hour and the fact that most of the court would be in the feasting hall.

He grunted and returned to the sofa, sitting on an arm. His casual posture belied the sudden tension in him. "Then I offer you, in exchange for your help, the one thing you so obviously want."

"The death of the king and my brother?" I said blandly.

"That might be a side result," he said. "But what I'm offering is the glass throne itself."

THREE

For several minutes I could only stare at him. Then I laughed. Harshly.

"You would go to war against all of Cannamore for a woman most courtiers consider no better than a common trull?"

"No, I would go to war for the one thing my people have long wanted. Independence."

There was a passion in his voice—a light in his eyes—that stirred something I'd long thought dead: interest. Not sexual interest, but rather the simple need to know more about this man and his people.

"I want the right to rule our lands as we see fit," he continued, "rather than be forced to obey the orders of a man and a people who do not know or love our lands, and who certainly do not understand her ways."

"If you think I'm going to be the one to give your people their freedom, you're sorely mistaken."

"That's more than possible, although the wind is rarely wrong."

I raised my eyebrows. "Rarely?"

He grimaced. "It was on her advice we signed the treaty. We have regretted it ever since."

"And yet in signing your people were gifted centuries of peace. Have you not regained strength and rebuilt your broken lands in that time? I wouldn't call *that* a bad deal."

"And there are many amongst the five tribes who agree with you."

But not his people, his tone suggested.

I drank some tonic and continued to watch him warily. "Why does the wind believe I'm the one who will make such a gift to you? *No* woman will ever hold that power. Not in this place."

He shrugged. "I cannot explain it; I only repeat what she tells me."

I snorted softly. "Then your mistress of air is seriously insane. Even if both the king and my brother *were* to die, I wouldn't be placed on the throne. It would likely go to whichever of my male cousins could draw the sword."

I couldn't help the slight edge in those last few words and his gaze narrowed. "You resent that."

"Yes."

"Why? As you said, no woman has ever taken hold of the throne, so why does your anger run so deep?"

"Because the ancient text above the throne never mentions a firstborn *son*."

"And yet history has gifted this land with the rule of one firstborn son after another," he said. "So why the anger when, as you said, the throne was never yours to sit upon anyway?"

"Because I was raised to believe I was every bit as worthy as my brother. And because—" The bracelets stirred to life, the heat burning into the thickened skin of my wrists. It was a warning I dare not ignore. I quickly downed the rest of the tonic and then added, "My anger, as you can see, is little more than thwarted ambition."

"Oh, I think it's a *whole* lot more than that."

This man was dangerous, if only because—unlike so many others who'd stepped into this room—he saw what lay beneath the surface. "So what, exactly, does your mistress whisper about me?"

"A rather obvious change of topic, Princess, but I shall indulge you for the moment—"

"If you expect to be rewarded for such indulgence, you're bound for disappointment."

His teeth flashed; once again I wasn't entirely sure if it was a smile or a snarl. "I have *no* desire to tumble another lady of this court. One has caused more than enough trouble."

"You don't want my body, and yet I can in no way deliver what you *do* want," I said. "I think your mistress has led you into a bad bargain, highlander."

He shrugged. "Even the wind cannot fully predict fate's path. Every decision, every action, alters the lines of what could be. She can only whisper of what might be."

"Then tell me what she's whispering about our tenure at the Karva Pass. Why did your father tell you to survive, no matter what?"

"We'll survive." There was a grim flatness in his tone that belied his words. "We *must*. Whether these lands will is another matter entirely."

Fear pulsed—not so much because of his words, but because of the weight the stirring air seemed to place on them. "Why would you believe our lands are in danger? The Skaran might harass our borders, but I've heard no mention that they were ready to launch a full-scale attack."

"It is not the Skaran we need to fear, but someone—some*thing*—else."

"Is that why you were here in Divona? Because of this undefined threat?"

"Yes. My father thought the king should be aware that a darkness stirs."

"So why not use a communicator? At least you and your brother would not have ended up in the eighth tower."

He smiled. "I did suggest that, but the wind advised otherwise."

"And yet she didn't warn you of the dangers of bedding a lord's wife? Your mistress is a fickle creature, it would seem."

"That can be said of most women, I believe." He drank some wine. "And, unfortunately, not even the wind can always see past the veils that hide the future."

"Then she really hasn't said anything more about the threat?"

"No. In fact, she's not inclined to say more than that darkness comes, and that war rides in on its coattails."

The apartment door opened and a tall woman with gray hair and a pleasant countenance entered.

"The ale arrives, and just in time," Donal said. "My thirst was becoming fierce."

"If I'm not mistaken, it was your damn thirst that led you into your current situation."

His gaze shot to mine, surprise evident, and then he laughed. It was a warm, rich sound that echoed oddly off walls that had not heard such a thing in a very long time.

"I suspect we refer to two very different thirsts, Princess, but your words nevertheless hold a deep grain of truth."

My maid placed the large flagon and two mugs on the

table next to Donal, and then glanced at me. "Will that be all, Lady Nyx?"

"Yes, thanks, Mary."

She nodded and departed.

"Lady Nyx?" Donal said, one eyebrow rising.

"I asked her to drop the formality and use my name. Lady Nyx is the closest she'd come."

"Ah." He reached for the flagon. "Do you wish some?"

"No, thanks."

He poured himself a drink then contemplated me for several seconds over the rim of the mug. "Why do you call your father 'the king' whenever you reference him?"

"Because he is."

"Yes, but you've never once called him Father, and that's unusual."

I shrugged. "He stopped being my father the minute he forced these bracelets on me."

His gaze dropped to my wrists. "What was the blue light that briefly lit those things when your father said he ceded your presence over to me?"

"I would tell you if I could. But I can't. Not in this place. Not until we leave Divona." I smiled, though it felt tight. "Is the war the wind whispers about the reason you offered me the throne?"

"In part, yes. But *that* is a discussion best saved for another night." He downed the drink and refilled his mug. "Is there only one bed in this room?"

I half smiled. "Yes, and you may have it. I'm comfortable enough on the cloudsaks."

Speculation briefly flared in his eyes. "You don't wish to share? Even *after* I've showered? I'm deeply wounded."

"This from the man who not a few moments ago stated he had no desire to tumble another lady of this court."

"Indeed. Princesses, however, are *always* a different matter entirely."

Amusement briefly stirred. Despite his words, it was obvious that whatever this man truly wanted from me— be it freedom for his people or something darker—sex *wasn't* part of the bargain. And that was a very nice change.

Whether it would remain that way *after* he'd gained control of my leash was something I'd know soon enough.

"Take the bed, highlander, and take your ale with you. I need to get some sleep. Tomorrow, I fear, is going to be an interesting day."

"Indeed." He grabbed the flagon and pushed upwards. "It's not every day a disgraced highlander lord and a princess of Cannamore are banished to the border for six months. It will undoubtedly cause a stir amongst the troops."

I had a bad feeling it would be my presence more than his that would cause the stir. Given *I* hadn't known who he was, it was unlikely any in the relief force would. But they'd all know me—maybe not my reputation, because those of the court would never share such gossip with common folk —but they'd certainly know me by look. I was very much my brother's twin, even if smaller in stature and female in form.

And *that* would undoubtedly cause problems in the weeks ahead.

But all I said was, "I hope you're not expecting special treatment, because the king is rarely the type to grant such favors."

"Oh, I'm fully aware of just how little your father is willing to cede. Thankfully, his daughter does not share the same unwillingness." His smile flashed as he bowed rather grandly. "I thank you for your kind gesture of gifting me your bed."

"You're quite welcome to it, believe me."

It wasn't like I ever slept there anyway. In fact, I'd curl up on ice before I'd ever willingly climb into that bed.

He must have caught the edge in my words, because once again speculation stirred in his eyes. But he didn't say anything; he simply gave me a nod goodnight and walked across to the sleeping platform.

I reached for a nearby blanket, tugged it over my body, and then shifted slightly so that one foot touched the warm tiles. Through them came the soft pulse of the earth. It was a strong, calm heartbeat of power—one that had kept the faint threads of hope alive in the darkest hours.

Despite Donal's presence in my room, sleep came, and for once, neither fear nor the memory of past degradations invaded my dreams.

We were woken on the cusp of dawn by guards delivering two backpacks and clothing for Donal.

Once they were gone and breakfast was had, I donned my old leather pants and boots, then tugged on a tunic and a hooded, weatherproof vest. In one of the packs, I stuffed two changes of clothes, some toiletries, and the bread and dried fruits that remained from our meal. Finally, I put the one thing in this entire apartment that meant anything to me: the glass knife my mother had given me—in secret—on the eve of the earth initiation ceremony. She'd said it had been given to the firstborn female in every generation of her family and was a symbol of the power that had once been theirs—and might one day be again.

Like the King's Sword, it was made from a blue-white glass that was all but indestructible. The blade was straight and had obviously been designed for close combat as much as throwing. It was also more elaborately decorated than the King's Sword, and had ancient runes running the length of its blade. This was the *only* indication that it was more than just an unusually made blade—it was, in fact, one enhanced by both earth magic *and* real magic. What exactly the runes said or did, I couldn't say. My mother had simply stated they were designed to protect, but from *what* had been long ago lost. And it wasn't like I could ask the king or my brother; doing so before I'd drawn the sword would have revealed the knife's presence—something my mother had bid me never to do—and afterward, I didn't dare. In the week that had followed her death, the king had destroyed absolutely everything in the castle that had been hers— burned anything that bore her likeness or retained her memory. Everything except this blade and me.

I had no doubt he was currently plotting ways to rectify the latter.

The one thing I *did* know about both this blade and the King's Sword was that they could be used as a breaker between the earth power and the user. By plunging either into the ground, you could channel the earth's energy to or from them, and thereby lessen the risk of being torn apart by the forces flowing through you.

I raised the knife to the light filtering in from the windows. Deep within the blue glass, a fiery pulse beat— one that not only matched the rhythm of my heart but spoke of its connection to the earth. I might not be able to access that power thanks to the bracelets, but the earth had not abandoned me as she had the king and my brother.

But that heartbeat had also been evident when my

mother had held the blade and, for the first time, I couldn't help but wonder if she'd at least been capable of hearing the earth's voice. Though she'd never given any indication of it, she'd been born in Gigurri—the last remaining stronghold of earth mages. And her sister now ruled that place alongside her earth-capable husband. If Mom *had* been able to hear the earth, it would certainly explain why she alone had been able to stand up to—and win—against the king.

But if that were true, why had she taken her life rather than fight his decision to deprive me of the throne? She'd spent my entire life standing up for me—why wouldn't she continue to do so at the one time it mattered most?

Or was it perhaps simply a matter of knowing this was one battle she couldn't win? That the king would make her pay an even *greater* price than he'd made me pay?

Whatever the truth, I hoped she was now in far better place than death and a pauper's grave had given her. Hoped that if she *had* been capable of hearing the earth, she was now part of that greater consciousness.

Because if she was, there was a chance I would one day be with her again.

I blinked against the sting of tears, tucked the blade securely into my pack, and then hoisted it over my shoulders.

Donal came down from the sleeping platform. Though I hadn't taken much notice earlier, he'd been given the black uniform of a commander rather than the brown of a regular soldier. He was also fully armed.

Perhaps the king was actually going to do the decent thing for a change and slot him into a position befitting his station as a highlander lord.

His gaze skimmed me and came up frowning. "Why are you wearing old practice leathers?"

"Because they're all I have that is suitable for such a journey."

"But your father—"

"Is an asshole who will give his unwanted daughter absolutely nothing." Nothing except unwanted partners, that is.

"A statement that deserves an explanation," he growled. "But I'm guessing it will not be forthcoming."

A faint smile tugged at my lips. "You learn fast."

"In a family of ten, you need to." He waved me forward. "Lead the way, Princess."

I spun around and headed for the door. "I do have a name, highlander."

"So do I. When you use mine, I'll use yours."

"Fair enough."

The door opened as we neared, revealing four guards instead of the usual two. Perhaps the king believed Donal wouldn't hold to his word. Although, given he and his brother had taken care of both Lord Brannon *and* seven of his guards, these four weren't likely to dent Donal's plans if he had been inclined to run.

We were led swiftly from the building and across the small yard to the waiting carriage. No one other than the usual allotment of royal guards stood in either the courtyard or on the walls, but tension nevertheless gathered within me. Just because the king wasn't here didn't mean he wouldn't be in the military zone. Didn't mean he wasn't playing some cruel joke, and that he wouldn't, at the very last moment, renege on giving me to Donal.

We both climbed into the carriage and, once the guards were positioned front and back of the vehicle, we left the castle proper and were soon making our way through the streets, heading for the heavy metal gates that separated the royal district from the rest. The first tier—where the military was housed—was a natural C-shaped platform that completely surrounded the royal tier and overlooked the rest of the city. It was a place of gray stone buildings and even grayer metal rooftops, but in the summer, the veins of quartz that ran through the stone glimmered and sparkled, lifting the austerity of the place.

It was not summer, however; between the gray buildings and even grayer skies, it was a grim and forbidding place, and it very much matched my mood. Until Divona, the king, and my brother were left well in my wake, I couldn't allow myself to believe that I might escape the city that had been both my hell and my prison.

The carriage came to a silent halt to one side of the gateway between the first and second tier. I looked out the window and my gut immediately twisted. The relief squadron was ready and waiting—two hundred and fifty men and women all staring directly at us.

I couldn't immediately see the king, but that didn't mean he wasn't here. Tension flowed through me, and I flexed my fingers. It didn't help. Nothing would. Not until I was free of this city.

"Ready, Princess?" Donal said quietly.

My gaze shot to his. "No. But like many things in my life, it's not like I have a choice."

"And if you did?"

"I'd leave this goddamn city so fast you'd only see dust."

He raised an eyebrow. "And what of your ambitions?"

"I have none beyond survival."

"And what of the throne?"

"That *isn't* an ambition. It's an impossibility."

The door opened, cutting off any reply he might have made, but the questions I could see in his eyes would undoubtedly appear thick and fast once we were free of this place.

"Lord O'Raen," a brown-haired, brown-suited man said. "Commander Gallego awaits. Please come with me."

He made no mention of me. He didn't even look at me.

"From this moment on, Princess," Donal murmured, "we present a united front and protect each other's back."

My gaze shot to his again, but I didn't ask why. There was no need. This might technically be a military outfit, but it was filled with what was basically Divona's unwanted—its murderers, cheats, thieves, and outcasts—and they would no doubt test us.

I climbed out of the carriage and stood to one side, surveying the gathered army with what I hoped was a mask of indifference.

Donal stepped down and, as one, we followed the soldier across the parade yard. There was absolutely no sound. A hush had fallen over the entire first tier and odd energy filled the air.

The only thing that wasn't quiet was the earth. Her rage was building, a frustrated force I could feel through the thin soles of my boots.

She didn't like what was happening, but she, like me, could do little to alter the situation. Since her abandonment of the king, she'd had no voice in this city.

Commander Gallego was a powerfully built man with bushy gray eyebrows, a thick shadow of gray around his chin, and a close-shaven head. His dark gaze briefly met mine and showed neither surprise nor annoyance. He'd obviously been expecting my presence here, but there was little indication as to what he thought about it.

"Lord O'Raen," he said, as we came to a halt in front of

him. "I've been ordered to hand control of the scouting division to you."

"And the man who was previously in charge of this division?" Donal asked mildly. "What does he think of this development?"

"He will act as your second."

"And is he a seasoned soldier such as yourself?"

"All divisional heads are—"

"Then with respect, we both know my taking his place will only lead to resentment. I'd prefer if we act as *his* seconds."

Surprise and amusement briefly touched the commander's weatherworn features before he shut it down. "We? I hardly think it appropriate the princess be given such a post. She has no experience beyond the walls of her castle, Lord Donal, and *that* presents a danger to us all."

A statement that confirmed my belief that the whispers about me—and the utter contempt in which I was held—had indeed been contained within the castle walls. No one beyond them knew—or cared—about the true state of my life there. Not even those here in the military tier.

"And yet, given her rank, it's hardly appropriate for her to be slated as a common soldier." He raised an eyebrow, his expression challenging. "Or did you, perhaps, have some other position in mind?"

The commander's smile held little in the way of amusement. "No, I did not."

"And the king? Has he given any orders regarding my presence?" I asked.

His gaze came to mine again. Even though there was no emotion in either his eyes or his expression, nothing but contempt emanated from him.

"The king has given me no orders."

Which all but suggested he *had* been given orders from someone *other* than the king.

"Then this matter is settled," Donal said. "Is my brother here?"

"He awaits in the guardhouse." The commander stepped to one side and motioned toward the small metal construct positioned to the left of the main gateway.

"Thank you." Donal glanced at me, and though he didn't say anything, it was obvious his "stick together" request didn't apply when it came to his family.

I crossed my arms and watched him walk away. And instantly felt a whole lot less secure—which was ridiculous. No matter what these people might think of my presence here, they wouldn't do anything within Divona's walls.

Once we were beyond them, however, all bets would be off. But no matter what happened, I'd have to deal with it myself. It was the only way I was ever going to gain any respect from these men and women.

Unless, of course, me gaining respect *wasn't* part of the highlander's plans.

Once Donal was out of sight, the commander glanced at me and said, in a hard voice, "If you, in any way, do *anything* to endanger my people, I will kill you myself, princess or no."

I met his gaze evenly. "Commander, I'm not sure what reasons you were given for my presence here, but I ask that you do not believe them. Nothing but lies comes from the glass court these days."

He didn't reply, but I nevertheless felt his scorn. But *that* was an emotion with which I was comfortably familiar. Even the waves of contempt flowing from those standing in silence behind us didn't really bother me.

It was the off sense of anticipation and avarice coming

from one very small section of the group that *did*. Its scent was so strong it stung my nostrils, and it was one that confused the hell out of me.

I resisted the urge to rub my arms and kept my gaze on the guardhouse. Why had Donal been so insistent on seeing his brother one last time? Granted, it would be another six months, at least, before they were in each other's company again, but I rather suspected that *wasn't* the reason. That it wasn't so much a goodbye he was interested in, but rather the wind and her whisperings.

The two men came out five minutes later. Aside from the newly healed wound that ran from the corner of his left eye down to the edge of his mouth—a gift from the fight with Lord Brannon and his men, no doubt—Donal's older brother was the spitting image of him.

They embraced briefly, then, without looking our way, the brother departed through the gates and Donal returned to us.

"Lord Donal, you and Princess Nyx are with Captain Marx at the front of hauler three." His gaze went past us. "Company, let's move."

Two hundred and fifty soldiers turned in a somewhat less than precise way and began a quick-time march up the main road. Donal and I fell in behind them and, in very little time, had reached the vehicle terminus. Hauler three was a five-pod vehicle and the smallest of the six gathered, but, like all of them, looked like a sleek metal caterpillar.

Donal walked up to the first pod behind the control unit, opened the door, and climbed inside. He didn't offer me a hand up, and I would have refused it if he had. We were being watched, and I had no desire for anyone to think the only reason for my presence was as a body to keep him warm at night.

Though I had no doubt that's exactly what they were thinking.

And what might yet happen.

The inside of the pod was sparse, holding little more than two long benches—one behind the other—and a small curtained-off area at the rear that I presumed was a privy. Donal had already claimed the back seat.

I swung off my pack, tucked it under the seat, and sat beside him. My stomach churned, and it took every ounce of control I had to maintain a calm front when all I could think about was whether or not the king was playing the ultimate game.

Because handing me the possibility of escape and then snatching it away at the last minute might well be the thing that finally broke me.

I licked my lips and then said, in an effort not to think about *that* possibility, "Is your brother heading straight home?"

He glanced at me, eyebrow raised. "What makes you think he'd want to stay in this wretched place any longer than necessary?"

"Oh, I have no doubt he's leaving Divona; I'm just questioning whether he's returning directly home, or if your mistress has other plans for him."

"The air guides his steps nowhere but home." He glanced past me. "Captain Marx, I presume?"

A black-haired, green-eyed, middle-aged man stepped into the pod and dropped onto the seat in front of us. "Yes. And I appreciate your willingness to step aside, Lord Donal, but it's unseemly—"

"That my station be put above your experience and familiarity with these men," Donal said.

A smile touched the captain's leathery features. "I seriously doubt *my* experience would be any greater than that of a Westal Wildman. Your people battle the Skaran full-time. Those of us assigned command of the relief squadron at the Karva Pass only do so on a six-monthly rotating basis."

"It is nevertheless prudent to retain the existing command structure. I'm not here to cause trouble, Captain."

"I appreciate that." His brief glance at me suggested that what he didn't *appreciate* was my presence here. But at least he didn't give voice to that opinion.

"What's happened to the unit leaders we're replacing?" I said.

"They were given last-minute orders to stand down and will be given duty next rotation. They'll also be on standby if we lose any unit leaders during the next six months. Familiarity is very much a bonus when it comes to survival beyond the Pass."

Suggesting he didn't expect me to last long. But then, he had no idea just how good I was at surviving.

"How many are there in the division all told?" Donal asked.

"We're thirty strong, which equates to six units. Five per unit seems to be the balance point. It gives the unit a greater chance of survival while still allowing some hope of slipping through the Wild Lands unseen." He hesitated. "I lost well over half the scouting division last go-around."

"That suggests a lack of training, Captain."

"Six months of training will never ready miscreants and murderers for either battle or survival in the wilderness." The captain's gaze came to me. Though there was little emotion to be seen, and I wasn't getting much on a deeper sensory level, it was nevertheless evident he considered me as unready as the miscreants—a point I couldn't really disagree with. "I have no idea why you're here, Princess Nyx, but I hope you're aware that you'll be afforded no luxuries or special consideration."

"All I want is to be treated with respect. Nothing more. Nothing less."

A somewhat ironic smile touched his lips. "Respect is won, not gifted. I hope you're prepared for *that*."

Which was a warning if ever I'd heard one. "I guess we'll find out, won't we?"

"Indeed, especially given you'll be expected to lead a small group of scouts into Skaran territory." He paused. "These men are the dregs, Princess. They *will* test you, and if they think they can best you...."

He didn't finish, but he didn't need to. I was well equated with what men—and women—could do when they believed they had the upper hand. And in the pink plushness of my bedroom, that had been more common than not.

"Then someone had best teach me how to use blasters and the like," I replied evenly. "Unless, of course, you've been instructed otherwise."

"I'll teach you," Donal said, "when we're off duty."

"There's an hour target practice allotted before each twelve-hour shift, but you'll be wanting to sleep when you're not on duty, especially until you're used to the long hours."

"No one needs to sleep twelve hours, Captain. There's time enough to train."

The captain raised an eyebrow, making me wonder if he *had* received some sort of order regarding me and weapons usage.

"Then be prepared to draw a curious crowd." He pressed the halo around his ear and then added, "Hauler three loaded and ready."

The door instantly slid shut and the secondary engine came to life. These haulers, like many other such vehicles—military or not—used a form of magnetic repulsion technology that drew on the energy lines crisscrossing Cannamore to move. But in cities as large as Divona—where there was heavy interference between the magnetic field and the exchangers not just in the form of buildings and roads, but in all the underground utilities—simple hover technology was used. Batteries and solar panels might have been quieter, but they were also far more expensive to install and replace. When it came to the outposts, sturdiness and reliability was the key.

Or so the Red Queen had once informed me.

The impeller roared to life, the sound not unlike a gale force wind. Despite the terminus being a place of stone, dust flew around the pod, cutting visibility to almost zero.

Almost.

Because between one wave of dirt and another, I glimpsed my brother. My stomach twisted and fear surged.

He stood in the middle of the terminus, untouched by the swirling clouds of gray, his right arm braced and his expression a weird mix of fury and satisfaction.

As our gazes met, he raised his left arm, made a gun with his fingers, and shot me.

Then he smiled.

A deep, satisfied smile.

I knew in that instant he'd decided to risk the wrath of Lokain and now had allies somewhere in the relief squad. Allies who would no doubt be well rewarded if I were "accidentally" killed in the course of the next six months.

I closed my eyes and tried not to panic. I'd survived twelve years of him doing his best to kill me, and I'd damn well survive whatever evil he'd unleashed within the ranks of these men and women.

Our hauler moved forward and took him from my sight. I crossed my arms, leaned back against the bench's metal back, and did my best to ignore the churning tide of apprehension as I stared out of the window.

Though I'd freely roamed the breadth of Divona when I was younger, I'd been restricted to the castle grounds for the last twelve years. There'd been a lot of growth within the city in that time, and many of the buildings I'd known as a child no longer stood, replaced by taller, grander ones. The streets, too, had changed—they weren't as pristine as I'd remembered, and were certainly a whole lot more crowded. Even the people were different, though how I couldn't really say. Maybe it was simply the fact that there was no joy in their faces as they went about their everyday lives.

But then, there was little joy in the royal district, either. At least there wasn't for those who served and protected. The king and my brother were not easy taskmasters, and lords and ladies of the court followed their lead.

It took half an hour for the military convoy to snake its way through the various levels, streets, and non-aligned gateways—a deliberate design to stop invaders easily moving from one level to the next. Eventually, though, we reached the massive metal gatehouse that was the main entrance on the Mauvaissian side of Divona. My heart raced as we moved down the long tunnel and then over the drawbridge that spanned the Merrigold River.

Freedom was close. So damn close.

The impeller units cut out the second we left the drawbridge, and the dust and noise faded as the magnetic exchange technology kicked in. The hauler surged forward with renewed speed and the landscape around us became something of a blur.

But it was a blur that had emotion crashing through me—emotion that was mostly disbelief and uncertainty, but entangled within those two was jubilation.

The impossible had happened.

I was *free*.

But even as that thought crossed my mind, fire flickered across the bracelets—an indication that control had switched from the king to Donal, and a stark reminder that I very much remained a prisoner.

Freedom was still a long way from being mine.

Donal glanced at my wrists and then me, and raised an eyebrow in silent query. I didn't answer. While the restrictions the king had placed on me speaking about the bracelets and my life would have fallen when control switched over, I had no desire to share such intimacies in the presence of a stranger.

Which, in very many ways, Donal still was, but I at least trusted him. I had no idea yet whether the same could be said about the captain.

After a moment, Donal looked at the captain and said, "How long will it take to get to the Karva Pass?"

The captain shrugged. "It's a three-day journey if the weather doesn't screw us around. We'll stop overnight at Druxdale and Uxa Waters."

Both were places I'd never heard mention of, which meant they were probably military encampments. The Mauvaissians roamed the length and breadth of their lands for three seasons of the year, and only retreated to Rodestat—the Red City—for the harsher winter months. But Rodestat was never completely devoid of people, as it was positioned *behind* both the Karva Pass and the military garrison there. From what the Red Queen had said, there was not only the required number of Mauvaissian guards living within its boundaries but many others who chose to stay, either because of age or because there was coin to be made from an encampment of men and women who had little to do in their spare time but sleep, eat, drink, and fuck.

"And Druxdale is how far?" Donal asked.

"Fourteen hours, give or take an hour or so."

Meaning we had a long day ahead. Thank the gods there were only three of us sharing the privy facilities in this pod. A wry smile touched my lips. I'd gone from simply sharing my body to sharing a bathroom *and* sleeping quarters, and it would definitely take some getting used to. But it was a trade I was more than happy to make.

I continued to stare at the window. The Mauvaissian plains were nothing more than a flat and endless wave of yellow grasses. It was a beautiful but sparse place, with little in the way of trees or habitations to break the lonely wildness. I had no doubt there *were* animals and other vistas to be found here, especially given the Mauvaissians had successfully carved a hunter-gatherer existence in these lands for as long as anyone could remember, but none of it was visible.

Which was undoubtedly intentional. Part of the treaty conditions between Divona and the Mauvaissians was a set course for any vehicular travel through their lands.

The day rolled on slowly. The captain offered us a ration pack around midday, which, while basic, not only eased my hunger but also saved the breads and fruits in my pack for later in the afternoon.

As flags of pink and orange heralded the arrival of night, the convoy finally slowed. I shifted position to get a better look of what might lie ahead but couldn't see anything in the way of formal structures.

I glanced across at the captain. "Is Druxdale a settlement or a campsite?"

"The latter. We three share a tent tonight." He regarded me steadily. "Is that a problem for you, Princess Nyx?"

"It's only a problem if you think sharing a tent also means sharing my body. Try *that*, and I will gut you, captain or not."

He stared at me for a moment and then laughed. "Interesting response from someone who has no fighting experience."

"I mightn't have formal training, Captain, but I suggest you don't, in any way, underestimate either my abilities or my determination to survive."

He raised an eyebrow but didn't give voice to the disbelief I could see in his eyes. He simply glanced at Donal and said, "The camping equipment is stored in the hold under the impeller bay. You and Nyx will set up our quarters beside this hauler while I see to the rest of our people. Dinner will be at nineteen hundred. We'll do the introduction to the rest of the team then."

Donal nodded. The doors opened as the hauler came to a gentle halt and the captain immediately disappeared out of them. A few seconds later, he was barking orders and making arrangements for the overnight stay.

"Let's go, Princess," Donal said, and climbed out of the pod.

I didn't immediately follow. Instead, I pulled my knife out of my backpack and strapped it to my right leg. While the need to keep it hidden remained—especially when I had no idea whether Vin's assassin had been ordered to report back—I wasn't about to go unarmed. The sheath at least kept the blade hidden, and few were likely to remark of the hilt itself, given it was not uncommon for ceremonial blades to have specially decorated or unusual hilts. A knife might be next to useless against the full weapon kits of the others, but it was all I had. And, to be honest, all I was comfortable with—at least until I got some training in gun usage.

I jumped down from the hauler but paused to glance around. Our vehicle had stopped in a small half circle rather than in a straight line, and there were close to thirty people in the immediate area, some setting up tents to complete the circle while others were erecting a makeshift kitchen and dining area in the middle.

Everyone had a job and knew exactly what to do, and it made me feel all the more useless.

I frowned and headed around to the rear of the pod. Donal had already opened the cargo hold and was in the process of pulling out a long, yellowish-green canvas bag.

"The tent, I presume?"

He nodded. "Grab the other end, will you?"

I did so, grunting a little at the unexpected weight of it. We carried it around the side of the pod and, with Donal instructing me, soon had it set up. The tent was oblong shaped and large enough to hold eight, with the sleeping platform held off the ground by sturdy metal poles. Maybe the critters I couldn't see were more prevalent and dangerous than I'd been presuming.

The rest of the scouts' portion of the night camp was soon set up. I followed Donal across to the tables and sat down next to him. We didn't speak and no one paid any great attention to us, though I had no doubt they were aware of every little move we made.

Dinner was soon ready. We lined up with everyone else,

were served a portion of meat stew and wild rice on a metal plate, given a slab of bread, and sent on our way.

When the meal was done and the plates collected by the wash crew, Captain Marx stood. Silence instantly fell—and that alone suggested Donal's decision *not* to take this man's position had been the right one.

"As most of you are now aware, Lord Donal and Princess Nyx have joined our ranks. They will be acting as my seconds, with Lord Donal being responsible for the princess's behavior."

Annoyance surged and I stood. "I apologize for the interruption, Captain, but *no one* is responsible for my behavior but myself. I grant that I'm little better than a raw recruit, but I'm willing and ready to learn, whatever it may take."

The captain raised an eyebrow, but all he said was, "Fair enough, Princess—"

"It's Nyx," I said. "I left my title behind when I left the walls of Divona."

"Nicely done," Donal murmured as I sat down. The wind stirred around us as he spoke, making me suspect not even those who sat close to us would hear our conversation. "You just set a challenge for every man and woman in this squad."

"If I'm to gain their trust and respect," I replied, just as softly, "I can't hide behind my title."

The captain continued on, issuing various orders and assigning watch duty to different groups. It appeared the scouting division was responsible for the safety of the *entire* camp rather than our immediate area. Donal and I were given the three to dawn watch, which—given the few smirks I spotted—was obviously deemed to be the worst time to be out.

Finally, he read out the names of the people who would come under Donal's and my command. If the murmuring that rose with one name—Dravan—was anything to go by, the captain had just shoved trouble my way. He was obviously intent on testing my resolve to be treated no differently to anyone else from the get-go.

When the captain had finished, people departed either to their various stations or their tents, leaving Donal and me sitting alone at the tables.

Donal snagged one of the coffeepots and poured us both a drink. "Tell me about those bracelets."

The bracelets instantly warmed, a warning to obey what was meant as a request but came across as an order.

"They're what's called restraint bracelets." The wind swirled and rose upwards, once again snatching my words away from all ears other than his. "They magically restrict my actions and words and force me to obey whatever order the person or persons who control the bracelets might give."

For several heartbeats, he simply stared at me. There was little emotion in his face or his eyes, but I nevertheless had a sense of his shock.

"What happens if you don't obey?" he asked eventually.

"It depends. If I'm ordered silent and attempt to speak, the words are burned from my lips and my brain, and I'm left little better than a vegetable for more hours than I care to think about." Despite my matter-of-fact tone, horror shivered through me.

"Is that what happened when you were thrown into the cell with me?"

A faint smile touched my lips. "No. That was a result of what is called witch fire and is little more than torture. It's a heat that burns through you—through every single cell in your body—until it feels like you're more molten ash than flesh. It can kill, but he would never go that far."

"He being your father, I presume?" Donal's voice was flat, emotionless, and yet there was disbelief in him.

"Yes."

"Why? What did you do?"

Bitterness touched my lips. "I did the unthinkable. I did what I wasn't supposed to do."

He studied me for a moment, and then said softly, "You drew the King's Sword."

"Yes."

A smile touched his lips. "At least now some of the wind's whisperings begin to make sense."

"She told you about that?"

"No. She only said that lies abound in the heart of Divona, and they are capable of destroying us all." He took a sip of coffee. "Did your brother also draw the sword? Is that why he's heir and you're not?"

"He didn't draw it when I did. Or rather, he couldn't."

"But he did a year later?"

"From a replica throne, not the real one."

There was incredulousness in his expression, but no disbelief. And *that* warmed something deep inside. Something I'd long thought to be nothing more than ice. "So when your father said he was ceding his rights and his power to my will and word, he was actually handing over his control of you?"

"Yes."

"Seriously?"

"Yes."

His lips twitched. "So if I ordered you to strip off right here and now, you would be forced to?"

"Yes." I met his gaze evenly, even though my stomach

was twisting and my heart raced so hard it felt ready to tear out of my chest. "Just as I was forced to bed every single man and woman my father wanted me to. Twelve years of no choice, Donal. Think on that for a while. And if you *do* order me to strip off or even fuck you, you had best also add an order not to take my knife to your throat in the middle of the night."

His expression shut down hard and fast. But he was angry. I might not be able to see it, but I could both smell it and taste it in the air.

"Give me your hands, Princess."

His voice was cold. As hard as his expression.

I obeyed. I had no other choice.

His fingers wrapped around mine and then he said, in an almost angry tone, "Princess Nyx, I cede my rights and my power to *your* will and *your* word. Let no one ever again force their desires on you."

I could only stare at him.

Twenty-five words.

Twenty-five simple words.

That's all it took to give me my life back.

FOUR

B lue fire flickered across the bracelets, something I felt more than saw.

I didn't say anything. I couldn't.

A myriad of emotions tumbled through me—not just disbelief and hope but, rather weirdly, fear *and* confusion.

I licked my lips and dropped my gaze to the bracelets. They gleamed in the fading light of day, a bright evil that had blighted my life for too many years.

"Why?" I whispered.

"The people of Westal Ranges may be considered little more than savages by the gentle folk of Divona, but even *we* do not believe in slavery." His voice remained harsh. "I *do* want your help, Princess, but I also want your willingness."

My gaze shot back to his. He must have seen the question in my eyes, because he immediately added, "With what comes, nothing more. And no matter what does happen—in the near future and beyond—the choice to deal with it or not is now your decision alone. As it should always be."

"Choice." My gaze dropped to the bracelets again. "A rare jewel indeed."

He didn't reply, but his anger bled into the air, filling her with heat and turbulence even if it barely touched me.

I tentatively ran a trembling finger across the intricate patterns that adorned the left bracelet—patterns that vaguely reminded me of the runes that ran down my knife's blade, and that I suspected might now be forever burned into the skin around my wrists.

I could find out, if I wanted.

I could release the bracelets and examine the scars that lay underneath. Scars I'd only ever felt.

If I dared.

The truth of the matter was, these things—and the restrictions that came with them—had become so much a part of my identity that I wasn't entirely sure who or what I'd become if their lock on my life had truly lifted.

I might have dreamed of this moment for a very long time, but now that it was finally here, part of me was very reluctant to take the final step—to the say words that would release the shackles and give me freedom.

I closed my eyes. Felt the turbulent air caress my skin, as if in encouragement.

Felt the pounding of the earth under my feet, an impatient heartbeat that silently begged me to get on with it. To reconnect.

I could do this.

I *had* to do this.

I took a deep breath and released it slowly. Then, very softly, I said, "Bracelets, unlock."

Once again, blue fire ran across their surface. A soft click followed and then, with little fanfare, my silver shackles released their grip on my wrists and fell to the table.

Free.

Something I'd long wanted. Something I'd long despaired of ever achieving.

Freedom.

To do what I wanted, to go where I wanted. To be with whomever I wanted. Or not, as was more likely.

Tears stung my eyes and I rapidly blinked them away. There'd been no tears in twelve years. There would *not* be tears now. Not here, in this place, where others might be watching.

I took another deep breath. It didn't do much to halt the trembling in my body or the turmoil still threatening to overwhelm me. I frowned and concentrated instead on my wrists. They were indeed scarred. Layer upon layer of successive burns had forced healing skin to follow the bracelets' pattern, so that it now appeared as if I wore leather imitations.

For now and forever, these scars would be a permanent reminder of the evil that now stained the might of the glass throne—an evil that might yet throw this land into darkness.

My frown deepened at the thought, but I had little time to wonder at its origin. Unhindered now by the restraint bracelets, the earth's energy surged, hitting me with so much force it blasted me from the bench seat down to the ground.

Where I remained, on hands and knees, my body shaking as fiercely as the earth under my fingertips. The ground grew so hot it felt like my hands were pressed against a furnace—one that didn't burn—and the night's scents and sounds sharpened almost to the point of pain. Still the power surged, a force I could not deny—didn't *want* to deny. But the earth was intent on reclaiming every part of me—every hair and cell—and she stormed through my body so fiercely it felt as if I was being stretched beyond the limits of life.

But oh, it felt so beautiful, so enriching, to once again be a part of such a force, to hear the welcoming cries of all those who had gone before me. Those cries pulled me deeper and deeper into the earth's warm embrace, until my mind spun, my connection to life weakened, and the desire to leave flesh behind and become one with them was a pulse that beat through every part of me.

It was tempting.

So *very* tempting.

"Princess," a distant voice said. "You must pull away."

No, a silent part of me screamed. *Not after twelve years of only hearing her heartbeat, of never truly feeling her touch or hearing her advice.*

But that other voice would not give up. Would not let me be. "You have to control it, Princess, or you'll destroy us all."

Destroy? The earth only ever welcomed; there was no intent to truly destroy in either her voice or her actions. Not unless I wished it.

"Princess, do you hear me?"

I hear. Not just his voice or his words, but the alarm that ran through both. It cut through the power haze, brought me back to myself.

I reached for my knife and drew it from the sheath. The glass hilt felt cool in my grip, and it tore past the final veils of heat and madness. The earth meant no harm, but in her exuberance, she *would* cause damage if I didn't control her.

I thrust the knife's sharp point into the hard ground, creating a channel through which the energy could reenter the earth.

It was as if a switch had been flicked. I was in full control and aware once again.

Around me lay destruction, and its cause was those few vital seconds in which I'd been at the earth's mercy, unable to control the energy that surged through and around me. That force had been so strong it had radiated out in waves, causing the ground to heave in response. The hauler seemed to have escaped with only minor damage, but there were tents, equipment, and people down everywhere else. No one paid any attention to us. They were too busy climbing to their feet and looking at the mess.

Donal knelt in front of me and, though his expression was concerned, he made no move to touch me. Which was good. I might now be in control, but that hyperaware state still lingered. A touch, no matter how gentle, would feel like a blow right now.

A fact he was no doubt very aware of. Earth and air might be very different mistresses, but the aftershocks of such a power surge were nevertheless similar. It was undoubtedly why he'd so quickly recognized what was happening.

"Are you all right?"

Even though it was softly said, it sounded like a shout. But that didn't stop the smile that touched my lips. "For the first time in twelve years, I can honestly say that I am."

"Good." He sat back on his haunches. "Why didn't you mention you're an earth mage?"

"Because you didn't ask, and because I'm not." I hesitated. "At least, I've not trained as one. I took the initiation ceremony, but the restraint bracelets were placed on my wrists not long afterward. I know the *theory* of control—I've read every old book about it that I could get my hands on—

but I've never really had the opportunity to put that theory into practice."

"The more I learn about your father," he muttered, "the more I want to kill the bastard."

"That's *my* task, not yours. Promise you'll not take it from me, highlander."

"An easy promise to make, though I do hope you'll allow me the pleasure of watching it happen."

"If I have my way, the whole damn court will bear witness." I pulled my knife from the ground then grabbed the edge of the nearby seat and pushed upright. The earth stirred past the thin soles of my shoes and curled up my legs, but there was no heat, no anger in her touch. It was a simple caress; it was almost as if she feared to release me lest something separate us again and she once again became mute in this land. "Do you think anyone will realize I was the source of this quake?"

"No, and not just because they see you as little more than palace fluff. Mauvaissia is often beset by quakes—Rodestat itself sits between two volcanoes."

I grunted. I guessed being seen as palace fluff was better than being considered the palace trull. The contempt with which I was viewed within royal circles had to be the worst of the king's actions against me. But both the unwanted suitors sent to my bed and his whisper and ruination campaign had been designed for one purpose only—to shatter my spirit to such an extent that I would do the one thing they could not.

In the bleakest hour of many a long night, I might well have contemplated ending my life, but never once had I actually taken a step down that dark path. I was far too stubborn to make things *that* easy for them.

And while none here would have heard the rumors

about me, it didn't mean much. Princesses were generally considered little more than blue blood breeders or bartering material by those who both lived within *and* without royal tier—and it was an honest enough view given that was generally our lot in life. At least it was in Divona.

"We'd better go help clean up the mess I just made," I said. "The last thing I need is to be seen standing here doing nothing."

He raised an eyebrow. "And you think I can afford that? Have no doubt that these men will test me as thoroughly as they test you."

Yes, but his tests would be ones of weapons and strength. Mine would no doubt be of a more intimate nature.

But at least now I could fight back.

At least now, I could say no.

I found the two bracelets, clipped them onto my belt, and then helped Donal right the tables and benches and sort the cooking area into some semblance of order. Thankfully, the damage wasn't as widespread as I'd first feared— only the camps on either side of us had been caught in the power backlash. The rest of the convoy remained intact. No one suspected the true cause of the damage, either. Most had, as Donal had said, placed the blame on a localized quake.

Once order had been restored, I dragged a sleeping roll from the rear of our hauler, retrieved my backpack from the front pod, and then retreated into our tent. I didn't unroll my bedding on the platform, but rather on the ground. I was too used to listening to the heartbeat of the earth to separate myself from her now.

But before I stripped off, I unclipped the bracelets and studied them. These things had ruled my life for the last twelve years and a part of me—a very *large* part of me—wanted nothing more than to open the earth and bury them deep inside. But that other part—the part where hate and anger still festered so fiercely—dreamed of returning these bracelets in kind to the king and my brother.

To force on *them* what had been forced on me.

I grimaced and shoved the bracelets into the pack. In truth, no matter how sweet such a dream might be, there was very little hope of it ever eventuating. Aside from the fact I only had control over the one set of restraint bracelets, the king would order me dead—and to hell with the god's anger—long before I got anywhere near him.

I stripped to my underwear and then climbed inside the bedroll. And went to sleep to not just the earth's heartbeat, but to her gentle assurance that none would come near without her forewarning me.

For the second night in a row, I felt totally and utterly safe.

Watch duty came around entirely too fast. I wiped the grittiness of sleep from my eyes and climbed out of the bedroll. The air was cold and the night still. Captain Marx was fast asleep, but Donal was already up and dressed, studying some paperwork on the small desk near the door.

"Morning, Princess," he said, without looking at me. "There's coffee on the heating element if you want something to warm your insides."

"I do. Thanks." I quickly dressed, then strapped on my knife and walked over to pour myself a drink. The coffee looked like sludge and smelled burned, but it was better than nothing. "What are you studying?"

"Duty stations, criminal records and photos, and the captain's dot-point thoughts of our teams." He picked up a stack of notes and handed them to me. "You might want to have a look."

I perched on the edge of the desk and did so. Three of my people—one woman and two men—had Sifft blood, which made sense given heightened senses would be a definite advantage in such a position. All three were nothing more than common thieves. Dravan, however, had nary a squirt of Sifft in his bloodline and was a murderous thug with a record eighteen years in the making. Given he was only twenty-five, he'd obviously started his bullyboy ways at a very young age. He also had a problem with authority figures—especially if that figure was a woman—with more than half of his convictions involving retaliation against those who tried to either tell him what to do or get him to conform.

Marx had added a "do not tread lightly around this man or pay the price" warning in big, bold letters at the bottom of his notes.

No wonder there'd been laughter when Dravan had been assigned to my team. He'd obviously already gained a fearsome reputation amongst the troops. If I couldn't deal with him, the next six months were going to be hell.

Which made me suspect Dravan might be the bullet my brother had fired when we'd left Divona. Or, at least, one of them.

"The caliber of men and women in this squad is even worse than I'd imagined," I muttered. "It's a wonder the Mauvaissians haven't complained."

Donal shrugged. "Would it make any difference if they did?"

"No, but I can't imagine it would be easy accepting scum like this into their society."

"Given the Mauvaissian love of a good fight, it probably isn't such a problem."

"I guess." I hesitated. "I think my brother has had some say in the composition of my unit."

Donal's gaze shot to mine, his concern evident. "What makes you think that?"

"The fact that he fired an imaginary gun at me when we left Divona." I shuffled Dravan's paperwork to the top and then held it out. "And the fact that this man is in the scouting division, let alone my squad, basically confirms my suspicions."

Donal briefly scanned the paper. "He's certainly an unusual pick to be a scout. I could speak to—"

"No," I cut in. "I'd rather he was close, so I can keep an eye on him rather than have him floating around causing problems out of sight."

"True enough." He paused and frowned. "If your brother fears you taking back what he has stolen, why hasn't he simply killed you? Even if he didn't want to do it himself, he surely would have had ample opportunity to order it done."

"Except that I'm cursed, and he fears the possible reprisals."

Donal's eyebrows rose. "You father did mention that, but in what way are you cursed? And why would he fear it?"

"I was branded at birth by Lokain, the god of war and the destroyer of houses. Neither the king nor my brother can kill me directly or even order it done, because Lokain's wrath would fall upon them. Whether that's true or not, I can't say, but it's the only reason I'm still alive."

"Is there a history of your war god doing this? Because it's rather interesting that you bear his mark at a time when change is coming."

"To be honest, I don't really know much more than what the legend states." I shrugged. "It's been both my bane and my savior, and I've never really thought about it beyond that."

"So what does this brand look like?"

I raised my eyebrows. "Given it dominates the lower part of my spine, I'm surprised you didn't notice it when we were both naked."

"We were in the cell for most of that time *and* it was night. It's safe to say I had other things on my mind." Amusement twitched his lips and touched the corners of his blue eyes. "Which is not to say I was oblivious to your state of undress."

I raised my eyebrows. "From where I was sitting, certain parts of your body did *not* reflect that notice."

His smile grew. "We highlanders have supreme control over our bodies. Remind me to give you an intimate demonstration one of these days."

I snorted softly. "If we survive the next six months, I might just consider it."

"Good." He motioned to Dravan's papers. "I think it would be wise to mention the possibility of Dravan being a plant to the captain."

"What if he's aware of it? What if he's in collusion with my brother?"

"I doubt it. The captain's a career soldier—"

"Career soldiers can just as easily be corrupted by coin as thugs."

"Yes, but in this case, I trust him. More importantly, so does the wind."

"If the order for Dravan's inclusion in my team came down from the commander—or even direct from my brother —there's nothing the captain can do about it."

"I still think he should be made aware of the situation."

"Maybe. Let's just wait and see what happens today. I might be wrong, after all."

I doubted it, but the last thing I wanted was to be running to the captain at the first sign of a possible problem. It would only firm his belief that I was out of my league.

Which I was.

I glanced back down at the papers again and studied the duty stations. My group had been assigned watch over the head section of the haulers; Donal and his men had the long, curved spine, and a third team watched our rear. Though putting me in charge of one of the smaller areas was undoubtedly a strategic move on the captain's part, it also meant we were beyond the sight of the main encampment. And *that* could be dangerous. Dravan's long list of offenses suggested he wasn't the type to deny his need for brutality for long.

Which meant that if I was to have any hope of controlling the man, I had to prove I was not only willing—and capable—to stand my ground but also to return like for like. But I'd spent the last twelve years watching the ruthless way with which my brother dealt with others, and I was pretty sure I could channel his arrogance and brutality if the need arose.

I put the notes back onto the desk and took a sip of coffee. "I should be just another soldier. I have no right leading these people."

"If you want to sit on the glass throne, Princess, you have to learn to lead."

79

A wry smile touched my lips. "Giving me freedom was easy. Giving me the throne won't be."

"I'm not giving you the throne. You'll take it yourself."

I raised an eyebrow. "So says the wind?"

"Yes." Amusement twitched his lips again. "Of course, we *do* have to survive not just this night, but every night for the next six months *and* whatever it is that comes to destroy."

"So she's still playing coy about this nebulous threat?"

"She is indeed." He picked up one of two halos sitting on the table and handed it to me. "Your call sign is Caracal One. Your team numbers from two to five. You tap once to talk to them, twice to contact the captain."

A caracal was a now extinct wildcat that had once inhabited the Westal Mountains. I wondered if it was a coincidence that I'd been given it, or if it had been a deliberate choice. Was my brother perhaps sending a message?

"So the captain sleeps with an activated halo?"

"Until we get to the Karva Pass, where communications are monitored twenty-four seven by the operations team, yes."

"This is why I shouldn't be leading. I don't know basics."

"Neither did any of the people in the relief squad until six months ago. You'll learn, and faster than them, I'll wager."

"Maybe." I hooked the halo around my ear and then pressed the pliable tail into my auditory canal. My inner ear tingled briefly, a sign the unit was now active. "What's the expected procedure for watch duty?"

"Your people report on the half hour or when a disturbance is spotted. There shouldn't be any problems, but if there is, you send out two people to investigate."

"And if that disturbance turns out to be hostile?"

"Inform the captain immediately and order your people out of danger."

"That all sounds simple enough." And I was betting it wouldn't be. Not with Dravan in the group. "What's your call sign?"

"Wildman One, which is rather appropriate, is it not?" He picked up his halo and pushed away from the table. "Shall we go?"

"Personally, I'd rather *not*." I finished the rest of my coffee and stood. "But I guess it's better to confront rather than delay the inevitable."

"Just remember that no matter what, you are unit *leader*. Demand their respect and back it up with actions, and they'll eventually come around."

I ducked out of the tent. "Eventually being an undefined time in which danger abounds and the prospect of ending up with a bullet in my back grows."

"Even the hardest of felons won't risk death by attacking a superior officer in the middle of a main encampment."

I snorted. "That's not exactly a comforting thought."

"If you survived twelve years of abuse at the hands of your father and brother, you can survive whatever hazing these people might fling your way."

I wasn't worried about simple hazing. Words could never physically break me. Guns, however, were another matter entirely.

They had them. I didn't.

But even as that thought hit, energy stirred under my boots. They might be armed, but I had something far more powerful to call on. And while the earth couldn't stop a bullet, *they* couldn't fire at me if the ground opened up and swallowed them whole.

"I'll see you at breakfast, highlander."

"Indeed you will, Princess."

He didn't add "good luck," even though I half expected him to. He obviously had far more confidence in my ability to cope than I did.

I spun around and walked through the camp, heading for my group's assigned meeting point at the nose of the first hauler.

All four were waiting for me. All four wore expressions of barely restrained contempt and—in the case of the woman—a whole lot of anger.

Sage was around my height with a sharp face, blonde hair that had been plaited into a long braid, and a whip-thin frame. Two of the men—Kaid and Nash—were at least four inches taller than me and had the brown skin and golden eyes that was often found in those of us with Sifft heritage. One was thin, the other not. Both exuded a high degree of confidence in their own abilities.

But it was the fourth man who truly drew the eye. Dravan was as big as my brother—a man-mountain with short-cropped red hair, a bulbous nose, and the freckled features of those from Guilderan, the lands on the south-western edge of Cannamore before she met the sea.

I stopped in front of them and resisted the urge to cross my arms. I did *not* need to appear in any way defensive. "I don't expect any of you to stand on ceremony in my presence, but, like it or not, I *am* unit leader, and you will respect that."

"I'll not respect someone who has no experience and no right beyond birth to lead us," Sage said.

"Says the woman who is only here because she had the

stupidity to break into a danseuse's house and steal her jewels," I replied evenly. "And who then compounded that stupidity by attempting to sell them within Divona."

Her lips thinned. "I've nevertheless been trained—"

"For six months," I cut in. "That hardly gives you a greater claim to the leadership role than me. That *is* what you're saying, isn't it?"

Whatever reply she might have made was stopped by Dravan stepping forward.

The earth's heat surged, warming my toes and tingling up my legs. She was ready and willing to answer the call to battle should I but ask. But I couldn't do that—not unless it was absolutely necessary. I needed to win these four over by word and deed, *not* magic.

I raised an eyebrow. "You have to something to say, Dravan?"

"Indeed, *Nyx*, I do."

His tone was pure insolence. I didn't respond in kind. I might yet have to back my right to lead with action, but I had to start as I intended to proceed—by treating them fairly and with respect.

At least until that was no longer enough.

"Then by all means, please proceed."

He flashed me a smile that was all teeth and no sincerity. "I will not obey the word of a woman who is considered little more than a trull by those within the court."

So. There it was. Not only an outright challenge to my authority before the proverbial ink had even dried on the paperwork but confirmation that Dravan *was* Vin's bullet. How else could he have heard about my reputation? The court simply *didn't* air its dirty linen within reach of the ears or eyes of common folk, especially in front of the likes of Dravan.

I took three steps forward to ensure I was within the strike zone—mine, which put me a whole lot closer to him than I really wanted—and glared up at him. This close, he smelled of smoke, sweat, and stale, unwashed flesh.

"We are a long way from Divona, Dravan." I kept my voice soft. Pleasant. "I'd watch what you say and do, because nothing but lies prospers in the Glass Court these days. Do not trust promises made, especially if my brother makes them. Do not *ever* bank on riches flowing into your hands after treachery has been done."

His anger surged, even as a hint of uncertainty flashed through his expression. Not a man who should play cards, I thought.

"And like all trulls, you speak nonse—"

I didn't let him finish. I just hit him. Not with the earth's energy but with a clenched fist powered by a long history of pent-up rage. The blow connected just under his chin and sent him staggering backward. It said a lot about his strength and balance that he didn't end up on his butt.

I doubted my action would, in any way, have been military-approved, and I didn't really care. Men like Dravan only ever respected one thing—power. If you didn't have it —or didn't show it—then you were little more than someone to be used or abused as they saw fit.

A lesson I'd been taught over and over again.

I glanced at the other three. "You got anything to add?"

"No," both Nash and Kaid said, amusement evident. Sage raised an eyebrow but otherwise remained silent.

Dravan wasn't about to let my action go unchallenged. He charged, his steps like heavy thunder echoing through the ground. I waited until the last moment then quickly stepped out of his way and pushed him sideways. He roared in frustration and swung around—only to find my knife sitting at the end of his nose.

"The next time you attack, Dravan, I won't hold back. This knife *will* taste your flesh." I glanced at the other three. "That goes for all of you—is that clear?"

Again they nodded. Dravan simply glowered at me. The next time, I knew, his attack would be a lot more circumspect.

"As I said, like it or not, I'm in control of this unit. Until that ceases to be the case, you will give me the same respect you give Captain Marx or any of the other unit leaders. Are we clear on that?"

Murmurs of acceptance followed. Dravan merely gave a short, sharp nod. I rather suspected it wasn't acceptance of my command but rather of the challenge I'd just given. I might have won the first round, but this was far from over. Still, I didn't push it. To do so when there was no overt challenge would only lose what little respect I might have gained—another lesson I'd learned by watching my brother. Besides, we had a job to do.

I sheathed my knife and stepped back. After assigning them their watch positions, I ordered them to report on the half hour and watched them stride away.

Only then did the shaking start. I took a deep breath, but it didn't do a whole lot to ease the sick churning in my gut. I wasn't cut out for this. I might be royal born, but I wasn't capable of handling this sort of shit day in and day out.

And yet I'd survived twelve years of this very *same* shit. The only difference was the fact it was being flung from a very different hand this time.

This belief that I wasn't good enough—that I would *never* be good enough—was *exactly* what the king had wanted. It seemed that while I might be physically free, mental freedom was a long way off yet.

I took another deep breath and then got on with the business of keeping watch. The hours passed by slowly, and my team members reported in as ordered—even Dravan. As dawn started spreading her golden fingers across the night sky, our relief came. I stood my team down and made my way back to the temporary kitchen. Once I'd collected my breakfast and coffee, I hesitated and looked around. Donal hadn't yet arrived back from his watch, but Captain Marx sat with three others—a man and two women—at a somewhat isolated table on the far side. I walked over.

"Nyx," he said, "let me introduce you to Celi, Merlyn, and Raj, unit leaders from the lunar, sitar, and ghost squads."

They all nodded my way. Celi had dark skin, dark eyes, and a muscular frame, while Merlyn was almost her exact opposite—a thin build, blonde hair, blue eyes, pale skin. Raj was typical Sifft in looks and was also much older than either the two women or the captain.

"Morning," I said. "Mind if I sit with you?"

"That's what this table is for," Celi said, her tone friendly enough. "We generally debrief over breakfast or dinner, depending on which shift we're on."

"A tradition that will continue once we get to the Karva Pass," Raj said. "Not that there's generally much to report given the halos are monitored twenty-four seven and an update sheet is handed to the captain at the end of each shift."

Comments that suggested this wasn't the first time any of them had done relief duty.

"How many rotations have you done at the pass?" I asked.

"I'm going onto ten now," Merlyn said. "Rather it than wall duty any day."

"Five rotations for me," Celi commented. "And wall duty is the pits—endless hours of watching the river race by is not my idea of fun."

Raj's grin flashed. "I'm the granddaddy here with fifteen rotations. It's fair to say I've been well blessed by the gods of luck."

"Being as sneaky as the fucking Skaran also helps." Merlyn glanced at me. "His squad was the only one that didn't lose people last rotation."

I raised an eyebrow. "Impressive."

"Not really." Raj grimaced. "I was just fortunate enough to be on patrol in some of the worst weather we've had in years."

"Meaning the Skaran don't attack in storms?"

"No, and just as well," Celi said. "They're like damn ghosts at the best of times, and they tend to hit and run. I lost three good people last time around."

"I'm sorry—"

"Fact of life beyond the border," Celi cut in, her gaze on mine. "A good half of this group will not live to enjoy the freedom they were promised."

"Then here's hoping Dravan Montaire is one of the first to go."

The captain made a sound that was suspiciously close to a laugh, though there was little evidence of it when I glanced at him.

"How did things go with your squad?" he said.

"As well as could be expected." I picked up a chunk of bread, broke it in half, and dipped it into my beans.

"So there were no problems?"

"Nothing I couldn't handle."

"Good." He eyed me for a moment. "I take it you're happy enough with your team's composition?"

"Would it matter if I wasn't?"

His hesitation was only very brief, but it nevertheless spoke volumes. "No."

"Then I'll deal." With Dravan. With whatever Vin had asked him to do. "Tell me, is the entire garrison replaced every six months? Because that's a rather scarier prospect than encountering the Skaran, given the inexperience of both the relief squad and unit leaders like me."

The captain shook his head. "Key positions—such as communications and weapons—are the sole responsibility of full-time military personnel.

"And thank the gods for that!" Celi said, with a laugh. "I don't think *any* of us would feel safe if the miscreants got anywhere near the armory."

"Present company not included in that miscreant tag," Raj said, grinning.

A smile tugged my lips. "Given my knowledge of weaponry stops at the sword and knife, my inclusion is certainly warranted."

"I'm surprised you even know that much," Celi said. "Being a princess and all, I wouldn't have expected it."

"It would be fair to say I'm not an ordinary princess."

"That's a certainty," Raj said. "Blue bloods don't often show their faces down in the military zone, let alone join a defense unit like ours. Was it by choice?"

"Raj, personal questions aren't approp—"

"It's okay, Captain," I cut in, and then added, "No, it wasn't by choice. But I have no regrets about being here."

Speculation stirred in his eyes, but a look from the captain stopped further questions. It made me wonder yet again just how much he knew about the whole situation.

I ate the rest of my breakfast in silence. Donal came in about ten minutes later and, once he'd collected his meal, joined us. He was introduced to Celi, Merlyn, and Raj and then gave the captain a quick report.

The captain finished the rest of his coffee, then rose. "Packing starts in ten, people. We leave on the hour."

He left, and the other three soon followed. Donal grabbed another chunk of bread and then said, "How did things go?"

I picked up my coffee and took a drink. It was no less sludgy than this morning's effort, but it was at least unburned. "Fine, if you don't count the fact that my fist and Dravan's jaw had an unfortunate meeting."

Donal blinked and then laughed. It was a rich sound that drew more than a few stares our way. He raised his coffee mug and clicked it against mine. "Well done, you."

I grimaced. "I fear I've only made myself a greater target."

"No doubt, but given what Marx said of the man, you really had little other choice. You had to show him—and the other three—that you were willing to retaliate, or the consequences would have been far worse."

"I'm well aware of that." Especially given the only real difference between my brother and Dravan was the nature of their birth. "The problem is, he's fully armed and I'm not."

"He won't shoot you," Donal said. "By sending him flying, you've issued a physical challenge. If he retaliates by shooting, he'd lose face."

"I think he'd rather *that* than get beaten—in any way— by someone like me."

"Then you need to win the support of the other three so they can help watch your back."

"Something else I'm well aware of." I hesitated. "Can you teach me basic weapon handling today? I at least need to avoid shooting myself in the foot."

He half smiled. "The side of your leg is in greater danger than your foot, given blasters are usually positioned at the hip. But yes, I can."

"Good. Thanks." I hesitated again. "How was your team?"

He shrugged. "Interesting. I think one of the men and two of the women fancy me, but that's only natural given I *am* a magnificent specimen."

I almost choked on the coffee. "And modest beside."

"Always." His eyes sparkled in the rising light of day. "In all seriousness, neither of us will really know how good —or bad—our units are until we get to the border and start patrols."

"A statement that also applies to me. It's not like I've had much experience outside the palace walls."

"No, but you can hear the voice of the earth. That gives you an advantage over *any* of the people here—other than me, of course."

"Can all your people hear the whisper of the wind? Can your brother?"

"No. My father can, as can two of my younger sisters, but it's not something that flows true through every generation." He scooped up the last of his beans and then mopped up the juice with a thick chunk of bread. "Can your brother hear the earth? As heir, he should, shouldn't he?"

"Yes, but I can't say if he does or not." I grimaced and took another sip of coffee. "He underwent the initiation ceremony the same time as me, but I've never witnessed him using it."

"He wouldn't have had reason to. Divona's a long way from the borders and the Skaran."

A humorless smile tugged my lips. "Yes, but my brother's temper is somewhat infamous. Either he has absolute control, or it no longer answers his call."

"What does the earth say to that?"

I blinked. "Aside from the fact I didn't have access to her until yesterday, I never thought to ask."

He raised an eyebrow. "She's obviously a far quieter mistress then, because the air has never been backward in voicing an opinion or giving advice."

"The earth speaks from a place of history, whereas the air is more about current and future possibilities. It's natural that she would be the more vocal of the two." I frowned. "If you hear the wind's chatter all the time, how do you not go crazy?"

"Who says I'm not?"

"After your behavior in the eighth tower, certainly not me."

"You wouldn't happen to be referring to my decision to walk naked through the streets, would you?"

"Indeed. And the speed with which you ditched your kilt rather suggests you were quite excited by the prospect of doing so."

"As you noted before, Princess, had I been excited, there would have been evidence of it."

"So, it wasn't extreme control, just a lack of lust." I paused. "Of course, that same disinterest *is* part of the reason I trusted you."

Though his amused expression didn't alter, something very serious touched his gaze. Once again, it was apparent that this man saw too much, understood too much. About what I said, and what I didn't.

He raised that eyebrow again. "Only part? What was the other?"

I shrugged. "That you could do nothing to me that would be worse than what the king or my brother had already done."

"Ah. And here I was thinking it was my winning personality, when all along I was simply a less heinous option."

"But prettier on the eye than either of them, I'll give you that." My smile finally escaped. "At least when you're clean and smelling less like a latrine and more like a man."

"That smell kept the bugs away, Princess."

I snorted softly and finished the rest of my coffee. Once breakfast was over with, we rose and helped break camp. Within an hour, we were on our way again.

Over the course of the long day, Donal instructed me on using a blaster—the everyday weapon of a common soldier—showing me not only how to load it but strip it down and clean it, as well as telling me the basics on how to fire. One thing quickly became evident—handling such a weapon was never going to feel natural to me. Maybe *that* was nothing more than simply being too used to the weight of either a sword or knife in my hand. And maybe it was simply the fact that killing with a gun seemed all too easy— all too impersonal. With a sword or knife, you felt the impact of steel on armor or in flesh. You felt the heat of splattering blood and gore. You were witness to life leaching away from eyes and body. I might never have actually *witnessed* the latter, but I didn't really need to—not when I'd come close to seeing exactly that when I'd severed my brother's arm, and not when I bore the scars of such intimacy with steel all over my body.

Of course, given I had no experience in the real world

beyond the practice yards, it was very likely I'd come to appreciate the value of a distant and impersonal death—especially if the Skaran attacked.

As darkness claimed the sky, we once again set up camp. Donal and I were assigned duty from nine to midnight, and there was little trouble from Dravan or the other three in my unit. Not that I really expected there to be —I had no doubt he was now biding his time, plotting his evil and sorting out the bugs in whatever plans he brewed until the perfect moment arrived.

And *that* would no doubt be when the five of us were well beyond the safety of the Karva Pass military base.

The following day was very much a repeat of the previous. Donal once again ran me through a series of drills with the blaster, until I could load, break, and clean the thing with my eyes closed. I wasn't fast by any means, but at least I wasn't totally useless.

Of course, I hadn't yet fired at anyone. No matter how much he assured me that the lack of recoil meant the blasters were very easy to keep aimed, I wasn't entirely convinced I wouldn't end up shooting either one of my teammates or myself.

And it *did* occur to me that my lack of experience would be the perfect excuse if I ever decided to shoot Dravan.

As dusk claimed the skies again, the convoy started to slow. I slid across the bench seat and peered out the window.

Huge, dark mountains now dominated the sky. The Karva Mountains, in all their brutal glory. From where I sat, I couldn't see either the pass's entrance or Rodestat, but as the skies darkened further, the warm glow of lights began to appear, all of them clustered to the very right edge of my viewing area.

"If you wind down the window, you can perch on the sill and watch our approach," the captain said. "The Red City is quite something to see the first time."

I immediately did so, gripping the inside sill with both hands as I leaned out. The hauler began a long, sweeping turn and, as the caterpillar in front of us disappeared into the curve, Rodestat came into view.

It was massive, and unlike anything I'd ever seen before. Not even the images in the few books I'd read about the place could have prepared me for its sheer size and splendor.

A massive wall that shone like dark glass stretched across the width of the Karva pass. It was at least seven stories high and, given there were vehicles atop of it, had to be at least fifty feet wide. Behind the massive wall, three- and four-story houses climbed up either side of the mountain, appearing—at least from this distance—to be made of red earth that gleamed like fresh blood in the day's fading light. A silvery curtain wall skirted the edge of this tide of houses; it was a continuous ribbon made of thin lines of metal and protected the city from any attack that came from the direction of the barren peaks.

Some distance behind the massive front wall were two metal towers. They stood on either side of the mountain pass and dominated the skyline, almost appearing to challenge the peaks for dominance. The two were joined by a vast red archway that soared across the city and from which multihued flags streamed out in the stiffening breeze.

"I didn't expect anything so permanent-looking," I said. "Not given the nomadic nature of the Mauvaissians."

"This is their winter home," the captain said. "And winter can be very harsh here, let me tell you. You'll have to requisition a full kit from the stores; otherwise, you'll be suffering frostbite once the winter snows hit."

I ducked down to meet his gaze. "We patrol on foot?"

A smile tugged his lips. "Yes. Scooters and carriages are both expensive to maintain and impractical to use in the rocky terrain of the Wild Lands beyond the pass."

"How deep does the snow get? I can't imagine it would be easy to traverse on foot."

"We use snow skids—they'll be part of your pack once winter starts."

I had no idea what skids were but didn't bother admitting it. I leaned out again and saw the huge metal portcullis that dominated the mouth of the forbidding front wall was opening. People were also lining the top of the red arch, though whether they were soldiers or citizens I couldn't really say.

I slipped back inside the pod and glanced at Donal. "You want to have a look?"

"Indeed."

As he moved past and peered out, I asked, "Does the garrison look anything like the city?"

"No." The captain grimaced. "It's not called the black heart of Rodestat for no reason."

"I take it you don't like the place?"

He shrugged. "It's a fortress built to withstand almost anything the Skaran can throw at it. The comfort of those who must man the place was a secondary consideration."

"As it should be." Donal came away from the window and sat down next to me. "It's only a six-month detail, and there's a major city on its doorstep."

"A city we can only access at set times, especially during winter," the captain said. "We're also restricted to certain areas—go elsewhere uninvited or unescorted, and you court death."

"Given the caliber of soldier that is currently being sent here," I said, "that's not entirely surprising."

Again a smile tugged his lips. "No."

It was another twenty minutes before we reached the city. The impeller activated once we went under the portcullis and into a long tunnel that led into the city. The Mauvaissians who were on the streets paid us no heed—in fact, most of them turned their backs on us as we passed.

The deeper we got into the city, the narrower the street became. Eventually, we went through another tunnel and the blood-colored houses gave way to sheer mountain walls.

I scooted across the seat and peered out. We were in a deep, sheer-sided canyon. Rodestat lay behind us and only darkness lay ahead. The canyon was a sterile place—there were no trees, grass, or even moss, and while a constant flow of water ran down the canyon's vertical sides, it disappeared quickly into the crevices that zigzagged across the canyon's floor.

I pulled back from the window and glanced at the captain as he pressed his halo.

After a moment, he said, "Understood. Scout leader out."

"Problem?" Donal said, before I could.

"I'm not entirely sure." His expression gave little away. "But it would appear rumors of your presence has reached Mauvaissian ears. The Red Queen has requested a private audience with you both on our arrival."

That was a meeting I certainly wasn't ready for. I might have enjoyed her presence in my bed more than some, but that didn't alter the fact that the choice had not been mine.

And *she'd* been well aware of it.

I flexed my fingers, once again trying to ease the rising tide of tension. I had no desire to die—not before I'd at least enacted revenge on both the king and my brother—but if I didn't watch my words or my actions, death would very likely take my hand this evening.

And yet I wasn't entirely sure I was capable of such restraint. Not now that I was no longer leashed.

I looked out the window again and saw we were in a V-shaped courtyard. Multilevel buildings pressed up against the sheer mountain walls; the ground level areas were obviously dedicated to everyday requirements—mess halls, kitchens, armories, and the like—while the six upper levels on either side of the V appeared to be barracks. The widest point was a massive curtain wall that was topped by a walkway. Underneath this was a series of windows—communications and command centers, more than likely.

The red-and gold-clad garrison was lined up in the courtyard, and there were certainly far fewer of them than us. The haulers came to a halt and the doors opened. We followed the captain out and lined up with the other unit leaders in front of the scout division. The garrison soldiers formed several lines behind us.

The garrison commander greeted Gallego; the two spoke quietly for a few minutes, then our group was formally welcomed. In very little time—and with very little ceremony—the old squadron was escorting the new to the various stations and bunkhouses.

Two men in loose red tunics with guns belted at their waists approached Donal and me, requested we follow them, and led us away from the group.

"I gather from your reaction in the hauler," Donal said quietly, "that the Red Queen was one of the people sent to your bed."

"Yes." There was little inflection in my voice. I hoped I could keep in that way.

"Then I'm sorry."

My gaze shot to his. "Why?"

"Because I asked my father to request this meeting. Had I known your connection with her, I wouldn't have done so. Not until you were ready."

"I'm not a paper flower in need of protection, Donal." The tension I was trying to control was very evident in those few words. I took a deep breath and then added, "But why would you ask to meet with her?"

"Because she is queen of this land and needs to know what the wind whispers." He glanced at me. "And I'm well aware you're steel rather than paper, but even steel has a breaking point."

"The Red Queen *isn't* mine." Though there was no doubt that both anger and hostility *would* be an undercurrent in my dealings with her. I guess we'd soon find out just how visible those undercurrents would be.

"So you'll not kill her, then?"

"No."

"Good, because I suspect we'll actually need her help in the future."

"Suspect?" I glanced up at him. "Is that intuition speaking or uncertainty on the part of your mistress air?"

"The air advises against killing unnecessarily. She doesn't mention the Mauvaissian queen specifically."

"Not killing her does leave me with plenty of other options."

"Nyx—"

"I'm joking." My grin flashed, though it felt tight. False. "There are plenty of others I'd rather kill first—and we both know *that* is hardly practical if I ever wish to sit on the glass throne."

We were led through a guarded doorway into a tunnel that was lit only in the area immediately in front of us, which gave the impression that we were chasing the light. The tunnel walls appeared to be made of the same glass-like material as the walls that guarded Rodestat, which suggested this tunnel played a vital part in the overall security of the garrison —an impression backed by the door and weapon slots regularly spaced along it. If invaders ever got this far, they could be locked into individual "cells" and slaughtered at will.

We eventually came out into what was basically a small, metal-lined antechamber. There was one door directly opposite the tunnel we'd just left, but little else. There certainly didn't appear to be any sort of security measures, although I'd bet my life *that* was a false impression.

Our two escorts told us to wait and then walked across to the door. They keyed open a panel to its right and pressed several buttons. Lights flashed and, a heartbeat later, there came a distant sound of rushing water and the grinding of metal upon metal. An odd vibration began to run through the steel under our feet.

"I'd heard whispers of places like this," Donal said. "But I didn't believe them to be true."

I frowned at him. "Meaning what?"

He met my gaze. "This entire room is a turntable."

My confusion increased. "Why would anyone put a turntable under a mountain? The tunnel into this place is foot traffic only—there's no way they could get a vehicle in here, so why would they need to turn it around?"

"It's not designed for vehicles, but rather as a life and death lottery. If what I've read is true, there are a number of tunnels leading off this room, but only one safe tunnel in and out. The rest are death traps. Key in the wrong coordinates and you die."

"Which is an impressive piece of engineering—one I'm surprised isn't being used in Divona and the other cities."

He raised an eyebrow. "The treaty may have given us a thousand years of peace, but that doesn't mean all secrets have been—or ever will be—shared."

"True."

The vibrations stopped. The guards punched a few more buttons, then the door opened to reveal yet another tunnel—one made of stone rather than the strange glass material or even metal. As we entered, the pulse of the earth came to life and her voice stirred, whispering of what lay ahead.

We were no longer in the garrison but in Rodestat itself. This tunnel had been built eons ago, when the Mauvaissians alone had manned the black heart of Rodestat. But it had not only been designed as a trap but also a means of escape for any royalty caught in the garrison compound during an attack.

We were soon approaching another door; in the room beyond, the earth whispered, was one person.

I had no doubt that person was the Red Queen. She'd never been one to need either a large entourage or protection detail. In Divona, only three had shadowed her movements. Here, in the heart of her kingdom, there was little need for it, if only because it was very unlikely an opponent's blade would find its way into her heart. That was not the way in which Mauvaissian society worked.

I flexed my fingers again, but it did little to ease the knot of tension growing in my gut. Power stirred through the ground under my feet, seeming to echo the turbulence within me. The earth might whisper for calm, might urge that I didn't react out of anger or hate, but she was nevertheless ready to unleash hell should I urge it.

Part of me really *did* want to unleash—and not *just* on the Red Queen.

As the guards keyed open the door, I closed my eyes and drew in a deep breath.

I could do this. I *had* to do this. The air might whisper of a future where I claimed the King's Sword and ruled from the glass throne, but for that to actually happen, I had to face every single person who'd ever taken their pleasure from me.

Face them and *not* kill them.

The door opened. She was not immediately visible.

Donal stepped to one side, allowing me to enter first. I felt no easier with him standing at my back. In fact, it probably would have better had he been in front—at least then he would have stood between me, the queen, and any temptation I might have to lash out at her.

I walked into the room.

She stood to the left of the door, in the middle of the room.

And despite the grip I had on my emotions, despite knowing I could *not* react in any way, the mere sight of her unleashed twelve years of festering anger and impotence, and there was absolutely nothing I could do to stop it.

As the earth under my feet began to rumble and the room shake, I grabbed my knife, took six long steps, and thrust upwards with the blade.

FIVE

I didn't kill her.

The point of the knife didn't even break her skin.

But it *was* pressed against her throat just under her jaw, and if she so much as twitched the wrong way, it would have drawn blood.

She didn't twitch.

She didn't even call for the guards.

She merely studied me, one dark eyebrow raised. She was typical Mauvaissian in build—muscular, with black hair, red-brown skin, and dark eyes. What made her stand apart—and gave her the Red Queen moniker—was the red stain that dominated the whites of her eyes, making it appear as if they bled.

"If you kill me, Nyx, I must warn that both you and Lord Donal will be dead a heartbeat later." Her voice was calm, her tone cool.

"If I was here to kill you, you wouldn't now be talking." My voice might be even, but my inner turmoil was very much reflected in the tremors that vibrated through the floor. "I'm merely satisfying a long-held desire while restraining deeper urges."

"Oh, I'm well aware of those deeper urges. We've explored many of them over the years."

"Yes, we did." I pressed the knife just a bit harder against her skin. A small bead of blood welled around the knife's point. She didn't flinch. It wasn't in her nature to do so. "But they were never *my* urges. You knew that, just as you knew I was wearing restraint bracelets and had no choice but to do as you wished."

"But did you not gain pleasure from those experiences?"

Her expression was utterly confident and for a very good reason—I had. But *that* was not the point.

"No amount of pleasure can *ever* justify the denial of choice, Marttia. In using the power of the bracelets to make me do as you wished rather than simply *asking*, you went against all teachings of the goddess Eisha. For that, there one day will be a reckoning."

I pulled my knife from her throat and forced myself to step back. The rumbling earth immediately calmed, but it was warning enough that until I was used to accessing and controlling her, I would have to watch my temper. Otherwise I might inadvertently kill someone.

"If that is Eisha's wish, then so be it," she said calmly. "I for one do not regret the time we spent together, even if I had the advantage."

"But it is one you no longer hold," I said. "Don't ever hope for a repeat, Marttia, or my blade will taste your flesh more fully."

"In these lands, that is considered a threat."

"In mine, it's considered a promise."

Anticipation gleamed in her eyes. Anticipation and

desire. I ignored the first and went cold at the thought of the second.

Behind us, Donal cleared his throat. "Ladies, as entertaining as all this is, we have greater problems to discuss."

Marttia's gaze jumped past me. "Forgive me, Lord Donal, for my rudeness. Welcome to Rodestat, though I am somewhat at a loss to understand why a highland lord would be a part of Divona's relief squadron, or why your father requested such secrecy for this meeting."

Donal stepped up to stand beside me. He was close enough that his arm brushed mine, and I rather suspected it was deliberate. A show of unity against the queen, perhaps.

"Please, call me Donal."

A smile touched her lips, though her gaze was speculative as it swept between the two of us. "Then call me Marttia—at least when we are not in more formal company. What brings you here?"

"The wind whispers of troubled times ahead. Rainer paid no heed to the warning, but I hope you *will*, given Rodestat will bear much of the brunt of what comes."

"How so?"

Donal quickly updated her on everything he'd already told me, and then added, "Whoever—whatever—comes will hit us sometime within the next few months. We need to be prepared."

She frowned. "Prepared for what, though? We have more than enough weapons, food, and water to outlast a winter-long siege, and there is very little chance of the garrison's walls being breached, let alone Rodestat's. The Skaran do not have that sort of technology to hand."

"It's not the Skaran who will attack. It's a completely new foe."

"There has been no unusual movement in the Wild Lands. I would have been notified if there had."

"This threat doesn't come from there, but rather from the lands *beyond* the Skaran borders." The air stirred and Donal hesitated. "It's currently fifty miles beyond them, in fact."

"Which probably puts it in the dead zone. Not an area we can access easily."

I frowned. "What's the dead zone?"

She glanced at me. "It's a once lush land that was totally destroyed by a volcanic eruption over nine hundred years ago. No one lives there."

I frowned. "Surely nine hundred years is more than enough time for regeneration?"

"Yes, and much of the area *has* recovered. It's really only a wide strip of land that runs directly from the old volcano that hasn't." She hesitated. "But even in the regrowth areas, there is—as far as we can ascertain—no wildlife. If animals are unable to survive there, it is unlikely any possible threat to us could."

"I take it, then, you don't have patrols out that far?" Donal asked.

"Indeed not. Not only are the Skaran in the way, but it's also impractical to carry the amount of provisions needed for such a journey. We cannot get vehicles through the Wild Lands or over the mountain passes—and any work done to make either passage viable for such movement would only make it easier for the city to be attacked."

I frowned. "Then how can you be so sure that those lands remain uninhabited?"

Her gaze flicked to me. "Because we've trained blue hawks to carry small vision recorders into both the Skaran lands and as far into the dead zone as possible."

Blue hawks were small birds of prey who were native to Cannamore as a whole, but more prevalent throughout Mauvaissia. In ancient times—before the development of halos and scribe pens—they'd been used in wartime situations to deliver messages between the front lines and the commanders at the rear. Part of the reason most armies no longer used them was the fact that their flight range was limited and they could only be used in the daylight hours.

Donal frowned. "Even so, we cannot ignore the wind's warnings—"

"I will not endanger my people or even the Divonian relief squad to seek out a threat that might not eventuate, no matter what your mistress says," Marttia said. "The Skaran fiercely protect their borders and will spot any incursion within hours. And with winter almost on us, the mountain passes are already close to unusable."

"Neither of which is a problem for a wind mage. We'll go *over* the Skaran—they won't even see us."

Marttia frowned. "But why won't the wind simply tell you what the threat is?"

"Because she can't actually see it—something blocks her in two locations."

That raised my eyebrows. "What can block the wind?"

His gaze met mine. If the ethereal glow in those rich blue depths was anything to go by, the wind still spoke to him. But it was the concern so evident behind the glow that worried me.

"Another air mage. Or magic."

"How likely is either?" Marttia said.

"Before I arrived in this city, I would have said virtually impossible." His voice was grim. "Few outside the Westal Ranges have the ability to speak to the wind, and even fewer can control her. As for magic—I don't think there's been a spell master in Cannamore for many centuries."

"Personal magic and small spell makers still exist here, though. And the great mages certainly left behind many items of magic—both the King's Sword and the restraint bracelets are evidence enough of that." I rubbed my arms lightly, but it didn't do much against the growing chill. "And how would we know if any spell masters *had* been born? It's not like anyone keeps track of the bloodlines anymore."

"That's because the last known grand master died without offspring." Marttia frowned. "If, however, that situation has changed, we need to know. This place is all but impervious to traditional weaponry, but it was never designed to withstand the forces of magic."

"None of our cities are," Donal said. "Which is why we need to start preparing."

If Mauvaissia fell, then my homeland would be the next one hit. With the earth no longer responding to the king, she would have to rely on nothing more than her walls and her people—and our walls were no stronger than those of Rodestat.

Of course, in such a situation, the earth *might* recant her withdrawal from the king. And with the earth at his disposal, there would be few enemies he could not defeat—even one armed with magic.

Warmth stirred under my feet, and then a deep, rich voice reached into my mind and said, *no.*

Tears briefly touched my eyes even as fierce, bright joy leapt through me. For twelve long years I'd been waiting to hear the voice of the earth again. To do so now—so loudly and so clearly—was something I'd almost given up on.

But the anger that ran through the denial had me frowning. *Not even if Divona was under threat?*

No. He is a betrayer and, as such, will not be tolerated and cannot be obeyed.

Meaning that on his death, his voice will not join yours?

The stain of evil will never be welcome amongst us.

I wondered if the king was aware of the consequences yet to come. Wondered if he'd even care. With his mind fragmenting, it was very possible he wouldn't.

"And how does one prepare against magic when there are no spell casters in these lands?" Marttia asked.

"I can't answer that question right now," Donal said. "But between earth and air, we're not exactly helpless."

"Earth?" Her gaze shot to me. "*You* were the reason for the recent tremor?"

"Yes." Despite my best effort, anger crept into my voice as I added, "Did you think the king forced those restraints onto me just so I could become a plaything for all and sundry?"

"I was given the impression all Divonian princesses wore them."

I snorted. "And who gave you that impression? The king? My brother?"

"Brother."

She reached out—whether to offer comfort or an even an apology I had no idea and really didn't care. I stepped back quickly and her hand touched nothing but air.

"Don't," I said, voice sharp. "Not ever again."

Her expression told me she both saw and heard the anger, but I was pretty sure she didn't understand it. Just as I was sure if she *had* intended an apology, it wasn't, in any way, related to her usage of me. That, like many other things, wasn't in her nature.

She let her hand drop and glanced at Donal. "I wouldn't wish to sanction a journey into those lands without first informing the incoming commander and scout captain. If Rodestat *is* in danger, they need to be made aware of the situation."

"I agree," Donal said.

"How soon do you wish to leave?"

"Sometime within the next week, preferably."

Marttia nodded. "There's a major storm forecast in three days; it would provide you with more cover and lessen the chance of the Skaran spotting you."

It also gave us more time with our respective teams, and that was vital—at least for me. Dravan was obvious assassin material, but I doubted he'd be the only one. My brother had always hedged his bets.

Marttia glanced at the wall to our right. "Hargon, please summon Commander Gallego and Captain Marx to the war room immediately."

"Yes, my queen," an unseen male responded.

"Soldiers hidden within walls?" Amusement twitched Donal's lips. "I thought the Red Queen was above such things?"

Marttia's smile warmed the dark depths of her eyes. "She is, but she isn't a fool, either. This way, both of you."

She spun on her heel and walked toward the far wall. A small section immediately slid to one side, revealing six soldiers standing either side of a bright hallway. They snapped to attention as Marttia approached, then turned crisply and gave escort. We wound our way through various halls and staircases; gradually the plain corridor gave way to wide red halls that were furnished with bright tapestries and lit by natural light.

After climbing a final, very long set of metal stairs, we approached a solid-looking door guarded by a man and a woman. Once the door was coded open, Marttia led us into a long room in which the opposite wall was entirely glass. The view beyond was amazing—we were so high up that both the Red City and the garrison lay before us. Had it been daylight rather than night, I suspected we might have been able to see the tree-covered hillside on the *far* side of the garrison wall. No wonder it was called the war room; from this vantage point, Marttia would see everything that went on without any sort of help—though I had no doubt there'd be all manner of communication devices here, even if they weren't immediately visible.

As we moved toward the long stone table that dominated the room, I spotted a metal tower to the far right and realized we were in the red arch that soared across Rodestat.

Marttia sat at the head of the table, Donal to her left. I hesitated, and then walked across to the window, staring out over the night-covered streets. We were so high up it was impossible to see if people were moving along them, but even if they were, they would have been little more than insects.

I crossed my arms and tried to ignore the insidious whisper that I was no better than those insects. That I had no right to be in this room.

Silence reigned for who knew how many minutes, but I could feel the weight of approaching steps through the stone under my feet and watched the doors via the reflection in the windows. They eventually opened; Gallego and Marx entered, and then stopped to incline their heads at Marttia—an informal acknowledgment of her rule and all she generally required. Had it been Divona's court, a full bow would have been given.

"Gentlemen," Marttia said, "please sit. Princess Nyx, I would prefer it if you also did so."

I turned and walked back to the table, but I didn't

immediately sit. Maybe it was childish, but I simply didn't want to be seen obeying her orders. I wasn't one of her people—I was her ruler. Or would be, if I ever gained the glass throne.

Commander Gallego's gaze swept me, but he kept a tight lock on whatever he thought of my presence in the room as he turned to Marttia and said, "May I ask why you've called this meeting? We've had no information about an incoming attack by the Skaran."

"Lord Donal requested this meeting. It is he who should explain why."

Donal immediately did so. When he'd finished, Gallego frowned and leaned back in his chair. "The recent skirmishes with the Skaran give no indication they are under threat from another quarter. If they faced a new foe, their attacks against us would have eased."

"This threat hasn't yet reached their borders. As I said, it lies at least some fifty miles into the dead zone."

"Impossible," Gallego commented. "There's no life in that blighted place, and no way to survive there. Even the water is said to be poisonous."

"And yet some regeneration *has* occurred on either side of the dead strip, has it not?" I said. "Given the flight range of a blue hawk, it's possible repopulation has occurred elsewhere even if it hasn't reached the outskirts of the dead zone yet."

"Even if that were the case," Gallego said, "it doesn't alter the fact that the Skaran would be aware of any imminent attack and would have reacted accordingly. That they haven't altered their thrusts against *us* speaks volumes of this unknown, unseen threat."

"If the area is as barren as you say, Commander," Donal said, "they'd have no reason to venture that far into it."

"So what is it you wish of us? The Wild Lands and the Skaran lie between this unidentified threat and us. We have no vehicles that can safely traverse either the Wild Lands or the Peaks, and walking is impractical given the distances involved. And I, for one," he added heavily, "am loath to waste time on something as insubstantial as the whispering of the wind. Sorry, Lord Donal, but the garrison's resources *are* limited."

"I think you'll find Lord Donal understands that," Marttia said, "and he's not asking for the garrison force to be used in a quest into the dead lands."

"Then what is the point of this meeting?" Gallego said.

"Aside from apprising us of a potential threat, you mean?" Her voice was deceptively mild given the flare of annoyance that made her eyes gleam with bloody fire. Gallego, I surmised, wasn't one of her favorite people.

"Yes, obviously."

"I want any maps you might have of the place," Donal said, "and any information you can dig up about the area, either before or after the eruption."

"The only maps we have of the area are archived ones," Marx said. "They'd be of little use now, given that the quakes that continue to plague this entire region would undoubtedly have changed the topography."

"There'd still be some markers in the landscape that remain the same," Donal said. "We'll also need basic survival supplies—"

"Enough." Gallego's voice was curt. "Forgive me, Queen T'Ivio, but approval for such a mission lies with me, not you. Aside from the fact we work in units of five for *good* reason, Lord Donal has no more rights within the squadron than any other criminal—"

"The criminals sent here in the place of true soldiers

cannot hear the whispers of the wind, Commander," she cut in sharply. "Nor can they control her mood and whims. I'm no more inclined to believe a threat could exist in the dead zone than you, but neither am I willing to discount the wisdom of mages past and present. And, as the commander of a garrison that will face this threat *if* it exists, neither should you."

"*That* doesn't negate the fact that Lord Donal shouldn't go out alone," Gallego said. "This venture is a fool's mission. Even with the help of the wind, there are too many unknowns between the Skaran and the heart of this so-called threat."

"I won't be going alone," Donal said. "Princess Nyx will be accompanying me."

Gallego snorted. "Then this is indeed a mission for fools."

Donal crossed his arms on the table, a casual motion that belied the sudden anger in him. But before he could say anything, I stepped forward and pressed my fingers against the table. The stone warmed under my touch, a pulse that spoke of readiness.

"Why would you say that, Commander, when you have no idea of what I'm—"

"Come now, you're a *princess*," he cut in. "And Divona is not Mauvaissia—"

"No, it isn't," I cut in softly—angrily—even as I conjured the image of stone cuffs encasing his wrists in my mind. "And I'm *not* an ordinary Divonian princess."

I raised a finger and unleashed the heat gathered underneath. That heat surged forward, raising the table's stone into a wave that raced toward Gallego.

"What the fuck—?" His gaze went from the wave to me and then back again. "What the hell is *that* thing?"

"Proof that I can defend myself."

"Okay, I believe. Just stop whatever it is—" He pushed up and away from the table.

But not fast enough. The wave reached the edge and splashed upward, catching his left hand and encasing it in hard stone.

"I warned you before we left Divona not to underestimate my abilities, Commander," I said softly. "I may not have the gun skills of even the newest recruit, but I *am* a master of both sword and knife, and I can mold the earth and its elements to my will."

"An impressive display, Princess," Marttia all but drawled. "And a lesson learnt, I believe. But can you please release him so we can get down to the business of planning this journey?"

I drew the stone back to the table, released the remaining energy, and watched the wave roll back to solidity. Only then did I pull out the chair next to Donal and sit down.

And tried to ignore the slight ache forming in the back of my mind. There was always a price to be paid for using the elements—for bending earth, rock, and even metal to your will. For earth—and undoubtedly air—mages, that price was personal strength. And if you used too much— went too far—your body could be thrown into a state of shock that could take hours, if not days, to recover from.

It could even kill you.

The wave I'd created would have taken very little out of a mage used to controlling elements, but I was very much a novice given I'd had little time to build my mage "muscles" before the restraints had been placed on me. Maybe it wasn't just my shooting skills I needed to work on.

For the next half hour, the three men and Marttia

discussed the journey and made plans. I kept silent. I didn't know these lands, didn't know the Skaran, and certainly had little to say when it came to what we might or might not need. And it made me realize that no matter how much I might have studied the laws of the land and the procedures of the court, I still had a lot to learn. Though I *did* have one advantage—I certainly knew more about each lord or lady's dreams and desires than the king or my brother *ever* would.

Of course, the time to worry about that sort of thing was when I was actually on the throne. It was pointless doing so now when I had six months and an unknown foe to first get past.

"Keep me informed of progress, Commander Gallego. Captain Marx, please retrieve whatever maps you have in the archives and give them to Lord Donal and Princess Nyx as soon as possible." Marttia glanced at us. "And I would truly appreciate it if you both came back from this mission alive. I have no desire to explain your deaths in lands far beyond our own."

"If death *does* find us, it won't be in foreign lands," Donal said. "It'll be here, fighting for Rodestat's freedom."

Marttia's gaze narrowed. "So says your mistress?"

"This time, no. It's simply a gut feeling."

She nodded and rose. The rest of us immediately did the same. "Hargon, please escort them to the outer court."

The door opened and a big man wearing the loose red uniform of her personal guards stepped into the room. "This way, please."

Without waiting, he turned and headed out. The four of us followed silently, Donal and I walking side by side behind Marx and Gallego. We were led down that long metal staircase then through a series of hallways until we reached a wide stone courtyard. Lights on long black metal poles lit some areas while leaving others to shadows and imagination. The air ran with the rich scents of breads and meats, and laughter rode the faint breeze. It brought back memories of the times my mother had taken me into the second tier, where the merchants, traders, and danseuse lived. It too had been filled with warmth and merriment, though I had to wonder if that was still the case after the brief glimpse I'd gotten of the area as we were leaving Divona.

We were led across to a simple metal carriage. Once our ride was underway, Captain Marx said, "We've assigned you both accommodation with the other unit leaders. While we need to mention this mission to them—especially given they'll be patrolling while you two are gone, and should be on the lookout for behavioral changes from the Skaran—it would be better done once everything is in place and ready to go."

I had no idea why that would make any difference, but perhaps Marx simply didn't want to start any untoward gossip and speculation.

"Both your squads and the relief unit are already out on patrol with the outgoing team in order to learn their assigned sector," he continued. "You'll be joining them for the next two nights; I want recommendations from you both as to which of your team would make a good unit leader while you're gone."

I snorted. "You can sure as hell bet I won't be recommending Dravan."

"Discounting someone because you don't like them is not how a good leader works," Gallego said, voice cold.

I met his gaze evenly. "Neither is placing a totally inappropriate person into a team, Commander, but I guess we both know you had little choice in that. Just as we both know why Dravan is there."

"I'm obviously missing something here." Marx glanced at Gallego. "Exactly *why* was I ordered to place that man into Nyx's team?"

"It was on the prince's order, not mine." He glanced at me. "But you're wrong in saying I know why. Perhaps you'd care to enlighten us all?"

I smiled. "Let's just say that if I have an unfortunate accident sometime in the next six months and Dravan is near or present when it happens, then it *is* no accident."

Gallego frowned. "I cannot believe—"

"Commander, you know as little about court politics as I know about military actions, so please go no further with that statement."

He stared at me for a second and then nodded. "I'll have him transferred to another unit if you desire, and deal with whatever consequences might come once we return to Divona."

An offer I certainly *hadn't* been expecting. Maybe I'd been reading Gallego wrong—although I very much doubted I was misreading his discontent at my being here. "Thank you, but it's always better to keep a gutter snake close rather than letting it attack from a distance."

"Indeed." His gaze switched to Donal. "Is this threat the reason you were assigned relief duty?"

The smile that touched Donal's lips held little amusement. "No, but it nevertheless achieved the desired result."

"And you seriously believe Rodestat is in danger?"

"I wouldn't be here otherwise, Commander. Trust me when I say that your king could not have forced me into this unit had I wished otherwise."

Amusement touched Gallego's expression, but it was

gone so quickly I couldn't help but wonder if I'd imagined it. "Then we will do whatever we can to aid you."

That raised my eyebrows. Given Marttia's orders, I would have thought his helping us was a *fait accompli*. But obviously, the commander hadn't. It made me wonder just what the setup was between the garrison and the city it protected—and who'd have the final word if the worst happened and the garrison fell. Could the commander override the queen when it came to something as desperate as a citywide evacuation?

Unease accompanied *that* particular thought; we hadn't even yet sourced a threat, but my thoughts were already moving to evacuation procedures. I hoped it was my natural pessimism kicking in rather than a partial whisper of the future from the earth. I didn't want to believe a city as mighty as Rodestat could fall, if only because it boded ill for Divona.

We soon arrived back in the garrison's courtyard. Captain Marx showed us where the Base Exchange and armories were, and then took us over to supplies so we could get kitted up. The scout leaders' accommodation, which was tucked into one corner on the third level, was just down from the bunkhouses that held the rest of the division. Our room did at least have privacy cubicles rather than simple rows of beds and footlockers, but the sides of those cubicles didn't stretch to the ceiling, and they had no doors, just a partial partition at the front.

Donal and I were assigned the ones on either side of the door, as far away from the privy and bathroom facilities as you could get—a result of being the last to arrive, no doubt.

There was only one other person present—a golden-haired, golden-eyed man with the olive-brown skin of a Sifft.

"Tal is the sixth member of our team and leads ice unit," Marx said. "All three Nightwatch teams have been assigned a half hour at the shooting range at 5:00 p.m., and I suggest you use it to sharpen your shooting abilities—you're going to need them. We reconvene at six for dinner and a debrief with Daywatch."

"And where does that happen?" I asked.

Marx smiled. "Mess hall. There's a garrison map in your cubicle—the layout of this place can take a while to get used to."

With that, he turned and left. I glanced at the two cubicles and then at Donal. "Have you a preference?"

"Ladies should always have first choice." He paused, and then added with a twinkle in his eyes, "At least when the two options are virtually identical."

I snorted and headed into the one on my right. It wasn't a huge space—little more than a six-by-eight-foot rectangle —but there was a decent bed, a small metal upright locker and a footlocker, and a fold-down table and a chair to the left of the bed. After I'd stowed what little I had away, Tal offered to show us both the location of the dining area as well as where the unit table was located.

Celi and Merlyn joined us after the meal and the rest of the evening was spent quite pleasantly in the garrison alehouse, drinking and chatting. But as I went to bed, I couldn't escape the notion the pleasantness wouldn't last.

That, as of tomorrow, the darkness would begin to close in.

Maybe the feeling was little more than pessimism and the knowledge that I'd once again be dealing with Dravan.

Maybe it was the stirring earth, and her whispers that all was not right out in the dead lands.

Either way, sleep, when it finally did come, was uneasy.

Weapons practice went better than expected—I hit every target even if most of them wouldn't have been classified as "killing" shots, and that was certainly better than spraying bullets across the walls or at the people around me. Dravan basically ignored me, although his hostility continued to stain the air. It might be a leashed force, but I had no doubt it would spill over sooner rather than later.

Dinner with Daywatch revealed there'd been signs that the Skaran were active in the Wild Lands, but no units had been attacked. I was introduced to Rennie, the outgoing unit leader for my watch zone and, in very little time, both his group and mine were kitted up and walking through the long exit tunnel. The Gateway Canyon beyond was a place filled with rocks, uplifted black stone and earth, and deep crevices—one of which split the canyon completely in half, separating the area immediately beyond the tunnel from the forested beginnings of the Wild Lands. A wide metal bridge spanned the crevice, and though I couldn't see any means of either raising or withdrawing the bridge, I had no doubt it could be done. The Mauvaissians wouldn't have built it without ensuring a means of destruction.

My patrol sector ran from the base of the Karva Mountains to the Quaih River—which divided the Wild Lands from the Skaran's land—and then did a sweeping turn back to the garrison. It was just over eighteen miles in total, and I had no doubt I'd be wiped out by the end of it. I might be physically fit thanks to the years of using sword and knife in the practice yards, but *that* was very different to walking through broken terrain carrying a backpack, ammo clips, and weapons. Which was part of the reason why I'd decided to wear my old, worn-in boots rather than the new ones I'd been allocated. Given our incursion into the dead lands in three days' time, blisters were the last things I needed. Thankfully, slow and steady was the aim for these patrols—or so Rennie informed me.

We were spread out in a wide, shallow V, with Rennie and me taking point. Three and a half hours had passed when I first felt it—the slight tremor in the earth. I touched my halo, ordered a halt, and then knelt and pressed my fingers against the ground. The vibration I'd barely felt through the soles of my feet jumped into sharper focus.

Footsteps, coming at speed.

I glanced up at Rennie. "Is there anyone out here other than the Skaran?"

"No. Why?"

"Then we have a party of six coming at us."

He raised an eyebrow. "And you can tell that by simply touching the earth?"

"I'm an earth mage. It's a talent that runs in the family."

Amusement briefly touched his expression. He raised his head and flared his nostrils, drawing in the crisp night air. "I can't smell them."

"They're coming at us from the left, into the breeze." I hesitated, splaying my fingers a little wider, trying to capture more information. "They're still a couple of miles away."

"Which isn't far, given the speed at which they can run." He pressed his ear circle. "Heads up, Balcor and Caracal units; there's half a drift incoming. Stay alert."

"A drift?" I asked.

He grimaced. "I know it's a term meant for boars, but it suits the bastards. A full drift is a company of twelve, but thankfully, they aren't often out in those sorts of numbers."

He drew his blasters and cautiously continued on. I

echoed his actions as silently as I could, every sense I had alert for the signs of danger I could feel in the earth. But my palms were sweaty, and my heart raced so badly it felt ready to tear out of my chest.

I hadn't trained for this. I wasn't ready for this sort of battle.

You are no longer restrained, a voice whispered through my mind. *You no longer have to rely on only your own strength.*

I briefly closed my eyes and breathed deeply. Not only was the earth *right*, but I wasn't the only one here facing this enemy for the first time. I had four team members who'd undoubtedly be feeling the same—even if someone like Dravan was never likely to admit it.

Musk began to stain the air, a thick, sour scent that made me want to gag. It was so strong—so invasive—that it clung to my skin and clothes and forced me to breathe through my mouth. And as that scent got stronger, so too did the vibrations running through the earth.

"One mile away, Rennie," I said.

He nodded and touched the halo again. "Balcor and Caracal units, stand ready. At the first sign of movement, fire, and don't stop, or the bastards will have you."

His warning to our units had my fingers tightening on the grips of my blasters. Tension wound through my limbs, but I did my best to ignore it—to concentrate on the ever-increasing closeness of heavy steps on the ground.

Then they stopped.

But they were close—so damn close. I could feel the weight of them through the earth. Was practically drowning in their odorous scent.

So why weren't they attacking?

I scanned the darkness, wondering if this was part of

their methodology—a game they played with their prey to heighten tension and fear before they attacked.

Or had they perhaps realized we were ten rather than five and decided the odds were not in their favor? But if that were true, why were they not retreating? Why were they simply standing there?

"No movement, no sign," a voice said into my ear. Sage, from the sound of it.

"If you can't smell them," Nash said, "you need your damn nose checked."

I tapped the halo and said, "Caracal two and three, maintain silence unless necessary and remain at the ready. They're two hundred yards away."

"And this is *not* their usual behavior," Rennie murmured.

"Perhaps our numbers are giving them pause."

He snorted. "The Skaran welcome greater odds—the more, the better. It's considered the mark of a great warrior to win such fights."

Then why weren't they attacking?

He'd barely finished when the earth screamed a warning—a sound that was all but drowned under an inhuman roar that shattered the silence and sent a chill down my spine.

I raised my guns in readiness.

I didn't have to wait for long.

Something big, brown, and hairy came flying out of the trees, its monstrous form little more than a blur as it came straight at me.

SIX

I immediately fired both blasters. The creature's body shuddered and twitched as it was hit multiple times, but it didn't seem to care. It certainly didn't stop. I kept the triggers pressed but switched aim to its head. The bullets ripped into flesh and bone, tearing the left side of the Skaran's face apart. Blood and brain matter flew, but the damn thing refused to drop. Even though it should have been dead, it kept coming at me.

I swore and dove to one side, hitting the ground hard enough to drive a grunt of pain from my lips. Metal claws grabbed at me—claws that *should* have had no force behind them—snagging the skin just under my metal-threaded leather protection vest and digging deep. I twisted around and fired again, demolishing the rest of the Skaran's head and scattering its remaining brains across the nearby earth. And then fired several more shots, just to ensure it really was dead.

When the blaster clicked over to empty, I scrambled up and away from the thing. Rennie swung around as I did so, his blaster centered on my torso, but relaxed when he saw me. "Balcor and Caracal units, report."

Answers came in. No one lost, all Skaran dead. Relief surged and, just for an instant, my legs felt like water. I took a deep breath in an effort to calm my racing heart, then reloaded the blasters and walked over to Rennie.

A second Skaran lay at his feet, a cavity where its chest and heart had once been. They were humanoid in form and had to be at least ten feet tall, with two yellow tusks that curled upwards from either side of their wide mouths and eyes that were as pale as the moon above. Downy brown hair covered its flat face and nose, but the hair on the rest of its body was thick, coarse, and at least a foot long—and even longer around its genital region, which indicated it was a he, not a she. His feet, like his hands, ended in metal claws; they weren't natural but something akin to metal gauntlets.

This close, their body aroma was even more horrendous.

Rennie drew a knife, cut the two six-inch tusks away from its mouth, and then clipped the bloody items to his utility belt.

I frowned. "Why did you do that?"

"Two reasons. The first and most important is the fact that the Skaran apparently believe a soul cannot move on if the body is defiled in such a way." His expression was grim as it met mine. "And trust me, they do *far* worse to our fallen."

Not something I wanted to think about. "And the second reason?"

"The tusks fetch a good price in Rodestat—they use them to make jewelry and the like." He shrugged. "We might as well profit from the bastards given the toll they take on our people."

I didn't like the idea of *anyone* profiting from death, but maybe that was an opinion born out of ignorance.

He glanced down at my bloody shirt and frowned. "How bad is that wound?"

"It sliced me but not too deep. I'll heal." I'd certainly had far worse over the years of fighting against my brother.

"It's still best to grab the medikit and spray it with antiseptic sealer," he said. "They aren't the cleanest creatures, and even their metal claws carry a multitude of germs."

I immediately swung off my pack, grabbed the kit, and treated the wound. It was deeper than I'd initially thought, and though my Sifft heritage would have healed it, it was better not to take chances.

Once I was done, he pressed the halo again and ordered everyone to move on. The rest of the night passed slowly and without further problem.

By the time we made it back to the garrison, flags of yellow and orange were streaming across the sky, and my body felt like lead. All I wanted to do was fall into bed and sleep away the pain of my aching legs, but we had to report to the captain first

Over stews laden with meat and vegetables—not exactly breakfast food, but appreciated by my stomach nonetheless—we learned that we were the only team attacked. Donal's unit—which had also included the relief team, who had to learn both territories as the watch worked on a two days on, one off basis—had seen no trace of them. From Marx's expression, I gathered this was unusual, and it made me wonder if it had anything to do with the odd behavior of the drift that had attacked us.

With the reports done and breakfast eaten, I grabbed a shower, collapsed into bed, and fell into the sleep of the truly exhausted.

I was woken by someone lightly kicking my foot. I muttered something unintelligible even to *my* ears and received a chuckle in response.

Donal. And he sounded far too cheery after such a long damn night.

"Up, Princess. Otherwise you're going to miss target practice."

"I did additional target practice last night. I'd rather sleep."

He tsked. "And here I was thinking you wanted to be treated like everyone else and *not* like a princess."

I opened an eye and glared at him. He was leaning against the outer wall, his crossed arms testing the strength of his shirt's stitching. He'd obviously taken a shower, because his dark hair was damp and, rather amusingly, still held away from his face by my silver clasp. "What's the time?"

"Four thirty."

I groaned. "I could have had another twenty minutes sleep."

"Up, lazy bones, or I will personally drag you out from under those covers."

"Take one step toward me and you'll find yourself encased in stone." I scrubbed a hand across my eyes, then threw my feet over the side of the bed and sat up. Everything protested. Everything ached.

"I'm *not* looking forward to tonight," I muttered, gingerly rubbing my calves. It didn't do a lot to help.

"The first couple of weeks are the worst. After that, you'll be fine."

"I'll have worn out my feet and legs by then." I pushed upright with a groan. "Why are you in such a jovial mood?

Has the wind been whispering good news rather than bad for a change?"

"Indeed she has." His blue eyes glowed and his expression was filled with delight. "My sister had her baby last night—a bonny boy."

"Congrats." I reached for my clothes and began to dress. "Is this the first time you've become an uncle?"

"No, but it *is* the first boy born. My sister has had five girls to date."

I raised my eyebrows. "And is this a problem?"

He laughed. "Of course not—girls are the key to our future, after all. But it is the boys who carry the *name* into the next generation."

I sat back down and dragged my boots closer. "And you? How many little highlanders have got running around at home?"

"You'd think such a magnificent specimen such as myself would have a handful by now, wouldn't you?" His serious expression was somewhat destroyed by the amusement creasing the corners of his eyes. "But in truth, I've yet to find a woman worthy of bearing a child of mine."

I grinned, even as an odd sense of relief stirred. "Meaning you've yet to find a woman willing to put up with your lofty opinion of yourself, not to mention your tendency to shed your kilt at the slightest provocation."

"Despite events at Divona," he said gravely, but with increasing amusement, "I can assure you that I do not shuck my kilt for all and sundry."

"For which," a female voice said from the other side of the cubicle, "we are all eternally grateful."

"Merlyn, of course, makes this statement without having seen me sans kilt."

Merlyn's pale face appeared over the top of the cubicle.

Given she was no taller than me, she had to be standing on the bed. "He does have an inflated opinion of himself, doesn't he?"

"Indeed." I finished tying up my boots and then rose again. Various bits still complained, but moving about did seem to be helping. "But then, that can be said of all men when it comes to *that* part of their anatomy."

"I've found the ones who boast usually have less reason to do so. It's often such a disappointment that I've given up men entirely."

"Perhaps you would have been better choosing a higher class of manhood," he commented.

"They're uncommonly difficult to find where I come from," she said. "But then, Reighton has double the number of women to men. The good ones are usually snapped up pretty early."

Reighton wasn't a place I'd ever heard of, but her thick accent suggested she was from the Seilia region. Faloria was the capital, and the lord who ruled it a weed of a man with icy fingers.

I shivered and shoved the memory as far back into the memory banks as I could. As I walked toward the cubicle exit, Donal pushed away from the wall and stepped back into the walkway. "Shall we move this discussion on to the shooting range, ladies?"

"As long as we're talking about guns," Merlyn said. "I'm all for it."

Donal opened the door and ushered us both through. I flashed him a smile of thanks and then said, "I don't think I want to ask what other type of range there could be."

"It involves man parts," she said, as she fell in step beside Donal and me, "and lots—and lots—of booze before the contest can begin. I witnessed it once in a Falorian alehouse."

"The Falorians are very easily amused," Donal commented. "And quite easily beaten."

My gaze shot to his. "You've participated in such an event?"

"I might or might not have had a drunken moment or two in a Falorian alehouse when I was younger," he said. "Only the wind knows for sure, and neither of you can hear her whispers."

"The Wildman is wilder than I imagined," I said.

He raised an eyebrow. "And do you often waste time imagining things about me?"

"Having seen you sans kilt, no, I do not."

"Oh, *that* is very wounding, Princess."

I grinned. "Yeah, I can see the tears forming as I speak. Shall we change the subject before you embarrass yourself with emotion?"

He raised an eyebrow. "Emotion is *never* something to be embarrassed about."

"Depends on the emotion," I said. "And the reason. There are definitely some that are better well leashed."

He didn't say anything to that, but the fading amusement in his eyes told me he understood. And, rather oddly, *that* understanding was accompanied by a wave of anger so fierce it made my breath momentarily catch.

He barely knew me, but he was angry for me.

Which was strange—and certainly not something I was used to, let alone knew how to handle.

Thankfully, the conversation moved on to safer subjects, and our banter continued through our practice session. Even so, I had an uneasy awareness of being watched. I glanced down the range a couple of times, but no one seemed unduly interested in me. Not even Dravan, who was sharing a firing cube with Sage.

Dinner and the daily debriefing followed, and then we were once again on our way. This time, Rennie had me lead the two teams *and* the relief team—a tough ask given I'd only walked our patrol route once, and an order I suspected might have come from Gallego. I had no doubt he was testing me—or rather, testing my memory. He might have accepted that I wasn't useless—that I *could* protect myself—but he still doubted my leadership skills.

But with the earth guiding my steps when my memory failed, I reached the location where last night's attack had happened—only to discover the Skaran bodies were gone.

"Are there scavengers in the area?" I said.

Because if there *were*, they were the tidiest scavengers ever. Nothing remained of the Skaran—not a scrape of hair or piece of bone.

"There's little life in these lands beyond birds, who can fly above the Skaran's capacity to climb and leap at them."

"So the Skaran retrieve their dead?"

"Always. They share some type of telepathic link and know the instant one of them dies." He grimaced. "It's part of the reason why they consume the brains of their victims—they believe it enhances the ability of their own minds."

"The more I learn about them, the less I like them," I muttered.

He shrugged. "All creatures do what they must to survive, and there isn't much in the way of protein out in the Skaran grasslands. The dead provide that."

I stared at him for a moment, not wanting to believe what his words implied. "They eat their *own* dead?"

I was all for doing what you had to for survival—it had

been my methodology for the last twelve years, after all—but eating your kin really was a step too far.

"They use everyone and everything," Rennie replied. "What isn't immediately consumed is either smoked or pickled for leaner times."

"Meaning they're far more intelligent than I'd given them credit for."

"That's a trap most new recruits fall into," Rennie said. "It's easy to view them as animals given their looks, but I've heard it said they're simply a branch of humanity that took a very different development path."

"Do they live in communities like we do?"

He nodded. "There are five neighborhoods within the Skaran lands, and two are within striking distance of Rodestat."

I skirted the edge of a small but deep crevice—one that had the trickle of water at its base, even though there were no streams in the immediate area. "Has the garrison ever mounted an attack against them?"

"Yeah, and it didn't go well for us."

"Was that because the terrain doesn't allow the use of vehicles, or because the Skaran can move far faster than we can?"

"Both." He shrugged. "For the most part, the commander and the queen are content to simply keep them out of the Wild Lands as much as possible."

"It's done at a pretty heavy cost, though, especially given the Skaran haven't the capacity to do major damage to either the garrison or Rodestat."

"Just because they currently haven't doesn't mean they won't," he said. "These encounters do at least give us some idea of any advancement they might have made."

"I guess it's not like they're using either Rodestat's or Divona's finest in those encounters."

He smiled. "Until you and Lord Donal came along, that was certainly true."

The rest of night passed uneventfully, and we arrived back at the garrison not only half an hour earlier than the previous night but to the news that Donal's team had been attacked and was still making its way back. They had three casualties, though apparently there was nothing serious and Donal wasn't one of the injured. Which was a relief.

Once we'd checked weapons and ammo back into the armory, I dismissed my team and then glanced at the clock tower. Thankfully there was still plenty of time for a long, hot shower before breakfast. Of course, a bath would have been even better for easing the aches, but they weren't exactly thick on the ground in the garrison.

None of the day unit leaders was in the bunkroom, although the steam that still floated in the air suggested I'd only just missed them.

I grabbed a couple of towels from the rack and headed into the stalls. The water was hot and, for several minutes, I did nothing more than simply raise my face and let it sluice down my body in an effort to wash away the aches. Then I picked up the soap and cleaned away the sweat and grime. But as I switched the water off, an odd sound caught my attention. A heartbeat later, the earth whispered a warning of ill intent.

Dravan was in the bunkhouse.

And he wasn't alone.

The earth couldn't tell me who accompanied him, but the weight of their footsteps made me suspect it was Kaid, as Nash walked lightly while Sage was somewhere between them both.

I flexed my fingers to keep a lid on the surge of annoyance, and then grabbed my grubby shirt and tugged it on. It clung to my damp skin, but I didn't really care. Once I'd quietly pulled on my pants, I tucked the knife into the waistband near my spine, and then strode barefoot out of the bathroom.

Dravan was halfway down the room but came to an abrupt halt when I appeared. Kaid was near the door, no doubt acting as lookout.

I stopped just out of the Dravan's reach and said, my voice scathing, "I expected this sort of stupidity from Dravan, but not from you, Kaid."

He raised an eyebrow. "Why? I'm in the garrison for a good reason—and it's *not* because I'm good."

"And also not too intelligent, given that being caught in this room without a legitimate reason is a chargeable offense."

Dravan sneered. "Charge away. I'd rather sit in a cell than fight those Skaran bastards any day."

I raised an eyebrow. "So the man who thinks he's stronger and faster than me is now afraid to fight? Interesting."

He scowled. "That's not what—"

"I don't care what you fucking meant," I cut in. "If you want to test your strength against mine, then have some goddamn honor and issue a formal challenge."

"We both know you wouldn't accept—"

"If, however," I continued flatly, barely controlling the cold rage that stirred through me and echoed through the concrete under my feet, "you were hired by my brother to kill me, then you sure as hell had better succeed the first time. If you don't, I will gut you and dance barefoot in the warm flow of your blood."

Anger flared in his eyes, but it came with a touch of confusion. "That's the second time you've mentioned your brother, and I still have no idea what the fuck you're talking about."

I snorted. "If you're as clueless as you claim, why call me trull? That's a slur only my brother would use."

My brother, and half the court.

Dravan waved a hand. "Maybe I heard a whisper or two. Can't remember where."

That last bit was a lie, but I didn't think the rest of it was, and confusion stirred. Vin had certainly ordered Dravan placed into my unit, but maybe he'd simply hoped the thug's natural dislike of female authority figures would achieve what *he* couldn't.

But the fact that Dravan knew the slur meant he'd been speaking to someone who hadn't yet shown their hand. Which at least made tactical sense—my brother knew just how well I could fight, and it was unlikely he'd leave my destruction to someone as volatile and stupid as Dravan.

I flexed my fingers and said, "So why are you in this room, Dravan, if not at my brother's bidding?"

He snorted. "Because no snooty, blue blood bitch is *ever* going to best me and get away with it."

And with that, he charged.

With little room to maneuver in the walkway's confined space, I leapt sideways, grabbed the edge of the nearest cubicle, and used the momentum to swing back around. My feet connected with Dravan's left side and sent him staggering. He recovered his balance altogether too fast, and I'd barely regained my footing when he was coming at me again. I ducked two blows but caught a third on the side of my face and, with a grunt of pain, was sent staggering.

Again, he came at me. I dropped, twisted around, and

hooked a bare foot behind his leg, using his momentum to sweep it out from underneath him. As his butt hit the ground, I swung around again, this time aiming for his head. But he somehow caught the blow with his hands and twisted my leg, forcing me to drop and spin with the movement or risk breaking bone. I kicked out with my other foot, but he avoided the blows and, with a soft chuckle, began dragging me closer.

I had no idea what he intended, and no intention of finding out.

As my belly and breasts scraped painfully against the floor, I grabbed my knife then twisted around and slashed at the hands that held me. The razor-sharp blade cut through flesh and bone as easily as butter, severing two of his fingers and cutting my leg in the process. I didn't care. As Dravan howled and my own blood spurted across both my hand and the knife's blade, I pulled my leg free from his grip. He tried to grab me again, but the blood that now slicked my skin gave him no purchase. I scrambled upright; he tried to do the same but was far too slow. I kicked him in the face with as much force as I could muster; the blow smashed his nose, shattered teeth, and knocked him backward. As his head smacked against the floor and he was knocked out cold, I gripped my knife tighter, stepped over his unconscious body, and strode toward Kaid.

He raised his hands and backed away. "Hey, this wasn't my idea."

"I don't *care* whose idea it was." My voice showed little of the rage still flowing through me. "You were here to enjoy the so-called fun, so let's make sure you *do* get in on it."

I imagined the stone rising up to encase his legs; the earth shuddered and instantly obeyed.

Kaid's gaze widened and his expression became one of horror. "What the fuck—?"

I stopped in front of him, my heart racing and my grip on the knife so strong my knuckles glowed white. Part of me wanted nothing more than to ram the gleaming blade up through his throat and into his brain. To start taking the revenge I'd been denied for twelve years.

But *that* was the rage speaking, and I couldn't give in to it. Once I did, I had a bad, *bad* feeling I wouldn't be able to step back.

"Didn't the military teach you to *never* underestimate an enemy?" I said softly. "I warned you all that I wouldn't hold back if I was attacked again. Did you think I just meant with the knife? Did you think I wouldn't use *all* the abilities at my disposal?"

He didn't say anything. He just stared at me.

"I am *not* any old princess, Kaid. I am a daughter of Bel-Hannon kings, and I have the power of the earth at my command. Next time you try a stunt like this, you can be sure I won't just stop at stone shackles. Understood?"

He nodded. My answering smile held no warmth. "Who else knows about this little episode?"

He swallowed. "Sage."

I guess *that* wasn't a surprise given her oft-expressed opinion she should have been unit leader. "And have you any idea who told Dravan to call me a trull?"

"No."

I cursed inwardly, but I guess it was never going to be that easy. "Please do feel free to pass my warning on to Sage, or anyone you might have discussed this bit of stupidity with."

I stepped back and walked into my cubicle to retrieve

the halo. When a voice answered, I reported the incident and requested Captain Marx be sent for immediately.

Then I went back to check on Dravan. He still had a pulse, which meant he really *did* have a thick skull. The force with which the back of his head had hit the floor would have killed most people.

I shackled his legs with stone and then rose and continued on to the shower. Once I'd stripped off my wet clothes, I dealt with the wound on my leg—which, despite the spurt of blood, had rather oddly already scabbed over— and then redressed in fresh clothes.

The quick tremor of steps vibrating through stone warned me of Marx's approach. I thrust my knife into its sheath, tossed my wet gear and towels into the laundry chute, and walked out.

Marx took in the situation and then looked at me. "What happened here?"

"Dravan attacked me. I retaliated. Simple as that." I met his gaze evenly. "I did warn him that my blade would taste his flesh if he attacked me again—"

"Again?" Marx said sharply. "This *isn't* the first time?"

"No."

"Why didn't you report the first incident?"

"Because neither they nor you would have taken me seriously if I had."

He grunted—an acknowledgment that I was right, I suspected. "Is he alive?"

"Yes. Though that hand needs urgent attention if you don't want him to bleed out."

The amusement that briefly flitted through his expression suggested he'd caught what I *hadn't* said—that I personally wouldn't have minded that particular occurrence. He glanced at Kaid and said, "What's your excuse for being here, soldier? And before you reply, be aware that we'll be checking security comms to see what they reveal about the lead-up to this event."

Kaid scowled. "It was just meant to be a little bit of fun."

"Define fun." Marx's voice was flat. Dangerous.

Kaid shrugged. Though his expression held an edge of defiance, anxiety rolled through his unwashed, musky scent. "We were just going to slap her about a bit. Nothing serious."

"Really?" Marx said. "I'm not sure what sort of lowlife raised you, but I personally don't think slapping *any* woman about is 'nothing serious.' And the military has an even grimmer view of it, be that woman a unit leader *or* common soldier."

Kaid scowled down at the unconscious Dravan but didn't reply. Maybe he realized he'd only be digging a deeper hole for himself.

Two medics and a couple of garrison security officers arrived. Marx motioned to the unconscious Dravan and said, "Terryl, Betts, get this man to the infirmary and make sure he's restrained. Xander, Roland, take Kaid to the brig and lock him up." His gaze returned to me. "Nyx, release them both."

I immediately did so, but as the stone retreated, the ache in my head began. I crossed my arms and leaned my shoulder against the nearest cubicle wall. I needed painkillers, but I wasn't about to get them until everyone had gone. It was a long-held habit of mine not to show any sign of weakness.

Once the two men were removed from the room, I said, "Dravan said he'd rather be locked up than fight the Skaran, so I'd like to request he be forced back into duty once healed."

"That can only happen if you don't press charges," he said. "And it's *not* something I'd recommend, given he'll seek retribution for this loss of face. And next time, he might just use a gun."

"Then swap him out to day duty. At least that way, our paths will only briefly cross here in the garrison."

"I'll inform the commander of the situation; it'll be his decision as to what happens." He hesitated, his gaze skimming me critically. "Are you okay?"

"Yes." I smiled, and this time it did hold some warmth. "I'm no wilting flower, even if I am a princess."

"*That* is becoming quite obvious," he said, with an answering smile. "I'll see you in ten minutes for debriefing."

He left. I made my way back to my bunk and sat down. The shaking immediately began. For several minutes, I could do nothing more than breathe deeply. I might be fight-hardened thanks to my brother, but fighting the likes of Dravan—and even the Skaran—was totally different to anything I'd done in the practice yards. I knew my brother and could generally predict how he'd react to any given attack. The same could not be said of anyone—or anything —else I was facing out here on the Mauvaissian border.

And despite my instinctive actions both here and the other night against the Skaran, the thought of battle—of fighting against greater odds—scared the hell out of me.

As did the thought that *that's* exactly what we'd be facing.

I closed my eyes for a moment and concentrated on the gentle heartbeat under my feet. It was strong and resolute— everything I'd have to be if I wanted to survive what was coming.

Though even the earth couldn't tell me exactly what *that* was.

The sound of footsteps approaching had my pulse rate leaping again, but I very quickly recognized the rhythm of those steps. Donal, not another attacker.

He stepped inside the room and then stopped when he saw me sitting on the bed. His gaze scanned me, moved briefly to the floor, and then returned. "What the hell happened here?"

"Dravan." I pushed upright. All the bits that had been aching before the fight flared up again with renewed vigor. "I asked Marx to transfer the bastard to day shift."

He didn't step aside as I approached, which forced me to stop. His gaze dropped to my cheek and concern flitted through his expression. "Is that the only wound you came away with?"

He brushed a thumb against my cheek, his touch gentle and oh-so warm. At any other time—with any other person —I would have stepped back. I didn't like unwanted contact—hadn't for a very long time. But for some reason, the highlander *didn't* set off my instinctive need to protect myself.

"It's just a bruise—"

"Actually, it's quite a bit more." He showed me his thumb—blood smeared his skin. "I'd get some antiseptic on it—who knows what sort of diseases a parasite like Dravan might be carrying."

I half smiled. "He won't be carrying anything for a good while. Not after losing a couple of fingers, anyway."

"It's a pity you didn't chop off the rest. It might have cooled his thuggish tendencies."

"I doubt it, given he'd still have his feet." I pressed a finger against his stomach, hitting muscles that felt like steel. "You, highlander, reek. Can I suggest a shower before the debriefing?"

Devilment sparked in his eyes as he stepped back and waved me past. "I'd *love* to have a shower with you, Princess. Shall we go?"

"Idiot." I squeezed past him and walked across to the broom cupboard. "Has either the commander or Marx said anything about our journey to the dead lands?"

"No." He started stripping off as he followed me down the walkway—something I heard rather than saw. "I rather suspect they're waiting for that storm to hit before they give final approval."

"And what does the wind think of this delay?"

"That every day wasted takes us deeper into danger."

I grabbed the mop and bucket out of the cupboard, and followed him into the bathroom. "What of the storm? Can't you create one or at least hasten its arrival?"

I handed him the bucket and he placed it under the tap to fill it. "I can, but it'll drain me. I'd be next to useless for hours."

I frowned. "Is it just summoning storms that has that effect?"

He shook his head. "It varies depending on what I'm attempting, and the level of control required. A gale force wind that tears apart everything is far easier to create than an isolated thunderstorm."

He handed me the now full bucket and then stepped under the shower. I watched the water run down his muscular body for several seconds and then mentally slapped myself for doing so. "Meaning using the earth is likely to affect me the same way?"

"Possibly." He grabbed a fresh bar of soap and offered it to me. "Care to wash my back while you're standing there?"

"Only if you don't mind the tail end of the mop being used, because I have no intention of getting wet again."

"Really?" he said, and lunged toward me.

I yelped and ran backward, sloshing water up my legs and across the floor. His laughter followed me out the door.

"Idiot!"

The comment was met by yet more laughter. A grin tugged at my lips, but it quickly faded as I remembered just how little fun or teasing there'd been in my life up until his arrival into it.

The king and my brother really did have a lot to answer for.

By the time I'd finished mopping up Dravan's blood, Donal was dressed and ready to go. We made our way to the mess hall and—rather unsurprisingly—found Marx and the other unit leaders waiting for us. Once we'd updated the Daywatch on everything we'd seen or heard during our patrols, Marx placed a dusty cylinder on the table in front of us. The label on the side said they were maps of region 9B-7. "Donal and Nyx have been assigned a mission into the dead lands to track down the source of possible activity."

Celi frowned. "Why just those two? Getting past the Skaran is dangerous enough, let alone stepping into those godforsaken—"

"You forget I'm an air mage," Donal commented. "The Skaran won't even see me."

"Which doesn't explain the princess's presence. No offense meant, Nyx, but you're not battle-hardened, let alone trail-seasoned."

"True on both counts, but I'm not there for either. I'm there because I can manipulate the earth."

She blinked. "You're an *earth* mage?"

"And it gives me an advantage over the most seasoned soldier."

"Huh." She glanced back at the captain. "What do you want us to do?"

"Keep an eye out for usual activity—or lack thereof. If these two are to get back safely, we'll need to keep them updated on any situational changes in the Wild Lands."

"The Wild Lands is one thing," Tal said with a frown. "How the hell are you going to get through the Skaran grass-lands without being spotted? Even at the narrowest point, you'd still have to traverse a hundred miles of Skaran territory; if nothing else, that gives rise to the ration problem."

"Not for an air mage, it doesn't," Donal said calmly. He glanced at the captain. "When are we set to leave?"

"At four this afternoon. The storm should be well underway by then, and that'll give you plenty of cover. I suggest you both sleep until then."

Especially given the point that—in an unknown land—a good night's sleep was likely to be a commodity we could ill afford.

"In the meantime," Marx continued, "have you any recommendations for your temporary replacement?"

"Nash," I said instantly. "He seems the most level-headed and also appears in tune with his Sifft heritage."

Marx nodded and glanced at Donal. "Margreet," he said instantly. "Tough as nails but sensible."

"Good." He glanced at his watch. "We meet at the external gate at three forty-five. Armory will have full kits ready by three thirty. Now, let's all get down to the business of breakfast."

144

The full kit was damnably heavy, and I couldn't help but wonder if my legs were going to stand up to the weight. Which, undoubtedly, was the thought of a sheltered princess, not the warrior I was trying to be.

At least my pack wasn't as heavy as Donal's—he was also carrying a pulse rifle, extra ammo, and a number of pomegranates. Which, despite the name, weren't fruits filled with sweet but crunchy seeds, but rather powerful fragmenting explosive devices.

As we fitted more specialized halo devices that would allow us to be tracked for a greater distance than the regular ones, I said, "Did you get a chance to look at the map this afternoon?"

He nodded. "There were two lots—the first ancient, the second a partial overlay developed from the blue hawk flights."

"Anything of note?"

"Only that the blue hawks' flights didn't get anywhere near the areas that restrict the air." He half shrugged. "There's mention of a large city on the old map midway between the Skaran border and the volcano, but there's no indication of what might lie between that and the volcano. Either they have simply never mapped the area, or there *is* nothing beyond it."

"So we're going in blind?"

"Into the two restricted areas, yes. But the wind can help us everywhere else."

When I raised my eyebrows, he grimaced and added, "I suspect our investigations into the restricted areas will lead to other questions—like, if we *do* find life, where does it come from?"

"A question *I* suspect won't be easy to answer."

"Hence my request for additional supplies."

"So you're the reason this goddamn pack is so heavy?"

"Indeed," he said cheerfully. "Consider it my contribution to building up your strength and stamina."

I snorted. "Thanks. Appreciate it."

"Anytime, Princess. Anytime."

We headed out into the rain and the wind and walked across to the gate. Not only were Gallego and Marx waiting under the metal awning that jutted out from the gatehouse but also Marttia and her two red-garbed guards.

"Are you still sure this mission is vital?" she said, as we came to a halt in front of them.

"Unfortunately, yes," Donal said. "The wind cannot see beyond whatever protects this threat, so we have no other option."

"Then may the gods favor you." Her gaze came to mine. "Be careful out there."

"I've spent the last twelve years being careful, Marttia. I'm not about to abandon that now."

She raised an eyebrow at the edge in my reply but otherwise didn't comment.

"Captain Marx informed me of the attack in your quarters and of your request that both men be transferred to day duty," Gallego said. "I'm afraid that will only give them more opportunities to cause problems, something we cannot afford if an attack *is* coming. They'll be sent back to Divona to serve out their full sentences in prison. I've requested replacements from military stock, not prisoner."

Given it was unlikely my brother would be informed of the replacements, it probably meant I wouldn't have to worry about them. But that didn't mean I could relax. Vin's harbinger of death remained in this garrison—I just had to find him or her before they got to me.

"Thank you, Commander."

He nodded and glanced at the captain, who immediately said, "I want regular reports once you step into the area beyond the reach of the blue hawks. Given we know next to nothing about the region these days, please provide a location and description of anything that suggests habitation or possible threat."

"Will do, Captain," Donal said.

The commander nodded at the guards, who immediately opened the gate. Donal and I stepped through, our footsteps echoing as we made our way down the long dark tunnel. The upper gateway closed when we were midway down, which allowed the lower to open. The thick breeze that swept in was as cold as ice, and the rain beyond the gateway was so damn loud it sounded like a full herd of ruminants coming at us. I quickly put on the antifog goggles and then pulled the rain jacket's hood over my head.

"You won't be needing to use either for long," Donal said. "The storm is severe over the mountains and Wild Lands, but it peters out beyond the Skaran plains."

"Did you miss that bit where Tal said there're a hundred miles between us and the end of those plains? That still gives us quite a bit of storm exposure."

"Except we're not walking, remember." He glanced at me. "I've never transported anyone else, though. I suspect it'll limit our range and knock my strength for several hours."

"The wind had better drop us somewhere safe, then."

"If there is such a thing in those lands. Come along, Princess—a bit of rain won't hurt you."

I snorted and followed him out of the gateway. A bit of rain might not have hurt, but *this* was a full-blown storm. It was so damn cold that it immediately snatched my breath away, and the rain so hard that even with the goggles, I was struggling to see anything. As for the wind... I staggered sideways for several steps before I caught my balance and was able to follow Donal.

Halfway between the gate and crevice that separated the garrison from the rocky, forested Wild Lands, he stopped and held out a gloved hand.

"You'll need to hang on to me."

"Why?" I asked, even as I twined my fingers through his. He tugged me closer then wrapped his arms around my waist. I raised an eyebrow and somewhat skeptically added, "Are you sure this isn't just an excuse to hold me close?"

He grinned. "I can't deny it's rather delightful to have you pressed so fully against me, but it *is* a necessity."

"So if I was male—"

"I wouldn't be enjoying it half as much." His smile faded. "Just trust me. I won't let you fall. Ever."

Before I could ask him to explain that particular statement, the wind whipped up hard and fast, surrounding us in a screaming whirlwind that tore at our clothes and skin. Its touch remained icy and, despite my coat and the layers underneath it, I shivered. Donal's arms tightened even as the wind retreated a fraction. In the tiny space between the whirlwind and us, opaque air began to form clouds of spun cotton that became thick enough to block our surroundings from view.

"Ready?" Donal asked quietly.

I nodded and instinctively wrapped my arms around his waist.

"Then let's go."

With those three words, we shot into the air and were then ripped sideways at speed. I have no idea how fast or how far we traveled, but it only seemed like a few minutes had passed when we began to slow and the clouds surrounding us dissipated, revealing the landscape far below. It was a black and broken strip of land that stretched right up to the foothills of the vast but shattered volcano. While the area immediately below us was empty and without life, there were large patches of green either side of it. There certainly wasn't anything even vaguely resembling a tree, but it was at least an indication that life *could* exist in this place.

The wind delivered us onto the ground, then gently eased away. It was only then I became aware of Donal's shuddering and the harsh rasp of his breathing.

"I think you'd better sit, highlander, before you collapse and drag me down with you."

"A situation I wouldn't normally object to." His words were little more than a wheeze of air. "But I would rather it happen in a more hospitable place—like a bed."

I snorted and stepped back enough to catch his wrists and help him onto the ground. He didn't say anything. He just dropped his head and sucked in air, his whole body shuddering with effort.

I opened his backpack, pulled out some trail rations, then unclipped his water bottle and handed both to him. He nodded his thanks and immediately opened the rations.

I switched my gaze to our surrounds. The earth really *was* as black as ink; it was also—at least in this area—almost unnaturally flat. The old volcano dominated the northern horizon, a jagged black monolith that bore a breach wound on its visible flank. That it was evident from this distance only emphasized how big that volcano was—and just how massive the eruption must have been.

I turned and studied the land behind us. It, too, was flat, but there was a dark line visible in the distance—trees lining the Skaran border, possibly.

I tapped the halo, made my report to the captain, and then squatted beside Donal, my shoulder lightly brushing his as I pressed my left hand against the ground. The earth was cool and its pulse extremely faint. I frowned and dug my fingers deeper into the ash-like soil. The heartbeat got no stronger. The soil in this black strip might not be dead, but it certainly wouldn't maintain much in the way of life—not when it was little more than nutrient-poor dust.

Whether that meant I wouldn't be able to connect with the earth's voice, I couldn't say—but I needed to try. I also suspected I needed a stronger—or at least deeper—connection than simply shoving my fingers into the soil.

I grabbed my knife, thrust it hilt deep into the ground, and then reached mentally. For a few seconds, nothing happened. Then what almost felt like static stirred through my thoughts and the earth said, her voice weak and distant, *What is it you wish?*

Does life exist on this strip of black land?

Life returns to the area wiped out by the eruption, but that will never be the case in the true dead zone.

True dead zone?

An ever-lengthening strip of ground that has been utterly drained of energy and warmth.

By the volcano?

No. By whatever moves beneath it.

Trepidation stirred. Or maybe it was fear. Both were certainly justified given the underlying fury in the earth's voice. *Underneath?*

Yes.

What sort of life are we talking about?

We cannot say, the earth replied, *because there is no response from the dead zone and only anger in the ground that immediately precedes it. The deadness is a canker that rolls slowly toward the Skaran Plains. It isn't natural.*

If neither earth nor air could venture close to the dead areas in this place, it had to mean there was a greater force at work here.

What blocks you? Another mage? Or magic?

Magic. A type we have not seen for centuries.

Which wasn't news I really wanted to hear. *How far ahead is the dead area?*

The anger zone lies ten miles directly ahead of your current location. How far beyond that the dead zone is, we cannot say.

How deeply under the ground does the movement occur?

A few hundred feet, perhaps. We cannot say with certainty.

Are there any exit or entry points in the areas you can access? Or maybe even air vents?

Surely there'd have to be the latter, at least. No matter what was creating this deadness—be it a human species or not—they needed to breathe. If they *were* boring through the ground, then they'd also need a means of getting rid of the waste.

If they exist, you will have to discover them yourself.

I swore softly, and felt Donal stir. "What?"

I updated him and then said, "There's probably only a couple of hours of light left. Do you want to set up camp here for the night? Or do you think it'll be better to move through the night and rest during the day?"

"Given the urgency in the wind's tone, I think it better we get underway ASAP." He drew in a breath and released it slowly. "Help me up, Princess."

I frowned. "Are you sure? Half an hour won't kill us—"

"Perhaps not, but the longer we're stationary, the more likely discovery is."

"True enough." Even if whoever was creating this dead zone *did* live underground, that didn't mean they wouldn't have some sort of sentry system on the surface.

I rose and offered him my hands. He gripped them tightly and then, after a pause, gave a sharp nod. I helped him upright but didn't immediately release him, wanting to be sure he was steady before doing so. His breathing remained too fast and ragged for my liking, and his skin a little too pale, but the gleam of determination in his blue eyes suggested he wasn't about to let weariness stop him.

After he gave another nod, I released him.

"You'd better lead the way, given you'll be far more alert for the next couple of hours than me."

I frowned. "Are you sure you don't want to—"

"I'll be fine, Princess. It's just part of the price we pay for using such forces—and one I hope you don't experience anytime soon."

"Unlikely, given the earth is utterly dead up ahead and won't be able to respond to any call for help I might make."

"Well, doesn't *that* just make this journey all the more exciting." He waved a hand forward. "Go. I'll be three steps behind you."

I hesitated, my gaze raking him briefly, sensing the tiredness he wouldn't acknowledge. Then I half shrugged and spun around. The highlander knew his limits far better than I did.

With every step, black dust plumed, until we were surrounded in a heavy cloud that tasted like grit and made breathing unpleasant. I didn't have a filter mask in my kit, so I tugged the neck of my undershirt over my mouth and nose and used it to keep out some of the muck.

Dusk came and went, and night settled in, but neither the moon nor the stars were visible thanks to the heavy layer of clouds. Hours passed, but neither Donal nor I spoke—this place was so vast, so empty, that even a whisper would have echoed. And while the earth had lost its voice, it wasn't completely silent. Tremors ran through the ground, accompanied by a rumble that sounded both frustrated and angry.

The earth here might not be able to tell me what was happening, but she certainly didn't like it.

We entered an area littered with stones and mounds of uneven earth. Some of these mounds were tall enough to tower above Donal by a good four feet while others were little more than strips of raised earth that ran in lines or formed box shapes—the ruins, I realized, of the civilization had been here before the eruption. It made me wonder if we dug underneath the larger buildings, would we find the people who'd once lived here, their bodies frozen in whatever the position they'd been in the moment when death—and the molten ash and debris that had rained down upon this entire area—had claimed them.

Up ahead in the distance, fireflies danced, tiny sparks of red and gold that gradually faded to black as they shot higher. If there were fireflies here, then there had to be other life, no matter what the earth had said. Firefly pupae were carnivorous, and the adults couldn't exist without at least some form of plant life.

The earth's trembling intensified, until it was strong enough to send stones rolling from piles around us. I stopped. Donal halted beside me, his gaze narrowed as he studied the bright show up ahead. "There's something odd about those fireflies."

"Aside from the fact they shouldn't even exist in this

barren place, you mean?" I kept my voice as low as his, but it still seemed abnormally loud in the silence.

His smile flashed. "Yes. They're not actually moving like real fireflies."

"I'll bow to your greater knowledge, having never seen them in anything other than books." I frowned. "I don't suppose the wind can tell you anything?"

"No, because there's some sort of barrier preventing her from sweeping the area."

Meaning it had to be some kind of magic, because there was no physical barrier evident. "Then she lasted a lot longer than the earth."

"Right up until the tremors became consistent, in fact. Whatever is stopping her seems to be connected to whatever is causing them."

"Machinery would have to be responsible for the vibrations, wouldn't it? No matter how many people might be underground, no amount of human—or nonhuman—endeavor would cause the earth to shake like this."

"Agreed." His voice was grim. "Unless, of course, whatever mage or magic is stopping the wind is also causing the vibrations."

"I don't know anything about true magic, but wouldn't its creation and usage be as telling on a mage's body as using the air's power to transport us was on yours?"

"I'd have thought so, but for all we know, they have a never-ending supply of mages or some way of countering the personal physical cost." His gaze met mine. "But I think those fireflies might give us our first clue in that regard. Shall we keep moving?"

We did. As we drew closer, the earth's trembling stilled. The resulting silence ramped up my fear rather than eased it.

It soon became evident that the bright shower lighting up the night *wasn't* fireflies. It was sparks.

They were rising from a shaft that was circular and at least five feet in width. I knelt close to the edge and carefully peered over. The air that flowed across my face and riffled through my hair was warm, the sparks little bursts of heat that hit but oddly didn't burn. The shaft itself was vertical and very deep, with a thin strip of molten gold at its very base.

Donal frowned. "Is that a form of strip lighting or something else?"

"Who knows? This thing is definitely a chimney of some sort, though."

"If they *are* boring under the ground, then they'd have to have some means of sucking out the heat the process can cause." He scanned the immediate surrounds. "It's hard to tell refuse from ruins in this darkness, but if they're using machinery, they'd need a means of getting rid of the spoil."

"Unless they're simply transporting it back to wherever they originated from."

"Possibly," he said. "But it would take a lot of vehicles to remove the rubble from a large tunnel, and we'd likely hear them given we felt the tunneling vibrations earlier."

"Unless they've harnessed the energy of the earth and are using a form of repulsion technology. It's relatively quiet."

"Which *this* is not." He thrust upright. "Either way, this shaft isn't going to provide a means of uncovering answers. We need to find an access point that's horizontal rather than vertical."

"If there is such a thing." I carefully skirted the edge of the shaft and then led the way again.

"There has to be an access point somewhere—that shaft

didn't have any means of moving people or even vehicles up or down."

Which didn't really mean anything if we were dealing with an entire civilization capable of magic—and if we were, Cannamore was in serious trouble.

As the night and our journey rolled on, we came across another three shafts; they were evenly spaced along the center of the dead zone, and none were lit in any way, suggesting they were either no longer in use or simple ventilation shafts.

As dawn began to color the night sky, we reached what appeared to be the center of the ruined city. The remains of old buildings towered above us, casting long shadows that weren't lifted by the growing dawn. The rubble-filled streets were laid out in a crisscross pattern I suspected might follow the earth's energy lines and very much reminded me of the layout in some of Cannamore's older cities.

Did that mean this area had once held human occupation? These ruins certainly suggested it was possible, but surely if it *had*, there would have been some record of it in Rodestat's archives.

Something flickered to my right—a flash of movement that wasn't repeated. I frowned, half wondering if I'd imagined it even though the stirring dust was evidence enough to the fact I hadn't.

More movement. Once again it was little more than a brief flash and a trail of dust, but it was indication enough that we were no longer alone. The tension rolling off the man standing beside me told me he'd seen it too.

I unsnapped the retention clips on both blasters in readiness and then murmured, "What do you want to do?"

"You keep moving forward. I'll go around and stop it."

"Be careful."

"Always."

He disappeared in the shadowed canyon between two buildings. For several minutes, nothing happened. Then a sharp, inhuman scream broke the stillness, quickly followed by the blast of a rifle.

More screams, more movement.

I kept moving, grimly fighting the urge to go help—to go see if he was all right. He was the seasoned soldier in this little outfit, not me.

Then I saw it—a blur of gray that was all but hidden in the rising cloud of black dust. It was coming straight at me.

I raised the guns and fired, but it didn't stop the creature. It didn't even check its speed. I cursed and threw myself sideways to avoid being trampled, hitting the ground hard enough to force the air from my lungs even as I rolled into a semi-kneeling position and kept on firing. The blaster was doing absolutely nothing. I thrust one away, grabbed my knife, and then rose.

A long strip of silver appeared out of the dust cloud and arced down at my head. I instinctively—and perhaps foolishly—raised the knife. The blade hit something solid and shock reverberated up my arm—no surprise given that strip of silver was actually a two-meter-long sword that would have cleaved me in two. Instead, it slid off the knife's short surface and dug into the soil near my left leg.

As more dust flew skyward, those screams sounded again, only this time, they were much, *much* closer.

A heartbeat later, three gray-skinned creatures of nightmare erupted from the ground in front of me.

SEVEN

I cursed and ran backward down the street, not wanting to turn away from them and hoping like hell I didn't crash into a building or fall over rubble. I exchanged the knife for the other blaster and once again, rained metal hell down on them. It made no more difference now than it had before.

They gave chase, their screams of fury high-pitched and grating and unlike anything I'd ever heard before. No human throat could make a sound like that, but then, the only commonality these things had with humans was the fact they used weapons and were upright beings that ran on two legs rather than four.

The nearest one raised a thick metal blade and slashed it toward me. I jumped back and instinctively sucked in my gut. The blade's sharp tip cut easily through the layers of armor and clothes, but I had no idea if it had also sliced skin —and no time to find out. I kept firing, kept running, and the constant barrage finally began to take a toll on the nearest creature. The armor plating covering its chest area was cracked, and a metallic—almost acidic—scent stained the air as black liquid seeped down its torso.

Donal appeared behind them, rifle raised. I immediately threw myself into the nearest building then rolled upright and raised the blasters in readiness. As the creatures slid to a halt and black dust plumed into the air, Donal unleashed on the three of them.

Blood, gore, and brain matter flew as the back of their heads exploded. They went down hard and didn't move.

For several minutes, neither could I.

I just kept my guns aimed at the creatures and sucked in air, trying to ease the burning in my lungs and the quivering in my limbs. The bipeds didn't move, and they certainly didn't come back to life as some insane part of me half feared. After a moment, I lowered my guns and walked back to the doorway.

"Where the fuck did those things come from?" Donal scanned me critically, his gaze narrowing. "How bad is that wound?"

"From the soil about ten feet in front of me, and I have no idea." I reclipped my blasters and then carefully unlatched the breastplate and peeled away the undershirt. A thin red line stretched across my stomach, but it wasn't very deep. I'd obviously sucked it in at exactly the right moment. "It's nothing major."

"Good, but given the dust, I'd seal it to keep it clean."

I nodded and immediately shucked off the pack to get the medikit. He knelt next to the biped closest to me and rolled it over. Its slightly bulbous, overly large eyes sat either side of the V-shaped armored plate that started at the top of its forehead and ran down the center of its elongated face. At the end of this, there was a small snout and under it a mouth. Its large ears sat on top of its head and were leaf-shaped.

I quickly cleaned and sealed the wound then packed the kit away again. "Have you ever seen anything like these before?"

He shook his head. "Never. And there was certainly no mention of them in any of the old history books that I've read, though the Skaran are mentioned plenty."

"You don't strike me as someone who spends much time in dusty old archives."

His smile was brief but bright. "I'm not, which is why my father used it as a form of punishment."

I snorted softly. "Do you think they're related to the Skaran?"

"It's possible, but I personally doubt it. Their physiology is very different, and, at a guess, I'd say these bipeds are nocturnal."

Which would explain why their eyes were so large. "The Skaran hunt at night."

"Mostly in the warmer months, and mainly because it's cooler. They're heavily coated, remember."

I nodded and studied the three bodies for a second. "Given all the armor plating on these things, we're damn lucky to have taken them down. The blasters certainly weren't—in any way—effective on them."

"Which is why I used the pulse rifle and aimed at the back or sides of their heads—there's no plating there." He stood and looked around. "I think we'd better bury them and then get moving."

"Where to, though? Aside from these things, this city appears deserted."

"Yes, but I don't think they came from here—not if the wind is to be believed."

"You're hearing her again?"

"Only faintly, which is why I didn't call on her to help." His gaze came to mine, his expression grim. "We need to know if we're dealing with more than armored bipeds, or if these creatures have further plans that could harm the city."

"I'm not entirely sure I *want* to discover the latter." I frowned. "If they're nocturnal, their main city might be underground."

"Maybe. Maybe not." He studied the horizon for a second. "Given the air was blocked near the vent that held the sparks and also at the volcano, I think that's where we need to go next."

"It's too far—and likely too dangerous—to walk there." Not to mention the fact we didn't have the supplies to do so. "And I'm not sure we can afford the toll on your strength."

"It won't take long to get there via the wind, and then we can rest."

I hesitated. In truth, we really did need answers, and fast. The tunnel wasn't all that far from Skaran lands and while I had no doubt they'd fight to the death against the bipeds, I also suspected they'd have as little defense against magic as us—*if* that's what we were dealing with. As yet, nothing was certain, especially given the bipeds who'd attacked us certainly hadn't used it.

"Do you want to report to the captain?" he added. "I'll get rid of these bodies."

He dragged them into the nearest building. Once I'd made our report, I helped shift rocks across the door to stop a casual glance from seeing what lay inside. Whether it was enough to stop the bipeds from smelling the death and decay, I didn't know and didn't really care. I was covered in sweat, and every muscle in my body ached. Even if we could have done more, I simply didn't have the energy.

But the dawn had shifted to full sun and the day was far from over for us.

I wearily picked up my pack and slung it over my back. "How far will we have to walk before you can use the wind?"

His shrug had strips of sweat-dampened hair falling into his eyes. He brushed them away and then said, amusement lightly creasing the corners of his eyes, "Remind me to buy you better hair clasps when all this is done. This one is next to useless."

"Aside from the fact my short hair makes them redundant, they weren't designed to control a mane like yours." I turned and moved out, wanting to get away from the dead as quickly as possible. "Although I have to ask—why do you highlanders have such long hair in the first place? Isn't it dangerous in a battle situation?"

"Long hair is considered a sign of virility amongst my people." He fell in step beside me. "And it's not like we've actually faced a serious battle situation for centuries."

"What about the Skaran?"

"They're too busy trying to rip you apart to grab a hair tail. If it *is* grabbed, it's easily sliced off."

"That's presuming you have the time to draw a knife."

"Indeed." His grin flashed again. "But Skaran are not the only ones who can move at speed when necessary."

We continued on in silence. The air soon spun around us though the earth remained mute—dead. Donal stopped and held out his hand. I twined my fingers through his and stepped close. Within seconds, we were wrapped in gossamer clouds and being swept sideways.

It didn't take long to reach the broken volcano. This time, though, the clouds didn't dissipate, even when we were delivered safely onto the ground—and *that* made me wonder what dangers lurked beyond the gauzy veil that protected us.

I stepped back, my gaze sweeping Donal critically. Though sweat ran freely down his face, his breathing wasn't as harsh as it had been previously. For whatever reason, moving the two of us hadn't affected him as badly this time, even though the distance we'd traveled was probably greater.

"This way, Princess."

Though his voice was little more than a murmur, his words nevertheless hung in the air, as if waiting for someone to hear them—someone *other* than me. I shivered and rubbed my arms. The stone under my feet was flat, black, and glass smooth. I had no idea if it was natural or not, and the earth's voice remained dead. As she'd warned, I wouldn't be able to call on her for help if it became necessary.

The ground soon began to slope sharply upward, losing much of its smoothness in the process. After a few more minutes, the light of day gave way to shadows. Donal stopped and the gossamer cloud finally dissipated. I halted beside him and looked around. We were in a cave—a small, almost triangular-shaped one that ran with water as dark as the walls and stunk of foul eggs.

I swung back to the light, but there was nothing to see except blue sky. I glanced back at Donal. "Where are we?"

"In a cave close to the point where the lava breached the cone."

I frowned. "Why are we here rather than in the cone itself?"

"Because this is as far as the wind could take us—we're just below the line of whatever is impeding her and, I presume, the earth."

"The earth's voice was extinguished at the beginnings of those ruins and that hasn't changed."

"Then let's hope we're not discovered, or we'll be in deep trouble."

He swung off his pack and walked up the slope to the cave's rear. While the entire lower section ran with little streams of water, the main source of all that moisture was a natural fissure that divided a five-foot-high ledge at the back of the cave.

I threw my pack onto the ground beside his and then rolled my shoulders. It didn't help a whole lot with the ache but then, nothing short of a long hot bath and several days of rest would achieve that—and both were unlikely to come my way in the near future. "I wonder why the deadness and restrictions affects the earth more than air?"

"Maybe the restricting magic is more earth-based." He unhooked his bedroll. "Rest, Princess. It could be a while before we get the chance to do so again."

I glanced at him sharply. "Is that the wind's judgment, or yours?"

"Both."

"*Not* what I wanted to hear."

"If I'd lied, would it have made you feel any better?"

"Probably not." A smile touched my lips. "And I wouldn't have believed you even if you *had*."

He made an aggrieved sound. "It's a sad state of affairs when a man's word is trusted so little."

"It's not so much a matter of trust," I replied, though the gods only knew I had reasons enough not to trust the word of any man or woman ever again. "But rather the fact your eyes give you away when you're less than honest."

He raised an eyebrow. "My many wins at the betting tables would refute that statement."

"Maybe I'm just a little more perceptive than those who throw their cash in your direction."

"I think *that's* the more likely answer." He flicked his bedroll out. "In fact, I think you're probably the most perceptive person I've ever met."

I snorted. "Then you obviously haven't met many people."

"Oh, I have—which is why I'm so certain you notice many more things than you'd ever admit, Princess."

"And I think you're insane."

His grin flashed, bright in the shadows. "That is also totally possible. After all, I am a Westal Wildman."

I snorted again. As he double-tapped his halo to report to the captain, I spread my bedroll out and then grabbed some rations—and promptly decided paper probably had more taste.

The stretching silence had me looking at him, eyebrows raised in question.

"It looks like we're beyond the range of the halos." He grimaced. "Which isn't surprising, really, given even these ones were never designed to bridge such a distance."

"No, but it's still damn annoying." If only because if we couldn't pass on any information about whatever we found tonight.

He climbed into his bedroll and settled down. After a moment, I did the same. It said a lot about my weariness that even though this was the first time in twelve years I was without direct contact with the earth, I fell asleep within seconds.

I woke abruptly hours later, my pulse racing so hard it felt like my heart was going to leap out of my chest. For several seconds, I simply lay there, listening to Donal's soft snoring and wondering what the hell had woken me. The deeper darkness of night gathered within the cave and, in the skies beyond its entrance, flags of orange and purple could be seen. I had no sense of movement—either in the cave or beyond it. No sense that anything or anyone was approaching. If there *had* been, surely the stirring air would have woken Donal rather than me.

I frowned and drew in a deep breath, sorting through the various scents within it, trying to find anything out of the ordinary. The foul scent of rotten eggs remained, but this time it was accompanied by the wildness of a storm. Thunder rumbled, a distant sound that held the threat of violence.

But it wasn't the storm that had woken me. Divona was a city living on the edge of the sea, and violent storms were something we were all well used to.

I pushed out of the bedroll and walked across to the cave's entrance. Donal almost immediately said, "What's wrong?"

"I don't know. Something."

"The wind mentions no threat."

He climbed out of his bedroll and joined me near the entrance. The land stretched out far below us, mile upon mile of black emptiness. Nothing moved in that forsaken thread of land—nothing we could see, anyway.

I carefully eased past the cave's entrance. The path we'd followed into this place continued on for a good one hundred feet or so then did a sharp left. It was empty as the land below, so I stepped out and looked up. What almost looked like a frozen black wave arched high above us and stopped me from seeing what was going on beyond it.

I glanced back at Donal. "The wind still sees no threat?"

"Indeed—but if one *is* approaching from up top, then

she wouldn't, given the barrier begins at that wave." He squeezed past me and then moved further up the narrow ledge. "There's no sign of movement."

"Would we see it even if there was?" I certainly hadn't seen the bipeds hiding in the ground until I'd all but stepped on them.

"Probably not—" He stopped and cocked his head sideways. "Do you hear that?"

"What?" I moved from under the black stone wave and stopped beside him. Only then did I hear it—a slow, bass-heavy beat.

"Is that a drum?"

"Sounds like it. And where's there's a drum, there's a drummer." He looked down at me. "I think we'd better go investigate."

"Well, we didn't come all this way *not* to."

I spun and hurried back into the cave. After reattaching the bedroll, I slung on the backpack and walked back out, this time following Donal. The path zigzagged up the mountain—the cave may have been under the lip of the breach, but that lip was a long one.

The crater's side grew steeper, rockier, and the ground less stable. Much of the path crumbled under our weight, sending mini slides of soil and stone leaping over the edge into nothingness.

The drumbeat got louder—closer. Donal motioned me to stop, and then edged past a jagged rock that jutted across the path and disappeared from sight. I shifted from one foot to the other, fighting the urge to ignore his order and go see what might lie beyond that rock.

After a moment, he reappeared and motioned me forward. I dug my fingers into small crevices and slowly edged around the rock, battling gravity and the weight of the backpack, both of which seemed determined to pull me over the edge into nothingness.

Donal clasped my wrist midway around and steadied me as I stepped onto the wide, shelf-like area that lay between two broken sections of cone's wall. The edge lay twenty feet away; there was nothing and no one to be seen beyond it other than the opposite wall of the circular crater —a wall that time and weather had severely eroded. There wasn't anything to even suggest life had *ever* existed within the walls of the volcano.

Nothing, that was, except that steadily beating drum.

"Did you look over the edge to see what's further down?"

"I can't." His voice was grim. "There's a barrier of some sort stopping me."

I studied the area between the edge and us but couldn't see said barrier or even any obvious sign of magic. But then, why would I? It wasn't like I had any familiarity with the stuff. "Wonder why we were able to move through the barrier that stopped the wind investigating the vents but not this one?"

"Not a question I can answer, given my decided lack of knowledge when it comes to magic," he replied. "But it does at least confirm *someone* around here is capable of it. Whether it's our armored attackers or perhaps even a lingering remnant of a bygone era is what we now need to uncover."

"I wouldn't have thought barrier magic would linger for centuries, especially in an area as unstable as this."

"I guess it would depend on what it was leashed to. The King's Sword survives, after all, and it holds magic, does it not?"

"Yes, but it's not at the mercy of unstable ground." Just

an unstable mind. "I have no idea what it actually does, though. I certainly never felt anything more than the earth power in the few minutes I held it. Where did you hit the barrier?"

"The midpoint between the crater's edge and here."

"It blocks the entire path?"

"Yes." He glanced at me, amusement creasing the corners of his eyes. "And before you ask, I can neither crawl under nor climb over it. I did attempt both options."

"Which would have been a *very* amusing sight. Shame I missed it."

I cautiously walked forward. As I neared the midway point, warmth flared against my thigh—one that grew hotter with every step. The glass knife had come to life, and was now throwing off a light so bright it made the leather sheath glow gold. I hesitated and then wrapped my fingers around the hilt. It didn't burn, although the fierce light crawled across my hand and totally enclosed it. I drew the knife free.

It wasn't the blade that was glowing. It was the runes that ran along its length.

"It seems the King's Sword isn't the only magically imbued item within Divona," Donal said. "And *this* one is obviously designed to sense what we cannot see."

"It appears so. Unfortunately, my mother died not long after she gave it to me, so I don't really know much about its use."

"That seems to be a developing theme, and one that may yet cost us all dearly."

My gaze shot to his. "I hope you don't hold me—"

"No." He clasped my arm, his grip warm and reassuring. "I only wish the wind had brought me to your doorstep sooner."

"I'm glad she *didn't*." I raised the blade and walked on.

Red began flickering through the golden glow of the runes. "Because then you would have been nothing more than just another who'd taken his ease with me, and I would have been forced to add you to the hate list."

"You can rest assured I will never be *just* another, Princess."

"Not to blow your own horn or anything," I murmured, amused.

"I wasn't talking about my skills as a lover, profound as they might be."

"Then what were you talking about?" I hesitated, and then grimaced. "Oh yeah, I forgot—all you want from me is freedom for your people."

"Perhaps." He motioned to the knife. "How about you concentrate on that rather than something that may or may not eventuate."

"Perhaps? You can't say something like that and then not expect to explain what the hell you mean."

"I can when expectations are nothing more than desires best-kept secret."

My lips twitched. "So does that mean you *do* desire me, despite previous statements to the contrary?"

"Concentrate, Princess. Now is *not* the time for such discussions."

"A simple yes or no is all that's required."

"You really *are* annoying sometimes, you know that?"

My amusement grew. "It's one of my many unheralded traits. And something you, highlander, have yourself perfected."

"Barrier. Knife. Concentrate."

I chuckled softly but nevertheless returned my attention to the glowing knife. With every step closer to the barrier we couldn't see, the red fire grew, until it all but smothered the gold. I stopped again and studied the air just beyond the blade's point. If the fire flickering down the blade was anything to go by, the barrier was now within touching distance.

I took another step and pressed the knife forward. My arm wasn't quite straight when the blade was stopped and the faintest shimmer appeared at its point. I pressed harder, trying to force the knife's magic through the other. For several seconds, nothing happened. Then the runes pulsed and the red flames gained life, crawling from the blade onto the surface of the unseen barrier.

Their touch was like acid to the opposing magic—it quickly peeled away from them, creating a hole through which the rest of the pathway and the mountain beyond were visible.

Revealing the fact that this barrier wasn't just magical—it was a *lie*.

The old crater *wasn't* empty.

It was filled to the cone's rim with buildings.

Big, rusty, metal and stone buildings.

"What the *fuck*?" Donal peered through the red-ringed gap. "Why would anyone in their ever-loving mind want to live in the crater of an old volcano, let alone build a city so fucking *huge*?"

"If they can create a barrier that hides their presence so successfully, then maybe they've found some way of controlling the volcano's eruptions. Or maybe they simply don't care." I paused. "Presuming, of course, that this city belongs to the bipeds and not someone else."

"Yes." His voice was grim. "Are you able to widen that gap enough for us to crawl through?"

"Possibly."

I swept the knife up and around; a glowing trail of red

followed the movement and formed an arched doorway. But the minute I pulled the knife away, it disappeared.

I cursed, repeated the process, and then glanced at Donal. "You go through first. I'll follow."

He unlatched the pulse rifle and then crawled through. I followed him, making sure the knife remained in contact with the barrier even though it required a little sideways shuffle. I had no idea what would happen if the magic reasserted itself when I was partway through, and no intention of finding out. At the very least, it might set off an alarm, and that was something we could ill afford given how far away we were from either the air or earth's help. We certainly weren't carrying enough ammo to take care of a city filled with armored bipeds.

Once through the barrier, I pulled the knife away and the gap immediately closed. I followed Donal across to the edge; the farther I moved from the barrier, the less intent the knife's red glow became. But the runes still shed golden light, which suggested it was still reacting to some sort of magic, be it the barrier or something else. I sheathed the knife to contain the glow and was oddly comforted by its warmth against my thigh. If magic in another form approached, I rather suspected it would burn brighter, and that, in turn, would give us time to react.

Or, at the very least, run.

I dropped and crawled the last few feet until I reached Donal. The stone and metal buildings were perched precariously on the crater's sides, their varied shapes and sizes seemingly dependent on the section of rock to which they clung. There were a series of bridges and stairs linking the various buildings on the same level, and at least twenty levels all told. These were accessed via a platform that zigzagged from the crater's rim down to its base. Interspersed along its length were silver poles topped by a flickering, yellow-green flame. They threw a very muted light across both the platform and the nearby buildings, but if this were the home of the armored bipeds, they wouldn't have needed much more.

Then I spotted them. They were stationed on every level, and all of them were carrying the long, sword-like weapon that had almost sliced me in two. They were obviously guards, but against what? Did other beings live within this dead zone? One whose culture either threatened or were at war with this lot? Or were they simply a precautionary measure, in much the same way as Cannamore's army was?

They weren't the only bipeds here, however, and these others were, in fact, more plentiful. They were long and pale, with limbs that were oddly stick-like and faces that weren't as angular as their armored kin. Those who were obviously male had bony plates of red on their heads while the females had red scales that ran down their spines and covered their rears.

A good portion of these were leaving their houses and heading down the walkway. The base of the old volcano was strangely flat and would have been little more than a black hole had it not been for the flickering, amber-green lights. The entire area was packed with both kinds of bipeds, but many also lined the walkway immediately above. In the center of the lit area was a raised dais on which two figures stood. The first was the drummer—an armored biped who, even from this distance, looked huge. The other was not only taller but one of the bipeds without armor. His head plate wasn't red, however, but the same brilliant color as the lights. He was holding a silver staff topped with a black stone and wore a chunky white necklace—which suggested he was a figure of importance given none of the others appeared to be wearing any sort of jewelry.

"We've obviously caught them in the midst of some sort of meeting," I whispered.

"Which conveniently provides *us* with the perfect opportunity to do a little investigating."

"I'm not entirely sure that's wise, Donal." I skimmed my gaze across the crater again. While most of those visible on the upper levels seemed to be watching what was happening below, it didn't exclude the possibility of others who weren't so entranced. "There's far too many of them and only two of us. If we get caught—"

"We'll be in a shitload of trouble," he cut in. "I'm well aware of that. But we need to know if the bipeds are responsible for the tunnel we discovered, or if that's someone—some*thing*—else. If there isn't a tunnel entrance here, then we really have no choice but to go back out and try to find it."

The last thing I wanted was to go underground—and not just because I still wouldn't be able to access my element. I simply had a bad, *bad* feeling we would never see daylight again if we did.

Which might just be fear rather than intuition, but I still wasn't about to ignore it. Not unless there was absolutely no other choice.

The drum's steady beat was getting louder, echoing off the cone's walls. The pale biped raised his silver staff and made a sound that weirdly reminded me of the guttural noises produced by groaners. That we even heard it above the resonating drum suggested there something enhancing his voice even if there was nothing evident.

Yellowish-gray light shot from the black stone on top of

his staff, a bright beam that arrowed past us and then flared out across the barrier, making the invisible visible. It was only then that I realized neither the stars nor the moon could be seen. The barrier not only kept prying eyes out but also any glimpse of the night sky. Given the muted lights that ringed the crater, maybe the moon was simply too bright for them.

A chant rose, softly at first but gathering in strength with each beat of the drum. No one appeared to be looking at the ever-spreading blanket of yellow light; instead, they seemed entranced by the two on the dais.

"If these creatures *are* responsible for the tunneling," I said softly, "the entrance will surely be underneath us given this is the point where the deadness would meet the mountain."

"There's only one way to find that out."

Donal pushed forward until a good portion of his body was hanging over emptiness. The edge started to crumble under his weight, so I shifted position, braced my feet against a rock, and then grabbed his legs.

"Thanks, Princess." He twisted left and right for several seconds and then added, "There's no obvious tunnel entrance that I can spot, but there's a large rock shelf directly below us. I can't see what might lie below it."

"Are there any buildings on our side of the cone?"

"None at all. Maybe it's too fragile."

Given how well anchored the other buildings appeared to be, I had no doubt they would have found a way around the fragility if they needed to. That they *hadn't* suggested they had other reasons for not using this side.

"Is there any sort of path that leads either down to that outcrop or further around the crater itself?"

"There's a track to our left, though it doesn't look very

wide. If we can follow that around, though, we should get a better view of the entire crater."

"Let's try that, then."

I helped him get back onto more solid ground and then rose and went left. The path began at the point where the lava breach ended and the volcano wall rose sharply upward again. It was little more than a goat track and looked even more fragile than the one we'd followed up to the breach point.

I swung my feet over the ledge and then, after a calming breath, dropped down. Black dust plumed around my boots and small stones skittered toward the edge.

I took a step and then froze as a crack appeared. When nothing else happened, I risked another step. The ground shifted slightly and the trickle of stones moving toward the edge increased.

"I don't think this ledge will support your weight, Donal. It's barely supporting mine."

"Give me your pack. That thing won't be helping."

I carefully tugged off the backpack, handed it up to him, and then took another step.

The result was the same—more cracks, and more stones sliding toward the edge.

"Hang on." Donal swung off his pack, dug out a rope, and tossed one end to me. "Tie that around your waist. At least that way I won't lose you if the ground does give way."

I quickly tied it on and then double-checked the knot to make sure it wouldn't come undone at an inopportune moment. Donal wrapped the other end around his body and then braced his feet against the volcano's wall. Once settled, he gave me a nod. I continued on, keeping as close to the wall as I could and pausing between each step so that the flow of dirt and stone toward the path's edge didn't become too noticeable.

The chanting grew louder; the bipeds who lined the walkway were joining in. The beam of light coming from the pale biped's staff was now pulsing and, overhead, a foot-wide hole had appeared in the dome of the magic that protected this place—something that was evident only because I could see pale stars shining in the black sky.

I continued to follow the path's gentle curve. Light from the yellow beam washed across the area directly ahead, and I didn't need the knife's increasing heat to warn me not to step into it. Even from where I stood I could feel not only the power of that beam but its foulness.

A few more steps took me to the end of the rope's length, but I was far enough around now to see the area under the stone shelf that had blocked Donal's view.

Though there were a lot of vertical fissures splitting the volcano's wall under the shelf, there was nothing wide enough to suggest it might be a tunnel of any kind. But at the volcano's shadowed base, close to where the crater's wall would have met the floor, a thin stream of molten yellow was visible—one that matched the stream we'd spotted at the base of the shaft lit by sparks. The thin stream dropped into a pool that slowly bubbled—a pool that didn't appear to increase in size despite that molten flow.

That pool was lava. It had to be.

But where was it coming from? It surely couldn't be an indication that the old volcano was active, because the flow was coming *into* the volcano, and that suggested an outside source.

Unfortunately, the diffused lighting lining the rest of the crater wasn't enough to provide even the smallest hint of what the shadows above the pool hid.

Those shadows deepened as the yellow beam of light went out. Both the heavy drum and the chanting stopped, and the ensuing silence was filled with anticipation. Chills slithered down my spine, and all I wanted to do was run. But that was the instinct of someone who'd spent nearly half their life protecting themselves, and one I couldn't afford right now.

Moonlight poured in through the ten-foot-wide hole the yellow beam had created in the protective barrier. It didn't diffuse as it should have, but was instead funneled directly down the middle of the crater. It hit the table on the dais, and spider-like veins of silver appeared in the black stone. They moved swiftly toward the edges, until the whole stone shone so brightly it was almost impossible to look at it.

The pale biped pointed his staff to the right. A door at the far end of the lit area opened and a pale female walked out.

A murmur rose from the waiting crowd—another wave of anticipation that was quickly silenced.

As the female moved up the steps, the biped mage thumped his staff three times on the dais. A bell-like sound rang out and the lights ringing the entire area flared brighter. They not only cast away the deeper darkness concealing the area around the southern edge of the volcano but also revealed what lay beyond—a cavernous, V-shaped cut in the crater's crumbling wall. It was in the right area to line up with the strip of deadness that had led us to this place and all but confirmed these bipeds *were* behind the tunneling.

I pressed back against the wall again and carefully edged back along the path. On the dais below, the female had walked to the shining table and stopped opposite the others. The mage lifted his staff again and the chanting resumed; this time it was a husky but haunting sound, and it sent another shiver down my spine. The steady thumping of the drum sounded like a heartbeat and maybe it was, because moonlight pulsed in time with it. With each heavy thump, the luminosity increased, until the beam of moonlight was all but solid. This time it flooded the old volcano and filled it with a surreal glow that made the black stone buildings gleam.

The bipeds made no move to protect their eyes, but none of them appeared to be looking at the moonbeam column, but rather what was happening on the dais below.

The chanting grew louder, the moonlight fiercer, its brightness washing across the path. It would only take one of the armored bipeds to look up and they'd see me as clear as day.

I hastened my pace, not wanting to remain on this crumbling pathway any longer than necessary. But the cracks were becoming wider and the flow of stones over the edge stronger. Sooner or later, someone was going to notice them. I had to reach the breach point before that happened.

Again the chanting stopped. Again the silence was eerie.

I glanced down. The mage lowered his staff and touched its black stone first to female's right shoulder, and then her left, uttering guttural sounds I presumed were either some sort of blessing or spell, but really could have been anything.

When he raised his staff, the female rose. The drumming immediately resumed; the female was rotated and then placed facedown on the silver-veined black table. The moonlight still pulsed in time with the drumbeat and the sense of rising power grew.

The ceremony was reaching its crescendo. I had a bad feeling I'd better be anywhere but on this ledge when it hit.

But the increasingly fragile state of the ground made going any faster virtually impossible. Instinct might be warning I'd better get off this ledge, but *falling* from it would be infinitely worse than whatever might happen when the spell hit its peak.

As the chanting grew in volume, the male biped gripped his staff with both hands and raised it above his head. His voice also rose, his chanting carrying easily over both the drums and the other voices. He stepped closer to the table; the female didn't move, didn't react. Perhaps she was locked into immobility by the pulsing light.

The thrum of power was so fierce it crawled across my exposed skin, small gnats of energy that bit and stung. I glanced sideways; there were twenty yards, if that, to go, and yet it might as well have been a mile. At least Donal was gathering the slack and keeping the rope as tight as practical. If I *did* fall, it wouldn't be very far.

His gaze met mine. He didn't shout at me to hurry, but the command was nevertheless in his eyes.

The chanting once again stopped, drawing my gaze downward... to see the pale biped plunge his staff into the spine of the female. She didn't react in any way. The mage slowly turned his staff, as if screwing it tighter into her flesh. The silver began to tarnish, turning a dark blackish red.

Blood, I realized.

The female's blood was somehow being sucked into the staff. The discoloration bled into the shaft of moonlight and flushed upward, staining the beam with its powerful putridity. As it rose, a deep rumbling began, one that grew louder and appeared to be chasing the bloody swirl.

A tremor.

It was a goddamn *earth* tremor.

I swore and gave up any pretense of caution, running for the ledge and Donal. The ground cracked and moved under every step, and an avalanche of stones and dirt poured over the side. I didn't care. I just needed off this path.

The red-black stain reached the top of the moonlit shaft and spread like fire across the barrier. Power surged, a wave so powerful I was blasted backward. I hit the crater's wall with a grunt and somehow shoved my fingers into a crevice to steady myself as my feet slipped.

"Nyx, move!" Donal's voice was barely audible over the increasing intensity and noise of tremor.

I thrust away from the wall and leapt toward him. But as I did, the path collapsed and I dropped into emptiness.

EIGHT

The rope snapped taut, stopping my fall with jarring abruptness. For several seconds I just hung there, gently swinging back and forth across emptiness, my heart racing and every digit I had crossed in hope that none of the bipeds looked this way.

But we'd been pushing our luck all day and it was inevitable it would give out at the very moment we needed it most.

From the other side of the crater came a fierce roar. I twisted around and saw several bipeds pointing their long swords at us. More roars soon joined in, until it became a wave of sound that rolled all the way down to the pale biped on the dais.

He didn't move—maybe he couldn't move, given his staff remained lodged in the female and her blood continued to be siphoned into the moonlight—but he barked fiercely at those surrounding him. As one, the armored bipeds flowed out of the lit area and began climbing, seeming to have little trouble finding purchase despite the fragility of the crater's wall.

There had to be at least a hundred clambering toward us. A mere three had almost killed us out in the dead zone.

We needed to get out of here.

Needed to find live earth and air to have any hope of surviving.

I swore, then grabbed the rope and began to climb even as Donal started hauling me up. Heat whizzed past my cheek and exploded into the rock face directly in front, sending shards of stone spearing into my skin. The knife's heat became fierce, not only burning my thigh but also sending thin beams of golden light spiraling into the bloody glow surrounding us. I had no idea what it was reacting to, but it certainly didn't stop them firing at me. Nor did it protect me from the sharp missiles of stone that sliced into the air with every shot that barely missed.

The rock shelf loomed large above my head. I released the rope, gripped the edge with both hands, and hauled myself up and over. Globs of yellowish mucus-like material chased me over the edge, hitting close to my heels and almost instantly liquefying the stone. It was some form of acid. Nothing else would affect rock like that.

I surged to my feet and raced to the next wall, once again climbing the rope as Donal pulled me up.

I reached the breach's edge, scrambled over it, and then quickly crawled away on all fours. But the long, cylindrical weapons the armored bipeds were using weren't hampered by distance, and the globs of mucus were getting ever closer.

I thrust up and then tried to undo the rope, but my fingers were shaking and the knot so damn tight it was next to impossible.

"Don't bother." Donal tossed me my backpack and motioned me forward. "At least if we're leashed together, if one of us falls from the ledge the other has some chance of saving them."

"Or being dragged to their death." But that was perhaps a better option than getting captured by the bipeds. I had a vague feeling our fate might be along the same lines as that of the female on the table.

I drew the knife as we neared the barrier. The bloody-black stain hadn't yet reached this point, but it was close. I didn't need to look up to know that—I could feel its foulness wash across the back of my neck.

I thrust the knife's point into the barrier and swiftly cut an opening. Once Donal had crawled through, I dropped to my knees and followed.

Something hit my foot, and the stench of burning leather began to sting the air. I swore, swung around, and saw the globule leeching into the heel of my left boot.

Then I saw the bipeds—they'd reached our ledge.

I pushed through the gap and quickly pulled the knife away. As the barrier closed once again, Donal grabbed my arm and hauled me upright.

"You okay?"

"No." I raised my foot and sliced the remains of the bootheel away. I repeated the process with the second heel to even my footing and then pulled away from him. "Go."

A guttural scream went up behind us. The bipeds, coming at us hard. I didn't bother checking whether they were able to get through the barrier—we'd know soon enough. Right now, it was far better to concentrate on getting down this mountain as fast as possible.

Donal reached the outcrop and started climbing around it. Something hissed through the air and I instinctively ducked. The globule aimed at my head instead hit the nearby wall and the rock began to melt. I drew a blaster, spun around, and fired. There were a dozen bipeds on the other side of the barrier, but only one of them had a cylinder weapon. The others were pacing back and forth, their weapons raised and their screams filling the night with anger and frustration.

The barrier no more stopped the blaster's bullets than it did the globules, but once again they made little impact on the creatures as they prowled the barrier's length. How long it would contain them, I had no idea. The blood ceremony was ongoing, given the stain still spread across the dome, but even creatures as tall as these bipeds only had a finite amount of blood in their bodies. When the female was drained, I very much suspected the mage would be able to open the barrier and unleash his forces.

"Nyx, come *on*."

I holstered my gun and knife and then ran for the jutting outcrop. At the halfway point, Donal once again grabbed my arm, dragging me the rest of the way and depositing me safely on the other side. A globule hit the rock where I'd been only seconds before and the stone began to melt. It wouldn't impede them as it had us—in fact, given the ease and speed with which they'd climbed the crater's wall, it probably wouldn't have provided much hindrance anyway.

"Move, move," I said.

He didn't. Instead, he swung his pack around, pulled out a couple of pomegranates, and lobbed them at the barrier. They passed through it as easily as the bullets and the globules, suggesting the barrier had been designed to stop light and flesh but not metal or their own weapons.

With a huge whoomp, the pomegranates exploded. Blood, flesh, and gore sheeted the barrier, but the furious roar that immediately rose said we hadn't got them all.

But then, there was a whole volcano filled with the bastards. A few pomegranates were never going to make much of a difference.

Donal shouldered the pack and then led the way down the hill as fast as practical. But it wasn't just the narrow nature of the path that made things difficult—it was the quake that continued to shudder through the old volcano and the dust and debris that fell like black rain all around us. It was damn difficult to see where we were going despite the fierce glow of the moon.

Somehow, we made it down three levels, then four.

From above came guttural cries that were a mix of jubilation and anger. I risked a look and saw one of the bipeds leap over the path's edge and arrow toward us. After several seconds, he twisted in the air and hooked onto the wall with one long hand. Others quickly followed and, within a heartbeat, there were half a dozen of them scrambling toward us.

"Princess, move it," Donal growled.

I raced after him, concentrating on putting one foot safely after the other, all the while aware of the steadily growing roar of anger coming from above—a very real indicator of how close those creatures were getting and how little time we had left.

Five levels down, then six.

On the path directly below us was the outcrop of rock that protected the cave in which we'd slept. If we could reach it, Donal would be able to call on the wind to help....

Another guttural cry erupted, this time just above my head. I instinctively looked up, only to see a biped coming straight at me. I swore and grabbed my knife, but he was far too close and I was far too slow.

He swooped in, gathered me in one arm, and then leapt over the edge into the night and emptiness.

I had no idea whether he intended suicide or if he was going to spin and grasp the mountain as I'd seen them do above—and no intention of waiting to find out.

As Donal's curse bit across the noise of the screaming bipeds still above, I thrust the knife as hard as I could into the creature's gut. It might have built-in body armor, but it was no match for the glowing glass blade, which slid into the biped's flesh as easily as a hot knife through soft cheese. As blood flowed and blade's golden fire began cindering its flesh, it bared its teeth and snapped at me. I jerked back instinctively, and only the wash of its dead-meat smelling breath caught me. I gagged but withdrew the knife and thrust it into his body again... and then again. Its grip on me went limp and its body fell away. The rope around my waist went taut and I once again stopped with gut-wrenching suddenness.

"Nyx, cut the rope and drop to the ledge."

I glanced down and saw it was little more than a couple of feet below me. I freed myself, dropped down, and then glanced up. Donal was tying his end of the rope around an outcrop of rock. Whether or not it would hold was a moot point. More bipeds were flinging themselves down the mountain. If he didn't get down here fast—or if he tried to use the path—he would be caught and killed.

"Throw me the pulse rifle," I shouted.

He immediately did so and then climbed over the edge and began to rappel down. I quickly sheathed the bloody knife and then caught the gun, flipped it around, and fired at the bipeds closest to him. The shots ricocheted across the night as blood, gore, and brain matter rained all around me.

It didn't stop them, but I didn't expect it to. I was just trying to ensure Donal made it to the ledge in one piece.

He released the rope and dropped the last six feet,

briefly sweeping his fingers against the stone platform to gain his balance before he grabbed my arm and pulled me forward.

"Come on, the air awaits. We just have to get off this rock."

The words were barely out of his mouth when there was a thump behind us. I twisted around and fired the rifle. Three shots took out two of the bipeds, but I missed the third. Before I could fire again, Donal all but threw me over the edge. I swore and landed awkwardly, stumbling forward several feet before I gained my balance. I swung around, saw him in midleap, and jumped back to avoid a collision—then spotted the biped only feet behind him.

"Donal, hit and roll."

I jumped back again to give him room and then raised the rifle and fired—and kept firing. The biped's body twitched and bled under the impact, but its momentum was such that he just kept coming. I swore and threw myself sideways, hitting the crater's wall hard enough to force a hiss of pain. I had no time to recover or gather breath. Donal grabbed my hand, stepped over the body of the biped, and ran down the path. The air began to swirl around us, a force that quickly gathered strength, throwing dust and grit into the air without ever touching us.

Multiple screams rose from the path above; I didn't look up. I didn't need to. Those screams told me how close the bipeds were—and how many of them were now hunting us.

The maelstrom grew stronger. Donal stopped and spun around so abruptly that I ran straight into his chest. His arms went around me even as he grunted at the impact and, a heartbeat later, we were wrenched sideways at speed. This time, there was no gossamer cloud to hide us; I guessed it would have been pointless given the night was clear and bright. A lone cloud would have been very obvious.

The guttural screams followed our departure, as did several globules. They hit the turbulent air surrounding us and were sent flying straight back at the bipeds, who scrambled left and right to avoid being hit.

But the ground below was alive with movement; the bipeds had come out of their crater in numbers. And while they might not be able to match the wind for speed, they were still damn fast.

The knife's heat increased abruptly, her light so bright sunbeams poured from the sheath. I wrenched the blade free; while the runes were glowing gold, whips of red were once again crawling down its length.

Magic, coming in fast.

But from where?

As if in answer, a glowing orb of yellow-green appeared, trailing sparks behind it as closed in on us. The wind jagged us sideways with such force that it dragged a gasp from my lips. The orb shot past and slowly arced back down to the ground.

More orbs appeared. The wind kept zigzagging, but the scent of sweat was now stinging the air and moisture was trickling down Donal's face.

As we were snapped left once again, two orbs came in from the right. I slashed at the closest and, as the blade sliced through it, the whips of red leapt onto the surface of the orb, quickly encasing and then consuming it. When it was nothing but dust, the whips leapt back to the blade.

The magic in this knife had definitely been designed for defense—and against *this* type of magic. It briefly made me wonder just what the King's Sword had been designed to do.

The orbs continued to chase us across the night sky, but we were slowly gaining distance on the horde, and they no longer provided an immediate threat. Which was good, because the sting of sweat was stronger and Donal was now shaking.

And I very much suspected it was more than just the effort of controlling the air. "Are you okay?"

His gaze met mine. "No."

"Then put us down—"

"Not until I absolutely have to." There was a grim determination in both his voice and his expression. "We need more distance between us and them—at the rate they run, they'll catch us in hours."

"Driving yourself to the point of exhaustion isn't going to help, Donal."

"It's not exhaustion. One of the goddamn orbs hit me."

"What? Damn it, highlander, put us down so I can check—"

"No," he said. "Now shut up and let me concentrate."

"Goddamn stubborn *man*," I muttered. "If you suddenly lose unconsciousness and drop us from this height, I'm going to make your afterlife hell."

Amusement crinkled the corners of his eyes, momentarily blotting out the gathering pain. "Well, if I'm going to be haunted by anyone, I can't say I'd be unhappy for it to be you."

"That is not exactly reassuring."

"What part of be quiet and let me concentrate did you not understand?"

I grinned. "You're the one that keeps answering me."

This time, he didn't bite. We continued on through the night and gradually left the bipeds and their glowing orbs far behind. As the first hints of dawn appeared on the distant horizon, we finally started losing both speed and height. I glanced down. The ground was littered with prickly cacti and tumbleweeds, and was scattered with rocks, both small and large. There was no water anywhere that I could see and nothing moving. If anything other than the bipeds lived in these lands, then they were either seeing out the night underground or were so small that they simply weren't visible from this height.

We began dropping at a faster rate. Donal was soaked in sweat and his entire body shook. But his eyes were narrowed and his expression determined. He was not going to lose control, no matter what the cost to him personally.

The ground grew closer and our speed lessened, until there were little more than a few yards separating us from the ground. Then the wind and Donal's strength gave out, and we dropped like stones. We hit feet first, and hard enough to jar my spine. Then Donal collapsed backward with a wheeze and dragged me down with him.

"Sorry, sorry," he said, his voice hoarse and filled with pain.

I rolled off him and scanned his length for the wound, but given how close he'd been holding me, it would have to be on either his limbs or his back. "Where were you hit?"

He didn't answer, just rolled slightly to the left. My eyes went wide. The wound was on his right butt cheek, close to his hip, and had to be a good hand's width in size. The orb had eaten down through his clothes and was now tearing into his flesh with tendrils of green-gold, creating an open sore that bled profusely.

If it got any deeper, it would expose bone.

I closed my eyes for a heartbeat, trying to control the surge of horror. This wasn't going to be fixed by anything we had in our medikits.

"Do something, Princess. I don't care what, just stop this goddamn pain."

I hesitated and then dragged out my knife. The runes flared to life again and the red tendrils of energy slipped down to the blade's point, as if in readiness.

"I'm going to try and counter the orb's magic with the knife's," I said. "It might hurt."

"It can't possibly hurt any more than it already is," he growled. "Just do it, Nyx. Please."

I hesitated again and then carefully pressed the knife's point into the wound—into the very heart of the pulsing mess of yellow-green that was eating his flesh.

He screamed, a sound that cut through the very heart of me. It was—mercifully for him—a sound that abruptly cut off. He was unconscious, which at least meant he wouldn't feel anything I now did. I pushed the knife's point deeper into the opposing magic. The runes flared brighter and the red tendrils leapt down to counter the yellow-green. For several seconds, the two magics fought each other, the tendrils lashing and counter-lashing, making his flesh and muscles leap and twitch in time.

Thankfully, the red won.

The blade's magic returned, leaving an open and bloody wound the size of my fist but thankfully *not* the depth of it. I sheathed the knife, then swung my pack around to grab the medikit.

After cleaning and packing the wound, I sprayed the entire area with a sealer. The false skin would help prevent infection and allow freer movement, but it wouldn't stop the pain. It was also doubtful he'd be able to move very fast. Not under his own steam, anyway.

I returned the kit to the backpack and then looked around. A faint haze of dust was visible on the horizon, suggesting the bipeds were still coming after us. But dawn was drawing ever closer and would hopefully soon force them underground.

Even so, there was little chance of us moving anywhere for some hours to come, and that meant constructing a shelter for us both.

I rose. There were plenty of stones around the area, but it would take me forever to create a shelter large enough to hide us both, and there was no guarantee it would prevent them from smelling us, let alone protect us for long against the acidic globules.

What we needed was a cave—one deep enough to stop our scent from rising and to protect us from the acid.

Which in turn meant I had to call to the earth. But creating stone shackles was vastly different to creating a deep cave. I'd never done anything like that before and had no idea of the protocols or even if there *were* any.

I shoved the knife hilt deep into the hard soil and then closed my eyes. The response, while still a little distant, was immediate.

What is it you wish?

I need to create a cave large enough to protect us.

Picture it, and it will be done.

I immediately envisioned a long deep cavern that was wide enough to hold the two of us, with an entrance that was short and steep. The knife pulsed and power surged up the hilt into my body, forming a deeper connection between the earth and me. Though she wasn't actually pulling on my strength, I nevertheless felt it slipping like rain from my body. This was the cost of the earth magic and one I was more than willing to pay if it kept us safe until Donal had recovered enough to move.

Dust plumed gently into the air as the earth set about

creating the chamber I was picturing. Sweat soon trickled down my body and my head started to ache, but I didn't release the knife. Not until the dust had stopped rising and the earth informed me that the cavern was done.

Thank you, I said, not sure of the protocols when it came to this sort of stuff. I took a deep breath that did little to counter my racing heart or the weakness washing through my limbs, and then freed the knife from the ground. Once I'd sheathed it, I rose. For a heartbeat, everything spun, and it was all I could do to lock my knees and remain upright. I took another deep but useless breath and then walked across to the cave's entrance. It was certainly steep, but there was enough roughness in the packed earth and stone to provide grip points to climb out. I took off my pack, tossed it down, and, after a slight hesitation, slithered after it to check the cave out.

It was deeper than I'd actually imagined and carved entirely out of stone, which should proof it against any sort of cave-in. It was about six feet wide and seven long—just wide enough to fit us both in comfortably.

Now I just had to get the highlander in here, and then figure out a way of blocking the entrance while still providing an air source.

I climbed out—a task made harder by my aching head and trembling limbs—and walked back to Donal. I knelt to check his pulse—it was a little faster than it should have been but nevertheless strong—then rose and grabbed his arms. I couldn't drag him butt-first thanks to the wound, and that meant holding him high enough so that his face wasn't scraped across the ground or the rocks.

But that made it infinitely harder—especially when the man *wasn't* a lightweight.

By the time I got him down to the cave's base, my breath

was little more than short, painful pants, and my head was spinning. I released him and slumped back against the stone for several minutes, dragging in air and trying to ignore the desire to just collapse and sleep. I wasn't done yet—creating the cave was pointless if I just left the front door open and allowed the bipeds easy access.

I pushed away from the wall, staggered over to the ramp, and dragged myself up it. Once at the top, I again thrust my knife into the soil. This time I imagined a thick slab of rock sliding across the opening but left a fist-sized hole on one edge and semicovered it with a small wave of stone to ensure there was fresh air coming in.

Again the knife pulsed, and again my strength slithered away. My heart was now racing so hard it felt ready to tear out of my chest, and my head was on fire. I could barely see through tears, but I didn't need to see to know what was happening—I could feel it through the knife. Stone flowed across the entrance, creating the door I imagined and enveloping us in utter darkness. But air still stirred, an indication the air hole had indeed been created.

We were safe.

Relief surged, my strength gave out, and unconsciousness swept me away.

I had no idea how many hours passed before I woke. I did know my head still thumped and that there was a matching ache in my right leg. I groaned and shifted, and almost instantly various other bits of my body started complaining.

I forced my eyes open and saw only darkness. I waited until they'd adjusted and then looked around. I was at the bottom of the ramp, meaning I'd tumbled down after falling unconscious. My right leg had been cut from my knee to near my ankle, but thankfully, the wound wasn't serious, even though it had bled enough to soak my pants leg. What I'd cut it on, I had no idea, but there were plenty of rocks on the ramp that were sharp enough. I certainly hadn't specified smoothness when I'd created it.

I warily checked my other limbs, but aside from various bruises and sore spots—probably a result of the tumble—there didn't appear to be anything major wrong. I'd been very lucky yet again.

I sat up, waited until the booming in my head eased again, and then glanced around, looking for the knife. It wasn't visible anywhere near me, but a faint flicker of gold had me looking up. It was still lodged in the earth, and that meant I'd have to retrieve it before I made any attempt to get further rest. If the biped mage came anywhere near our hideaway, the knife's reaction to his magic might just give away our position even if the air hole wasn't particularly large.

But I had no intention of doing anything until I'd looked after my leg. One of us had to be fully mobile—although in truth, if Donal couldn't haul us out of here on the air, we were in serious trouble. While I could certainly provide a shoulder to lean on, the sort of speed he'd be capable of wouldn't get us far. And it wasn't just the bipeds we had to worry about, but also the Skaran. Presuming, of course, we actually did get across the Skaran border. Right now, things weren't looking good.

I shuffled forward on my butt until I reached my backpack. After treating and sealing the cut, I gingerly got to my feet and climbed back up the hill, retrieving the knife and tucking it safely into its sheath. A lone sliver of daylight shone through the small air gap, but gave me little indication of the time. There was no noise out there—nothing to indicate the bipeds or anything else were even remotely close. Of course, that wasn't so surprising given the bipeds appeared to be nocturnal.

But we needed to be out of here by night to have any chance of putting distance between them and us. If Donal hadn't recovered sufficiently by that time, then it might be better to remain here until the *next* sunrise. The last thing we needed was for his strength to give out halfway across Skaran lands. Even if we called the captain for help—

The thought froze me and I swore. We hadn't updated the captain since we'd left the ember-lit shaft and gone beyond the range of the halo.

I immediately double-tapped the device, but there was no response other than static. Either the unit was broken or we were too deep under the earth for it to work.

I carefully slipped down the ramp, then grabbed my pack and limped across to Donal. I did a quick check of his pulse, discovered it was back to normal, and then pressed a hand against his forehead. He didn't have a fever and there was no redness developing around the sealed wound. The fierce tide of relief that ran through me was telling—in the brief time I'd been in this man's company, I'd come to rely on him more than anyone else currently in my life.

I eased his backpack off, shifted him into a more comfortable position, and then tucked the sleeping roll under his head. The cave was warm enough that he didn't need to be covered.

After unclipping my own sleeping roll, I took the time to both eat and drink. Neither particularly helped ease the ache in my head, but I suspected only time and sleep would do that. I settled down, crossed my arms, and gradually drifted off.

I woke to an awareness of being watched; while there was no hint of threat in that sensation, tension nevertheless gathered. I opened my eyes, but before I could say anything, Donal's hand touched my shoulder—as if to gauge my position—and then he leaned close, his breath warm on my lips as he whispered, "The air warns of movement."

"How many, and how close are they?"

"An advance party of three, but the main group isn't far behind them."

Meaning we either got out of here now or we took the risk and stayed. "What do you think is our best option?"

"I don't think we can risk any further delays," he said. "Now that the bipeds know we're aware of their presence, they may give up the tunneling and just attack."

"Except the tunnel might be a means of protection rather than a method of concealment. It wouldn't be practical to expect a sizable army to dig themselves shelter every night."

"Perhaps, but we still can't risk remaining here. The garrison will need to prepare for a possible attack."

I wasn't entirely sure there *was* any way to protect a city made of stone and metal from a substance that melted both, but I guessed time would at least give us a chance to discover if there was any information about the bipeds or their magic in either the Mauvaissian archives or the larger libraries within Divona.

"Will you be able to control the air long enough to get us back to the garrison?"

"Yes."

I snorted softly. "I suspect you'd say that even if you were knocking on death's door."

Amusement briefly crinkled the corners of his eyes.

..oubtedly, but we have little other choice. I can't run—not very far, at any rate."

I wrinkled my nose. "How bad is the pain?"

"It hurts like a bitch, but there's nothing either of us can do about that, so I'll just have to ignore it." His amusement grew. "And to do anything else would ruin the stoic reputation we highlanders have."

"It's better to ruin a reputation and be alive than not. Trust me on *that*."

His amusement faded. "I have no intention of dying, Princess, either here or in the Red City. I want to watch the reaction of Cannamore's so-called finest as you claim the sword and your rightful place on the throne."

"If we don't beat these bastards at the Karva Pass, then that's something neither of us might live to see." I hesitated and cocked my head sideways. I couldn't hear anything, but the knife's light was flaring to life again. There was magic out there, somewhere.

I pressed my hand against the stone and the earth immediately spoke. *Another biped has arrived; he thrusts one of their long staffs into the soil and uses it to seek.*

I swore softly. *How far are any of them from our cave?*

Half a mile. They inspect each of the larger stone deposits and then move on.

Meaning they suspected we were hiding and would undoubtedly find us sooner rather than later. I returned my gaze to Donal. "We need to get out of here."

"You clear the way and then come back down. If we leave direct from this cave, there won't be the usual dust devil to give our position away."

I nodded, rose, and grabbed my pack. I didn't bother retrieving the sleeping roll—it was just one more thing for Donal to carry and I suspected that, despite his bravado, he was skimming far too close to the edge when it came to strength.

I scrambled up the ramp and then shoved the knife into the earth and quickly pictured the stone slab silently retreating. Once again, the knife's hilt warmed and energy began to flow. The night slowly became visible, the stars bright in the blackness. We'd be visible the minute we left this shelter.

With the stone back in its original position, I slid back down the ramp and limped over to Donal. He frowned. "What did you do to your leg?"

"Had a bit of a blackout last night, so I can't really say. It's only a scratch, though."

"Says the other master of understatement in this little outfit." He held out his hand. "Shall we go?"

I placed my fingers in his and let him pull me close. Once he'd wrapped his arms around my waist, the air stirred, whirling silently around us until its force was enough to lift. It twisted us around so that we were horizontal, and then shot us out of the cave and into the night.

Ten seconds.

That's all it took for the bipeds to spot us. They were closer than half a mile, but fired neither their globule weapons nor the yellow-green tendril mass. The three of them simply chased us. What they intended I had no idea; maybe they just wanted to see where we were going.

The remaining biped—a mage, although a different one to the one we'd seen earlier, as he was shorter and wasn't wearing the thick white necklace—knelt and wrapped both hands around the staff. It came to life and sent a beam of light arcing back to the volcano. Some form of communication, perhaps?

Once again, we slowly drew clear of our pursuit; the

ground beneath us changed, becoming less arid and far greener as we drew close to the Skaran border.

The Kanjoi River—the demarcation zone between the dead lands and the Skaran—soon appeared. The landscape didn't instantly change—while there were thick pockets of trees, it was for the most part as flat as the dead lands. But aside from the occasional black scar—reminders of just how far the volcanic eruption had reached—the land was lush and green.

Our pace began to slow. Donal's expression was again determined, but his sweat soaked my clothes and his arms trembled. I didn't say anything—there was little point. He would get us as far as he could. Beyond that, it was up to me.

Buildings started dotting the landscape. At first, they were little more than huts on the edge of fields that were laid to cropping—though what, exactly, they were growing wasn't clear from our current height. Gradually, though, the fields gave way to a city that was ringed by a wide, deep ditch, and a fence that appeared to be made of swords—ten-feet-tall, rusted metal swords. The Skaran were capable of smithing, something I really hadn't expected—although I was not entirely sure *why* given I'd witnessed firsthand the detailed gauntlets that covered their hands and feet. They certainly hadn't purchased *those* from any of Cannamore's smiths.

Their buildings were far less sophisticated, being circular in shape and made mainly of stone, with what looked like thick straw as roofing material. All the buildings —be they large or small—were positioned around what looked to be a circular meeting and marketplace situated in the center of the fenced area.

There were hundreds of Skaran out and about—not

only fierce-looking warriors but also men without tusks, women with thick black manes and fur covering their genitals, and naked children who ran, screamed, and played in much the same manner as children all across Cannamore.

Then we were past them and skimming across treetops. Once we'd crossed the Quaih River, we were over the Wild Lands and close—so close—to safety. But our height was again dropping; the swirling wind kept the branches at bay as we dipped down below the treetops, but I could see the ground now and it was coming at us way too fast.

"Donal—"

"I know," he all but ground out.

At the last possible minute, the wind braked and we were deposited gently on the ground. Donal sucked in a deep breath and released me. A second later he was kneeling on the ground, his whole body shaking and the stink of his exhaustion staining the air. I grabbed his water bottle and handed it to him, and then hit the halo.

"Garrison, this is Caracal One. Wildman One and I just arrived back in the Wild Lands and are in serious need of escort and help."

For several seconds there was no response other than static. I tapped the unit in frustration, shoved the link tail deeper into my ear, and a woman's monotone voice finally came online. "—you, Caracal One. We have a unit close—they'll be with you in an hour. Stay at your current location if you can."

"As long as the Skaran don't attack, we will."

"There's been no sighting of them by either team tonight," she replied. "But keep an eye out. The bastards move fast."

"So I discovered. Caracal One out."

I squatted in front of Donal and studied him.

"What?" he said, after a few seconds.

"You look like shit."

"That's because your ass is heavier than it looks."

I grinned. "If you're flinging insults, then you're stronger than you look. Do you think you can shuffle back to the tree?"

He glanced over his shoulder; the tree in question was a thick old black pine that would, with a little earth reinforcement, provide the perfect shelter to wait out the arrival of the rescue party.

Without comment, he took off his pack and shuffled back until his spine rested against the tree trunk. Then he closed his eyes and sucked in air, his whole body shuddering. He remained on his knees though—trying to keep additional pressure off the fist-sized hole in his butt, no doubt. Given the toll moving two of us took on him, it was a wonder he was even conscious. I certainly wouldn't have been.

I pressed my hand against the earth and imagined a heavy earth and stone cave rising up and around the tree, with a small open entrance that faced the pathway. If the Skaran did attack, then at least we had a defensible area.

The earth pulsed and warmed under my fingertips, and a tremor ran through the ground as it rose to fulfill my vision. By the time the cave was finished, my head was again aching, but at least this time unconsciousness wasn't a threat.

I took off my pack, crawled in beside Donal, and then grabbed the pulse rifle and made sure it was ready. Once I checked and reloaded my blasters, I leaned back against the tree trunk, listening to the silence and the soft heartbeat of the earth.

Nothing approached. Not for at least an hour. Then,

gradually, came the soft tremor of steps—light steps, which suggested a scouting team rather than a Skaran hunting party, as the latter walked heavier on the earth.

The steps paused about twenty feet away from our cave and then a voice said, "Caracal One? You there?"

"Yes."

I shifted slightly and peered out. I didn't recognize the woman who spoke, meaning it was Donal's team who'd come to our rescue rather than mine. She lowered her gun and grinned. "Welcome back. The higher-ups were getting a bit worried about you both."

"It's a worry we shared, let me tell you." I glanced back at Donal and saw that he was awake. "You able to move out, highlander?"

"If you'll give me a hand—I think the legs have gone to sleep sitting like this."

I grabbed his hand and steadied him as he rose and limped out of our cave. His eyes were little more than narrow slits of blue, but he didn't say anything about the pain I could practically smell.

"Margreet," he said. "Anything of interest happen while we were away?"

"Nary a thing." Her gaze swept him critically. "How bad is the injury?"

"I'll be all right."

"No doubt, but I'm more interested in the speed with which you can move, as I'd really like to get back to the garrison before midday."

"You set the pace, I'll keep up."

"Determination. I like it—even if it is a lie." Her gaze met mine. "And you?"

"In full working order."

"Good. Between us all, then, we should be able to get

the boss back to the garrison in quick order." She clicked her fingers and two men walked around her and approached Donal. "You *will* need help if I'm any judge, so don't argue and just accept it."

I couldn't help grinning at her no-nonsense attitude. I liked this woman.

Donal didn't argue—not only was he ultimately a sensible man but he also wanted to get back to the garrison ASAP to report our findings. He placed his arms on the two men's shoulders as they locked theirs around his waist. With little fuss, they chair-lifted him and we were on our way.

We moved out quickly. While I did my turn of carrying Donal, I certainly didn't have the strength to last anywhere near as long as even Margreet.

It took us just under an hour to reach the garrison, and we'd barely cleared the tunnel when Captain Marx approached. His gaze scanned us both and then he said, "You up to delivering a full report?"

"I am. The highlander needs medical care."

"No—"

"Donal, we need you at full strength if the bipeds hit, so shut up and just go to the medical center."

He raised his eyebrows, a small smile touching his lips. But all he said was, "Yes, ma'am."

As he was hauled away, I returned my gaze to the captain. "You might want to call in the commander and the Red Queen. They'll both need to hear what we found."

"They already await. Follow me."

He spun around and walked to the nearby set of stairs, bounding up them with far more energy than I could dredge up.

Two guards stood either side of a heavy metal door at the level underneath the rampart; they keyed the door open for the captain to go through, and then held it until I arrived. The hall beyond was gloomy and unlit and ended in a T-intersection. The sign on the external wall said communications was to the left, briefing and command to the right. We went right.

After we were keyed through another metal doorway, we stepped into a long, windowless room that was ten feet wide and at least triple that in length. The commander and Marttia were already seated at the table that dominated the room; the captain moved around to sit beside them, but I was motioned to sit opposite—a position that instantly made it feel a little like I was on trial.

"So." The commander leaned forward and interlaced his fingers. "What happened? Why were you out of contact for so long?"

I took a deep breath and then detailed everything we'd seen and everything that had happened. By the time I'd finished, their expressions were a mix of disbelief and horror.

"They have the ability to melt rock?" Marttia said. "Just how powerful is this substance?"

"We didn't hang around long enough to find out," I said. "But the globules were about fist-sized and turned stone into fluid. How far the melting went, I couldn't say."

The commander frowned. "They would need plenty of such a substance to weaken the garrison walls—they're twenty feet thick."

"They wouldn't have to hit the whole wall," Marx commented. "All they'd need to do is create an access point *into* the garrison."

"At which point they would be met by a barrage of metal."

"Which may eventually stop the bipeds, but it *won't*

stop the yellow-green tendril orbs that eat into your flesh," I said. "Donal's damn lucky to be alive."

"How did *you* stop the orb?" Marttia asked curiously. "There was nothing in the medikit that would have been of much use against that sort of magic."

I drew my knife. Just for a moment, golden light sparked along the runes, sending sun-like beams of brightness spinning through the gloom. "I'm an earth mage, remember, and the King's Sword isn't the only magical item remaining in Divona. The magic in this knife was able to counter the other, and undoubtedly saved Donal's life."

A smile teased Marttia's lips, though her eyes were cold. "I admit not noticing the blade when you drew it on me, and I'm rather surprised such a weapon was gifted to you considering the circumstances."

I swallowed the bitterness that rose at her comment and said, as evenly as I was able, "That's because the king doesn't know it exists—in fact, it would have been destroyed if he had, simply because it belonged to my mother. The knife has been handed down to the firstborn female in her family for generations."

"Which is all very informative," the commander said, "but I can't really see how it relates to our situation here. One knife will not make a difference if these bipeds attack us."

"True," Marttia said. "But I think you miss the point, Commander. That knife countered a magic we've never seen before—there's nothing in either our written *or* oral history that even vaguely resembles the magic described. And that means her mother's people must have encountered these bipeds before—why else would that knife be able to destroy their magic?"

The commander's gaze snapped back to me. "Where did your mother hail from?"

"Initially from the Isle of Whyte, but they have long since lived in Gigurri."

The commander frowned. "Wasn't the Isle of Whyte laid to waste by a volcanic explosion?"

"So Cannamore history claims."

Marttia raised an eyebrow. "Your mother told you different?"

"She used to tell me stories about her people when I was much younger, so my recollection might be vague." I hesitated. "While I believe the volcano *was* the reason the island was laid to waste, it wasn't a natural occurrence."

"So they destroyed their own island?" she asked. "Why?"

I shrugged. "She never said. Maybe she never knew."

Marttia frowned. "Was your mother an earth mage?"

"The ability ran in her bloodline, and I now believe she could hear the earth's voice. Whether she could also command it, I can't say. Certainly I never saw her do it." I hesitated again. "There might be some mention about either the bipeds or their magic in the old texts held in Gigurri's history museums. Whether we have the time to request them, let alone go through them, is another matter entirely."

"I'll nevertheless contact Lady Helena and request she do an urgent search."

Lady Helena happened to be my aunt. She'd been a frequent visitor to Divona when my mother had been alive, but totally absent in the years since her death. I couldn't help but wonder now if that absence had been deliberate, or a result of the king's rampage in the aftermath my mother's death.

"I'll also contact the caretaker of the Antiquities Library in Divona and see what records they hold—"

"I wouldn't bother," I cut in. "There's little in the old archives that mentions either the earth power or the reason why earth mages fled their island home and became refugees in our land."

She raised an eyebrow. "And how would you know this?"

"Because over the years, I've had plenty of time to read and research." Not just about the earth power and her origins, but also the laws and treaty documents. When I did eventually claim the throne, I wasn't about to rely on the word of others. "When you speak to Lady Helena, also request the help of their mages."

Marttia raised an eyebrow. "I was under the impression the Gigurrian mages were little more than pale imitations of their former greatness."

"I bet the king told you that." When she nodded, I added bluntly, "Gigurri remains the last true mage stronghold, though their numbers are indeed dwindling. But the earth still hears and obeys them, and they will, at the very least, be able to bolster and repair foundations."

And with them protecting the city, I could concentrate on destroying the biped mages. Or, at the very least, destroying their staffs and ending their access and abuse of the earth.

"Even if they agree to help, it will take time for them to get here—time these bipeds may not give us," the commander said. "We need a plan of attack if they do decide to hit."

"Well, the most obvious way to counteract acid-like globules would be to make use of the old water channels that run across the top of the wall," Marx said. "Releasing fresh water at the first sign of an attack should render them harmless."

"These globules are based in magic, Captain," Marttia said, "so that rule may not apply."

He glanced at her. "It's still worth a shot given we've little else to run with right now."

"Agreed—make immediate arrangements, Captain."

"Is there anything else you can tell us about these bipeds?" the commander said. "Anything that might provide another means of countering their attack?"

"They're fast and they're dangerous. Blasters won't take them out, so you'll need to issue all on the wall with pulse rifles, at the very least. If you have blast cannons, I'd ready those as well." I hesitated and glanced at Marttia. "I'd also be making evacuation plans."

"Living on the cusp of a volcanic zone as we do, our evac plans are well bedded down." Her voice was cool. "But I honestly cannot believe it will come to that."

"I hope you're right." But *I* honestly believed that she wasn't.

The commander grunted. "Thank you for your assistance and advice, Nyx. Go get some sleep. We'll contact you if we need anything further."

I rose, nodded at all three, and then turned and left. Once outside, I drew in the cool morning air and looked around. Part of me wanted to go check Donal was okay, but I was walking too close to the edge of exhaustion. If I wanted to be in a fit state to go out on patrol tonight, I needed to rest.

I headed down the stairs until I reached the third level and then walked around to our bunkrooms. Merlyn was, unsurprisingly, the only present, and she was fast asleep. I stripped off, dumped my clothes into the laundry chute, and had a long, hot shower that at least eased the ache in my bones if not the overall tiredness. I slipped my knife under my pillow, feeling a weird need to keep it close, and then climbed into bed and went to sleep.

I was woken by singing—soft and very off-key singing. I lay there listening to the sound, trying to place the voice without much success. After a few moments, I gave up and got up.

The singer immediately stopped. "Sorry, did I wake you?"

"No." I stretched the kinks out of my back and then walked across to the doorway and peered out. The singer was Celi.

"What time is it?" I glanced out the door; dusk hadn't yet settled in, so at least I wasn't late for the dinner briefing.

"Five thirty-five."

I grunted. If I'd slept any longer, I would have been late —especially given I wanted to go see how Donal was progressing. I quickly dressed. "Did you have any problems out there today, Celi?"

"No, but then, we rarely do given the Skaran generally don't hunt during the day in summer or autumn. It's a wonder they don't rotate the teams around every few weeks and give the night teams a break."

"Maybe they figure it'll cause too many problems with everyone's circadian rhythms."

"Maybe." She appeared in the doorway and leaned a shoulder against the screen. "Rumor is that you and Donal hit some problems out in the dead lands."

"You could say that."

"Anything we should be worried about?"

"Maybe." I glanced at her. "I can't say anything, Celi. That's up to the captain."

She grunted. "There's some armament changes up on the wall, so obviously something is going on. Hopefully the cap will enlighten us sooner rather than later."

"He will." It was said with more confidence than I actually felt. I had a vague feeling that neither the commander nor Marttia would believe the true gravity of the situation until the bipeds actually attacked.

If they attacked, that was. Maybe the only reason we'd been chased was the fact we'd intruded on both their lands *and* their ceremony.

And maybe tomorrow the king and my brother would drop dead, allowing me to reclaim the throne without any sort of problem.

But at least the weapon upgrades were happening. They may not in the end make much difference, but it was better than nothing.

I strapped on my knife belt, sheathed my knife, and then headed for the door. Celi stepped to one side and allowed me to pass. "I'm heading to medical to check on Donal. I'll see you at dinner."

"You will," she said and returned to her off-key singing.

I clattered down the stairs and walked across to the other side of the courtyard. The medical unit was—according to the signs—on the second floor. A smiling nurse directed me to the third curtained section down the long room. Donal was lying on his stomach the wrong way around on the bed, his arms crossed and a look of sheer boredom on his face.

But at least he smiled when he saw me.

"Princess," he said cheerfully, "aren't you a sight for sore eyes."

I raised my eyebrows as I snagged a nearby chair and sat down at the end of his bed. "And why would you say that when, from what I can see, there's plenty of pretty nurses about to ease the plight of said sore eyes."

"But all of them stand in awe of my magnificence and I've become rather accustomed to your blasé attitude and quick retorts."

"Careful, highlander, or I might begin to think you actually like me."

He grinned. "You—quite literally—saved my butt. Of *course* I like you."

I chuckled softly. "Have they said how long you'll be stuck in here?"

"They've got the healers coming twice a day, and they're saying the wound should be fully repaired within a day or so," he said. "How did the commander and Marttia take the news?"

I gave him a rundown on everything they'd said, and then added, "So basically, exactly as you'd expect."

He frowned. "I might ask my father to check our archives—I know we temporarily took in some of the Isle of Whyte refugees, so there might be a mention as to what—or who—they were fighting when they destroyed their island."

"It's worth a shot." Whether any of the investigations would bear worthwhile fruit before the bipeds attacked was another matter entirely. I glanced at the clock—it was five to six, and time to go. "Do you need anything? I can bring it over in the morning, after I've finished tonight's patrol."

He shook his head. "Just be careful out there—this is a long way from over."

"I will." I touched his shoulder lightly. "Don't give the nurses too hard a time just because you're bored."

"I'll be too busy listening to the wind's chatter as she updates me on events."

"Has she said anything about the biped's movements? And does she know what these things are?"

"No, but that's not surprising given it appears it's only your ancestors who have come across them before. Perhaps you should ask the earth about them."

"I will." Once he was mobile enough to be there and keep watch while I did. "And the bipeds?"

"Have gone underground—"

"The three who were chasing us or the main group?"

"The three. They're in shallow graves on their side of the Kanjoi River. The bulk retreated to the tunnel they were digging." His expression was grim. "The dead zone moved a mile overnight, which suggests they are pushing their machines and people harder."

And being underground, they didn't have to stop for daylight. "How long do you think it'll be before they reach us?"

"How long is a piece of string?" he retorted. "It would also depend on whether they decide to keep tunneling once they hit the Kanjoi River. I doubt they will."

"Is that the wind's wisdom or a hunch?"

"A hunch, but a logical one. If attack *is* their intent, then they won't want to give us much time to prepare."

"That's presuming they think along the same lines as we do. They might not."

"Even fire ants prefer to swarm on unsuspecting prey."

"Then I pity the Skaran."

He raised an eyebrow. "The Skaran are a scourge—"

"Yes, but they no more deserve extinction than we do," I said. "And if either the highlanders or the Mauvaissians thought differently, something would have been done about them long ago."

"I doubt we'd have the capacity to do that *now* let alone

214

centuries ago. And given the Skaran have more than one settlement, extinction *isn't* likely."

"Even so, there were a lot of women and children in that settlement, Donal. I have no desire to see any of them fall victim to the bipeds."

He grunted. "You, Princess, have a surprisingly soft core under the steel."

Which few people ever saw, simply because up until *this* man, I'd never let my guard down. But then, protecting my heart and letting nothing but hate and anger simmer had been a key point of surviving the last twelve years.

"Don't let that snippet get out, or you'll ruin my reputation." I pushed up. "I'll drop by in the morning and update you."

"Hopefully that update will hold nothing but an uneventful night."

"Hopefully."

I touched his shoulder again and then headed across to the mess hall. Once I'd grabbed a meal and some cutlery, I joined the others at the table. The day leaders reported, and then Marx briefly mentioned the results of our mission and the activity we'd discovered. "We're currently on a simple watch brief until we learn more about these bipeds. Even if attack is their intent, they'll have to go through the Skaran first, and we all know that will be no easy task."

"A watch brief doesn't explain the pulse cannons being fitted up on the ramparts," Raj commented. "That's getting ready for an attack."

"Indeed, because I'd rather be safe than sorry." Marx glanced at me. "Stay sharp when you and your team get close to the Quaih River; the bipeds might just skirt the Skaran settlement to come at us, and that means your patrol will be in the way."

"If that happens, we're dead, Captain. Blasters don't kill the bastards."

"Which is why all patrols are being issued pulse rifles," he said.

"Good." Between the rifles and the earth, we at least had a fighting chance. Whether either would ensure survival was another matter entirely. "Have Dravan's and Kaid's replacements been added to my team?"

"We sent out an in-house call for volunteers until the replacements arrive." He tossed me a couple of folders. "Their names are Finn and Orli."

"I take it they're career soldiers without Sifft heritage?"

He nodded. "But we'll give them night circlets, which will magically enhance their sight enough for them to see almost as well as you."

Good, because the last thing the team needed would be two soldiers next to useless in the dark. "Thanks, Cap."

He nodded. "Be careful out there—the Skaran rarely go more than three days without an attack, so you'll likely get hit tonight."

I nodded and flicked through the folders as I ate the rest of my meal. Once I'd finished, Margreet and I walked across to armaments to get our kits and pulse rifles, and then joined our teams at the exit tunnel.

Nash greeted me politely, but Sage's expression was sour. "Nice of you to finally grace us with your presence," she muttered.

"Hey, you were more than welcome to take my place on the mission into the dead lands." I kept my voice mild, even as annoyance stirred within. "Of course, you would probably now be dead given you're not an earth mage and can't summon her power to either protect or attack."

She snorted. "No matter what the rumors might be

saying about you, only the king and his heir can summon the earth, and we all know you ain't *that*."

"I love the certainty with which you say that," I said. "Now if you could just muster that sort of conviction and effort into your job, you might make a good soldier one day."

Her gaze narrowed, but she had the sense not to comment any further. I glanced past Nash to the two newcomers. The night circlets were very similar to the ones communicators wore, but black in color. "I'm Nyx, leader of this motley group."

The two men nodded and introduced themselves. Finn was a wiry, gray-haired man in his midfifties while Orli was swarthy in build and coloring, and even older than Finn.

As the tunnel gate opened, I said, "I want sharpness out there tonight. It may not be just the Skaran we have to worry about."

"Is that what your mission in the dead lands was about?" Nash asked.

"Yes, and they're not dead."

"Great." Nash fell in step beside me. "So what, exactly, is out there?"

I hesitated. Given neither the captain nor the commander had updated the scouting group as a whole, I probably shouldn't say anything—but I didn't want them walking into the Wild Lands and possible trouble without some sort of forewarning.

"Bipeds that are faster and meaner than the Skaran, with body armor that renders blasters next to useless."

"Well, didn't *we* choose a fine time to volunteer for a short tour of duty out here," Finn said cheerfully and motioned toward the rifle strapped across his back. "If the buggers attack me, they'll be hearing lots of noise from my metal friend here."

I smiled but didn't say anything. Truth be told, if the bipeds attacked in any sort of force, five pulse rifles weren't going to make a whole lot of difference.

We left the tunnel and crossed the bridge into the Wild Lands. As we entered the deeper darkness of the forest, I said, "We'll keep to a tight V-formation tonight, with me in the lead. I want everyone within eyesight of each other."

Nash frowned. "If the Skaran attack, you'll be taking the brunt—"

"No, because the earth will inform me of their approach long before any of us can smell them."

He raised his eyebrows but didn't question me further. With him and Sage to my left and right, and the two soldiers behind them, we moved out. The night was silent and empty, and the hours went by slowly. Despite this, the sensation that something was off-kilter grew. It wasn't originating from the Wild Lands, but rather the Skaran.

I stopped at the Quaih River and scrambled up a large rock, hoping to get a better view of the distant settlement. The place was dark and silent, both of which struck me as odd given how much activity had been evident last night.

"Is there a problem?" Nash asked, as he and Sage stopped at the base of the rock.

"Maybe."

I scrambled back down and then knelt and pressed my fingers into the soil. *What happens in the settlement on the other side of the river?*

Deadness, came the reply.

I frowned. *Meaning they're all dead? The whole settlement?*

Surely that wasn't possible—aside from the fact the bipeds were nocturnal, the Skaran settlement was huge.

We cannot say if they live or not, because the deadness

that was present in the dead lands surrounds the whole settlement.

Alarm stirred. *The bipeds have tunneled that far already?*

No, their tunnel approaches at speed, but they have not reached the river yet.

And the bipeds themselves? Where does the bulk of their weight lay?

They do not press against us, so they are either in the dead earth surrounding their tunnel or in that settlement.

I swore and thrust up. Nash opened his mouth and then shut it again when I raised my hand. I tapped the halo and said, "Base, this is Caracal One."

"Go ahead, Caracal One."

"We've reached the Quaih River. The Skaran settlement is dark—I think we need to investigate."

"Negative, Caracal One." It was the captain's voice. "The Skaran have employed similar lure tactics in the past to capture patrols."

"This isn't a tactic, Cap—not when it involves the whole settlement. There's something wrong out there, but the earth can't tell me what it is."

"Then we'll investigate in the morning, when light is on our side. Move on, Caracal One. That's an order."

The morning would be too damn late—the certainty of that echoed through every fiber of my being. Whatever was happening, whatever the bipeds were doing over there, we needed to see it.

Or pay the price in lives for our ignorance.

"Fine. Caracal One out." I hit the switch and met Nash's gaze. "You're on point from now on. I'm going to investigate."

He frowned. "But Marx said—"

"I know precisely what he said, which is why you and the team are going to obey him."

"But you can't go there alone—"

"It's easier for one person to escape their notice than five," I cut in. "And we all know I'm less likely to gather flack for disobedience."

"Getting any closer to the Skaran home base is nothing short of suicide," Sage muttered. "If she's happy to go alone and get herself killed, I'm all for it."

"Sorry to disappoint, but I have no intention of getting dead." I returned my gaze to Nash. "Control will undoubtedly realize what's happened sooner rather than later, so inform them you're obeying my orders and that I've said under no circumstances are you or anyone else to come after me. I'll report once I hit the settlement. And remind them I'm better able to protect one than five."

Nash hesitated, clearly unhappy about the situation. But he didn't argue; he simply glanced at the rest of the team. "Let's go, people. Standard close formation for the rest of the night."

I pulled the halo out of my ear and tucked it into a pocket, then spun around and followed the river, keeping to the shadows as much as practical. The Skaran encampment was at least a couple of hours of walking away, but despite the urgency beating through my veins, I wasn't about to hurry. The settlement may be silent, but that didn't mean there weren't Skaran hunting parties out in these woods. The earth would warn me if any approached, but I'd hear that warning a whole lot clearer if I was walking rather than running.

I was an hour into my journey when the halo vibrated lightly. I ignored it. It was undoubtedly the captain with an order to forget my current course of action, and that was something I had no intention of doing. The unit buzzed several more times and then fell silent.

Fingers of yellow and rose were beginning to light the sky by the time I started climbing the longish hill that separated me from the Skaran encampment. The Quaih River had long ago left my side and a mix of trees and long grass currently surrounded me—neither of which provided much cover. Not that I needed it. There was no movement, no sound, and no sign of life. I was alone out here.

As I neared the top of the hill, I dropped down and crawled the rest of the way. The long grass bent around me, almost as if it was determined to give way rather than be crushed underneath me. Or perhaps it was the earth attempting to make my movements easier. The deadness that covered the Skaran settlement and prevented her from feeling what was happening had tendrils reaching up this hill, but for the moment, they weren't strong enough to prevent me from hearing or reaching for her.

I stopped at the top of the hill. The Skaran settlement below was as still and silent as the surrounding land—unlike last night, there were no adults moving about, and certainly no children playing. There was also absolutely no sign of the bipeds, be they armored or mage.

For all intents and purposes, this settlement looked abandoned.

And yet no matter how fast the Skaran were, surely not even *they* could evacuate a settlement this large in the course of a day and a night.

Of course, it was totally possible the captain was right and this *was* some form of trap. But if that were the case, I suspected it wasn't one the Skaran had laid—and that *they* were the intended prey, not those of us who patrolled the Wild Lands.

I reinserted the halo and then said, "Base, this is Caracal One. I've reached the Skaran settlement."

"You are in such deep shit when you return, Princess," an all too familiar voice said. "To say the captain and commander aren't happy is something of a major understatement."

No doubt—and I really *didn't* care. "Donal, what the hell are you doing out of bed? You need to be resting your broken butt—"

"Which was impossible to do after the wind told me what you were up to."

"That still doesn't explain why you're answering comms and not the captain or the comms team."

"Marx is currently off duty and the shift captain has graciously allowed me to stay."

Which was Donal code for he would not be moved no matter what, and the shift captain was wise enough to know it.

"What's happening out there, Nyx?" he added.

I returned my attention to the settlement. "Absolutely nothing."

"Clarify nothing."

"No sign of movement or life. No smoke from the chimneys. Nothing to indicate anyone or anything ever lived there. According to the earth, the strange deadness we encountered over that tunnel now surrounds the Skaran encampment."

"Any sign of bipeds?"

"No." I paused and studied the hill immediately below me. "And no indication that they've buried themselves for the oncoming day. I'm going closer to investigate."

"Be careful."

"That's my middle name."

I slithered down the hill. Halfway down, the long grass stopped moving to one side, which meant I was now leaving a trail of crushed vegetation behind me. I doubted it mattered, because I really didn't think there was anyone within the settlement to notice or care.

As I drew nearer, the earth's pulse died, but it was replaced by the same angry trembling that had been evident as we'd drawn closer to the spark-lit shaft out in the dead lands. Whatever had been happening out there was now happening here.

I reached flat land and paused, sweeping my gaze across the rusting metal wall of swords that divided me from the settlement's interior. They were unscarred—untouched. There was no indication that *any* weapon—not even brute force—had been used on them.

There was no sign of fighting inside the wall, either. There wasn't even any form of disorder—not even random bits of abandoned rubbish—and surely there would have been if the Skaran had left in any sort of hurry.

I studied the ground between that metal fence and me but couldn't see anything untoward, no matter what instinct might be suggesting. I pushed up and ran forward, still keeping as low as possible despite the fact there appeared to be no one and nothing around.

I wasn't far from the sword fence when the knife flared to life; a heartbeat later, I ran straight into something solid. I bounced back and hit the ground butt first, hard enough to elicit a grunt of pain.

I sucked in some air and then rose onto my knees, carefully reached out with one hand, and met a wall—another invisible one. I might not be able to see the bipeds, but they'd certainly been here. I pressed the halo again. "Base, this is Caracal One. I just hit an invisible wall."

"The same sort that we discovered at the volcano?" Donal asked.

"Yes. I haven't explored the full extent of it, but I'm guessing it completely surrounds the settlement." I paused. "I'm going in."

"Nyx, that might not be—"

"We need to find out what the hell is happening," I cut in. "If you can figure out an easier and safer way to do that, please let me know."

He made a low noise that very much sounded like a growl of frustration. "You know I can't, but I still think—"

"The earth thinks otherwise, Donal. I'm not about to gainsay her. I'll let you know once I'm on the other side of the barrier."

"Be fucking careful—and remember, the earth can't rescue you in the dead zone."

"I'm well aware of that, highlander. Caracal One out."

I drew my knife. The runes instantly came to life, their golden gleam almost rivaling the growing day for brightness. I carefully pressed the delicate point into the barrier; once again the runes pulsed and the red flames came to life, crawling down the length of the blade and onto the surface of the unseen barrier. As it began to melt away, I swept the blade around in an arc to create a doorway. After carefully crawling through, I released the knife and then turned around.

And once again saw the truth.

Only this time it wasn't civilization.

It was destruction.

Bloody, brutal destruction.

NINE

The sword barrier had certainly been breached—and in multiple places. In some areas it had utterly melted, while in others the heavy metal swords had simply been parted or flattened. They might well have been twigs for all the respect the bipeds had shown them.

And in the settlement itself....

I briefly closed my eyes and fought the surge of my stomach. The Skaran certainly *hadn't* evacuated their city; in fact, it was rather apparent that they'd barely even had time to realize they were in danger.

There were bodies everywhere; some were whole, but most were not. Those closest to me not only had the tops of their skulls sliced off but also fist-sized holes in their chests. There was no heart inside that cavity, just as there was no brain inside their skulls. The bipeds had obviously taken them as trophies.

I swallowed heavily. As much as I wanted to do nothing more than turn and run, I needed to see the full extent of this destruction—needed to know whether it involved the entire settlement, or if some here had managed to escape.

Though I doubted it. The pall of death hung too heavily over this place.

I touched the halo again. "I'm inside the barrier. The Skaran settlement has been destroyed."

"What level of destruction are we talking about?" came the captain's voice.

"On first indication, it appears the Skaran have been annihilated. Buildings are untouched."

Marx swore. "And the bipeds?"

"Other than their shield, there's no sign of them. I'm going deeper."

"Negative, Caracal One—"

"Captain, we need to know—"

"I understand that, Nyx, but you're to hold position until Donal gets there."

"But he's injured—"

"And apparently as incapable of obeying orders as you." Marx's voice was grim. "So damn well hold position until he arrives."

"Will do, Cap."

I crawled back through the barrier, pulled my knife free, and then swung my pack around and grabbed some trail rations. It was no substitute for bacon, eggs, and chunky bread, but it at least stopped my stomach from grumbling.

Dawn had given way to full sunshine by the time the wind picked up strength. I glanced up and saw Donal dropping rapidly toward the ground. He landed near the base of the long slope—which was probably as far as the wind could take him given that was pretty much where the earth's pulse faded.

I pressed the halo. "Donal just arrived, Cap."

"Good. Keep the halo open and describe what you see once you get back into that settlement."

226

"Will do."

I rose and watched the highlander walk toward me. His stride was long and strong, and though he was favoring his right leg a little, it obviously wasn't bothering him too much. He had two pulse rifles strapped across his back, additional ammo clipped to his belt, and was holding a third rifle.

"You've come prepared for battle," I commented. "Although I really wish you'd stayed at the garrison and let that wound fully heal."

"You are *not* going into a Skaran settlement alone, Princess. Not when you're without your most dangerous weapon."

I swung around and walked toward the barrier. "They're hardly a threat when they're all dead."

"You can't say that with absolute certainty given you've only seen this perimeter." His voice was grim. "And given the wind's whispers about your importance in the upcoming war, I'm not about to risk everything by letting you fall."

I squinted up at him. "So it has moved from a threat to an all-out war now?"

"Yes." He waved a hand toward the wall we couldn't see. "But let's concentrate on one thing at a time."

I grunted and slashed open the barrier. Once we were both through, I rose and stood beside Donal, sweeping my gaze across the bloody and broken bodies that were absolutely everywhere. Having seen it once already, it shouldn't have affected me as much this time, but it did.

"*Fuck.*" Donal's whisper was filled with the horror that ran through me. "I've seen a lot of destruction over the years of fighting Skaran, but never have I seen anything like this."

"No." I scanned the buildings up ahead. "Do we skirt the perimeter or go straight in?"

He hesitated. "Let's move toward the center. If there's anything alive here, that's where it'll probably be found."

"I'm not sure we actually need to find survivors, especially given they're likely to be a little pissed off."

He glanced at me, eyebrow raised. "Do you honestly think we'll find anyone living here?"

"No, but the point remains."

Donal raised his pulse rifle and moved forward cautiously. I sheathed my knife and pulled my rifle free. If other magic existed here, then the runes would sense it, whether or not the knife was in my hand.

But I couldn't help hoping it *didn't* sense anything.

As we moved deeper into the heart of the settlement, I started describing what we were seeing for the captain. I tried to keep my voice monotone, but it was a task that grew harder and harder. The sheer number of bodies meant it was next to impossible to avoid stepping on their broken, bloody remnants. Some of those remnants held weapons, but most did not. The Skaran really *had* been caught unawares, and that struck me as odd. They were warriors and wouldn't have relied solely on the strength of their sword barrier to protect them. They would have had sentries, at the very least.

The knife began to pulse as we drew close to the center of the settlement and a T-intersection, and the trembling in the earth grew stronger.

Donal glanced at me. "The last time the earth reacted like this, we were approaching that spark-lit shaft. I can't see anything like that here."

"There may not be a shaft, but there's definitely another source of magic here, because the knife is reacting."

His gaze dropped briefly to my hip. "Can you use that reaction to find a location?"

"I don't know." I drew the knife and then turned slowly around. The flicker disappeared when I was facing the way we'd come but came back came to life as I continued around.

"That's handy," Donal said, voice dry. "It's reacting equally to both the left and right paths."

I frowned at the blade and wished there was some way to understand what the runes were trying to tell me. But all I had was the strength of its reaction. "I think whatever it's sensing either has some distance to it or lies underground."

"Neither which is overly helpful right now." He studied either direction for a minute, then shrugged and headed right.

I sheathed the knife again and followed. This section ran around the open area dominating the center of the encampment and was crammed with circular houses. We took the time to check each one, wanting to be sure there was nothing and no one lying in wait. All we found was more death—women and children, mostly. The bipeds had no boundaries when it came to their mutilations and certainly hadn't shown any compassion, not even to babes. And while my sense of horror and anger continued to grow, I couldn't help but wonder how much kinder the forces of Cannamore might have been had an attack been ordered. Especially given that garrison troops collected tusks to sell and considered the Skaran to be more animal than human.

We continued to move around until we'd reached the opposite side of the open area and yet another intersection —this one four-way. I stopped and did the circling thing again—the knife glowed fiercer when pointed to both the right pathway and the one directly ahead.

I put it away again. "Checking up ahead would be the logical option."

"I hear a 'but' in your tone."

"That's because my gut is saying we need to go right first—even though it would make more sense to ensure there's no one left alive here to threaten us or the garrison."

"It's only midmorning," he said, "so there's plenty of time left to check this place later. Let's trust your gut."

We moved past several large globs of rusted metal that would have once been the sword fence line and in very little time reached the barrier again. I pressed the knife's point into it and created a circle large enough to peer through.

"Anything?" Donal asked.

"Nothing but empty grasslands." And huge swaths of crushed grass.

"And yet the knife still pulses."

That it did. Something was definitely out there; we just couldn't see it. "Should we continue?"

He raised an eyebrow. "We both know you have no intention of doing anything else, so why even ask?"

I half smiled. "I'm not the one with the broken butt."

"My butt is just fine, but thanks for the concern." He motioned toward the barrier. "Open her up fully, Princess."

"I want you both back at the Skaran encampment by one," the captain commented. "And on your way back to the garrison by four."

"Sorry, Cap," Donal said. "But until we've found whatever the knife is sensing, we're not going anywhere."

"The last thing we need is you two getting yourselves injured or dead—especially when the pair of you could be the difference between this garrison standing or falling."

"There are plenty of air mages in the Westal Mountains," Donal replied.

"But how many earth mages are there?" Marx retorted.

"I can't actually envision the king or his heir racing here to help us."

"*That* is a fact," I muttered. "But I'm sure Gigurri would send help if asked."

"And let's not forget," Marx continued, either not hearing my comment or simply ignoring it, "that the Skaran appear to share some kind of mental connection. It's very likely the other settlements are aware of this destruction and will come to investigate. You don't want to be anywhere near that settlement if that happens."

"No, we certainly don't," I said. Which *wasn't* a confirmation that either of us would actually obey his order.

I cut another doorway through the barrier and once again followed Donal through. We continued along the wide road of crushed grass as quickly and quietly as we could, but there was no sign of the bipeds. If they'd gone underground to wait out the day, then they weren't doing so anywhere near here.

The sun tracked higher and the day grew warmer. Sweat trickled down my spine and the stink of it stung the air. Winter might be approaching fast, but autumn's warmth hadn't finished with us yet. Donal's limp had become noticeable, but he refused to stop or rest. When it came to stubborn determination, he'd obviously stood in line twice.

Still....

"Are you able to hear the wind's voice yet?" I wasn't able to hear the earth, but that wasn't entirely unexpected.

He glanced at me. "Yes—why?"

"Then ask her to carry you along—it might help prevent the wound getting any worse."

"I'd much rather save my strength for an emergency dash out of here." Amusement lurked around the corners of his eyes. "You seem awfully concerned about the state of my butt."

"Well, it *is* a fine one, as far as these things go."

The captain cleared his throat. "You are on an open line, remember."

"Yes, but I'm positive the highlander won't in the least mind if everyone in comms knows how fine his posterior is."

"Indeed," Donal said, his amusement growing. "Although they should also know my magnificent butt—and everything that goes with it—will be unavailable for the foreseeable future."

I raised my eyebrows. "Has the wound affected your sexual prowess?"

"Nothing short of death would affect *that*—we highlanders have a hearty reputation for good reason. No," he added, rather loftily, "I have simply decided to save myself for the right woman."

Laughter echoed down the halo's line. Apparently I wasn't the only one who found that funny.

"Concentrate, people," Marx said, his voice loud enough to suggest it was directed not only at us but at those around him. "If you *must* discuss Donal's attributes, Nyx, please do so in your own time."

We continued in silence and the miles slipped by uneventfully, until it was way past time we should have turned back. But the earth's heartbeat was now pulsing through my shoes and the knife's golden glow was becoming stronger. We were finally close to the magic it was sensing.

What was interesting, however, was the fact that it had been able to detect it from such a distance when it had needed closer proximity up on the volcano. What had changed? The strength of the magic? Or was it perhaps a simple matter of the knife becoming more attuned to our world—and to me?

I really wished I knew.

Wish I could ask my mother. I blinked. She was part of the earth's voice now, so while I might not be able to talk to her directly, her knowledge should be available to the greater consciousness.

But it was a question I could ask later. Right now, I needed to concentrate on what the knife was sensing rather than why. I knelt and pressed my fingers into the warm earth. Her response was swift.

The bipeds lie in front of you.

I scanned the empty horizon with a frown. *Are they underground?*

If they were, why was there no sign of it? Given the numbers that must have attacked the Skaran settlement, surely there should have at least been some evidence of digging somewhere. Unless, of course, they were using magic to hide their presence.

There is another shield ahead, which is why you cannot see them.

Meaning you don't know what lies behind it?

They do not draw on the earth's energy to power this shield. Their weight is vast—there are hundreds, at least.

Hundreds, not thousands.

Hundreds to defeat a settlement that had to be at least triple that number.

If we couldn't figure out a means of countering the magic of these bastards, we might end up as dead as the damn Skaran.

Do they sleep?

They do not move. Some have burrowed.

Can you kill them?

Yes, but to kill so many at once could be fatal. Taking life also drains life, and the knife you hold is not designed to counter that force being entirely taken from you.

Which was why I'd felt so weak the few times I'd used it as a buffer. *Is the King's Sword capable of such a feat?*

We believe so.

Which was no doubt why the wind's whisperings were filled with dire warnings about the king bringing doom upon us all. He held the sword, but it was now useless in his hands.

I repeated what the earth had said about the bipeds to Donal and Marx, who immediately said, "Which means you have the information you were after and can now return."

"Negative, Captain." I pushed up and moved on. "These barriers are obviously portable, which means we need to confirm *how* they're created if we're to have any hope of destroying them."

Marx didn't reply. Either he agreed or he simply knew the futility. Ten minutes later we reached the barrier. I sliced open a small section and peered through.

To be met by shadows.

The barrier that couldn't be seen by the eye blocked the sunlight—everything aside from the light streaming through the gap I'd created, that is. Thankfully, there weren't any bipeds sleeping close to where we were standing.

In what I presumed was the middle of the thing was a raised platform. On this was an old stone table on which a body lay—a body that had been pierced by a metal staff topped with a black stone. Three bipeds with yellow-green head plates sat in a triangle formation around the body, but whether they were awake and monitoring it I couldn't say. They were simply too far away.

But this was exactly what we'd seen up in the volcano, so why had the earth lost its life both there and along that strip of land that was the tunnel, and *not* here?

As my eyes adjusted further to the darkness, I saw the rest of the bipeds. Or, rather, saw the mounds of earth that covered them. Beside each mound lay either a long sword-like weapon or the hollow tubes.

"What can you see, Princess?"

I stepped aside rather than answering. He peered through the gap for several seconds and then glanced at me. His expression was grim.

"If we take out the mages and destroy that staff," he said, "the sunlight might just take care of the bipeds."

"There's one major flaw in that theory, and that's the hundreds of bipeds that lie between us and that damn staff." All it would take was one wrong move—one wrong sound—and the entire encampment would awaken. "It *is* a shame the garrison has no vehicle access through the Wild Lands. Handguns might have no impact on the barrier, but tank cannons might be a different matter."

"Except tanks are made of metal, and the Skaran's boundary fence proved just how susceptible metal is to the bipeds' weapons."

"I'm betting the tanks have a longer range than the biped's tubes. A few well-placed shots might make all the difference."

"Given they were firing at us from the other side of the volcano, I wouldn't be entirely sure of that."

I grunted and withdrew the knife. "I really don't think we should or could do anything more here."

"Then we at least need to check out the other bit of magic the knife was sensing."

"With that, I agree—although I'm not entirely sure confirming they're capable of multiple types of magic is going to help our situation."

And no matter how powerful the runes on either my knife or even the King's Sword were, how could two weapons counter the might of multiple mages?

We needed answers—and we needed them fast.

Whether we'd have the time to find them was another matter entirely.

"Better to know than not," Donal commented, falling into step beside me. "And we've got to go through the encampment anyway to get back to the garrison."

It took us longer to go back, and not just because of Donal's wound but also because of my lack of fitness. The level of conditioning I'd acquired fighting against my brother in the yards was a very different level of fitness to this. The yards were short, sharp bursts of energy, with nothing more than your sword and knife. *This* needed both stamina and strength, especially with full battle gear on and the fact I'd now been on the move for something close to twenty hours.

It was nearing four by the time we reached the encampment, and the stench of death had increased tenfold thanks to the day's heat. I somehow managed to keep my stomach in check and once again used the pulse of the knife's runes to guide us. Though the earth was again mute, she was trembling, and I still had no idea why. We followed the road that ran around the perimeter of the marketplace until we neared the far end of the oblong encampment. As red began to flicker through the gold, I stopped. While there were a number of grander round houses here, there was one building that towered above them all. Not only was it large but also rectangular—a meeting hall, perhaps. I couldn't hear anything moving around, and the stench of rotting meat was so damn strong it was unlikely I'd smell anything else, even if there were an entire battalion of bipeds here somewhere.

"Given there are no windows in that hall, I'm thinking it might be the perfect place to hide." Donal glanced at me. "Shall we check?"

"You know the sane answer to that question would be no, don't you?"

He grinned. "Then it's just as well you and I aren't sane."

I snorted but nevertheless followed him over to the large building. I stopped on the other side of the rusting metal door, then shoved the knife away, drew my rifle, and nodded. Adrenaline pulsed through me, making my heart race and my muscles tremble in readiness.

He gripped the handle and thrust the door open. I half expected it to squeal in protest, but it made no sound. Sunshine poured in through the opening, lighting the interior for several yards before giving way to shadows and then darkness. The scent of death stirred past my nose, but it held none of the viscosity of the rest of the encampment. The only other detectable smell was smoke, although if there was a firepit in this hall it had long gone out.

Donal slipped inside and stopped to the right of the door. I went left and pressed my back against the cool stone. There was no response to our appearance and absolutely no sound.

I swept my gaze across the shadows, studying the long hall's sides, looking for any sign of life. There was nothing here... and yet it didn't feel empty.

I pulled the knife free and it immediately flared to life, sending rays of golden light spearing out from its blade. Dust filled the air, drifting down from the thatched ceiling and coating the backs of the seating benches. There were three wide aisles—one down the middle and two that ran along either wall—and some sort of stone platform at the far end.

There was no evidence of life here, and no evidence of death despite the smell.

I glanced at Donal and raised an eyebrow. He motioned me to the left edge and then pointed toward the platform. I nodded and moved out, keeping as close to the wall as practical, the rifle gripped in my left hand and the knife in my right. My hold on the blade's hilt was so fierce that my knuckles practically glowed.

The smell of smoke became more pungent the deeper we went into the room. I couldn't see its source, but the closer I got to the platform, the grimier the walls became. I had a strong suspicion the staining wasn't caused just by smoke.

The light pouring from the knife became so intense it was almost painful to look at. But the flickers of red remained faint, and I had no idea whether that meant the magic here wasn't as strong, or if—given the other magic had been based in sacrifice—this one *wasn't*.

The rectangular platform at the end of the hall was made of stone and was several feet taller than even Donal. There were stairs at either end and, after a brief hesitation, I carefully climbed the nearest ones. It wasn't a platform but rather a two-foot wide wall that surrounded a massive firepit. Thankfully, the pit was empty aside from a thin layer of ash, coal, and what looked to be bones.

Human bones.

I shuddered and studied the length of the hall with more than a little confusion. There might be evidence of human sacrifice here, but it wasn't the source of death I could smell. And yet, this place was absolutely empty. So what was knife reacting to?

I turned and looked at the rear wall. The thick muck coating the stones seemed to absorb rather than reflect the knife's golden light, which made it hard to pick out inconsistencies. Even so, there didn't appear to be a secondary exit from the building.

I frowned and joined Donal on the other side of the pit. "Anything?"

He shook his head. "Perhaps the knife is simply reacting to the barrier's presence."

"Maybe."

He glanced at me. "But you don't think so?"

"No. The death scent hangs in this room, even if it's not as strong as outside. Yet there is no sign of bodies anywhere."

"That's not surprising given how pervasive the goddamn smell is."

"I know, it's just—"

I stopped as I caught sight of an odd protrusion on the left edge of the otherwise smooth sides of the pit. I knelt and held the knife out to illuminate the entire pit. It was a door handle—and a rather ancient looking one at that.

"Well, I'll be damned," Donal murmured, and jumped down.

"We just might be if we tempt fate and enter wherever that door leads," I said, even as I joined him.

"As long as your knife keeps pretending it's a mini sun, we should be all right. You want to open it?"

"What door are we talking about?" came Marx's comment.

"One that rather oddly sits in the side of what looks to be a ceremonial firepit, and which I suspect is an entrance into an underground passageway or crypt," Donal said. "Which begs the question, how did the bipeds know about it?"

"If they're capable of restricting the earth, it's possible they can sense where she *doesn't* exist," I said. "But we don't know that the bipeds *do* know about it."

He glanced at me. "Whatever you knife is reacting to isn't this room. It's pretty reasonable to presume that something lies beyond this door."

"Whatever might be going on," Marx commented, "once you head into that tunnel we'll be briefly out of contact. Notify me once you hit the surface again."

"Will do, Cap." I moved past Donal, gripped the handle, and then looked back. "Ready?"

He nodded and raised his pulse rifle, his finger resting lightly on the trigger. I took a deep breath and then pushed the door open.

Nothing jumped out at us. Nothing moved.

I released my breath, but tension still rode me. Before us lay a wide, high tunnel that had been hewn out of the earth and shored up with thick slabs of metal. The air running past my nose was heavily scented with death, though it was nowhere near as bad as the stench outside—not surprising given this tunnel appeared to run deep.

"You and the mini sun go first," Donal said. "I'll follow close on your heels. If anything moves into the light, drop so I can shoot it."

"Just remember my threat to haunt you and don't get too trigger happy before I can duck."

"If you can be sure of anything, Princess, it's the fact I'd rather have you alive than dead."

I stepped into the tunnel and held the knife in front of me, letting its light burn away the shadows. It would give away our presence if there was anything alive at the base of this tunnel, but it would also give *us* time to either react or flee, given that both the bipeds and the Skaran appeared to have an aversion to light.

The tunnel sloped down sharply. The deeper we got, the hotter it grew and the stronger the tremors became.

And while the voice of the earth remained mute, I slowly became certain of one thing. Those tremors were an expression of anger at what was happening up ahead.

At what she was being *forced* to do.

And that left me with a horrible possibility—that the bipeds were capable of not only *restricting* the earth with their magic but also *using* her. If that were true, then we were in even more trouble than I'd initially presumed.

The urge to simply run from the death and destruction that was marching inexorably toward the Red City and Cannamore was so damn fierce that I actually paused. Donal swore softly, did a quick sidestep to avoid running into me, and then raised an eyebrow in question.

"Sorry," I muttered and forced my feet on. I might want —with every bone in my body—to do nothing more than escape this place, but I had a bad, *bad* feeling we needed to see exactly what the bipeds were doing here.

Up ahead, the tunnel gave way to what looked to be a cavern. Red flickered down the blade's length and instinct had me sheathing it. Its light muted, and the shadows closed in ahead.

Shadows, not utter darkness.

There was a light source somewhere in that cavern, but

it wasn't the one fueled by a blood ceremony. This light was a fierce red-gold glow that hummed with power.

Earth power.

Or something very similar to it.

I licked my lips and edged closer to the end of the tunnel. The cavern that opened before us was both deep and natural, made of a black, glass-like rock that glistened and gleamed in the red-gold glow emanating from its base.

That glow was molten earth.

Lava.

It bubbled up from a wide pit in the middle of the cavern. Three mages surrounded it; each held a silver staff that was thrust deep into the black stone and topped by a red stone that was linked by a bloody beam of light to those on either side. Power thrummed through the air, a force so foul it made my skin crawl.

But they weren't *just* creating a pit of lava.

They were raising it, shaping it into a thick, wide ram of liquid hell, and pushing it into a tunnel at the base of the wall opposite us.

A tunnel that was the same shape and width as the ram of molten earth.

"They're using the lava to create a fucking tunnel," Donal whispered. The air stirred around us as he spoke, taking the words back up the tunnel rather than toward those below.

"I'm guessing it runs toward that attack party we discovered."

"It seems a whole lot of trouble to go to when this settlement is already theirs," Donal said. "And it didn't take a damn tunnel to achieve it."

I pressed my fingers against the nearby wall. The earth couldn't answer me, but that had never stopped me sensing her emotions. What I felt now wasn't anger; it was muted, agonized, suffering.

She was *dying*.

In using their lances to melt the earth and create the lava ram, they were completely and utterly draining the earth of her spirit, her power, and her life. This area, like that long strip that ran from the volcano, would never recover.

And there was no way to stop them. Not here. Not now.

I clenched my fist against the urge to try anyway, and said, "Maybe the attack party isn't their goal. Maybe their aim is to connect with the wider tunnel we discovered in the Dead Lands."

"Then the deep shit the wind has been whispering about for the last couple of months really *will* hit." His voice was grim. "Is there any way you can stop them?"

"No. In creating the lava, they drain the earth of her voice and power. The longer they draw on her, the wider and deeper the death."

He frowned. "If they're capable of commanding the earth, why go to this extreme to create a tunnel? Why not just order it done, in the same way as you can create an earth shelter?"

I hesitated. "It's a guess, but I think they're drawing on the heat *within* the earth rather than her energy, as earth mages do. In doing so, they drain the earth of any ability to sustain life far quicker than drawing on her power ever would."

"Which is why I could hear the wind's whispers in much of the dead lands and you couldn't hear the earth."

I nodded. It was also the reason why the air from the chimneys had been so heated, and why the earth trembled so fiercely. She was expressing her anger at being so used in the only way she knew how.

"Why now, though?" Donal asked. "They've obviously been in that volcano for eons—why have they suddenly become so hell-bent on destruction?"

"Maybe it's got something to do with the actual tremors that started a couple of months ago. Maybe they were as dormant as their volcano until then."

I shifted and looked away from the lava pit—and in that moment not only caught movement but also the source of the death scent. Over fifty armored bipeds were devouring the remains of the Skaran—remains that were not warrior class, but rather men without tusks, as well as women and children. Which suggested this cavern wasn't a crypt but rather a shelter. They'd probably come down here seeking safety but had instead succeeded in doing nothing more than trap themselves.

I hoped their deaths had been swift, but I very much suspected that had not been the case. Not given there was some who still moved, even as they were being consumed.

Despite the heat of this place, a deep coldness began to creep through me. I rubbed my arms and stepped back from the ledge. "We'd better get—"

I stopped abruptly and snapped my head around, staring into the darkness of the tunnel behind us. Nothing but silence met my gaze, and yet I had the feeling that we were no longer alone in this place.

After a second, I heard it again. The soft brush of metal against stone—a sound that wasn't caused by the earth's tremors further up the tunnel.

I glanced at Donal, raised one finger, and then pointed into the tunnel. He immediately raised his rifle and then stepped forward, lightly pressing his cheek again mine to whisper, "Your senses are sharper, so you lead and I'll follow. The minute we're close enough, blind them with the light and get out of the way."

I nodded, my heart racing so hard it was practically tearing out of my chest. It could only be either a Skaran or a biped, and neither was something I particularly wanted to meet in the confines of the tunnel.

I wrapped my fingers around the hilt of the knife, oddly comforted by its fierce pulsing as we moved back into the tunnel's darkness. Silence wrapped around us and though there was no immediate repeat of that metallic sound, the air ran with a scent that sat uneasily between rotten meat and bitter acidity. I'd smelled the latter once before—when we'd killed the armored bipeds in the ruined city. Which meant the biped that approached was wounded—but where the hell had it come from? There were no arteries off this tunnel, and there'd been no indication of any sort of burrowing in the meeting hall. But that only left the possibility it had come from outside and meant that, no matter what we'd thought, the daylight wasn't deadly to them.

The smell grew so strong that even Donal couldn't have missed it. My fingers tightened on the knife's hilt. It was very close now.

A stone scuttled toward us, bouncing lightly off the wall. The noise was like a rifle shot in the tense silence.

That was close enough.

I dragged my knife free, raised it high, and stepped aside. As the golden light banished the darkness, the biped hissed and raised a hand, instinctively protecting his eyes. Donal released three quick shots and the biped's chest exploded.

A scream rose from the cavern behind us and was soon joined by others.

Donal grabbed my hand and hauled me forward so damn fast that for the first couple of steps he was all but dragging me. Once I'd caught my balance, I ripped my hand free from his and raced past him. He might have longer legs, but I was fueled by fear. We ran up the long incline and out into the pit. Donal boosted me and then tossed me his gun and jumped, catching the edge with his fingertips and dragging himself up. I put the knife away, handed back his rifle, and drew mine.

Movement, to our left.

I swung around and fired.

The biped screamed as the blast tore a hole through his hip, but he kept on coming. I fired again, and again, until he went down in a spray of blood and bone.

More screams echoed across the silence and the ground began to move. This time it wasn't the earth or her anger, but rather buried bipeds coming out of hiding. We might not have seen them, but the bastards were certainly here.

"Run!" I leapt off the edge of the pit and raced for the door.

Several shots boomed out and then Donal was beside me. We ran up the center aisle and out into the sunshine but didn't stop, heading directly across the empty meeting area.

Screams had my head snapping around. The bipeds were following us. They might not like the sunshine but, as I'd feared, they weren't hampered by it.

Donal nudged my shoulder, gently pushing me to the left. I frowned up at him.

"A test," he murmured.

The bipeds didn't immediately follow our change of direction but instead kept running directly ahead. Then the one nearest us raised his nose, drew in a deep breath, and barked an order. As one, they changed direction and came after us again.

They were using scent, not sight.

Then the knife pulsed to life. I pulled it free and the blade immediately gathered brightness.

Donal all but groaned. "Not again."

"I'll get you through the barrier, then I'll chase this—"

"Not on your goddamn life," he cut in brusquely. "Go."

I spun and ran right, chasing the magic that the knife was sensing. It looped us back toward the old hall but didn't lead us inside—I wouldn't have followed it if it *had*—but rather behind. Sitting within a ring of black stone between the old hall and the barrier, and partially buried in the soil, was a silver staff topped by a clear stone. Though it didn't appear to be emitting any sort of energy, it was certainly present—the force of it was so strong it felt like gnats were nipping at my skin.

I slid to a halt and glanced behind us. Our pursuers hadn't yet caught the most recent change of direction and currently weren't in sight.

"You keep watch. I'll see what I can do with this thing."

"Are you sure this is necessary?"

"As necessary as anything else we've done today."

He grunted and shoved a fresh clip into his rifle. "Try not to be too long. We've five minutes, if that."

I didn't waste time answering. But the minute I stepped closer to the ring of black stones, the ground within it began to stir. Once again it wasn't the earth—it was a biped.

As one of the mages with the yellow-green head plates began to emerge, I quickly raised my rifle and fired. The stones flared to life and the pulse speared off sideways, hammering into a nearby roundhouse and exploding something within.

"They're coming," Donal warned. "So whatever you need to do, do it fast."

The only thing I could think of doing was using the knife. I shouldered the rifle, then gripped the knife with both hands and thrust it as hard as I could into the heart of the nearest black stone.

For a heartbeat, nothing happened. The biped continued to emerge from the ground, but its movements were slow and there appeared to be some sort of film over its eyes. It was looking around in what appeared to be confusion and its gaze slid past me without any immediate alarm.

But just because it couldn't see me didn't mean it soon wouldn't.

The knife began to pulse against my palms and its light grew until it became so fierce I couldn't look at it. A heartbeat later, the entire black stone circle exploded, sending me sprawling as sharp shards of rock sliced through the air and into my skin.

I swore as what seemed a million pinpricks of pain erupted across my body, but it was a sound lost to the boom of Donal's pulse rifle.

Our time was up.

I scrambled to my feet and then lunged at the biped as it reached for its staff. The knife trailed golden fire as I slashed down at the biped's hand; the blade met armored flesh and sliced through it as easily as water. As blood spurted from cut veins and the biped screamed in fury and pain, I twisted around and thrust the blazing knife into his chest.

The creature exploded into flame. Between one heartbeat and the next, it became little more than cinders.

"Nyx, we need to go."

"Coming."

"Now."

"On my way."

I twisted around and, more out of instinct rather than anything else, shoved the knife into the middle of the staff. The blade treated the metal as contemptuously as it had the biped's flesh, and energy crawled across the staff's surface. The crystal cracked and the prickly sense of power died. I wrenched the staff out of the ground, pulled the knife free, and then ran toward Donal.

"Go," he said and fired several more shots at the oncoming bipeds before he spun and followed.

We raced over the globs of metal fencing and continued on unhindered. The invisible barrier had obviously fallen when I'd cracked the crystal.

Was that the key to their magic? Or rather, the key to *breaking* their magic?

The wind began to stir, quickly picking up speed and power, surrounding us in a whirlpool of dust. Donal grabbed my hand and hauled me close; I grunted as we collided and would have fallen if he hadn't caught me, steadied me. A heartbeat later, we were picked up and flung skyward.

Safe.

We were finally safe.

Relief hit and left me shaking. I closed my eyes and leaned my forehead against his chest as I sucked in air and tried to control the ridiculous urge to cry. I hadn't given in to such an emotion in twelve years; I wasn't about to do so now, even if the inner me—the me that had, by necessity, been so thoroughly caged since my mother had died—felt oddly safe in the presence of this man.

It didn't take very long to reach the garrison. The wind placed us gently on the wall, but Donal didn't immediately release me. Instead, he stepped back and scanned me.

Whatever he saw didn't please him, if the darkening of his expression was anything to go by.

Before he could say anything, the halo came to life, and Marx said, "I want you both in the briefing room ASAP for a full breakdown of events."

"I'm sorry, Captain, but the princess is dead on her feet. She's been on the go for close to twenty-four hours—she needs to rest before she does anything else."

I opened my mouth to protest but was silenced by a stern glance. Truth be told, it was taking all my effort to remain upright. I really did want to do nothing more than to grab a hot shower and then climb into bed for several days.

"Fine," Marx growled. "Donal, you report. Nyx, go rest and we'll talk in the morn."

"And the night patrols?"

"Have been pulled. We're not risking them now that the bipeds have overrun the Skaran—we'll use the blue hawks to keep an eye on them instead."

If the blue hawks were capable of successfully monitoring the Wild Lands, I suspected they would have been used well before now. But I kept my mouth shut and simply said, "Thanks, Cap."

He grunted. "The Red Queen is on her way. Don't be long, Donal."

I plucked the halo out of my ear and then handed Donal the mage staff. "They'll want to see this, but don't let them take it apart. I think I've rendered its magic inert, but I'd nevertheless better be the one to fully examine it."

He nodded. "Do you need any help getting back to the bunk room?"

I half smiled. "I might be physically and mentally exhausted, but I'm not an invalid."

"I wasn't suggesting—"

"I know." I touched his arm lightly. "And I appreciate the offer. But I've never had—"

"Anyone to lean on or trust for the last twelve years, and find it difficult to do so now. Believe me, I know."

I didn't say anything. I couldn't, in all honesty, because what was there to say to someone who so effortlessly saw through all the barriers I'd raised? Someone who understood me so completely?

It was scary, this connection between us. Scary, and yet oddly exhilarating.

And I wasn't sure if I could—or should—do anything about it.

I pulled my hand away and stepped back. Something flickered across his face—an emotion too fast to define—and then he smiled. "I'll see you tomorrow sometime."

"Yes." I hesitated and then walked away, aware of his gaze following me; it was a heat that pressed into my spine long after I'd actually moved beyond his line of sight.

I slipped the pack from my aching shoulders and held it by the straps as I clattered down the steps and walked across the yard to ammunitions and supplies. It didn't take very long to sign everything in, but it nevertheless seemed to drain the last remnants of my strength.

Perhaps that's why it took me so long to hear the earth's urgent warning.

When I finally did, I paused and looked around. There were people everywhere, all of them going about their business without paying any particular attention to me.

So why was the earth so convinced I was in danger? What could she see that I couldn't? There was only one way to find out, and that was to ask.

I clattered up the rest of the steps, walked across to the nearest building, and pressed my fingers against the stone.

But before I could do anything more, the metal walkway abruptly shifted, throwing me sideways. Something hit my shoulder with enough force to spin me around and my head smacked into the wall. Blackness hit, and swept me away.

TEN

I woke to a gentle, rhythmic beating. It took me a few minutes to realize it was a sound that matched my heartbeat, which meant I had to be in the hospital.

I did a mental check of body parts, and then gently wiggled toes and fingers. Nothing was missing; everything responded as it should—although there was a niggling ache in my right shoulder and I couldn't move it with any sort of ease given it appeared to be tightly wrapped.

But why?

Even as that question rose, memory hit. I gasped and pushed up—or at least tried to. A hand pressed lightly against my left shoulder and stopped me. My eyes flew open.

"It's okay." Donal's expression was a mix of concern and anger. The latter, I sensed, wasn't aimed at me but rather the situation. "You're safe."

"You're here, so of course I am." I couldn't help the note of irritation in my voice. "But why are we in the hospital?"

"Because you were shot."

"I was?"

His eyebrows rose. "You can't remember it?"

I hesitated. "I remember the earth's warning and the walkway buckling, and then something hit me. After that, everything is decidedly fuzzy."

"The earth saved your life," he said. "By intervening as it did and throwing you off balance, the shot that should have blown your brains apart hit your shoulder instead."

Which certainly explained the tight bandaging across my right shoulder. "Do you know who the shooter was?"

"No. There were no witnesses, and by the time anyone realized what had happened, they'd slipped away."

"And Dravan? Was he still locked away?"

"He was sent back to Divona several days ago. It wasn't him."

Suggesting that either Dravan *hadn't* lied when he'd said my brother wasn't responsible for his attack on me or that my brother *had* set his hunting bow twice, and I'd yet to meet Vin's other agent.

Not the sort of news you wanted to wake up to.

"How long have I been out?"

"Only a day. You were kept unconscious while the medics and healers patched your shoulder. It was pretty much a shattered mess."

If it had taken both surgery and healing magic to fix it, then I really *was* lucky to have retained use of it.

"Were any weapons unaccounted for?"

"No, and the bullet they dug out wasn't standard issue. The shooter must have brought the weapon in with them." He grimaced. "The captain has ordered a full search done, but I don't think they'll turn up anything. The shooter is too canny to be caught out so easily."

"Which means I'm a walking target for as long as they are free."

"Yes, which is why Marttia has sent you this." He reached behind him, picked up a small, plainly wrapped parcel, and handed it to me.

I accepted it with a frown. There was little weight in it, which was puzzling if whatever lay inside was meant to protect me. "What is it?"

"I don't really know. She handed it to me in secret, said I wasn't to tell anyone else about it, and that such garments have protected her in the past."

I raised a somewhat skeptical eyebrow but nevertheless tore open the package. Inside was a gossamer shirt of silvery gray. I held it up; against the light, the needle fine threads of metal gleamed. This gorgeous undershirt was apparently a form of bulletproof vest—although how the Mauvaissians had managed to make it so sheer while still retaining its protective properties, I had no idea.

"Even if something like this can stop a bullet in its tracks, it not going to protect me from another head shot."

"If your attacker has any sort of sense, they'll try something up close and personal next time—like a knife."

"Isn't that something to look forward to," I muttered. "I'm surprised Marttia didn't deliver this herself, though. She's the type to use such a situation to her advantage."

Donal raised an eyebrow. "I get the feeling that despite this tendency, you do not hold her in the same low esteem as all the others."

I smiled, though it felt tight. "If you're asking if I like her, then yes, I do. She and I could have been a good pairing had circumstances been different. But they aren't, and I'll never forgive her actions. I'll never forgive *any* of them."

"Which will make your task of ruling them all the more difficult."

"I'm well aware of that fact." I placed the shirt and packaging to one side. "What's happening with the bipeds?"

"No sign or movement from them. The wind is monitoring the entire area but cannot see any obvious sign of advancement."

"She wouldn't if they're going underground."

"Which is why it's so vital we keep you safe *and* alive. You're the only one here who can detect the deadness that comes with the tunnel."

Which was undoubtedly why Marttia had been so secretive about giving me the gossamer body armor—the easiest way to draw out an assassin was to make them think their target was without any obvious form of protection. But I also couldn't help thinking that, at least in part, she'd wanted the garrison kept unaware that her people were capable of creating such a delicate but vital piece of protective armor.

I carefully shifted into a sitting position and for the first time noticed I was in a private ward with guards on the door. They really *were* serious about protecting me, which was pretty funny considering how desperately the king and my brother wanted me dead.

"Aside from certified hospital staff, only myself, the captain, the commander, and of course Marttia have permission to enter this room," Donal said, obviously seeing my surprised amusement. "Anyone else will be shot first and questioned second."

I snorted. "That's a bit extreme, isn't it?"

"No. You lost so much blood that it was a close call as to whether you'd live or not." He reached out and wrapped his hand around mine. "Thankfully, you're a stubborn wench who refuses to let even death get the better of her."

"As I keep saying, I'm not going anywhere until I get my goddamn revenge."

"I don't care what keeps you alive, just as long as you are."

He squeezed my hand and then released me. I found myself mourning the loss of his touch—another first for me. "How long am I going to be stuck in here?"

"The healer will be back later tonight—he has a couple more muscles to work on. All being well, they'll release you for light duties in the morning."

I raised my eyebrows. "Light duties? Are they not aware of the trouble headed our way?"

"Yes, but it just means you'll be restricted in what you can carry."

"Well, I can't say I'm sad about not having to haul a backpack around. I'm sure that thing was loaded with goddamn rocks."

He grinned. "Fully loaded packs are something of a test for all garrison newbies, I've learned. A means of sorting out the wheat from the chaff."

"Most of the relief crew are criminals, for gods' sake. There's nothing *but* chaff."

"Which is why they're tested. Better to know up front who is going to get on with the task, and who is likely to cause problems."

"Which doesn't explain why *we* were tested."

His smile grew. "I was sent here as a criminal remember, and you were thought to be nothing more than my floozy."

I raised my eyebrows, a smile lurking about my lips. "Floozy?"

"A rather quaint local term for a man or woman of loose morals."

"So a trull."

"No, because a floozy doesn't accept coin in exchange for his or her services, and are generally—but not always—married."

"Then either they aren't very good business people or they merely follow the decree of the goddess and therefore do not deserve the term."

"You skipped over the whole 'married' part of the explanation."

"Meaning the Westal mountain men do not approve of such extracurricular activities once the bonds of marriage have been made?"

"The Westal mountain women do not approve of it, either, and husbands who stray are most likely to find a knife aimed at their nether regions."

"If straying is such a rarity, why is there even a term for it?"

"Because it's not so rare amongst those who come from the Arkon region. They have a far more liberal view of matrimonial bonds."

"And you?" I kept my voice light even if it was something I was suddenly desperate to know.

His expression gained an odd sort of intensity. "The woman I intend to marry should have fully explored the extent of her desires and needs before she commits to me. Once I give my heart, it will not stray, and I expect the same in return."

"Which is as it should be," I said softly.

His smile was quick and bright. "I'm glad we agree on something as vital as the marriage bond. It is, after all, the foundation on which many great things have been built."

My eyebrows rose again. "Like what?"

He waved a hand airily. "Dynasties and the like."

I snorted. "You're talking to someone who comes from a long line of arranged marriages, and a dynasty that has declined in might over the years."

"Which is a sad statement about arranged marriages more than anything else."

I guessed it was. I glanced around at the sound of footsteps. A woman carrying a tray loaded with covered plates approached; she was quickly scanned in and gave me a nod of greeting as she approached. She placed the tray on the nearby table and then wheeled it across to my bed. With another nod, she spun around and left.

I glanced at Donal. "They're a rather serious and noncommunicative lot here, aren't they?"

Donal cleared his throat. "*That* could have something to do with my presence."

"Why? What did you do to her?"

"Not her but rather the entire hospital staff. I threatened to rain weather hell down on everyone who worked in this place if they let you slip away. I think I scared them."

"That's hardly fair given—"

"I know, but fear does sometimes make one act out of character. I apologized, but I think the damage is done."

The wind's message of oncoming doom had to be pretty intense if Donal had done something like *that*. I might not have known him long, but I was damn sure such a reaction was well out of character.

"Has Marttia had any success contacting my aunt?"

He nodded. "A search of the old records is underway. If anything is found, they'll contact us via a communicator."

"I hope to gods she impressed the urgency of the matter on them." I pulled off the lids from the various trays, revealing a mix of meats, cheeses, breads, and vegetables. There was enough food here to feed my entire squad. "Did she say anything about our request for additional earth mages?"

"No, but that doesn't mean anything. The Gigurrian court is a little more scattered than most, and it takes time for them to gather."

"We haven't got time, Donal."

"I know. And unless the earth's voice has suddenly become mute within the Gigurrian borders, then I daresay they're also aware."

"If they are, why aren't they already here?" Frustration and anger edged my voice.

"Perhaps for the same reason there are no additional air mages here as yet—the distance."

A reasonable enough answer but one that didn't ease the frustration. Gigurrian mages might be thin on the ground these days, but the last I'd heard there were at least a dozen earth-sanctified mages aside from my aunt and uncle. A dozen mages could be the difference between Rodestat surviving or not.

"Marttia's people are also going through their archives, but much of their early history was lost in a volcanic eruption and the subsequent aftershocks that all but destroyed the city eons ago."

"Surely if they had any knowledge of the bipeds, it would have at least been spoken about. They're not something easily forgotten."

"You say that, and yet haven't the history and capabilities of the King's Sword been forgotten?"

I grimaced. "To be fair, it's possible that the knowledge simply hasn't been shared with me. I wasn't supposed to draw the sword, remember."

"Considering how vital the sword is to our safety, even *that* is inexcusable, if for no other reason than the fact that knowledge shared is knowledge not lost."

"You're still putting a whole lot of faith in the capabilities of one sword."

"The wind is, not me."

"So why doesn't she know more about the sword?"

"That I can't say." He motioned with his chin to the trays. "Eat. You need to replenish your strength."

I ignored him. "Has Marttia contacted the king? Divona needs to be aware—"

"There have been communications. I get the impression they didn't go well."

I snorted. "In other words, the king doesn't believe this problem to be Divona's. We need to get there—"

"Until we know more about the bipeds and their intentions—"

"I think their intentions are already pretty clear."

"We cannot risk returning to Divona as yet," he continued, ignoring me. "Right now, we have nothing more than the whispers of the wind and the destruction of one Skaran settlement. Cannamore's court will need more than that to back the removal of a king."

"Cannamore's court is unlikely to *ever* back me against the king, no matter how much evidence we gather." And the more time we wasted here, the greater the danger.

And yet, Donal was right. To have any hope against the bipeds, we needed to know more about them—where they came from, what they wanted, and, most importantly of all, what they were truly capable of. Until we had a clear idea of at least the latter, there was no point in making any attempt to reclaim the sword.

Which didn't ease the frustration or the deep need to reclaim what was mine sooner rather than later.

"Your time will come, Princess," Donal said softly. "In the meantime, you need to eat and regain strength."

Because you're going to need it. He didn't say that, but the words nevertheless seemed to hover in the air. I slid a plate toward him. "Only if you share. I have a healthy appetite, but there's no way I'm going to finish all this."

"I'll eat what you can't finish." Amusement creased the corners of his eyes. "And you have no idea how pleased I am to hear your appetite is healthy."

"*I* was talking about food."

"Oh, so was I." But the innocence in his expression was totally spoiled by the wicked glint in his eyes.

I shook my head and got down to eating. Donal kept me company for the rest of the afternoon, only leaving to grab some sleep—at my insistence—once darkness had fallen. The doctor came in not too long after that, ran a medical scanner over my shoulder, and declared the bones had healed sufficiently to begin light duties. The healer then appeared not long after. He manipulated my shoulder for several seconds and then grunted, looking less than pleased. He motioned me to sit upright and then, after placing his hands on either side of my shoulder, closed his eyes. After a few seconds, his hands warmed and pressed heat into my skin, making the muscles tingle and twitch. He was accelerating my naturally fast rate of healing.

By the time he'd finished, his face was ashen and his hands were shaking. Healing magic took a fierce toll on those capable of using it, which was why most only lasted between ten and fifteen years in the business. The magic they used to heal others couldn't be used on themselves, and that meant most were faced with either giving up their profession or a shortened life span. Thankfully, given what was coming at us, healing magic was one of the few magics that *weren't* scarce in Cannamore.

"Don't push yourself for the next couple of days." His voice held a deep note of exhaustion. "The muscles have knitted together rather nicely, but it'll take another day or so before the new connections will withstand abuse."

"It's not like I abused it this time, healer. I was shot."

He dismissed the comment with a vague wave. "Indeed, but the advice remains the same."

I nodded. "Thanks for your help."

With a tired half smile, he spun and left. No one else came into the room; after eating my evening meal, I drifted off to sleep.

Morning brought more food, and then a nurse appeared, dumping fresh clothes on my bed before escorting me across to the shower—where she stood, refusing to leave while I turned on the taps. Donal appeared just as I stepped under the water and laughed at my obvious annoyance.

"It's standard practice in most hospitals." He dropped the toilet lid and then sat down. "But I'll make sure she doesn't fall, Mary, if you want to move on."

"You sure, m'lord?"

Donal nodded and she bustled away. I raised an eyebrow. "M'lord?"

He shrugged. "She found out who I was and refused to call me anything else. Not right, she claimed."

"She and my maid have a lot in common then." I switched off the tap and caught the towel he tossed me. "Why are you here?"

He raised an eyebrow. "Why do you always think I have a motive for seeking out your company?"

"Because you quite often do." Apart from his presence

here yesterday afternoon, that was. That had been nothing more than a desire to keep me company, and one I'd appreciated more than he'd ever know.

"Sad but true, although hopefully, that won't always be the case."

"Let's worry about surviving the present before we start even thinking about the future."

But even as I said that, I couldn't help doing it. Whether it be a short-term fling or something infinitely more, there was a deep, altogether too-long leashed part of me that hungered for the possibilities in the offering.

Even if those possibilities had only vaguely been acknowledged, at least on my part.

I tossed him the wet towel and then padded across to the bed. He didn't move, but his gaze once again pressed heat into my spine.

Once I'd pulled on underclothing, I reached for Marttia's gossamer armor and put it on. It sat so lightly on my skin that I couldn't help but hope she hadn't overstated its capabilities. I finished dressing and then turned around—and caught the glimmer of desire in his eyes a second before it disappeared. I'd seen the same look in many an eye over the years, but this was the first time it didn't fill me with dread.

"Where to now, highlander?"

He pushed up and walked toward the door. "Marx wants the two of us to run a check through the Wild Lands."

I frowned as I fell in step beside him. "Why? I can ask the earth that question without us risking life and limb."

"Yes, but the earth cannot tell you whether the dead areas are a result of their ability to restrict her or their drawing her heat to create their tunnel."

True enough. "And our scout teams?"

"Have all been assigned to the wall instead. It's not worth the risk of life given the bipeds now know we have weapons that can shatter their body armor and are likely to attack in greater numbers to counter that." His expression was grim. "At least you and I have a means of either stopping or escaping such an attack."

"My ability to stop them is dependent on how much heat has been drawn from the earth."

"Yes, but the lava-based deadness does not affect the wind."

Which was at least *something* to be grateful for.

"And remember," he continued, "the bipeds attacked the Skaran encampment without using their tunnels or magic. The barrier only appeared *after* the destruction, and was done more to hide it—and them—from our eyes."

"It'll take more than an advance party of a couple of hundred bipeds to destroy the garrison walls." And yet I had to wonder if it was true given the weapons they had at hand. "Besides, won't the wind alert you to their presence?"

"Only if they're moving above ground."

We left the hospital and strode across to the armory. I was handed a pulse rifle and issued two ammo clips that attached to my belt rather than across my back. The docs had obviously relayed the order I was not to be weighed down. Donal was fully kitted up.

Marx was waiting for us at the exit tunnel. "How are you feeling, Nyx?"

"Fighting fit, Captain."

He grunted but refrained from saying the obvious—that I'd need to be. "While we need some idea how far away the bipeds are, I don't want either of you taking any risks. At the first sign of movement, I want your asses hightailing it back to the garrison." He glanced at me, his expression steely. "Is that clear?"

Hightailing it back wouldn't give us the answers we needed. Wouldn't give us a timeframe with which to work. But all I said was, "Yes, Captain."

He studied me for several more seconds, disbelief evident, and then swung around and motioned the guards to open the gate. Once we'd left the tunnel and crossed over the metal bridge, I bent and pressed my fingers to the ground. *What happens with the deadness?*

It marches two ways.

So they're tunneling toward us now?

Yes.

Can they tunnel into the city itself?

No. The chasm is too deep.

Which was at least something. *How close to the Wild Lands are they?*

They approach the Quaih River.

I swore softly and repeated the information to Donal. He didn't look all that surprised. "In what direction?"

The deadness extends in a direct line from the Skaran encampment, came the answer.

And the bipeds? Can you feel their weight anywhere else?

They have not shifted from their protected area.

I frowned. Surely it would have made more tactical sense to move to the Skaran encampment, given the large cavern would have protected them from sunlight and kept them out of our sight?

And the tunnel we saw being created in the Skaran's cavern?

Its deadness will link up with the wider one in their own lands within a couple of days.

Was that why the bipeds who'd attacked the Skaran hadn't moved? Were they waiting for reinforcements? Or did they simply believe that, while we were now aware of their presence in the Skaran encampment, we didn't know about the assault party hiding beyond its boundaries?

I rose. "Do we continue? The earth has told us more than we'll probably ever see."

"Maybe," he agreed equably, "but it never hurt anyone to double-check information."

I glanced at him. "Do you ever double-check the wind's information?"

"Probably not as much as I should." His amusement was evident. "If I had, I might not have ended up in the cell with you."

"So despite your protestations to the contrary, you *did* have an inkling Lady Vivian was married."

"As I said, I chose to believe the lady." He shrugged. "I had no idea she was Divona's version of a floozy."

Never a truer word had been said, I thought in amusement. Marriage certainly *hadn't* curbed Vivian's enthusiastic pursuit of pleasure, though whether that was due to Lord Brannon failing to keep her satisfied or simply a desire for more than he could ever offer, I couldn't say. I'd never really had much to do with either of them—something that *would* change if I ever gained control of the throne. Lord Brannon was the man currently in charge of the treasury and, by all accounts, pretty canny when it came to all matters money.

Of course, that sort of cunning wasn't going to be of much use to anyone if we couldn't stop the bipeds here at Rodestat.

We moved through the Wild Lands in silence and, eventually, the earth's rage-filled tremors gave warning that we were nearing the tunnel's location. The only trouble with *that* was the fact it *wasn't* just close to the Quaih River —it had crossed it and was now in the Wild Lands.

Either the bipeds had an unending supply of mages capable of using and shaping the earth, or it didn't affect them the same way as it affected me.

We continued on; the earth lost her voice but gained an even deeper sense of rage. Eventually, her hostile trembling stilled; we were in the dead zone, and above the actual tunnel.

There were no obvious signs of either and certainly no sign of the bipeds themselves.

I bent and pressed my fingers against the ground. It was not only silent, but very, *very* cold. It might well have been ice under my fingertips rather than ground that only hours ago had held heat and life.

I looked around; the nearby trees looked drained, their leaves hanging limply and more gray than green. It was almost as if ash had covered them.

Was that what the bipeds wanted—or even needed? They were creatures who lived in the ashes of a volcano, after all. Perhaps the vibrancy of other life—these trees, the Skaran, and us—were an affront on their sensibilities.

I rose. "What now?"

"We follow the line of deadness to the edge of the forest and see what the rest of the bastards are up to."

"What, isn't the air speaking to you or something?"

"She's being cryptic again."

"Does she not understand the severity of the situation?"

He glanced over his shoulder, amusement evident. "Considering she's been warning us of approaching doom for months, she certainly does. But not even she, despite being everywhere, can always see everything—especially when they're underground and she's being restricted by magic."

We moved in silence and the trees quickly gave way to the grasslands that rolled to the river and the Skaran settlement beyond. There was nothing and no one visible. The entire area was empty and the only sound to be heard was the rustle of grass. But that grass was brown—life had left the soil, and now everything that had depended upon it was dying. The river itself seemed unaffected, but I guessed that was unsurprising. Even if the ground were icy enough to freeze water, gravity and the constant push of the warmer waters from upstream would keep it at bay.

We crossed the river and walked up the gentle incline. I was sweating by the time we reached the top, but that was more a result of the day's heat than overexertion.

Below us lay the Skaran encampment, but it was once again untouched by any sort of death or destruction, despite the rotten scent that now clung to the air. The bipeds had raised the damn shield again.

"Why would they even bother?" I accepted the water bottle Donal handed me and took a long drink.

"They've obviously got something they need to hide."

"It can't be their presence—they know *we* know they're here." I swapped the bottle for a strip of jerky and then added, "They also know we're capable of getting through that shield. Besides, if they were so damn worried about discovery, why haven't they got guards posted?"

"That would be *our* immediate response to an incursion by an enemy, but they may not think the same way we do." He glanced at me. "Shall we move on?"

"I don't know why you bother to keep asking that question when you already know the answer."

"It's always better to ask rather than presume."

"In many situations, I'd agree. This is different."

"As someone is rather fond of saying, the point remains."

I nudged him lightly and then headed down the hill. The knife once again let me know when we got near the barrier; I drew it free and sliced open a peephole.

And saw what the bipeds were concealing.

They were constructing tubes.

Hollow tubes.

The type that had spat the stone-melting globules at us, only much, *much* bigger.

I swore softly and stepped to one side so Donal could have a look.

"Oh, *fuck*," he muttered.

"I don't think the captain's idea of running water down the walls will work against cannons *that* size."

"No." He looked at me. "We need to get hold of one of them."

I blinked. "In case it's escaped your notice, those things are *huge*."

"Not those ones but one of the smaller ones. They're obviously built along the same lines, so if we can dismantle it, figure out how it works, we might be able to counter it."

"*If* we had the time, and I'm thinking we don't, given how fast their tunnel is moving."

"Yes, but even if Rodestat falls, we'll need a way of countering their weapons if the rest of Cannamore is to have any hope."

I hesitated, and in that moment, the decision was taken out of our hands. A gong sounded, and a dozen bipeds swung around and ran straight at us. I stepped to one side, keeping the knife pressed against the barrier and the window open. Donal fired. Several bipeds went down, but the rest kept coming.

Then a globule whizzed through our window, missing Donal's face by mere inches.

"Time to retreat to wind zone," he said.

I didn't argue. I just closed the window and ran as hard as I could for the base of the hill. The screams grew louder; I looked over my shoulder and saw the barrier shimmer as several bipeds crashed through it. They'd obviously adjusted their magic.

Globs of yellow-green began to chase our heels, sending acid-like droplets spraying through the air. The gently stirring wind kept the worst of it away, but the occasional droplet broke through and hit my boots. Whether it burned my skin as easily as it burned the leather, I couldn't say. I was too busy concentrating on simply keeping ahead of the bipeds to worry about such a thing.

The wind grew stronger as we raced up the hill, hitting our backs and forcing us into greater speed without ripping us up and away. I had no idea what Donal was waiting for, but I trusted him enough to keep my questions to myself.

Something whooshed through the air and I instinctively ducked. A sword soared over my head and burrowed into the ground several feet beyond me. The wind ripped it out, twisted it around, and flung it back. I had no idea if it hit anything. I simply didn't want to look. It was bad enough that I could hear the rasp of their breathing; I didn't need to see just how close they were getting.

The roar of the wind increased until it felt like we were standing in the eye of a storm. Donal stopped and swung around. I immediately did the same.

The wind had swept the bipeds off the ground and was shaking them violently from side to side. Weapons clattered to the ground—swords, knives, and hollow tubes. Donal flicked a finger and a sliver of wind wrapped around a tube and carried it over to us. He grabbed it and then released the bipeds. They plummeted to the ground, hitting hard enough that I not only heard bones breaking but also saw it.

None of them moved.

They weren't unconscious. They were dead.

The wind swung around and got us the hell out of there. We were met by two soldiers at the garrison and were once again led down to the windowless debriefing room. Gallego sat at the head of the table and Marx was to his left. A woman and two men were on his right, and the mage staff I'd stolen lay on the table, the broken crystal gleaming softly in the room's harsh lighting.

Marx quickly introduced us and then said, "What's happening out there?"

Donal filled them in on everything we'd discovered and then stripped off his pack and placed the tube on the table. "And that, ladies and gentlemen, is the thing that's is going to cause all the damage to the city."

"I take it it's one of the acid-spitting weapons you mentioned earlier?" Marx said.

"Yes," Donal said, "But they're currently constructing cannons ten times larger than this in the Skaran encampment."

Hilgar—the woman in charge of engineering—carefully drew the tube closer and examined it. "At first glance, it appears rather primitive. The shot is loaded into the chamber at this end and is fired by this button here." She pointed to a slight indentation on one side of the metal. "It doesn't seem to have any sort of guidance attached. It is, quite simply, a point and shoot weapon."

"One that can turn stone into liquid," I commented.

"We need to find a way to counter the acid shots, because the bastards will be here within the next day or so."

"How can you be so sure?" The commander's voice was harsh.

"Because they're already in the Wild Lands. Or rather, their tunnel is. Their main force hasn't yet arrived at the Skaran encampment."

"Is that the force you spotted in the volcano?" Wrest, the man in charge of the Garrison's permanent army, asked.

"Yes," Donal said. "They'll have easy access into the Wild Lands once the two tunnels join."

"Is it possible for them to bypass the wall and emerge somewhere in the middle of the city?" the commander asked.

"No," I said. "The chasm is too deep. They'll have to resurface at some point to set up their camp and attack."

Jancin, the man in charge of munitions, said, "What's to stop them going under the mountains or even attacking from on high?"

"Nothing," I said. "But their course has not deviated in all the miles between us and their volcano. I think it's safe to presume they'll not do so at the last minute."

"We dare not work on presumptions right now." The commander glanced at Marx. "Alert all the watchtowers. Tell them to raise the cannons in preparation."

"And warn them that tremors confined to a specific strip of land is one of the first signs of a tunnel approaching," I said. "It may be the only warning they get."

Marx activated comms and immediately began issuing orders. The commander switched his gaze to Hilgar and Jancin. "I want you two to take that weapon apart and figure out some way to counter it."

"And the mage staff?" Hilgar asked.

The commander glanced at me. "Any ideas?"

I shook my head. "But given they use it to access and control the earth, it's obviously a form of magic not dissimilar to that in both the King's Sword and my knife."

"Which doesn't exactly help us, given such magic has long disappeared from Cannamore." Gallego thrust a hand through his hair. "Nyx, take the thing and see what you can uncover. If either of you sense any further movement out there, inform Marx immediately."

Which was an obvious dismissal. I picked up the mage staff and followed Donal out the door.

"Is it safe to take that thing apart within the garrison?" he asked as he led the way back to ammunitions.

"I deactivated it, so it should be." I handed over my rifle and ammo.

"I hear another 'but' in your tone."

I grimaced. "That's because I don't know enough about *our* earth magic let alone this one."

"So we'll need to be somewhere somewhat isolated before we attempt anything." He scanned the area for a moment and then said, "There're no real options here. Let's try the canyon between the garrison and the Red City. That area is pretty lifeless already, so it's not going to matter much if we unleash something."

The gates were open, but the guards stopped us from leaving. After a quick conversation, they contacted Marx and we were allowed through. The chill in the air immediately increased and moisture swirled. The heat we'd been getting over the last couple of days had obviously melted the early snow further up the mountain, and it was now pouring down the canyon's vertical sides, creating a long waterfall that sounded like thunder. Water lapped at our boots as we made our way toward the center—there was so much coming down from up high that not even the deep splits that crisscrossed this no-man's land could contain it.

Once I'd reach a small but dry mound of stone near the center of the canyon, I placed the staff on the ground and squatted beside it. The staff was made of some sort of metal *other* than silver, which was slightly odd given silver was apparently the better conduit for magic. The end that went into the ground was pointed and sharp and appeared to be made of a glass-like material similar to that of both my knife and King's Sword. The crystal that topped the other end had multiple cracks marring its surface, and it wasn't emitting any sort of power.

"Any revelations?" Donal squatted opposite me.

"No, and that's rather frustrating." I carefully touched the crystal; it was as inert as it looked. "I really wish my mother had told me more about the history of her people."

"Her people are your people," he commented. "Their blood runs in your veins."

"Yeah, but so too does the blood of the king."

He grunted. "But if she's now part of the earth's greater consciousness, it might be possible to talk to her. Even if it's not, her knowledge will be available to you."

"Except I have no idea if she *did*, given the manner of her death. Besides, it's not like I've had much time since the bracelets were released to ask that sort of question." And I certainly had no desire for anyone to witness me doing so—not even Donal. I'd spent a very long time controlling my confusion and anger over her death, but it was more than possible that—if she were able to talk directly to me—the mere sound of her voice would shatter that leash.

I drew my knife. Fireflies flickered down its blade. The stone might be inert, but there was still something here, however faint.

I pressed the blade's tip under one of the three metal clamps holding the crystal in place and carefully pried it away, then repeated the process until the stone fell free and rolled toward Donal. He picked it up and examined it.

"Is it possible for stones to represent different types of magics?"

"Anything is possible." I carefully picked up the staff and examined the area that had cradled the stone. Its surface was smooth and, like the rest of the staff, appeared at be made of metal. "Why?"

I started to flip the staff over to check the pointed end when something slid from the center of the cradle and raced over the edge. Though it looked to be little more than a grain of sand, I nevertheless felt the impact of it through the earth under my feet. I frowned and peered more closely at the base—and discovered a hole little larger than said grain.

"Because," Donal said, "both the mage in the volcano and the ones positioned with their advance force used blood sacrifice and a black crystal. The three making and controlling the lava used red stones, and this one—which was the source of a barrier that prevents entry and presents a false image—is clear."

"I guess it's one way of not mixing up the different staffs they're using for each of the magics."

I half flipped the staff; more sand appeared, hitting the ground with a weird heaviness.

"Yes, but where are they getting them? The black stone might have come from their mountain, but I very much doubt the others would have." He paused, studying me—something I felt rather than saw. "What have you found?"

"Sand. The staff appears to be filled with it." I tipped the staff again, allowing more golden grains to drop onto the ground. "The earth shudders each time the sand touches it."

"Which suggests it's powerful." He placed a hand under the gentle dribble and caught some of it in his palm. "And yet it feels no different to the sand found on any shoreline. Is it, perhaps, some sort of conductor between the earth and the crystal on top?"

"Let me ask the authority on all things earth." I placed the staff on the ground and then splayed my fingers across the stone. *What can you tell me about the sand that leaks from the staff?*

It is old.

How old?

It comes from a continent that was lost long ago to volcanoes and ash—Atlan.

Which was a place I'd never heard of, and its fate a somewhat eerie echo of what had happened to Isle of Whyte. *The bipeds come from there?*

As did many of the mage lines that remain in Cannamore today. But the Volker did not create the earth staffs—they simply adapted them to their needs.

I blinked. *If you knew their name and origin, why have you never told me before now?*

Because the eons that have passed buried the knowledge deep, and that meant time was needed to retrieve it.

I hadn't really thought about it before now, but it did make sense that the sheer amount of information that came with each new soul entering the collective consciousness would—by necessity—mean older information would be "stored" until needed. *So why did the Volker attack then? Why do they attack now?*

We do not think they have any real reason, other than the fact they believe they are a superior race, destined to rule above all others.

They wouldn't be the first or the last to think that.

Certainly more than a few wars throughout Cannamore's long history had been started because of that very same belief. *If the staffs were designed by earth mages, how did the Volker get hold of them?*

Treachery. More than that, we cannot say, as memories of that time never became part of the greater consciousness.

I frowned. *But surely the knowledge of those who weren't traitors would have.*

Sadness ran across our connection—an emotion so fierce tears stung my eyes.

The great mages were too secretive about the staffs they created—that was in part what led to their downfall. The dark magic that corrupted and then betrayed also consumed them, body and soul.

That still doesn't explain how the Volker got hold of them, let alone how they can use them.

Again, we cannot fully answer that. But they are creatures born into the deeper recesses of the earth, and her heat runs through their veins. They are also capable of magic based in blood and use staffs similar in design to the earth mage ones. It's possible that in mining the deeper energies of the earth to augment their weapons, the earth mages woke an evil they had no understanding or control over.

More than possible, given what we'd witnessed in the volcano. *Which still doesn't explain how the Volker can use the staffs in the first place. Blood magic is not of earth and it should preclude them.*

Unless the souls of the corrupted are held within each mage stone, and that is what provides the link between the two.

Meaning if I *did* attempt to destroy these staffs, I'd be going up against the might—even if in spirit form—of the greatest earth mages to have existed. That didn't fill me with a whole lot of hope.

If we can destroy the staffs, will that stop them from using the earth against us?

Yes. But destruction was tried before, the earth commented. *It failed.*

Because the staffs were too strong?

Because life was too weak without proper conduits.

I frowned again. *Why didn't you have proper conduits? Wasn't the King's Sword and my knife designed for that very reason?*

They were created after *the Volker forced the volcano awake and the eruptions destroyed the island. We have no knowledge of them.*

Why not?

She who held that knowledge never joined the consciousness.

I was tempted to ask why not, but it really wasn't important right now. *Why wasn't the eruption stopped?*

It was thought the Volker would be trapped and destroyed with the island. It worked no better this time than it did the last.

The last being Atlan, obviously, and that raised a whole lot of questions as to why lessons hadn't been learned. *And the Volker that attack us? How are they related to that original group?*

They are not related. They are the same.

I blinked and automatically said, "Impossible."

"What is?" Donal said immediately.

I raised my free hand and then silently said, *The island was destroyed nine hundred years ago—how could they possibly be the same?*

The slow walkers of the barren Tardigradus region can

hibernate for over a hundred years and only need a solitary drop of water to be revived.

A hundred years is very different to a thousand.

The slow walkers are also much smaller. If creatures the size of a coin can survive one hundred years, why couldn't the Volker survive a thousand?

Put like that, I guessed it *wasn't* impossible. *Would I be able to use a staff?*

Only if the crystal that tops it is unbroken, and only if the staff is buried within live soil and unprotected by the magic of their mages. But it is dangerous.

Why?

Aside from the corrupting magic that might overwhelm you, the staffs are all connected. Any attempt to use one will be felt by those controlling the others.

Which was a risk worth taking if there was absolutely no other choice. *And the King's Sword—you really can't tell me anything about it?*

No. Racinda's soul, like those of the great mages, never became part of the greater consciousness. We do not know what happened to her.

Racinda had been, according to what I'd read, the queen of the Isle of Whyte and her strongest mage—and if *she* couldn't stop the bipeds, what hope did we have?

I swore softly and told Donal everything the earth had said about the bipeds.

"As much as I love the idea of going after the mages, they'll be fiercely protected and an almost impossible target."

"I wasn't so much thinking about the mages but the staffs. The Volker might not be able to access their full powers, but we could."

"Except for the corruption factor. I might not know

anything about actual magic, but even I know blood magic is not something the sane want to trifle with."

"We might not have any other choice, Donal."

He grunted. Whether that meant he agreed or not, I couldn't say. "Did you ask about the King's Sword?"

"It's a conduit able to withstand the full force of the earth magic and allows the user to destroy without being drained unto death. But there's no certainty I'll be able to use it, even though the knife is responding to me."

He frowned. "Did you ask how the sword ended up in the hands of your father's ancestors?"

"No, because it's not information the earth has." I thrust up. "Let's head back to the garrison—I need to eat."

After first reporting my findings to Marx, we did just that. The other scout leaders started questioning us as soon as we arrived back at our quarters—the garrison had finally been informed about the Volker, though the commander hadn't gone into great detail.

A good hour had passed before I was finally able to retreat to my cubicle. I wasn't particularly tired, but I also didn't want to be falling asleep during watch duty.

Donal woke me close to six and we walked across to the mess hall. There was no news on the tube we'd brought back and the search for more information about the Volker remained futile. But in my mind, the real question that needed answering was, if my mother's people had destroyed their island and then fled, why hadn't the Volker immediately followed them? Why had they instead moved into the dead lands, set up home in another volcano, and gone into hibernation?

It didn't make any sense.

Night swept in. My team had been assigned the area immediately to the left of the pulse cannon that protected

the tunnel gateway, and were spaced at twenty-foot inter-
vals. The Wild Lands were little more than a deeper blob of
darkness against the night sky and as silent as a grave.

The night wore on without incident. As dawn began to
creep across the sky, I smothered a yawn and shifted from
one foot to the other.

That's when I saw it—an odd glimmer deep in the heart
of the forest. I tapped the halo and immediately said, "Did
anyone else see that?"

"See what?" Sage said, her tone bored.

"A flash of light in the forest."

"No," echoed down the line.

I frowned into the fading darkness, my uneasiness growing. Despite the fact no one else had caught the glimmer,
the notion that something was very wrong was building. I
placed a hand on the wall, seeking clarification, but the
earth couldn't tell me what was happening in shadows
underneath the trees.

Not because she didn't know, but because she was being
restricted.

Which meant the bipeds were out there, and in force.

Even as that thought crossed my mind, the glimmer
appeared again, gaining size and brightness as it arced
toward us.

It was a globule.

A stone-melting globule the size of a goddamn groaner.

ELEVEN

The cry of "incoming" echoed along the garrison wall, but there was little most of us could do except watch it. Only the wind responded, gathering speed and power, throwing dust high as Donal created a swirling barrier of air between the globule and us. It hit the turbulent air mass and was flung onto the ground where it splattered wide and began melting stone, turning it into little more than black water.

For several minutes, nothing else happened. Tension crawled through me, and my grip on the wall became so fierce the rough edges were tearing into my fingers, making them bleed.

Deep in the forest, light glimmered once again.

"Three more on the way," someone farther along the wall yelled.

Again the wind battered the globules right and left, protecting us even as it deepened the river of stone running along the canyon's floor.

A third barrage came; again it amounted to nothing.

Then the stone under my feet shuddered. I leaned over

the parapet and looked down. There was no light, no glimmer, but dark water ran from the base of the wall, and a cavernous hole had appeared where there should have been solid stone. While we'd all been watching the sky, the bipeds had assaulted low with concealed globules.

But I wasn't the only one who'd noticed; an order was barked and the water that had been pumped up to the storage tanks behind us was immediately released. As more globules lit the predawn skies, water poured into the decade-old channels and flooded down the wall. The first wave hit the area of wall that was being eroded; steam rose, but the stone continued to melt, a dark swirl washing through the clear water as it hit the canyon floor and raced toward the nearest crevice.

"Donal," I screamed, hoping he'd hear me over the howling of the wind. "The base! We need more water at the base of the wall."

The water flooding the length of the wall immediately switched direction, racing in from the left and the right, rising in speed and force until it formed waves. They crashed into the holes the globules were creating; steam exploded from all three and the flow of black water stopped. I placed a hand against the wall and gathered stone and earth, pressing it into the holes, repairing the breach as best I could.

The assault once again stopped. I stared uneasily at the distant forest, knowing they were out there, knowing this wasn't the end of their tests despite the growing light of day. I clenched my fists and wished I could simply order the earth to destroy them, even if such an order might mean the end of me. But the restrictions on the earth around the bipeds' base prevented that possibility—not surprising given they now knew they faced at least one earth mage.

The minutes ticked by. Sweat trickled down my spine despite the coolness of the air. I hated being up here, hated being able to do nothing more than watch. We had to find a way to neutralize both the bipeds and their weapons, and we needed to do it soon. Water had successfully extinguished the globules, but the tanks only held a finite amount. More could be pumped in, but that took time.

And time was the one thing we didn't have much of.

A minute passed, then two, then five. Fear pounded through my veins and the stink of it stung the air—though it wasn't mine alone.

Overhead, thunder rumbled and lightning crackled across the storm-clad sky, an echo of the tension assailing the man who could control both, perhaps.

Another minute slipped by.

Then they hit us.

Hard.

Globules sprayed out of the forest, a fierce rain of spitting yellow-green. The wind flung them left and right until the canyon was awash with rivers of stone. The barrage kept coming, filling the skies with its evil and battering the wall of wind with increasing intensity.

Despite the best efforts of the wind and Donal, some got through. They not only hit the curtain wall but also the walkway, eating swiftly through the stone and then dropping into the rooms immediately underneath. Screams rose, horrid screams, as men and women were hit and burned. As an evacuation order went out for all areas under the walkway, I pressed my hands against the wall, pouring every ounce of energy into strengthening and repairing. Nothing I did seemed to make much difference. The wind's fierceness was waning, and too many globules were causing too much damage now.

285

Once again thunder cracked overhead, then lightning splintered down, hitting the forest and setting it alight. At the same time, rain hit the garrison, a force so fierce it drowned me in an instant. The wind sent it scuttling in multiple directions, dousing the globules swiftly and efficiently.

As the fire caught hold in the forest, the barrage ceased. The rain's force immediately lessened and the howling wind fell silent. I spun and raced along the wall, ignoring the protests of my aching head and trembling limbs as I leapt over gaping holes and multiple bodies. Just as I drew close to Donal, his strength gave out and he collapsed. I lunged forward, thrusting my arms under his, and took the brunt of his weight as he fell backward. Pain ripped through my shoulders and my legs buckled. I swore but went with the fall, my knees smacking hard against the stone. But better them than his head.

For several seconds, I didn't move. I couldn't move. My head was pounding, my breath was little more than ragged gasps for air, and there were dark spots dancing in front of my eyes.

Thick smoke filled every breath and momentarily blunted the stench of burned flesh and fear. I hoped like hell the fire burned the bipeds as thoroughly as they'd burned us, though I doubted it would actually stop them. But a reprieve, however brief, was welcome.

I wearily looked around. There were bodies, and bits of bodies, everywhere. Between the regular garrison troops and the scout teams, there'd been close to seventy-five people manning the weapons and keeping watch on the wall, but a good third of those appeared to be down. At *that* rate of attrition, the bipeds would wipe the garrison out in a matter of days.

Medics were already treating the worst of the wounded in situ while others were being stretchered away. No one as yet worried about the dead or those who were barely recognizable as human.

Bile rose and I swallowed heavily, trying to control the strengthening urge to just get out of here. To run.

But if we didn't stop them here, Divona would be their next target. If I was sure of anything, it was the fact that this assault was little more than a test run. A means of discovering what we were capable of.

Now that they knew, far worse would come.

I glanced around at the sound of approaching footsteps and couldn't help frowning. "What are you doing away from your post, Sage?"

"What do you think I'm fucking doing?" Her voice was tart. "I was ordered to help."

My frown deepened. "Who told you I needed help?"

"Who do you fucking think? You two are the captain's precious pets."

I didn't bother biting back or explaining just why the captain was so keen to keep us alive. I simply didn't have the energy.

"Fine—you can help me get Donal back to the bunkhouse. Grab his arms."

She did so. With his weight off me, I was able to climb to my feet. My knees were bloody and raw, but that was nothing compared to the destruction that lay around me.

I moved to Donal's right, slipping my good shoulder under his before locking arms with Sage. Between the two of us, we were able to drag him off the wall and down the stairs. A number of globules had soared into the courtyard, but they hadn't hit anything important and the rain had stopped them burning too deeply. Those holes were already being filled. The garrison might have been hit, but there was little panic—everyone was still doing their job.

As we stepped onto the walkway that led around to our bunkroom, the earth began to tremble and her anger pulsed through my feet. I hoped the cause wasn't the bipeds doing what she'd said was impossible—burrowing under both the chasm and the wall—but I simply couldn't risk stopping to ask. It was taking all my concentration—all my strength—to keep going.

As we neared the entrance into our room, Sage said, "What happens after this?"

"What do you think happens? We're soldiers. We go back to the wall and we fight."

She snorted. "I think tonight has already proven the uselessness of *that*."

"So what would you rather do? Run?"

"And you don't? I'd figured you to be smarter than that."

"If they break through here, Divona will be next. And if *she* falls, there'll be no safe place to run."

"I won't be running into Cannamore. I'll be grabbing passage across to Gallion and getting well away from this godforsaken place."

"And how do you plan to do that? Aside from the fact you're stuck here with the rest of us, passage isn't cheap, and all your assets were seized when you were convicted." I couldn't help the sharp note in my voice. I really wasn't in the mood for her nonsense right now. "Donal's cubical is on the left, just inside the door."

Once we'd gotten him onto his bunk, she stepped back and said, "I don't need money because passage has already been paid for. I just have to show up."

I rolled my shoulders, trying to ease the ache. "If you prebooked a means of escape out of Divona, you either weren't very confident of your thieving abilities or simply a rotten thief."

"In this particular case, I'd say both are true." She shrugged. "Anything else you need help with?"

"No. Go rest."

She snorted. "As if anyone is going to rest knowing those bastards are out there."

She moved past me, but as she did, something hit my side and pain flared. I frowned and glanced down; caught the flash of silver sliding away from my body.

A knife.

A goddamn *knife*.

Sage was Vin's assassin.

That's what the earth had been trying to tell me.

The blade hit again and was once again thwarted by Marttia's sheer vest. I swore and lashed out with a clenched fist, but Sage was faster than me and ducked the blow. Again the knife hit; this time, the blade slithered down to my thigh and drew blood. I swore again and dropped, sweeping a booted foot around, trying to knock her off her feet. She jumped over the blow and came after me, the knife a blur as she cut and parried, her face intent. I twisted, blocked with my own knife, and ducked her blows, but my strength was low and my reactions slowing. Then she switched the knife from her right hand to her left and punched hard. I pulled back but not fast enough; the blow skimmed my chin and sent me flailing backward. I hit the partition wall and somehow remained upright, looked up to see the blur of approaching steel, and threw myself sideways. I hit the ground with a grunt and felt the immediate response of the earth. I ordered her to rise, to lock the other woman in stone, and then scrambled away. Soft laughter followed.

"Not so tough now, are you, Princess?"

I didn't answer. I didn't have to.

In utter silence, a two-foot wide trunk of deadly intent rose behind Sage. Multiple branches of stone swiftly sprouted from it and lashed around her body, pinning her arms to her torso and immobilizing her legs. She screamed for help and fought to escape, but no one came to her rescue, and for the same reason why she'd chosen this moment to attack. There was no one near to help.

And no escape for her.

Not from the stone.

Not from me.

Not from the death that would soon hit.

I leaned against the partition wall, shoved my knife away, and then hugged my knees close to my chest. Everything hurt and my vision blurred. Unconsciousness loomed, but as much as I wanted to give in to its unfeeling embrace, there were questions that needed answers.

Sage soon realized the uselessness of fighting and growled, "Fucking release me."

"What's in it for me if I do?" I replied evenly. "Nothing but death, I'd wager."

"I'll give you the name of the person who hired me."

"I already know that."

Her skin was pale, almost ashen, but it wasn't in response to my reply. The stony fingers that held her so securely were drawing ever tighter across her chest, and her breathing was now little more than short, sharp pants. But viciousness remained in both her expression and her voice. "If you knew, why didn't you stop me?"

"Because while I knew an assassin had been employed, I wasn't sure who it was. Tell me, was Dravan working with you?"

Her snort was filled with contempt. "As if."

"But it *was* you who told him my court nickname and who needled him into attacking me, wasn't it?"

"If I answer your questions, are you going to release me?"

Which was answer enough. "No. I'm going to sit here and watch the earth squeeze every last drop of air from your lungs."

"You ain't got the—"

I flicked a finger upwards. Stone flowed from her chest to her neck and then across her mouth and nose, cutting off her air. Her eyes went wide and she screamed, a muffled sound that didn't last long. As death claimed her, I closed my eyes and let unconsciousness do the same to me.

***

I woke to the awareness of being in bed rather than on the floor. I was also being watched, but there was no threat in the sensation and the earth was silent. I drew in a deeper breath and sorted through the various scents within it. The only person currently in the bunkhouse was Donal—and *he* was in my cubicle. And given I no longer wore the vest that had saved my life, had more than likely stripped me.

I opened my eyes. He'd swung the small desk chair around and was sitting on it backward, his arms crossed on the backrest. His skin had lost its ashen color, and though faint shadows remained under his eyes, he nevertheless looked far stronger than he had last night.

"You should be resting rather than watching me."

"I find watching you very restful." A smile teased his lips. "How you feeling?"

"Probably the same as you."

"I didn't have to protect myself from an assassin after expending all my energy repairing the wall. The bitch deserved the death she got."

Maybe she did and maybe she didn't, but at least for the moment, I didn't have to keep looking over my shoulder. "Is she still a life-size ornament in your cubicle?"

"Yes, because the stone locks her to the floor."

I grunted, touched the wall above my head, and asked the earth to release her. She pulsed in response and, a heartbeat later, there was a crash from the other room.

Donal tilted forward; his frown turned into surprise. "She just hit the ground and shattered."

I blinked. "Literally shattered?"

"Indeed. I had no idea human flesh could actually become stone."

"Neither did I." And it just made me wish I knew more about the earth power. Turning flesh to stone would certainly be a very handy weapon against the bipeds. "What time is it?"

"Five in the afternoon."

"And the bipeds?"

"No sign of them, but they're out there."

"Waiting for night, no doubt."

"Night, and their main force. They're only a mile or so out from the Wild Lands now."

I raised an eyebrow. "The wind can track them?"

He hesitated. "No. But it *can* track the location of both the concealment shields *and* the areas that it can't traverse."

I grunted. "Once the two forces come together, we'll be in trouble. You and I haven't the capacity to keep them at bay, Donal."

"I know. I've asked my father to send reinforcements, but it's going to take them a couple of days to get here. The distance is simply too far to bridge over the course of twenty-four hours."

Meaning we had to hold them off for at *least* that long, and I really wasn't sure it was possible. Not given we'd barely survived what was little more than a probing attack.

"I need to go get the sword, Donal. It's our only hope."

What I was going to do once I got it, or how I was even going to achieve that, I had no idea. The earth might be on my side, but Cannamore's elite never would be.

"That may be true," he said, "but the wind is still advising patience—"

"The longer we hang around here," I cut in, "the deeper the danger grows for the rest of Cannamore. Time isn't on our side, and we both know it."

"Agreed, but moving too soon might be as disastrous as waiting. At the very least, we should wait until a reply comes from Gigurri."

If a reply came from Gigurri. It was rather ominous that there'd been no response from them as yet despite the urgency of Marttia's request. Still, Donal was once again right. Now was not the time to be making rash decisions—and I certainly hadn't spent the last twelve years plotting my revenge to waste it all with hasty action. "Has Hilgar had any success breaking down the acid tubes or finding a counter?"

He shook his head. "Aside from water, no. She's been talking to her counterparts in Divona, though, and it appears both water and platina wire might nullify it."

I raised my eyebrows at the edge of excitement in his voice. "And this is good because...?"

"Rodestat's fence and much of her rooftops are made of a mix of platina wire and iron."

"Which won't protect the walls from either the acid

globules or the bipeds themselves. They'll just tear through the wire fence or scramble up and over it."

"Except that the fence can be electrified. If those bastards touch it, they'll fry. And that will give us time."

But not much, I suspected. Still, even a few hours extra was better than nothing.

I shifted and stretched, trying to ease some of the niggling aches. My thigh twinged and the area around it felt tight—a result of being sprayed with wound sealer, I suspected, which meant a medic had tended to the wound rather than a healer. That wasn't really so surprising given the healers had far worse to tend to than a rudimentary knife wound.

The earth murmured a warning and I looked around to see Marx walk into the room.

"Ah, good, you're both awake." He crossed his arms and leaned against the outer wall. "I can guess what happened with Sage, but you'd nevertheless better make a report."

I did so. When I'd finished, he swore and said, "If you hadn't taken care of the stupid bitch, I most likely would have."

I raised my eyebrows. "Even *I* know the military doesn't believe in an eye for an eye."

"Except in exceptional circumstances. These times are certainly that." He studied us critically for a moment. "The commander and Marttia wish to speak to you both ASAP. I'll arrange for Sage to be removed—"

"That will simply take a broom," Donal said. "The princess broke her when she disconnected the stone locking her to the floor."

"Broke?" Marx briefly looked over his shoulder and then added, tone dry, "Remind me never to get on your bad side, Nyx."

294

"I'm reserving the whole flesh-to-stone thing for very special enemies. You're pretty safe, Cap."

"Good." Amusement briefly touched his lips and just as quickly fled. "So, twenty minutes? That should give you time to shower before the meeting."

"I think he's saying you stink," Donal said.

I slapped at his knee and he laughed. "Twenty is fine, Captain."

He nodded and left. I flung off the bedcovers and got up. "You, highlander, can sit right there. I shall have my shower in peace and alone."

His response was a deep, somewhat martyred sigh. "Deprived of viewing your loveliness in what could be my final hours alive. You're a cruel woman, Princess."

"You can watch my butt as it disappears out the door, if you like."

"Oh, I will, trust me on that."

I grinned and gathered my clothes and Marttia's mesh vest. It had certainly lived up to promises made, and I wasn't about to go anywhere without it now. While I doubted my brother had more deadly surprises waiting within the regiment, I wasn't about to bet my life on that.

Once I'd showered and dressed, we headed across to the briefing room. Gallego and Marttia once again sat on one side of the table, but this time, the far end seat was occupied by a thin man wearing the blue uniform and silver circlet of a communicator.

Marttia motioned us to sit down opposite her and then said, "Ragstaff, please connect with the Gigurri communicator."

Ragstaff closed his eyes and, after a moment, the circlet began to shine.

"Lady Helena," Marttia said, "I'm here with your niece,

as requested. Please proceed with the information you've found."

There was a pause as the message was passed on and then Ragstaff said, in a voice that held so many echoes of my mother's that tears briefly stung my eyes. "Nyx, you have no idea how happy I am to learn you've escaped your father's grasp."

"A grasp *you* did nothing about." I took a deep breath in an attempt to control the bitterness, and added, "Did you find anything on the Volker in the archives?"

There was a long pause, then, "There's little information available from the time of the fleeing; the old records were too numerous to be carried, and there wasn't time to call in aid from the air mages. The great libraries were destroyed with the island."

The communicator's tone suggested my aunt was upset by my response, but what else did she expect? She'd not only left me alone in what had very swiftly become a hostile environment, but hadn't in *any* way attempted to contact me in the last twelve years. Even a note of support slipped to me during my uncle's infrequent visits to court would have left me feeling a little less alone.

"We did find some information in Racinda's final journals, which accounted for the last two years of her life," she continued. "It emphatically states that raising the earth's molten core against creatures born on the outer edges of such heat was not the answer—that it had now failed twice and should not be tried again."

"I think it's safe to say we're *not* going down that path." Marttia's voice was dry.

"Did Racinda's journal offer any information about the mage staffs or offer suggestions on how to destroy them?" Donal asked.

"There were twelve staffs, one for each of the great mage houses of old. Each was topped by a black crystal and was tied to the earth with earth," my aunt said. "And if we'd known how to destroy them, young man, we would still be living on our isle."

"Then why were the King's Sword and the knife my mother gave me created if not as a counterpoint to the staffs?"

"They exist thanks to the fact that, in the Isle's dying minutes, the magic hampering us using the earth's force died, and Racinda was able to capture two staffs. She deconstructed their magic and then used that knowledge and power to create the sword and knife. Whether they will actually work against the remaining ten mage staffs is unknown, given the Volker have only recently resurfaced."

"The knife certainly does," I said.

"Which does give us hope the sword will also work."

But was no guarantee, her tone implied. Obviously, there was more dark news to come, at least when it came to my use of the sword.

"Why were only the two created?" Marttia asked. "Surely it would have been more logical to at least create as many counter weapons as there were staffs."

"It would indeed, but perhaps she simply ran out of time."

"Then why create two different weapons?" I asked. "Why not two knives or two swords?"

"We don't really know. But one of the very last entries in the journal mentions the fierce and all-consuming nature of the magic that stains the staffs. We suspect that in her efforts to understand and provide counterpoints for it, she was drawn deeper and deeper into its thrall and simply ran out of time. Had she not realized what was happening and

297

locked herself in endless sleep, she would have joined great mages in that darkness."

I raised my eyebrows. "I thought no one knew what happened to her?"

"No one truly does, but such an action would make sense for one such as she."

"If the greatest earth mage of the day couldn't control or destroy the darkness within the staffs," Donal said, his gaze meeting mine, "then it's certainly not something you should be trying."

"There's no darkness in the knife, Donal. It may not exist in the sword, either."

"Perhaps, perhaps not," came my aunt's reply. "The final line in that last journal suggests that to destroy all you must first be linked to all."

I frowned. "How the hell am I supposed to link either weapon to ten mage staffs?"

"I thought you'd already destroyed one?"

"I destroyed a staff, but it was topped by a clear crystal, which means it wasn't one of the old earth mage staffs but a Volker copy."

"But you destroyed it?"

"By shoving the knife into its core and shattering the crystal," I commented. "I'm unlikely to get that close to the rest of them."

"You might not need to," my aunt replied. "Not if the staffs are embedded in earth, and you are able to disrupt the magic that restricts your access to her power."

Which was what the knife appeared to do—at least on a small scale. But there was still altogether too much being left to conjecture and "might nots" for my liking. "Did Racinda leave any information about the sword's capabilities?"

"There wasn't a great deal. She said that both must be bound to you by blood for you to use them."

"But the earth doesn't demand blood...." My words trailed off. The earth mightn't, but the Volker's magic *did*. I licked suddenly dry lips and tried to ignore rising trepidation as I added, "I didn't bind the knife to me."

"You blood must have stained the hilt at some point if the magic now answers your call."

Given the number of times I'd used it lately against both human and bipedal adversaries, that was more than possible. "So I simply have to bleed on the King's Sword to unleash its power?"

"In theory, yes. But being able to use the knife is no guarantee you'll be able to unlock the sword's true capabilities."

I frowned. "Why not? I drew it from the glass throne—"

There were gasps from several in the room, but my aunt didn't seem surprised, which made sense given she would have heard the truth from the earth itself.

"Countless of your ancestors have done that," she cut in. "It's unlikely any would have been able to access the power, given few of your father's line have joined the greater consciousness."

"Great," I muttered. I thrust a hand through my hair and then added, "Did she say anything else about it?"

"No."

"Then why was it given to the Bel-Hannon kings rather than being gifted to her heirs, as the knife was?" Donal asked.

"A means of protecting these lands if the Volker attacked again was the price for our resettlement. Over the centuries since, the Bel-Hannons have deliberately sought marriage to the earth mage lines to bolster their power and their ability to use the sword. But they will never be able to fully access it."

"Which leads me to the one question that's been bothering me," Marttia said. "Why now? Why has it taken them so long to attack us again?"

She hesitated. "It could be a number of things, but I suspect that, given the sword was created in part by Racinda's knowledge and in part by her possible use of Volker magic, they simply became aware there is currently no true heir to wield its power."

"Except I can use the knife. If they can sense the sword's presence, however tenuously, why wouldn't they also sense the knife?"

"I have no idea. Perhaps it is simply a matter of the sword having more power." She hesitated. "But if you *can* use it, doing so may well kill you."

A "may well" at least left room for a "may not" possibility. Still.... "Why?"

"Because using blood to bind yourself to the blade you might also unleash that darker energy. The sword was created in the last days of Racinda's life, remember, when the darkness was beginning to tell on her strength and determination. It's very possible she wove the threads of that darkness into the sword's fabric."

"Is there any way to counter or protect myself against that possibility?"

"None that we're aware of."

Meaning the one weapon we had against the Volker magic might be the one weapon we dare not use... but even as that thought crossed my mind, I knocked it away. If the sword was capable of destroying the mage staffs, then it had to be tried, no matter what the personal cost.

"Anything else?" Marttia asked.

The communicator shook his head. "As yet, no. We'll continue to search through the records and journals, but I doubt we'll find anything relating to the Volker or their magic. It seems both Racinda's sacrifice and any information about the bipeds has been deliberately pushed from the consciousness of those who survived the Isle's destruction."

Either that, or it was a result of the dark power Racinda had unleashed when she'd dismantled the mage staffs and created her two weapons. Perhaps as well as nearly consuming her, it had dulled the memories of those around her. While I had no idea what was and wasn't possible when it came to magic, if a healer could draw on personal energy to fix the broken bodies and minds of others, why couldn't a darker force alter collective memories?

"What of my request for additional mage assistance?" Marttia said.

"We are sending five of our strongest. Whether they will get beyond Divona remains to be seen. The king has placed a temporary ban on travel into Mauvaissia, citing unrest."

I snorted. Unrest was an oversimplification if I'd ever heard one.

"I'll contact him and request they be allowed passage," Marttia said. "Please notify us immediately if you do uncover anything else about the bipeds."

"I will. But I would have a private word with my niece before we break communication, if that is allowable."

Marttia raised her eyebrows and glanced at me. I shrugged in reply.

"If this has anything to do with the Volker, their magic, or the mage staffs, I'm afraid that's a request I cannot—"

"It is a personal matter," my aunt replied. "No more."

"Then we'll retreat."

She and the commander immediately rose and left the room. Donal made to follow, but I touched his arm, silently asking him to remain.

"They've left, Aunt, so you can say whatever it is you need to say."

The communicator hesitated and then said, in a softer tone, "Be wary if you return to Divona, niece. And be aware there'll be consequences for us both if you attempt to reclaim what was taken."

For several seconds, I could only stare at the man who gave her voice. Then a mix of anger and uncertainty surged, and I snapped, "And what else would you have me do given the threat we all face?"

"All I'm saying is that your actions *will* have consequences. You need to be prepared this time, that's all."

Something in her reflected voice—an edge that was both fear and something else—had me frowning. "Meaning what? Now is not the time to be evasive, Aunt."

"If I could tell you more, I would. But I can't, for much the same reason you were unable to react in any appropriate manner against your father's treatment of you over the last twelve years."

It was such a simple statement, but one that once again turned my world upside down. I swallowed heavily and then said, my voice somewhat hoarse, "Why would he restrain *you*, of all people?"

"Because he feared losing control."

I frowned. "I'm still not getting—"

"Your father knew we would not stand by and watch an imposter wield the sword." The communicator's face twisted. "The bracelets were a present, gifted to me on our arrival minutes *after* you'd staked your claim on the throne.

I had no idea what they truly were until it was too late—and by that time, greater evil had been done."

Greater evil.... The words echoed harshly through my brain and my grip on the table became so fierce the stone melted around my fingertips.

"No," I denied. He couldn't have. He wouldn't have... and yet, if he *had*, it explained so much.

"Yes," my aunt replied softly.

I closed my eyes and slumped back into the seat. All these years of believing my mother had taken her life to avoid the shame of a daughter who flouted both tradition and expectation when in fact nothing could have been further from the truth.

She hadn't been ashamed of me at *all*.

She'd been killed—murdered—by the bastard who'd helped give me life.

That was why the earth had abandoned him. It wasn't because of his treatment of me—although I had no doubt that played some part given the anger I so often felt in the earth—but rather his murder of my mother.

But why take her life in the first place? Was it a simple matter of doing to *her* what he *couldn't* do to me, thanks to his belief that I was marked—and protected—by the god of war?

Or was there something deeper at work?

"I felt her passing, Nyx," my aunt said softly. "She bid me to protect you, but no matter how much I wanted to, I couldn't."

Because she'd also been trapped by the restraint bracelets. Her absence in my life made so much more sense now. Tears stung my eyes but it was rage more than regret that ran through me. The king would pay for his treachery—

even if I couldn't save Divona or Cannamore, I would ensure *that*.

Donal placed his hand over mine. I shifted our grip and twined my fingers through his, drawing comfort and some sense of calm from his touch. Whatever happened, I was not alone in this fight.

I took a deep, somewhat shuddering breath, and then said, "Are there others in the same position as you?"

"No. Only Gigurri. He controls our lands—controls Jedran—through his control of me." She paused. "But you must do whatever it takes to save this land and her people, Nyx. However diluted it may be, Racinda's blood still runs in your veins, and it will help you when all else fails."

"You're being cryptic again."

The communicator's smile was faint and, while it was little more than a reflection of my aunt's reactions, had images of my mother rising. Though there'd been two years between my mother and aunt, they could have been twins, so alike did they look.

"Yes, and I'm sorry, but much of the past knowledge has been lost and what remains has been handed down verbally from generation to generation." The communicator's mouth twisted again. "In the retelling, small details often get lost."

"If we survive this, that has to be rectified."

"I agree."

Her tone told me she didn't expect to survive and that deepened the anger stirring within. He'd taken my birthright, murdered my mother, and made me believe I'd been abandoned by everyone else who mattered. He would *not* take anything else from me. Not ever again.

"All magic has limits, be they time or distance. If you stay in Gigurri, he cannot use the force of the bracelets against you, right?"

"Yes, but even with the sword in your hand, you will need someone you can trust to back you—"

"I know," I cut in. "Which is why—when the time comes to act—I want Jedran to be present but not you."

She hesitated. "Jedran's control over the earth isn't as strong—"

"It doesn't have to be. I want him there because he's respected by the other lords." My mouth twisted. "Let's face it, many of them are going to be too worried about how I'll react to their treatment of me in the past to listen to anything I might say about the immediate future. But they'll listen to him."

"I think you underestimate your own strength and presence, niece, but I agree Jedran's attendance could be vital. Send word when you leave for Divona. Jedran will be there to back you against whatever might happen."

Trepidation stirred, but before I could question her further, the floor shuddered violently and dust rained down from the ceiling. I pressed a hand against the table, seeking a connection to the earth, trying to find out what was happening. But there was no answer from her. No link. Just anger.

She was being restrained.

The bipeds weren't waiting for sunset.

They were *here*.

An alarm rang out, a claxon sound that made me jump. I shared a quick glance with Donal then thrust upright.

"We're under attack, Aunt. We'll talk again soon."

"Be careful, Nyx," she said. "And remember, when you get to Divona, show your father exactly what he expects to see; otherwise, you won't get anywhere near him."

There was little point in answering—not when we first had to survive the Volker's latest attack before we worried about how the king would react to me returning to Divona.

As life returned to the communicator's face, Donal and I rose and sprinted for the door. Another deep shudder ran through the thick stone that surrounded us, throwing us sideways for several steps. The door jammed before it fully opened, forcing us to squeeze through sideways. Neither Marttia nor the commander was nearby, and the guard had no information as to what was happening. I pressed the halo, but either communications were down or everyone was too busy to answer my request.

Donal was already racing for the outside door. The earth heaved again, sending us staggering. I grabbed at the nearby railing to steady myself, and swore as a rain of dust and stone debris fell around me.

"Is this a quake or the bipeds?" Donal pushed away from the wall and headed for the stairs.

"The earth's being restricted, so the biped mages are up to something."

"I thought the earth said the chasm was too deep for them to cross?"

"It is." I bounded up the stairs after him. "But you saw the bastards up on the volcano—it's not like the sheer walls of the canyon would contain them for very long."

The earth shuddered again, throwing us both sideways. Donal flung a hand at the nearby wall and steadied me with the other. More stone and dust rained down as a large fracture appeared in the wall above us. This garrison might have been designed to cope with earthquakes, but if I couldn't figure out a way to stop the earth's violent response to whatever the bipeds were doing, the whole place could collapse.

We hit the walkway at the top of the stairs and were confronted by chaos. There were so many globules in the air that the fading blue of the evening sky had become a wasteland of greeny-yellow. Men and women were scrambling to their stations even as the deadly missiles fell around them, but the pulse cannons were of little use against the globules. The walkway was awash with liquefied stone and deep trenches had opened, allowing the acid to drip down into the lower levels.

Donal swore and raised a fist; the wind instantly responded, swiftly becoming a cyclonic force that gathered strength and speed, ensnaring the globules and funneling them down to the canyon's floor. Dark clouds formed overhead and thunder rumbled, a gathering promise of relief that might not arrive in time.

The cannons began to bark, a continuous rattle that was met by a guttural, inhuman cry of fury.

I ran across to the wall and looked out. While the globules continued to rain out of the forest, a couple of hundred bipeds now lined the crevice's far side. They were making no attempt to cross it, which was odd given the spiderlike way they'd clambered up and down the walls of their volcano home or flung themselves down the mountainside after us. Most of them weren't even firing their weapons. They just raised gauntleted fists to the sky and unleashed what I presumed was their war cry.

It was almost as if they were daring us to try and kill them.

The wind whipped up around me, sending me staggering. I grabbed at the wall, catching my balance, and twisted around to see a globule explode through the stone. If I'd been standing there, I would have been cut in two.

I glanced at Donal. "Thanks."

He nodded, his expression intent. The ground lurched again, and more fractures appeared in the thick walls surrounding us.

If I didn't do something, this whole damn place would come down.

In desperation—and with little hope of it actually working—I drew my knife and thrust it has hard as I could into the wall. The blade sliced into stone as easily as flesh, but for too many seconds, absolutely nothing happened. The earth continued to voice her anger in the only way she knew how, and was now a greater threat to the garrison than the few globules still slipping through Donal's storm.

Damn it, if the knife had been designed to counter the mage staffs, why wasn't it breaking through the magic holding the earth mute?

As if in answer to that question, the runes on the blade flared to life and a distant, fury-filled voice said, *What is it you wish?*

Show me what's happening.

What came wasn't pictures; it was emotion and sound. I heard the rolling thunder of hundreds of feet echoing through my ears as the bipeds stamped and jumped and taunted us from a distance. Felt the agony of stone as the acid melted its layers and washed them away, and the rise of a heat so deep and fierce it was as if I'd stepped into a furnace.

Or into a rising tide of magma.

The globules might be coming from the Wild Lands, but the biped mages weren't there. They were here, on our side of the canyon, attempting to liquefy the earth and sink the entire garrison.

Can you tell me where they are?

The heat spreads from the western edge, close to the point where the fortifications meet the canyon wall.

I ripped the knife from the wall, but the runes remained

alive; energy pulsed through my fingers and up my arm, a heartbeat that matched the fury of the earth.

But there was no time to wonder what it meant. I touched Donal's arm to grab his attention; his gaze came to mine, his eyes bright and filled with lightning.

"The mages are attacking the foundations," I said. "I'm going down to stop them."

Although, given I was without the King's Sword, I had no idea how I was going to achieve that. Frustration stirred anew, but I pushed it aside. Right now, there was nothing else I could do.

"Call if you need help," Donal said. "I'll hear, no matter what else might be going on."

I hesitated, and then rose on my toes and dropped a kiss on his cheek. "Be careful, Donal, and be ready to run."

His smile flashed, quick and bright. "Have no fear, Princess. I have no intention of dying until well *after* I've seen you claim your vengeance and your throne."

An odd mix of disappointment and annoyance surged, the latter aimed just as much at myself as him. "And your lands their freedom."

"If you think I do this solely for that, you haven't been paying attention. Go, and be safe."

I hesitated, then turned and ran for the stairs. As I clattered down them at breakneck speed, I tapped the halo and said, "Command center, are you there?"

For a frustrating second, there was no response, and then Gallego said, "Go ahead, Caracal One."

"The biped mages are attempting to liquefy the garrison's foundations. You need to warn Marttia, and then issue a garrison-wide evac order for nonessential personnel."

I half expected an argument, but once again I'd

misjudged him. As a secondary siren started up, he said, "Can you stop them?"

"I don't know. I'm about to find out."

"Not without armed support—"

"It's too dangerous—"

"Nyx," he cut in, "you *cannot* go out there alone."

"If I don't, this garrison falls."

"Which doesn't negate my statement," he said. "Scout teams one to six, meet Caracal One at the tunnel exit immediately."

There was little point in arguing and not enough time left anyway. The earth's rage grew but so too did the heat emanating from it. Steam was now rising from fissures that were rupturing the courtyard, a sure sign we were approaching the point of no return.

I flew down the remaining stairs and raced across to the tunnel's entrance. There were half a dozen men and women already waiting and more undoubtedly on the way, but we couldn't afford to delay. I motioned for the doors to be opened and then said, "Keep the bastards off me for as long as you can. Retreat into the tunnel if you need to."

"Scouts don't leave their people behind," a voice at the rear muttered. "We retreat or die together."

I didn't reply, but the likelihood of the latter was altogether too high.

The gate guards tossed me their pulse rifles. I slung one across my shoulder, held the other in my left hand, the knife in my right, and headed into the tunnel. Red flame dripped from the knife's point, giving the thick dust that filled the tunnel a bloody glow. Water and gods only knew what else flowed freely from the multitude of cracks in the ceiling, and the walls were beginning to rupture, spilling blocks of stone into the tunnel. We wove through, and around the broken mess, the sound of our steps lost to the thunder of the earth, the rattle of the pulse cannons, and the screams of the Volker.

I tightened my grip on my weapons and tried to ignore the fear that had my heart galloping and the voices screaming inside my head. I'd lived with those voices for a very long time now, and no matter how much they said I couldn't do this, that I was a nothing, a nobody who would, in the end, get us all killed, I refused to give them any credence.

After all, if they'd had their way, I would have been dead long ago.

The door leading into the canyon slid open, but there was no immediate response from the Volker—either they hadn't yet noticed or they simply didn't care.

Another shudder ran through the ground and, with a sharp crack, the ceiling above the door came crashing down, accompanied by a thick river of brown water that was earth and gods knew what else.

We edged past the mess and followed the sludge out of the door. The Volker continued to taunt the garrison from the far side of the crevice, but I was beginning to suspect it was nothing more than a show—a means of diverting our attention away from the greater evil they were currently attempting.

The earth's shuddering became more violent. I swung left and raced along the base of the wall, keeping to the shadows as much as practical while trying to avoid erupting fissures and falling debris.

There was still no response from the Volker. Either they really hadn't seen us or they didn't think we provided much of a threat to their plans.

We ran on, but with every step, the ground became

more heated, until it felt as if the soles of my boots were starting to melt.

The ground heaved again, sending me staggering sideways for several steps before I caught my balance. Another fissure erupted to our right and thick steam billowed upward; huge chunks of stone tumbled down the wall. But instead of hitting hard and bouncing away, they started to sink

The earth was liquefying.

Time had almost run out.

I couldn't see the Volker mages ahead, but that wasn't surprising if they were using a shield. I had no doubt we were closing in on them, if only because the energy pulsing through the knife had become so fierce my muscles were twitching in response.

Then the blade went completely red.

It was a warning I dared not ignore.

As more of the wall began to crumble and sink, I told everyone to stop and hold and then leapt for the nearest stone. It immediately dipped into the soil, but I only remained long enough to catch my balance before jumping over to the next one. It was a process I repeated, until the canyon wall appeared close enough to touch and the fury pulsing through the knife was so strong it was a scream that ran through my entire body.

I paused, gathering balance as the slab of rock under my feet dipped and wobbled, then raised the knife and slashed the air from left to right.

Except it wasn't just air.

It was a shield.

Hiding under its cover were three mages; two of them held staffs topped by red stones while the third held one that was clear. With them were four armored bipeds.

I pulled the blade away to close the shield, swung the rifle I was still holding over my shoulder, and then knelt. My perch wobbled alarmingly and settled deeper into the ground. As brown sludge seeped over the rock's edges, I raised a hand to locate the unseen barrier, and then followed it down to the point where it met the ground. Then, after crossing mental fingers and quickly praying to every god I could think of, I plunged the knife into the soft soil at that exact point.

I wasn't entirely sure what I'd been expecting to happen, but it certainly wasn't an explosion.

The blast was so fierce it ripped my grip away from the knife and sent me tumbling backward. I hit the almost-too-hot liquefying soil and started to sink, and blindly groped for the nearest rock. Then hands grabbed me, hauled me upright, even as a scream of fury rent the air.

The Volker on the other side of the crevice were no longer ignoring us.

And while the shield had been destroyed and both the mage who'd created it and the biped guards were down, the two earth mages hadn't moved and their dark magic was still liquefying the ground.

We had to stop them. *I* had to stop them.

But to have any hope of doing that, I had to reclaim my knife.

The wind picked up speed and began to howl; I looked up to see a stream of globules being battered left and right. Some hit the ground and began to bubble and hiss, while others simply sank silently out of sight.

Our plight, if we weren't very careful.

The armored Volker scrambled upright and charged. As one, we fired. Bullets ripped into flesh and gouged huge chunks out of plated chests, but it didn't stop them.

I swore and knelt, firing relentlessly at a biped's knees, trying to incapacitate rather than kill. But *my* knees were now sinking into ground that had been solid only a heartbeat before. The rate of liquefaction was increasing; we surely didn't have too much more time before the foundations holding this section of the wall upright were melted away.

Once that happened, the garrison was lost. I might be able to command earth to solidify and stone to rebuild, but I was only one person and it would all take time. The Volker were unlikely to give us that.

The biped's knee exploded and he crashed to the ground with a scream of fury. I immediately switched aim, firing several rounds into the back of his head. As it blew apart, the other three leapt high into the air. A hail of bullets followed their movements, shredding armored stomachs and spraying black blood and gore all over us. It didn't stop them. They tumbled over us and landed some twenty feet away, effectively blocking our retreat.

A scream went up. Not from these three but from those lining the crevice.

They were coming.

As I'd feared, the wide crevice was no real barrier for them. They were simply flinging themselves into it and dropping down. I had no doubt that at some point their momentum would allow them to catch the other edge and climb back up.

We had, at best, ten minutes.

"I'm going to stop the mages. Hold these bastards for as long as you can." I had to scream to be heard against the howl of the wind and the battle cry of the Volker. "Retreat back to the canyon wall if necessary."

"There ain't no escape from these bastards there," a

familiar voice said. Orli, the gnarled veteran who'd only recently joined my team.

"There will be," I said.

And hoped I could live up to the statement.

I swung around and ran toward the biped mages. But the earth had become so wet that with every step I sank deeper and deeper into the soil, until I was all but swimming through the muck. There was no life in it, no response, and desperate fear began to pound through my body. I couldn't command earth that held no voice, and that meant even if I *did* stop the mages, I still might not prevent the wall from coming down.

And yet both the knife and the mages sat high and dry on an island of solidity.

As the wet soil began to creep up my neck, I made a desperate lunge for the knife. My wet fingers slipped down its hilt and the blade sliced into my flesh. But I didn't let go and, as my blood began to pool around the point where blade met earth, I hauled myself up and onto solidness.

As I sucked in great gulps of air, a distant voice said, *We hear.*

The earth. Despite the fact I was surrounded by a sea of death, she was somehow hearing me.

Blood, she said. *The knife counters and the blood revives. Not far, not enough to save, but we hear.*

I had no idea if she meant save us or the garrison itself, and right now, didn't really care. *Can you contain the mages?*

The clear biped staff remains active. It restrains us.

I twisted around; while the mage who'd used it was down, his staff remained planted into the soil and the clear crystal, though cracked, still glittered with power.

Then get ready to react the minute I—

315

I stopped as an ominous rumble cut across the surrounding noise, and then looked up sharply. The goddamn curtain wall was beginning to subside.

I hit the halo, ordered a retreat, and then wrenched the knife free from the soil and thrust upright. Light whipped out from the clear crystal, lashing my body, slicing through clothes and down into skin. I swore and lunged for the staff, my knife held in front of me like a lance. Red fire flicked out from the blade to meet the white, catching and destroying each whip before they could do me any more damage. Then the tip of the blade sliced into the staff and the white light died as the crystal completely shattered. I rolled to my feet and slashed wildly at the other two staffs. The blade cut through them with ease, but as the red crystals shattered and earth spilled like blood from their hollow insides, their mages screamed and, as one, attacked. I swore and scrambled upright, only to be sent flying backward as the first mage hit hard. We thudded against the ground and air whooshed from my lungs as stars briefly danced. The mage screamed and began to bite and tear at my flesh with teeth and talons. The knife lay between us, embedded deep into his gut; I bucked in an attempt to shift him, but he was so damn heavy I barely lifted him half an inch and was now struggling to breathe.

I swore, but it was little more than a guttural wheeze of fury and fear. I jerked away from several snaps at my face, somehow pulled one hand free, then quickly shoved my thumb into the corner of his eye and gouged deep. Blood gushed over my face, and his eyeball popped out of its socket, hit my forehead, and bounced away. My stomach rose and I gagged but nevertheless smashed my hand into his other eye, destroying the rest of his sight as I forced his head up and away from me. Then, without warning, he was unceremoniously pulled from me.

The earth had finally come to my rescue.

I scrambled upright and swung around, bloody knife raised and at the ready. The second mage wasn't a threat; it had been cocooned and was slowly being smothered. The earth had vengeance on her mind.

A faint sound had me swinging around. The remnants of the scout group were struggling through the mush, trying to make it to solid ground.

And at least a dozen bipeds were now hauling themselves over the crevice's edge on this side of the canyon. I swore, knelt, and shoved the knife into the ground. *Create an earth bridge out to those men.*

The earth obeyed. As a foot-wide sliver of solid ground began to extend across the liquid soil, I unslung a pulse rifle and fired at the bipeds. They were too far away for the weapon to do much harm, but I didn't really care as long as it slowed them down enough for the scouts to reach my bridge.

A slow shudder went through the vast wall behind me— something I felt more than saw. Then, with little warning, it began to sink, slowly at first but with ever-increasing speed, until a hundred-foot length of it splintered away from the rest and began to fall vertically.

Straight at us.

TWELVE

As the scouts scrambled madly onto the sliver of solid ground I'd created, I screamed, "Run!"

I grabbed my knife, thrust to my feet, and pelted toward the sheer canyon wall. Our only hope for survival lay in me creating a shelter strong enough to protect us from the mass of stone now tumbling toward us.

I gripped my knife hard and envisioned a deep cave being punched into the black surface. The blade pulsed, the earth shuddered in response, and a fissure appeared in the wall, growing wider and deeper with every step I took toward it. Huge chunks of stone began to thunder all around me, the force of their impact shuddering through the ground. But they were little more than a warning—the main bulk of the wall was still coming. I could hear the whistle of it falling, could see its ever-increasing shadow gather all around me.

Seconds. That's all any of us had left.

I swore and dove for the fissure, tumbling through its entrance and scrambling back to my feet. I swung around, saw a dozen scouts racing toward me. Where the others were, I had no idea—the earth bridge I'd created no longer existed and the liquid soil was awash with waves as ever-larger chunks of stone thundered into it. There were no bodies in that turbulent sea, and no Volker evident beyond it. Even those who'd clambered out of the crevice had halted their charge and were currently raising gauntleted fists to the sky with what looked and sounded like glee.

One scout made it into the fissure. Then two. Three. Four. Another threw herself toward us in desperation, only to be knocked sideways and crushed under a huge slab of wall.

Two more figures appeared out of the dust, both of them bloody, the woman all but dragging the man. I shoved the knife into the nearby wall and tried to extend the stone outward to give them some sort of shelter from the deadly rain. Pain began to pulse through my head, and the hilt of the blade was slick with blood. My blood, coming not just from my sliced hand but the multiple tears and bites across my arms and shoulders. The man stumbled and fell. As he did, he wrenched himself away from his partner and pushed her forward. Hands reached past me, grabbed her, pulled her inside.

The man never made it.

He disappeared under a mountain of stone that hit the ground so hard it sent a wave of dirt and debris rolling toward our cavern. I swore, wrenched the knife free, and quickly followed the others deeper into the fissure.

Darkness enclosed us. Darkness, and air so thick it was almost choking. For several minutes none of us moved; the mountain above us groaned and shuddered, and the cries of the Volker grew in intensity.

They'd broken the garrison's spine. A full attack could be only minutes away.

Nash moved out of the gloom and stopped beside me. "We can't stay here. The garrison's going to need every soldier still standing if we're to have any hope of beating these bastards off."

There was little enough hope of that happening, and we both knew it. But all I said was, "I know."

I raised the pulsing knife. Her golden light flowed across the dusty darkness, an indication there were no mages or dark magic in close proximity.

But it also revealed the wall of rock that now filled the fissure that had saved us. We weren't getting out the same way we'd gotten in. Aside from the fact it would probably take more strength than I currently had to move that wall, doing so would only put us in the path of the Volker and death.

I took a deep breath, ignored the wash of weariness, and studied the rest of the small cavern. A number of fissures littered the surrounding walls, some of them wide enough to pass through, providing the tantalizing possibility that this cavern was, in fact, part of a deeper system running through the mountain. "Nash, see if you can contact comms, and tell them what's happened. I'll see if the tunnel over there goes anywhere."

"And the rest of us?" Orli asked.

"Tend to your wounds and grab some rest. You're not going to get much chance to do either if we do get out of here."

As they obeyed, I walked across to the largest fissure and carefully edged inside. There was very little room—I still had a pulse rifle slung across my back, and in an effort not to damage the thing, I was instead scraping my damn breasts. The uniform's tough material and the vest underneath were both offering some protection, but if the wall got any rougher, the uniform, at the very least, would start fraying.

Thankfully, the fissure opened into a wide tunnel and then into a cavern with almost cathedral-like proportions. Water tumbled down the slick black walls and a large lake dominated a good portion of the area. I walked around the water's edge, picking my way across rocks that were wet and slick with slime. Another tunnel led me away from the water cavern and sloped upward. I trudged on wearily, battling exhaustion and the desire to just give up and sit down, vaguely hoping that I wasn't getting lost and this tunnel would lead somewhere.

As it turned out, it did.

I turned a sharp corner and was confronted by a door. A metal door that was thick with slime and rust, giving every indication that it hadn't been used in years.

Even so, relief surged so thick and fast that my knees threatened to give away. I flipped the knife around, stepped up to the door, and hit the rusted metal as hard as I could with the hilt of the blade. A gong-like sound echoed loudly across the silence, but there was no immediate response. I hit it again; again, the sound echoed.

There had to be someone out there. Had to be.

I leaned back against the wall and pressed the halo. But either I was too far underground or the damn thing was on the blink again, because there was no response, which left me with the choice of waiting or forcing the thing open. Given the growing tide of weariness, I decided on the former—a good decision given that, after a few more minutes, footsteps approached.

"Who's there?" a gruff voice said.

"Caracal One. I've injured people down here—we need a medic ASAP."

"Step away from the door."

I did so. After a moment, and with a huge amounted of protest, the old door swung open, revealing not just one man but ten. All of them wearing the red gowns of the queen's guard and all with weapons pointed straight out me.

And they didn't relax even when it was blatantly obvious I was the only one in the tunnel and no threat to them.

One of their number raised a hand and pressed the circular disk sitting close to the lobe of his ear. "My queen, the intruder claims to be Caracal One." He gave her a quick but accurate description, and then added, "Can you confirm identity?"

She obviously did, because all ten guards immediately relaxed. The man in charge gave me a quick smile and then said, "How did you find yourself in this cavern?"

"That's neither here nor there. I've got injured people in the cavern beyond the underground lake, and I need to know what has happened to the garrison."

"How many are we talking about?"

"Five."

He didn't immediately answer, and his expression suggested Marttia was speaking. After a moment, he unhooked the disk from around his ear, handed it to me, and then ordered all but one of his people forward. The remaining guard motioned me to follow him and walked away without waiting to see if I did. I hooked what I presumed was the Mauvaissian equivalent of the halo around my ear and then said, "Marttia, what's happening?"

"Chaos. Why did the wall collapse? I thought you went out to stop it?"

"By the time I got there, the ground around the foundations had already liquefied. There was nothing I could do."

"You couldn't solidify or repair it?"

We came out of the tunnel into the harsh brightness of a red wall walkway, and I realized abruptly where I was—in Rodestat. "No. What happens at the garrison?"

"Despite the breach, the bipeds are being held."

That was something of a miracle given their greater numbers and the hundred-foot expanse of wall that had fallen.

"And Donal?"

"The wind rages on, but its force is waning."

I swore softly. "I need to get over there."

"No, you don't. You've already said the wall can't be repaired, and I cannot allow you to put—"

"You can't *stop* me," I bit back. "I'm the goddamn queen of Cannamore by *right*, and I'll do whatever needs to be done to protect these lands and *all* her people."

There was a brief but shocked silence before she said, amusement evident, "And the monarch finally rises. *Good.* But don't ever use that tone with me again or you and I will start your reign on very unfriendly terms."

I snorted. "Let's survive the next few hours before we start worrying about shit like that."

"I agree, which makes it all the more imperative that you—"

"Marttia, if we're going to beat these bastards, we need the King's Sword. To get that, I need to grab the restraint bracelets because the king will not let me anywhere near Divona without them."

And to get near Divona with any sort of speed, I was going to need Donal's help.

The guard turned left, into a wider corridor. An open door lay at the far end, and beyond it stars glimmered. Night had fallen while we'd been trapped underground.

"Ah," she said. "*That* is an entirely different matter. I've just ordered a transporter to take you there, but it will wait—"

"I'm not abandoning the garrison. Not unless it becomes absolutely necessary."

"Which it will," she snapped, and then took an audible breath. "But fine. Do as you wish."

I half smiled. For the first time in a long time I'd actually won a battle of wills, and no matter how slight it was, it felt good. "Have you begun evacuating Rodestat?"

"Yes, and don't presume to tell me what to do when it comes to the safety of *my* people."

Her people were also mine, but I bit the comment back and simply said, "Do you send them to Divona?"

She snorted. "That place will undoubtedly be the Volker's next target. The bulk of our population is going to Ogdour Cove, where we have a fleet of barges at anchor. They'll carry them offshore if it becomes necessary."

Meaning I had a lot to learn when it came to the territories I might one day rule. I had no idea that the Mauvaissians were, in any way, seafarers.

A carriage pulled up as we exited the corridor. I ran down the steps and climbed inside. The driver immediately took off, his speed such that I was thrown backward into the seat. He'd obviously been told to hurry.

The main street was quiet and empty, and the houses and buildings on either side dark. It was only when we neared the no man's land that divided the city from the garrison that we slowed, and it quickly became evident why —there was a steady stream of people and vehicles coming into Rodestat from the garrison.

As the driver wove his way through the exodus, I opened the window and leaned out; thick black smoke billowed from the section where the wall had come down, and flames leapt skyward, bright in the darkness. Lightning flashed overhead, but it barely held enough power to illuminate the top of the remaining curtain wall, let alone any of the soldiers who were up there fighting for survival. Another flash peeled through the darkness, but this time it was more over the peaks. And in the fading glow, there was movement.

An ashy gray mass of flesh was crawling silently down the mountainside toward the garrison.

Panic surged and I hit the ear disk. "Marttia, are you in direct contact with the commander?"

"Yes—why?"

"There's a massive force of Volker coming down from the top of the mountain—the breach attack is a ruse. The garrison has ten minutes, if that, before they're swamped."

"May the gods help us all," she muttered before the line went dead. I hoped it was because she was contacting Gallego and not because the bipeds had somehow disrupted communications.

I thumped the wall between the driver and me and ordered him to hurry. As the vehicle lurched forward once again and people scattered and swore at us, I swung the rifle from my shoulder and restocked the chambers with what little ammo I still carried. Then I drew my knife and took a deep breath in a somewhat useless attempt to calm the fear and growing sense of horror.

As preparations went, it was pretty goddamn useless, but there was little else I could do. Raising the earth wasn't going to work—I simply didn't have the strength to make a wave of rock and stone large enough to swamp the sheer number of bipeds now coming at us. I doubted if even the king and my brother *combined* could do that—even if they had been capable of controlling the earth—especially given that Racinda and her people had failed to stop these creatures not once but twice.

Our best chance of survival was to regroup behind Rodestat's solid walls—and then find some way to stop the Volker doing to *that* city what they'd already done to the garrison.

What did surprise me was the fact they hadn't already attacked Rodestat, especially given they'd clambered up that mountain without anyone actually noticing. But maybe they simply wanted to deliver a killing blow on the garrison first, thereby destroying the city's most obvious defense before they turned their attention and their resources to the city itself. If the utterly straight line of the tunnel they'd created through both dead lands and the Skaran grasslands was any indication, they were creatures who didn't believe in any major deviation from a set course.

The carriage swept through the garrison gates into the chaos Marttia had mentioned. Thick black smoke filled the air and there were people, bipeds, and bodies absolutely everywhere. The pulse cannons were still barking, an indication that soldiers remained on the curtain wall, but most seemed to be either on the various levels or here on the ground; they were all still fighting, still trying to win.

I flung the door open, caught sight of several stretcher-bearers, and waved them over. "Use the carriage and get as many as the wounded out of here as possible. The whole place is about to be overrun."

Their faces went pale, but they the nevertheless hit their halos and began a rapid series of orders. The carriage driver started to protest but shut up at my glare.

I spun and ran for the nearest stairs. A fierce scream shattered the silence and jerked my gaze up—a biped had launched from the walkway two flights above and was arrowing straight at me. I didn't stop; I simply raised the rifle and fired until his blood and brains rained around me and his body slapped onto the steps behind me.

I didn't look back. I just kept on running. Another Volker came at me. I ducked his blow and used the knife and the force of his momentum to gut him. He screamed in fury, twisted around, leapt again; I rolled underneath him, somehow avoided his slashing talons, then spun and fired at the back of his head. As his brains joined his intestines on the walkway, I ran into our bunkroom, grabbing the edge of the door to steady myself as I spun around the corner and into my cubicle. But as I wrenched the locker open and slapped on the restraint bracelets, the garrison halo came to life. "This is a code one evacuation order for all personnel. Follow retreat procedures immediately and leave all possessions behind."

I hit the halo and said, "Commander, this is Nyx. Have you heard from Donal?"

"Not for at least ten minutes, but he was still up on the wall last report."

I swore and ran out of the room. The black smoke was even thicker and the walkways more crowded as remaining personnel began to evacuate. But the Volker weren't about to let anyone slip past their talons without a fight, and multiple flashes lit the darkness, some of them green-yellow, others the bright white of the pulse rifles.

I scrambled down to the courtyard, raced across to the stairs that led to the top of curtain wall, and pushed my way through those coming down as quickly as possible, but many of them were badly injured and being carried, and that by necessity slowed me down.

Then a familiar voice yelled, "Nyx!"

I looked up, scanning the bloody features of those above me for several seconds before I recognized one. "Raj, have you seen Donal?"

"He and his team are providing cover for the retreat. Where are you going? Didn't you hear the evac order?"

"I did, but I'm needed up top." I squeezed his arm as I passed. "Keep alert down there—the bipeds have infiltrated the garrison."

If he made a reply, I didn't hear it. I was already pushing on. The higher I climbed, the thicker the smoke became, and the more the air stunk of fear and death. The wind was little more than a whisper now and provided no relief from the gritty soot staining the air. And that could only mean Donal's strength was giving out.

A heartbeat later, the rattle of the cannons silenced, replaced by the pulse of rifles. But there were too few of them, given the weight of bipeds coming at us.

I swore and raced up the remaining steps. Two bloody figures dragged an unconscious Donal toward the stairs while another seven—including Margreet, Donal's second—held their ground and fired at what looked like a wall of ashy flesh and glistening talons.

I swung the rifle over my shoulder then shoved the knife into the wall and said, "Rise up and smother the bastards."

A rumble ran through the stone, gathering speed and intensity as it raced toward the oncoming Volker. It passed the scouts and then rose up in a wave that drowned the Volker in stone.

But the walkway under my feet vibrated with movement—there was at least a hundred more Volker climbing the broken wall. We had minutes, if that.

"Scouts, retreat," I yelled.

As the scouts obeyed, gauntleted fingers appeared at the

top of the break point, and then several Volker hauled them-selves up. I took another of those deep, shuddering breaths that did very little to bolster my strength, but just as I was about to order another wave, a metallic creaking caught my attention. I frowned, stepped away from the wall, and looked up. Several of the struts holding the old water tanks in place had bent, and both of them had gained a rather precarious lean. If they gave way....

I grabbed Margreet's arm and said, "The cannons—are they out of ammo?"

"The ones near the breach are, but it's possible those down further aren't." She frowned. "Why?"

"I'm thinking the bipeds are in need of a bath."

She glanced up and then grinned. "I like your thinking. Roz, take over and get clear of this place."

As the other six rattled down the stairs, her gaze returned to me. "Let's do this."

I freed my knife and then ran after her, leaping over rocks, acid trenches, and broken bodies until I'd reached a cannon. I checked it was loaded, hit the standby button to activate it, and then swung the heavy weapon around and up. We fired as one—Margreet at the Volker who were scrambling over the breach and me at the compromised supports holding the tanks up. My arms shook with the force of each shot and my head was beginning to pound in time with the cannon's rattling, but the struts were far stronger than they looked. Then, with what sounded like the groan of a dying beast, two supports on the first tank gave way and it began to topple, slowly at first and then with gathering speed. Water spilled over its edge and thun-dered down to the walkway; rather than run through the torrent, the Volker turned and sprinted for the safety of the breach, flinging themselves over the edge, as if desperate to get away. A third strut gave way and the tank came down with a massive clang, a noise that reverberated through the stone as the walkway gave way under its weight and several battlements were shattered. The rest of the water whooshed out of the tank, a fierce tide that flooded the wall and poured over the edge. The Volker who'd escaped the first wash were snatched up by the second. Their screams filled the air as they were swept over the edge and cast to the ground far below.

I switched aim to the second tank; after a dozen hits, it too began to fall. As a backwash of water swirled around our feet, I released the cannon and said, "Let's get out of here."

Margreet didn't argue. She simply took off with the speed of a horned swift. We'd barely reached the stairs when the second tank came down; already stressed stone gave way under its impact and huge chunks of both wall and walkway were sent flying in all directions. But it was the huge whooshing that had me quickly looking back; a wall of water was sweeping down the stairs toward us.

"Margreet, wrap your arms around the railing and hang on!"

I lunged for the metal, locked my arms around it, and then braced as best I could. The water hit a heartbeat later; the sheer force of it snatched my breath and swept my feet away. My arms slipped down the metal and thudded hard into a support. I gritted my teeth against the scream that tore up my throat and hung on grimly as water, stones, and even bodies pummeled me. It seemed to take forever for the flow to ease, though in reality, it was only a few seconds. I regained my footing and did a quick check; a few cuts and scrapes but no major injuries. My knife was still in place, but the rifle was who knows where. Then I remembered

Margreet and quickly twisted around; she was nowhere in sight. I released the railing and then ran down the stairs as fast as I dared. The last thing I needed with several hundred Volker about to gatecrash the garrison was to fall and break a leg.

I found Margreet two levels down, squashed into the corner of the landing. I quickly pressed my fingers against her neck but couldn't find a pulse. I swore, turned her head so the water could drain from her mouth, and then began resuscitation. After only a few seconds, she started coughing and vomiting up water. I pushed her onto her side so that she didn't choke, well aware that I might be doing more harm than good if she had other injuries. But if she didn't regain full consciousness, didn't start moving, we were both dead. The bipeds attacking the main wall might have been swept away, but that didn't mean anything when there was a greater force coming at us from above. I had no idea why they hadn't hit us yet, and no intention of finding out.

After another few seconds, her eyes opened and she said, voice hoarse, "Did a fucking house just fall on me or what?"

Despite the tension rolling through me, despite the knowledge that the Volker were coming, I smiled. "You able to stand?"

"Yeah," she said, and began to get up.

I rose with her, steadying her when she wobbled. She didn't say anything else, just gripped the railing and moved down the steps, slowly at first and then with increasing speed and confidence. Pools of water now covered much of the courtyard, oily expanses in which bodies lay, some of them human, many not.

There was no one else in the courtyard. No one alive, at any rate. But the gates into no man's land were still manned and there was a force of ten red-clad soldiers running toward us. Marttia had sent her finest to our rescue.

The Volker's howls filled the air and blobs of yellow-green splattered all around us; some melted the ground while others disappeared into the nearby pools, causing the water's dark surface to bubble and steam.

As Marttia's soldiers dropped to one knee and provided cover fire, I swooped to pick up a pulse rifle to replace the one that had been pulled from my shoulder. A quick check of the chamber revealed fifty rounds. That was all that stood between me and possible death. Fifty rounds and Marttia's soldiers.

It would be enough.

It *had* to be enough.

The ground started shuddering under the weight of the approaching Volker. They lined several levels now, but not all of them were armed or firing. Which was probably just as well—the twenty or so who *were* made our retreat difficult enough.

A flash of yellow-green flew past my ear and hit one of Marttia's soldiers. He started screaming, but it didn't last long as his face, neck, and vocal cords melted away. As he fell, another took a hit in the arm; she immediately dropped into the water and steam rose as the acid was neutralized.

I risked a look over my shoulder; the Volker were everywhere. Racing along the walkways, crawling down the walls, or leaping from level to level. And yet none of them were venturing out onto the courtyard.

Why?

There was so damn many here now that they could overrun us with very little loss of life. And yet they remained on the upper levels, for the most part content with screaming at us.

It made no sense.

Then I remembered the bipeds who'd run from the water spill long before the tanks had actually come down, and my gaze fell to the black pools covering much of the courtyard. Maybe it wasn't just their weapons that were neutralized by the water.

Maybe *they* were.

Given they were born out of the deep heat of the earth, it certainly made an odd sort of sense. It also gave us another means of protecting our cities.

We reached Marttia's guards; they rose as one, surrounded us, and continued to lay cover fire as we all retreated. I unleashed the rifle, but my shots were lost in the noise of nine other weapons and had little impact on the bipeds.

We weren't going to stop them—not with these weapons, and especially not when their numbers were so much greater. The minute one went down, three others took its place. And, right now, they were racing for the rear wall; if they reached that, they could avoid the water in the courtyard and get to the gate.

If they reached it before we did, we were all dead.

The knife began to burn against my hip. I switch the rifle from my left hand to my right and then pulled the knife free. Rays of golden light spun through the darkness and energy pulsed through my fingers—one that matched the rising heartbeat of the earth.

I might not be touching her, but we were nevertheless connected. *Seal the cracks*, she whispered.

My gaze went to the still open gates and the broken, water-slicked landscape beyond it.

"Stop shooting and run," I shouted. "We need to get into no man's land before they do."

"That won't stop them," one man replied.

"No, but I think water will—if there's enough of it."

His quick frown suggested he either didn't believe or didn't understand, and there was no time to explain. But the halo remained open and Marttia was undoubtedly listening. I had no doubt she *would* know exactly what I meant—and what I intended to do.

We ran as hard as we could for the gates. The Volker screaming got louder, and across the various levels, the stream of ashy gray racing for the wall increased. It was going to be tight.

The gate guards stepped inside and began firing. Bipeds fell from the upper levels, but it didn't stop them. Hell, even reaching the gates and no man's land wouldn't. Not until the fissures were all blocked.

Order it done, said the earth.

I gripped the knife tight and did so. The earth shuddered and shook, and the knife burned brighter as energy flowed from my body, a wave that would only weaken me further. One that would kill me if I weren't very careful. But better that death than the one the Volker would give me.

We made it to the gates. As they locked into position, I spun around, shoved the knife into one of them, and ordered stone and metal to fuse. The ground flowed upwards and sealed the doors. My head was now pounding so fiercely spots were beginning to dance in front of my eyes and my vision wavered. But I wasn't finished yet.

I spun and ran after the others. Behind me, the Volker screamed. I didn't need to look around to know they had reached the rear wall and were now flinging themselves down it.

We had a couple of minutes, if we were lucky.

The rattle of a pulse cannon started up and the air began to sing with the sound of their bullets. But the garrison wall was heavy with the weight of the bipeds, and even a dozen pulse cannons were never going to be enough to take them all out. Not when there were hundreds more still coming down the mountain.

We were splashing through an inch of water now, and the earth wasn't finished yet. As more and more of the fissures closed up, I stumbled and would have fallen had not one of Marttia's men grabbed my arm and not only kept me upright but hauled me on. Rodestat's gates loomed high above us, and the pulse cannons continued to rattle—but those flashes weren't flying over our heads now. They were aimed at the canyon walls on either side. The Volker were climbing high and going around the source of the water.

"I hope that wire fence holds," Margreet growled. "Or this escape is going to be a very short-lived one."

"It'll hold," a rather swarthy-looking woman said.

"If it doesn't, the city is gone," I said.

She looked at me, her expression grim. "It'll hold."

I wasn't entirely sure who she was trying to convince—herself or me.

The huge gate swung open. Soldiers flowed out of it, holding what appeared to be pulse rifles, only twice their size. They didn't open fire. They didn't need to. A good three inches of water now covered the canyon floor and the bipeds weren't going anywhere near it.

My guess had been right.

We hit the safety of Rodestat. Relief swam through me, followed swiftly by exhaustion so deep that I probably would have fallen if not for the grip of the soldier. All I wanted to do was lie down somewhere and drop into a deep coma, but my job wasn't done just yet. As the mighty metal doors clanged shut, I pulled my arm free, staggered over to them, and dropped heavily to my knees. Pain reverberated through every inch of my body, but I dredged strength from who knew where and shoved the knife into the ground, ordering the stone to rise on the other side of the door and meld onto the metal, sealing the city against the rising tide of water. Then, as my strength faded and the darkness of unconsciousness loomed, I ordered a channel be created halfway up the canyon's vertical wall so that the rising water had an escape and wouldn't flood over the wall and into the city.

With my heart laboring and my head feeling like it was about to explode, I wrenched the knife free and somehow shoved it home. As the screams of the Volker and the rattling booms of the pulse cannons echoed, I finally gave in to the looming darkness and collapsed.

When I next awoke, it was once again to the awareness of being watched. A smile tugged at my lips, but I didn't immediately open my eyes, instead listening to the murmur of the earth and to the weight of movement both close and distant. Neither spoke of danger.

As relief stirred, I opened my eyes. Donal lay on his side in the bed next to mine. He had a sheet across his hips in what I presumed was a vague attempt to protect his modesty, though I very much doubted he'd actually put it there, given the man didn't seem to know the meaning of the word.

"Hey," he said, with a smile that creased the corners of his bright eyes. "We survived yet another encounter with the Volker."

"Which is proof that miracles do indeed happen." Or, at the very least, proof that I was indeed favored by the god of war. I reached for the glass of water sitting atop the nearby bedside table; various body parts greeted this movement with a resumption of pain, and a muted ache remained in the back of my head. But for the most part, I felt pretty good.

His gaze dropped to my wrists and his smile faded a little. "I see you're wearing the bracelets again—why would you do that given all they represent?"

"Because we'll need them if we're to have any hope of getting near my father or the King's Sword." I paused. "Do you know what happens outside?"

Thanks to the murmurings of the earth, I was well aware that—aside from several attacking arms made up of at least fifty bipeds—their main force was still hunkered down on the other side of the garrison. But the earth couldn't tell me what they were doing beyond the fact they no longer tunneled, nor could she inform me what had happened in the Red City while I'd been unconscious.

"Rodestat's fence holds against the bipeds," Donal said, his smile fading slightly, "and the dam you created has prevented them from using no man's land."

"And the globules? Has Rodestat sustained much damage from them?"

"No, because for some reason, they're not firing."

Once again relief stirred. It might be a short-lived reprieve, but it at least gave us time to regroup and plot our next course of action.

"Given the sheer volume they used on the garrison, maybe they're waiting for supplies to be restocked." I gulped down the water and almost immediately the dull ache in my head eased. I grabbed the nearby jug and poured myself another. "Or maybe they're just figuring out a different means of getting into the city."

"Possibly." He shrugged and sat up. The sheet slipped from his hips and I tried to avoid staring, which was ridiculous given I'd already seen all the man had to offer. "My father sent word that eleven air mages are on their way—it's as many as he could send without completely stripping the five tribes."

That many air mages would definitely give us an advantage against the bipeds and their globule weapons. And yet, if the biped mages decided to bunker in and dig, we'd still be in very big trouble. "How long before they get here?"

"According to the wind, about five hours."

Surprise had my eyebrows rising. "How long have we been out?"

"Close to twenty-four."

"No wonder I'm goddamn hungry."

"I noticed."

It was said so blandly that my gaze jumped to his. "For food."

"Of course."

His tone was disbelieving.

I grabbed my pillow and tossed it at him. He caught it with a laugh, and then said, "When and if we survive what still comes, you and I will be having a serious discussion about that hunger of yours. In the meantime, there's food over on the table."

"You know where you can shove your serious discussion, don't you, highlander?"

I flicked off the blanket, then rose and padded across to the table. It held several platters of meats, cheese, and delicious-smelling, still warm flatbread, and my belly rumbled in happy anticipation.

The *other* hunger would have to wait until survival was ensured.

Donal rose and approached. A delicious sort of tension wound through me and my breath caught. He stopped behind me, so close that his breath brushed the back of my neck and the heat of his body rolled across my skin. Pinpricks of delight skittered down my spine, but he didn't touch me. I didn't know whether to growl in frustration or sigh in relief.

Now was *not* the time for passion.

But that was the sensible part of me speaking. The long-ignored, long-caged part that had been given no choice for far too long wanted to revel in her freedom, to turn and pursue desire while it still existed, and while it still could. It very much felt as if the two parts of my soul were at war, and I wasn't sure which would win. Or which one I *wanted* to win.

Because it wasn't just a simple matter of choosing desire. Not with this man.

"If you don't want a discussion," he murmured, "what do you want?"

You. The word lingered on my tongue, but I just couldn't say it out loud. Which was beyond stupid given I'd waited twelve long years to be free to feel anything this strongly—to choose whom I wanted to choose, and not be forced to bed someone at the will of the king.

But maybe *that* freedom was part of the problem, if only because once I'd delved the depths of passion with the man standing so very close behind me, I might never want to lose it.

And we were two very different people with two very different agendas.

Or was *that* nothing more than fear speaking? Was it a

decade of restraining emotions and fearing to take what I wanted because pain would undeniably follow?

I really *didn't* know.

"You didn't answer the question, Princess."

Warmth teased my neck, a touch so light it could have been his breath. But it wasn't.

I licked suddenly dry lips and said, "What I want doesn't matter right now."

"What you want will *always* matter." *To me.* He didn't say those words aloud, but they seemed to hover in the air anyway.

That featherlight touch moved down my spine. I shivered and crossed my arms, fighting the desire to just turn around and take.

Now was *not* the time.

Not when we had so little of it.

And yet, if I didn't take the time now, I might well regret it in the future.

I took a deep breath that did nothing to calm the racing of my pulse or the deeper down ache.

"That still doesn't answer my question, Princess."

The featherlight touch left my skin and disappointment screamed through me.

I briefly closed my eyes, gathered the unraveling wisps of control, and said, "Time. I want time."

"To decide?"

I turned and placed a hand on his chest. His skin was warm under my fingertips, his heartbeat strong. As strong as the man himself. As fierce as the desire I could see.

"No. I want time to explore. To know every bump and bruise on your body intimately, to feel your reaction to my touch, to taste your desire as it beads your skin." I raised my gaze to his and saw the heat of desire and the glitter of understanding. He knew what I was about to say, but I said it anyway. Because I not only needed him to know what I wanted, but also what I feared. "But most of all, I want the time *and* the courage to explore what might lie between us *beyond* the realms of mere passion and sex."

For too many seconds he didn't say anything. Then he simply raised my fingers from his chest to his lips. His kiss was light, barely a brush of heat over skin, but it nevertheless held an odd sort of promise. One that had my heart racing and my head spinning.

"That is also my wish."

"Good."

I ordered the bracelets to release and let them drop to the floor. The last thing I wanted was them on my wrists; they held too many memories—and far too much heartache and darkness—to be worn at a time when the choice of sex was finally mine.

I raised my lips to his and kissed him. He released my hand, wrapped his arms around my waist, and then drew me even closer as our kiss deepened. It was a long, slow exploration intensified by the close press of our bodies. I could feel the heat in his skin, the fierceness of his desire, the rapid beating of his pulse. Knew that he could feel the same in me.

But a kiss, however deep and satisfying, wasn't enough now. I wanted more, a whole lot more. I broke away, kissed his neck, his shoulders, his chest, and then followed the long line of hair down his washboard stomach, tasting and teasing and nipping. I explored every inch of his body with hand and tongue, until he quivered with desire and the scent of his need stung the air. Only then did I let him do the same to me. And when the desire that burned between

341

us became so fierce the air practically hummed, I pushed him back onto the bed and straddled him.

But I went no further; instead, I leaned forward, kissed him gently, and said, "Thank you."

The intensity of his gaze said he not only understood the intent behind my words but also suggested he'd do far more if I only asked.

But all he said was, "I'd say you're welcome, but I'd rather not have any sort of conversation at this particular point in time."

I raised an eyebrow, a grin twitching my lips. "I thought highlanders were renowned for their stamina?"

"We are. But the particular form of stamina we're talking about involves two people and an intimate connection. The latter is sadly lacking as of this moment."

"So you're saying, in a roundabout but polite way, to shut up and get back to business?"

"Indeed I am, Princess. Indeed I am."

I sighed, a heavy sound that made it seem the whole situation was nothing but an ordeal. "Only if I must. And only if satisfaction is guaranteed."

A smile twitched his lips. "It is, Princess, but if you'd rather not proceed, we can always—"

"Don't you *dare* even think about moving, highlander."

And with that, I shifted position and drove him deep inside. It felt so good, so perfect, so unlike anything I'd ever experienced before that for several heartbeats, I held still and just enjoyed. And then desire surged with renewed force and that moment was gone, swept away by the gathering tide of need. We moved, slowly at first, then with increasing urgency. Pleasure was a wave that rose ever higher, until it felt like every part of me was thrumming with desire and my body was wound so tightly I'd surely shatter. I couldn't think, could hardly even breathe.

Then rapture hit, everything did shatter, and oh, it was glorious.

For several minutes afterward, neither of us moved. I don't think either of us *could* move.

Eventually, I slipped to one side and propped up on one arm. "Well, that was certainly a pleasant way to waste half an hour or so."

"It was indeed." He raised a finger and traced the line of my cheek down to my lips. I kissed it lightly. "Had we more time, I'd suggest we waste a few more hours. But the wind informs me Marttia is on her way, so we'd best go take a very quick shower and get dressed. She might be well aware of your splendor, but she has never witnessed mine, and I won't flaunt what she can't have."

I raised an eyebrow. "This from the man who only very recently admitted brazenly flaunting his wares to all and sundry at a Falorian alehouse?"

"All too true, and if she were alone, I would indeed gift her a glimpse of my magnificence. But Rutherglen accompanies her, and he's known for his strong views on protocol and nakedness."

Rutherglen was a name I'd heard only once in passing—he was one of four nominated heirs who'd go into battle for the throne on Marttia's death. "Meaning you have no desire to advertise your wares in the presence of an unappreciative audience?"

"Precisely." He rolled off the bed, then caught my hand and tugged me upright. "Come along, Princess. They'll be here in five or so minutes."

"Five or so minutes is not long enough by half."

A wicked grin touched his lips. "You might be surprised at what can be achieved in five minutes."

As it turned out, I was. Pleasantly so. By the time Marttia appeared, we were both sitting at the table and the bracelets were back on my wrists. Her gaze swept us and a slight smile touched her lips. But she didn't immediately say anything, just walked across to the table and sat down opposite us. Rutherglen—a powerful, thickset man with a shaved head and cold black eyes—sat to Donal's right.

"We've word the Westal air mages will be here later this evening," Marttia said, her gaze on Donal. "Will their presence enable you to bring the full force of the elements against the bipeds?"

"To a point," Donal replied. "But if their mages use shields, as they have in the past, then no."

"Meaning we need to stop the mages before we can rain hell on these bastards," Marttia commented. "Rodestat's fence line will hold back any who attack from ground level, but it cannot stop those who go under or over."

"You've had no word from my aunt?"

"Not as yet." She frowned. "And the fact of the matter is, whether or not they arrive is irrelevant. Neither they nor the air mages can cause any great harm to the Volker until their mages are taken out. And *that* means you have to return to Divona and claim what is yours."

My gut clenched. What she said was nothing less than the truth, and something I'd wanted from the moment the king had taken what was mine and then destroyed my world. But now that the moment for confrontation had finally arrived, all the fear—all the hurt and self-doubt driven by years of being told I was unworthy, that I didn't matter—rose like a ghost, threatening to smother me.

I pushed my plate away and crossed my arms on the

table. And hoped, with every inch of my being, that the inner turmoil didn't show. "There's one major problem—the king has threatened to incarcerate me the minute I return."

"He wouldn't dare—not when you're a part of an official Mauvaissian delegation."

I snorted. "If you think that, you don't know the king very well at all."

"Whatever his reasons for refusing our request for additional resources, he won't act against a delegation. He can't afford the unrest it will cause amongst the others."

A statement I would have agreed with little over a year ago, but these days, his decisions were governed more often by emotion and mood. My gaze flicked to the silent Rutherglen. "I gather that's why an heir accompanies you? He's leading the delegation?"

"Indeed," she said. "Rutherglen is well-known and respected in Divona. Your father has already agreed to my request for a meeting of the full council—it's set for tomorrow evening."

"Such agreement actually means little," I said. "He's just as likely to send either my brother or another representative to speak on his behalf as attend such a meeting himself."

The real problem, however, was the fact that the council only rarely met in the great hall. And despite the fact that Vin often used the sword in our practice sessions, he didn't generally carry it on his person. It was instead kept in an ornate but very secure display case near the glass throne in the great hall—a gilded reminder to all those who attended him there of the power he could no longer actually control. "Besides, it takes three days to get—"

"For Divona's haulers, yes, because the treaty only grants you access along set energy lines and areas. We, of course, have no such restrictions. The sprinters will get you there by dusk."

Of course, they didn't, and it was stupid of me not to have realized that.

"When do we leave?" Donal asked.

"Within the hour."

She rose, as if that was all there was to be said—and I guessed to a woman who'd won her crown by taking the life of her sister, it was.

"You do realize," I said softly, "that what we plan here amounts to treason against a sitting king."

"The treason was committed twelve years ago," she said bluntly. "We merely seek to right a wrong."

"That's not how it's going to be viewed by many."

She shrugged. "Their view isn't important right now. Claiming your birthright and saving this land *is*. They'll soon come crawling forward offering acceptance and seeking forgiveness once the true depth of the danger is known."

I hoped she was right about one but wasn't sure I'd ever be capable of the other. But there was little point in saying anything, especially when I had no more choice in my actions now than I did when the restraint bracelets were keeping me in check.

If I wanted to save this land—and I did—then I would have to find courage and do the one thing that had kept me going through the darkness of the last twelve years.

Confront the king.

And perhaps even kill him.

THIRTEEN

I rested my head against the sprinter's wall and watched the city of my birth grow larger on the horizon. Dusk was settling in, and the long orange streak of metal that was Divona's mighty wall gleamed brightly against a sky filled with hues of yellow and pink. Lights glowed atop the evenly spaced towers, and although we were too far out as yet for the eye of any of them to fall on us, I had no doubt our presence had been noted and reported.

My gaze drifted up the city's tiers to the castle. Divona's strength had never truly been challenged—not after the Westal Ranges had fallen to her rule—and it had led to a belief that Divona, her people, and most importantly, her king, were unstoppable. Unbeatable.

The Volker had certainly proven just how wrong that belief was. But would me taking up the sword and revealing the true depth of the lies the king and my brother had told over the last twelve years convince the council to believe otherwise?

Or would they be in such fear of my reaction to their

abuse that they'd side with the king even in the face of a greater threat?

I suspected the latter, and that, in turn, meant no matter what else happened, there *would* be casualties in my quest to reclaim what had been taken. If I was sure of nothing else, it was the fact that the king—once he realized what was happening, what I intended to do—would go down fighting.

But there'd be even more casualties—possibly a whole continent of them—if I just walked away, as some dark inner corner of my soul begged me to do. Even if I could live with the guilt of such an action, it wasn't like I'd remain safe for very long.

At least we'd have one ally in the council's midst. I'd sent word of our departure via the earth to my aunt and had been told Jedran had already left for Divona. I really hoped his support would calm the other lords, because the last thing we needed right now was a true bloodbath.

I flexed my fingers, trying to ease the tension gathering within. It hadn't helped the dozen or so times I'd tried it in the last hour, and it didn't help now.

The small movement seemed to wake Donal, because he stirred and said, "Are you okay?"

"No, I'm not."

He took my hand in his and twined our fingers. "He will *not* hurt you. Not ever again. Not while I still have breath in my body."

His words had that inner part of my soul—the part I'd so fiercely protected for so long—rejoicing. "I'd really prefer you not dying, Donal. It would be rather inconvenient given future plans of seduction."

"Oh, I have *every* intention of fulfilling those plans of yours, of that you can be assured." He paused, his expression contemplative. "Although there has been many a tale of

Wildmen rising from the dead. It would seem the promise of great sex has great power."

"Only a Westal Wildman would even believe something like that was possible," Rutherglen commented.

He was sitting on the opposite side of the carriage, his arms crossed and eyes closed. His expression gave nothing away, so it was hard to tell if he was joking or not. I suspected, given what Donal had said about the man, that he wasn't.

"That's because we are great believers in the fact that anything is possible if you want it bad enough," Donal said evenly. "And I've actually witnessed love snatch life from the jaws of death."

Rutherglen snorted and opened his eyes. The coldness remained, despite the hint of amusement playing about his mouth. "I daresay there was a healer or medic involved in that feat somewhere."

"Indeed, but sometimes neither is enough. The will has to be strong for life to remain."

"You know," I said casually but with a tightness gathering in my throat. "I'd rather not be discussing the ins and outs of death when we're about to meet two men who have tried to do nothing *other* than kill me for the last twelve years."

Rutherglen's ungiving gaze met mine. "Then let's instead discuss what happens if a representative takes the king's seat at the council meeting rather than the king himself."

I smiled, though it felt tight. "Simple. You don't deal with whoever is sent and demand an audience with the king. You are not only Marttia's representative but one of her heirs and have the right to such if so requested."

He nodded. Though his expression still wasn't giving

anything away, I suspected he was probably more aware of his rights than me. That it had been a test, however small. "And once we get that audience?"

"The earth will rise—"

"The air will defend," Donal cut in.

"—and I will claim what is mine," I finished, gently squeezing his hand. "But neither the king nor my brother will go down without a fight."

"And that's what you plan?" Rutherglen said evenly. "To take them both down?"

"I don't believe I'll have any other choice, although I would prefer to keep my brother alive."

Rutherglen raised an eyebrow—a small movement that hinted at contempt. "After all he has said and done?"

"All he has said and done is the *reason* I want him alive." Though my voice was flat, it nevertheless ran with deep fury. "I want to visit on him *exactly* what he and the king gave to me."

"Ah," Rutherglen said. "*That* is most excellent news."

His response wasn't what I'd been expecting. "Why?"

"Because he has in the past rebuffed both Marttia's overtures and mine."

Surprise ran through me—not because Rutherglen had propositioned Vin, but because *Marttia* had. "Really?"

"Yes." He uncrossed his arms and sat upright. "He did in fact say that he would rather lie with dogs than barbarians such as us."

"I'm surprised she allowed him to live after a statement like that."

"She *was* tempted to gut him but decided revenge was a platter best served cold."

"When did this happen?" I glanced briefly out the

window; the drawbridge was lowering. The churning in my gut grew stronger.

"Three years ago."

Which was well into her "relationship" with me. "Given her preference runs to women rather than men, I gather she was after something other than just sex?"

He smiled, though it held little in the way of warmth. "What can't be won by force can sometimes be gained by succession."

I blinked, and then laughed. Only Marttia would be devious enough to try and gain the glass throne by bearing my brother's bastard.

The carriage rolled onto the drawbridge. The magnetic exchange technology cut out, replaced by the noisier impeller units as we moved into the long tunnel that led into Divona.

Had it only been weeks since I'd left this place? It felt like a lifetime longer. So much had changed—both within me and without—and those changes hadn't yet finished. But no matter what happened over the next few hours, I was no longer alone—and that was the most welcome change of all.

"Once we reach the royal district," I said, as the carriage began to weave its way through the tiers, "neither of you are to look at me or speak to me. The king has to believe I've been cowed by Donal, or this will all be for naught."

"What happens if you're forbidden to enter the council chambers?" Rutherglen asked. "Or he follows through with his threat to lock you up?"

"We'll deal with it when and if it happens. But given that—as far as he's concerned—I'm here at Marttia's request, I doubt he will. Not immediately, anyway." It was said with a surety that I wasn't feeling. If the king was anything, it was unpredictable.

"If for no other reason," Donal commented, "than to bask in the glory of his own cleverness and superiority."

Rutherglen raised an eyebrow. "I would disguise your dislike of the man far better than you currently are, highlander, or we'll all end up in the hangman's keep rather than the great hall."

"He's already locked me up in that wretched place once; he'll *not* do it a second time." Donal's gaze came to mine. "How do you plan to gain access to the sword?"

I hesitated. "It will depend on where the meeting happens."

And *that* very much depended on the king's mood. On whether he felt the need to remind Marttia's representatives of his position and power.

But it also depended on how much more his mind had degenerated in the brief time I'd been away. I suspected his grip on reality had fallen greatly, because surely no sane and sensible king would ignore the warnings of his frontline commanders or their urgent requests for additional troops.

"But no matter where it *is* held," I continued, "he's going to be wary—"

"Then we do our best to put his mind at ease," Rutherglen said. "And give the appearance that this is nothing more than a plea for help instead of the intended treasonous takeover of a sitting king."

"It's only treasonous if we fail," Donal commented, amusement evident.

"Once we *do* move," I said, with a wry look his way, "we'll have to contain the situation quickly. If we're in the council chambers, we'll have to force everyone into the hall. The only way any of them will believe the truth—especially given their opinion of me—will be for them to witness the inability of both the king and my brother to draw the sword. And *that* means we first have to get the sword from him, and then return it to the throne."

"Are you one hundred percent sure neither of them are capable of redrawing the sword?" Rutherglen asked. "Rainer is after all the current king because he *did* do so initially."

"There's no guarantee when it comes to my father," I said, meeting his gaze evenly, "but the earth no longer acknowledges him or answers his commands, and the sword is an extension of the earth power. But it was never my brother's. It's just another blade to him."

Rutherford grunted. "Containing the council will be far easier in the chambers than the great hall, given the latter has three exits and at least a dozen permanent guards within the room."

"There're actually four exits—there's an escape passage hidden behind the glass throne—and a dozen additional guards armed with pulse rifles watching from aeries hidden throughout the rafters."

"The wind can counter the guards easily enough," Donal said, "but you'll need to ensure all four doors are locked before we make a move."

"No one is getting in or out of that hall unless I will it." I hesitated. "But we will have to be fast. The king might no longer command the earth, but he will sense its use and react accordingly."

Neither man seemed overly concerned by that prospect. I wasn't sure whether to be worried or reassured.

"How likely is it that any of the council will act to protect their king?" Rutherglen said.

"Jedran is the only one who'll be on our side. The rest

believe the king was chosen by the sword to lead, and they all fear the power of the earth. Until I prove *I* hold that power, they will defend him with their lives."

Rutherglen raised an eyebrow. "Will they do the same for your brother if he's present?"

"He's the sword's heir as far as they're concerned, so yes." I smiled, though it held little more than cold satisfaction. "Vin won't be involved in any fighting that happens, though. He won't have fully recovered from having part of his right arm chopped off."

"A man in need of revenge is always the more dangerous opponent," Rutherglen said. "What if either of them orders you killed the minute the earth answers your call?"

"They won't; they'll simply order you two shot and hope I get caught in the crossfire."

Rutherglen frowned. "Why?"

"Because I bear Lokain's mark, and they fear the curse that comes with it."

"I wasn't aware that the god of war had marked you as his own." For the first time since I'd met him, Rutherglen's smile actually touched his eyes. But it was a fierce thing that sent chills down my spine and made me thankful he was on our side. "It makes me more hopeful for a positive outcome, both here and at our border."

"I'm afraid the other lords view it more as a portent of doom."

"Even Jedran?"

"Gigurri and her mages pay little more than lip service to Cannamore's gods. The earth mother and the voices of all those who have gone before them is the only form of divine wisdom they ever need."

I glanced out the window again; we were moving through the gates into the royal quarter. My gut clenched and my heart raced a whole lot faster. Fear, excitement, dread, uncertainty—it all churned through me even as the voices started in my head. Voices that said I wasn't worthy, that I'd never be worthy. Not of the earth and certainly not of the throne.

But those voices were part of a past in which I'd held no power.

That was no longer the case.

It was time to prove that.

To them. And to me.

"If that is the case," Rutherglen said, "the sooner you call to the earth and secure either the hall or the chambers, the better it'll be."

I nodded. "As soon as the doors are closed, I'll raise the earth and lock them. If the god of war is indeed riding with us, the king will be too busy deriding my presence or plotting to kill me to notice."

Rutherglen grunted and glanced out the window. "We're here."

The carriage came to a halt in front of the plain, rectangular building that was the great hall. I quickly unbuckled the knife sheath and tucked the blade into the waist of my pants, so that it was resting against my spine and out of sight. I'd stab myself if I wasn't very careful, but better that than its presence giving our game away before it had even begun. The king might or might not be losing touch with reality, but he'd know what the knife was the minute he spotted it and would react accordingly.

We needed to have the great hall secured before that happened.

Four guards approached the carriage, all of them armed and wary—a reflection of my father's mood, perhaps. The carriage dipped as the driver climbed out, and then the carriage door opened.

Holt Karland—the court chamberlain—bowed and then said, "The king has assembled the council in the great hall. Please follow me."

He turned and walked away without waiting for a response.

"It would seem your god is on our side," Rutherglen murmured as he moved past.

"Let's hope it remains that way," I muttered.

Donal gripped my knee in brief but silent support, then rose and followed Rutherglen out of the carriage. Neither looked back at me. I took a deep breath then stepped from the vehicle and looked around at the place in which I'd been born and raised. And oddly felt as if I no longer belonged.

It was a feeling amplified by the contempt that rolled from not only the four guards waiting for me to move but also from those stationed around the exterior of the great hall and on the wall.

Would that contempt ever be fully erased?

Probably not. After all, I *had* earned it, even if my actions had been forced rather than by choice.

But perhaps the real question in this situation was not whether I could change opinion but rather, did I even want to try? Or was this place as dead to me as my father?

I frowned and thrust the question—and the uncertainty that rose with it—away. I had a whole damn mountain of problems to overcome before I started worrying about things like *that*.

I hurried after the three men. Rutherglen's guards fell in behind me, and the king's escort behind them.

We stepped into the vestibule—an area so large it could easily hold several hundred people. But it, like the exterior of the building, was dour and cold; the walls were bare of plaster, the stone painted a simple white. There were no adornments on the walls, no heating or cooling, and the chairs were simple wooden benches—all very deliberate choices. All designed to make those wishing an audience with the king ill at ease—a feeling that would only be amplified once the doors into the great hall were opened and the sheer extravagance of the room was revealed.

Three doors lay at the far end of the vestibule. The largest and plainest led into the great hall. The one on the left led into the various antechambers—including the council chambers—that ran along that side of the great hall. The other led to the various service departments and privy facilities.

Our footsteps echoed on the polished concrete floors, a heavy beat that matched the pulse of the earth. All I had to do was express what I wanted and it would be done—but that same pulse was dangerous if the king was paying attention. And that, in turn, could certainly explain the tension so evident in our escort.

Sweat trickled down my spine, but it had nothing to do with the heat coming from the knife. It was fear, tension, and the need to get this over with—to either claim what was mine or die—all combined into one gut-churning, pulse-racing sensation.

The guards directly ahead opened the plain but sturdy double doors, revealing the interior of the great hall. The entire room—walls, floor, ceiling, as well as the soaring arches that supported it and gave the great space the feeling of a cathedral—were made of white stone through which thick veins of gold glittered. Brightly hued tapestries hung from the walls, interspersed with flags that represented the twelve territories. Wall sconces provided the entire room with a warm glow, though their flames were electric replicas rather than the real thing.

Twelve plush seating stalls—six on either side—dominated the dais half of the room, each large enough to hold the highest-ranking members from each territory's court. All of them were occupied with either the current lord or lady being present along with at least two other representatives. The stalls closest to the dais and the throne—a position that indicated the esteem those families were held in—were full, which was unusual given the hastily called nature of this meeting.

The Gigurri stalls were positioned on the left side of the room midway down, an indication of just how far out of favor her people had fallen from the king's good graces. My uncle sat in the front row, his posture casual and arms crossed. He was a typical Gigurrian in looks—a tall, broad-shouldered man with brown hair and skin. In many respects, he could have been blood related rather than via marriage, so similar in coloring was he to my mother.

There were five others with him—two men and three women. I vaguely recognized two but the other three were strangers—no real surprise since my last journey to Gigurri had been at least fifteen years ago. But I had no doubt that—given what my aunt had said—all five were mages. While I had no idea how adept they were at using the earth power, their presence at least gave us an edge.

It was an edge we were going to need, given that the number of guards within the great hall had been doubled.

My brother sat in the stall that was reserved for Divona's royal elite. I didn't recognize any of those sitting with him, but they were wearing the colors of the five main families. Vin's expression was nothing short of murderous, and I had no doubt that if he'd been capable of shooting me at that moment, he would have, consequences be damned. But he'd never been adept at using weaponry with his left hand and his right hand was now mechanical—which was surprising, as I'd thought his Sifft heritage would have been enough to save his real hand. I doubted he'd become proficient at its use in such a short period of time.

And while he was now forever maimed—thanks to the fact that mechanical hands could never replace the ease of use and dexterity of a real hand—that didn't make things even between us. Not one little bit.

Close to Vin's stall, at the far end of the room, was the long and simply constructed wooden dais. On this stood the glass throne—an ornate and beautiful piece of artistry that shimmered like a rainbow in the hall's flickering light. The king sat upon it, dressed head to foot in black, a dark blot against the brilliance of the throne. The combination made his brown skin appear almost sallow but had the opposite effect when it came to his eyes. They were as vivid as the wall of gold that rose behind the throne.

But it was the elaborately decorated, blue-white glass sword he idly spun on its point that caught my attention—as he'd no doubt intended.

The King's Sword. Out of its case and in his hand.

Was he mocking me? Or was he not so subtly daring me to go ahead and try to claim it?

Our footsteps echoed loudly in the otherwise silent room. The gathered lords and ladies watched us with varying degrees of disinterest, which suggested they had no idea as to why this meeting had been called.

Jedran, I noted, wasn't one of those studying us, though that was no surprise given he knew well enough why we were here. But I could see the tension in him, could see it also in the guards that lined the room and the way their gazes seemed to be trained on *me* rather than the two men in front.

The sword was definitely a dare.

Challenge accepted, I thought, even as my gut twisted and my heart began to beat so fast anyone would think I was climbing a mountain.

But in many ways, I was—one that had been twelve years in the making.

My gaze rose to the ancient text that dominated the golden wall behind the throne. *Whomsoever draws the sword from the ancient seat of this land shall rule it, and they shall bring peace and prosperity to its people.*

Rather oddly, as I silently finished reading the prophecy, peace descended upon me. All the fear, all the doubt, and all the tension inside stilled.

As did the earth's pulse.

Not because she was in any way abandoning me, but because that pulse had been a reflection of my own fears and anger. *Her* anger hadn't in any way abated. I could still feel it in the heat of the knife, in the warmth radiating through the polished stone under my feet, and fervently hoped that the king *didn't*. At least the dais on which the throne sat was made of wood rather than stone or metal; it didn't conduct the earth's energy as strongly. The king might be aware that her voice had stilled given how strong it had been, but there was less chance of him sensing the heat.

But Jedran would. And he, like the earth, would be readying for action.

The chamberlain stopped a third of the way down the room, forcing us to do the same. "My king and councilors, I present Lord Rutherglen T'Annor, Lord Donal O'Raen, and Princess Nyx."

"Bid them come closer."

The king's expression was as bored as his tone, but to believe that was to believe a lie. The presence of the sword and the tension in the guards were evidence enough of that.

As the chamberlain once again led the way forward, the doors behind us closed with an ominous clang. The heat pulsing through the knife increased, as if in anticipation.

Fuse metal and stone to prevent the four doors from opening, I silently ordered. *But do it as quietly as possible.*

The blade's heat increased and a tremor ran through the floor. My gaze jumped to the far end of the room, but there was no indication the king had noticed.

We continued walking down the hall. The closer we drew to the dais, the more the guards' tension increased. It made me wonder what he'd ordered—and whether whatever he'd told them to do in any way involved my brother. Given Vin's fury was now tempered by the glitter of satisfaction in his eyes, I suspected it might. It wouldn't be the first time blood had stained the pristine whiteness of the great hall. While the current king hadn't shed life in this place, the same couldn't be said for many of his ancestors.

We were three-quarters of the way down the room when he said, "Far enough."

The chamberlain bowed and backed away. For several seconds, no one else moved and no one spoke. The sharp scent of anticipation rolled from both Donal and Rutherglen, although their stance remained easy.

The king finally stopped twirling the sword and instead placed both hands on its hilt—a casual move most here wouldn't think twice about when in truth it was a deliberate reminder that while I might be the sword's chosen heir, both it and the throne were still *his* by right.

I carefully reached back under my jacket and wrapped my fingers around the knife's hilt.

Your wish? came the earth's voice.

The minute I speak, reach up and quietly leash the sword with stone.

The earth didn't reply, but the tremor that ran through once again spoke of her gathering readiness. Again, the king gave no indication he'd felt it.

That is because he cannot, the earth said. *He is blind in mind.*

And my brother?

Same.

"Lord Donal," he said, "I thought I'd made clear the penalties for bringing Nyx back into Divona."

My father's tone remained bored, but his golden gaze was on me rather than Donal. One eyebrow rose—a move that was both a silent taunt *and* a challenge. He might not be aware of the force gathering against him, but he had no doubt about *my* reason for being here.

He *wanted* me to move against him. And I had no doubt as to why—the minute I did, his guards would shoot, and he could claim self-defense to avoid the god's wrath.

"Indeed you did." Though Donal's voice was even, the air stirred. It was only light—little stronger than a faint brush of breath—but it spoke of a readiness as fierce as the force thrumming through the floor. "But there are some things totally unavoidable."

"I gave you full control of the restraint bracelets, highlander. Nothing is unavoidable; all you have to do is state your wish and she has no choice but to obey. Ask any of the lords here to confirm it—they have, after all, enjoyed the same privilege these last twelve years, if only for their assigned night."

It was both a reminder of my status in this place and of my reputation, one designed to hurt and embarrass. But as barbs went, it was poorly aimed. I'd heard variations of the same comment so many times that I'd become somewhat immune.

But what *was* interesting was the uneasy stir that went through the gathered lords. It suggested my father had kept the true purpose of the bracelets secret; that, aside from Marttia, few had been aware of my lack of choice.

"Unlike many here, I believe in freedom of choice." Donal's voice was even, without emotion—the highlander at his most dangerous. "Forcing your will on another always comes at a price—a fact many here will learn soon enough."

The king raised an eyebrow. "Is that a threat, highlander?"

"No," he replied evenly. "It's not."

Rutherglen cleared his throat and, with a narrowed glance Donal's way, stepped forward and said, "My king, we're here—"

"You've already had my answer to your queen's request for more men, Lord Rutherglen. She has wasted both your time and mine by coming here."

"I came here to plead our case to the assembly. If Divona won't help us, perhaps those gathered here will. After all, if Rodestat falls, these lands will be next in line for attack."

The murmur that swept briefly through the room told me no one here—other than the king, my brother, and Jedran's contingent—knew the true situation at Rodestat.

"A dire situation indeed, but we all know that won't

happen," the king returned evenly. "Just as we all know *that* is not the real reason you are all here."

"My king, I promise you—"

"Enough, Rutherglen. The game was up well before it had truly begun."

My grip on the knife tightened. The heated power running through the floor ramped up several notches, but it wasn't just my doing. Jedran and his mages were preparing to unleash and restrain.

"This is *no* game," Rutherglen said grimly. "It's a matter of life or death."

"Truer words were never spoken." The king's gaze switched to Donal. "What did I say before you left this place? Did I not warn that nothing but lies ever leaves her lips?"

"I think the lies began long before the princess was ever gifted the restraint bracelets, Rainer."

"Indeed they did," the king replied. "They are a deep part of her nature and the reason she is marked. Her god does *not* want peace, Donal. Both you and Marttia have been played for fools and *will* pay the price. Guards—"

Go, I said to the earth, even as I said out loud, "Move at your own peril."

I pushed past Donal and Rutherglen and strode toward the king. The wind came with me, a force of gathering strength. "You're right, Rainer, the game *is* up. It's time for you and Vin to come clean—"

"Donal, restrain her. Otherwise, I'll be forced to take action."

"If you want me restrained," I said, "do it yourself. And if you want me dead, then have the guts to raise that sword and strike the blow yourself."

He raised an eyebrow. "It's not the role of a king to personally take out insurgents."

"I'm not an insurgent. I'm the true heir to the glass throne and I'm here to claim what is mine."

"Did I not tell you she was mad?" he drawled, even as his eyes glittered with satisfaction. I was giving him exactly what he wanted—a justifiable reason to be rid of me. "By what right do you think you can claim this throne, when all here were witness to my son drawing the sword?"

"*Any*one in this room could have drawn the sword from that throne given it was a replica created specifically for that purpose. The real throne—the one on which you now sit—is made of the same impervious glass as the sword and the knife."

He frowned. "Knife? What knife?"

"I mean Racinda's knife, and the blade that is the other half of that sword."

I pulled it free and raised it high. The runes along the blade's length came to life, the ancient text glowing fiercely; a heartbeat later, the sword answered. Flames rolled down her sharp edges and deep in the heart of the blue-white glass, a phrase appeared. It was written in the same ancient text that ran down the length of the knife, but I nevertheless understood what it said.

To defeat death and darkness, you must first accept it.

My gaze returned to my father. Saw his contempt. Not just for me, but also for the power I held in my hand and the power he held in *his*—a power that had protected this land for so long. My gaze dropped again to the sword and the words that burned deep in its heart.

So be it.

"Acknowledge your lies, Father." I said it quietly, but the wind picked up my words and tossed them loudly around the room. "Acknowledge the fact I'm your true heir and that the sword is mine by right, not Vin's."

A cool smile touched his lips. "No."

"Then I will take what you will not give."

Which was exactly what he'd been waiting for.

With a flick of one finger, he unleashed a storm of metal. The guards in the aeries fired with deadly purpose—not just at Donal, Rutherglen, and me, but also at my uncle and his people.

Anger surged. He'd denied me access to their support for twelve long years. He would *not* make it permanent.

As the councilors scrambled to find cover, I ordered the earth to lock those above us into stone then sprinted toward the king. Bullets chased me, nipping at my heels and cutting through clothes. But they didn't bite deep, thanks to the fact I was still wearing Marttia's shirt.

The king hadn't moved; he was simply watching me with a disdainful smile. I realized why soon enough—a dozen men appeared in the periphery of my vision, coming at me from both the left and the right. *That's* why the stalls nearest the king had been filled—they were disguised guards, *not* councilors.

I dropped, shoved the knife into the stone, and used it to pivot around and knock the nearest four guards off their feet. The rest leapt at me, pinned me, their weight and numbers making it difficult to move, to breathe. A scream that was both fury and fear rose up my throat but came out as little more than gargled growl. My lungs were burning, my head pounding, and the knife's blade was being pressed into my side and somehow cutting deep, despite the vest. Or maybe the vest was simply no match for the power of the blade. Fear rose, its taste bitter, but with it came determination.

He wouldn't win.

Not this easily.

And certainly not when the knife gave me easy access to the earth even as it sliced me open. But even as I reached for her, familiar footsteps approached, and a fierce flurry of air unceremoniously sucked the men upwards. Donal grabbed my arm and hauled me upright.

"You okay?"

"Yeah."

He snorted. "You'd say that even if you were half dead. Go. I'll take care of this lot."

I spun and ran at my father, caught movement to my right and was sent flying sideways before I could react. My head hit the side of the nearby stall; stars danced in front of my vision and warmth flooded down my face. The thunder of approaching steps echoed and I groggily thrust the knife into the floor and sent a wave of white stone flowing toward my attacker. A scream rent the air—a scream filled with so much hate it sent chills down my spine. I forced my eyes open. Saw Vin in the air, leaping *over* the wave even as it reached for him.

I swore, pushed upright, and all but fell over the stall's wall, putting it between Vin and me. It wasn't much, but it gave me breathing space. Gave me time to recall the wave and send it chasing after him.

He hit the ground and lunged at me, every movement filled with the force of his anger. I pushed back and slashed with the knife, slicing open his one good arm. As his blood splattered across my face and stung my eyes, I glimpsed metal. Swore, and threw myself sideways. Heard the retort of a gun, felt slivers of wood slice into my face as bullets slammed into the seating inches from my head. Envisioned the stone reaching up, pinning his one arm to his body and leashing him to the floor. Imagined the same happening to my father.

The earth answered so swiftly the entire building shook. Cracks appeared in the floor near my feet and fanned out rapidly, racing up the walls and across the graceful arches, until dust rained down and the ceiling became a myriad of cracks. If they joined, it would all come down on top of us.

Part of me wanted that.

Wanted to watch all those hiding under benches squashed under the weight of stone and guilt.

But there were innocents here—people who didn't deserve to die amongst the scum.

Donal. My uncle and his people. Rutherglen.

I took a deep, somewhat painful breath, then shoved my anger back in its box and put a halt to the force threatening to tear the hall apart. My head was booming, my vision was fading in and out, there was blood in my eyes and matting my hair, and my side ached.

But I was alive, and that was something of a miracle.

I gripped the seat, hauled myself upright, and saw Vin. Fingers of white stone had wound up his body in a criss-cross pattern, giving him enough leeway to breathe but little else. The rest of the room was a mess of broken furniture, broken men, and scattered guns. But, for the most part, it appeared that the lords and ladies of the high council had escaped unscathed. My uncle and his people were moving toward the three external doors, and it was only then I became aware of the booming echo of metal against metal and the shudder running through the main doors—the guards outside were attempting to break in.

Rutherglen was nursing a bloody arm, had stone dust coating his hair and shoulders, and a cut running down his left cheek—a wound that looked to be caused by falling stone rather than a bullet or blade.

His gaze met mine and he nodded. Once.

An indication I'd finally won his approval, I suspected, but I couldn't dredge up enough strength to even smile.

The one person I couldn't immediately see was Donal. But even as fear gripped my heart and squeezed tight, he rose from a tangle of broken men and swung around. The relief that swept through me was so intense that, for several seconds, I couldn't even breathe. There was a cut across his forehead and blood staining his left thigh, but he was alive and so was I, and that was something of a miracle.

The wind stirred around me, bringing me his words even though he didn't speak out loud. *You're hurt.*

I ducked my head so no one could see my reply. "As are you."

It was very softly said, but the wind carried it across to him regardless.

Do you need help?

"Yes, but I can't accept it. I have to confront them alone, Donal."

They had to see—had to believe—that no matter what they thought of me personally, I *was* the true heir to the throne and the sword.

The stage is yours then, Princess. Go claim your throne. We'll protect your back.

I took a deep breath then turned to face the king. Fingers of stone had punched up through the dais and were wound like ropes around his body, pinning him to the throne. He still gripped the King's Sword tight, but so too did stone. With the earth no longer answering his command, he had little hope of freeing it.

His expression, like Vin's, was furious.

"This is *treason*." His face was a mottled purple-red, sweat trickled down the side of his face, and his breathing appeared rapid. "Your aunt and uncle will pay a heavy price for their treachery, but you, daughter, will be hung by the neck until the breath leaves your body and the birds pick your bones clean."

"You always were such a caring and considerate parent." I kept one hand on the half-wall as I moved toward the stall's exit. Though my vision had stopped fading in and out, my limbs were shaking and my head was filled with fire. I had no idea if the cause was weariness, blood loss, or perhaps even the knowledge of what was still to come. In truth, it didn't really matter. I couldn't and wouldn't call for a healer or medic. Not until I'd done exactly what I'd come here to do. "And if *that* is the penalty for treachery, then rest assured I will be more than happy to apply it."

"The rule of this place is *mine*." His skin, I noted, was beginning to take on an odd sort of sheen. "You may have the backing of the Westal Wildmen and the Mauvaissians, but Divona and her allies have defeated them once, and we will do so again."

"I daresay you're welcome to try, but be aware that both the Mauvaissians and the Wildmen have honed their fighting skills against the Skaran and now the Volker while the rest of Cannamore has grown soft." I glanced at the assembled lords. They were watching with varying degrees of concern and surprise, but there was little fear in their eyes and seemingly no understanding of what was really going on. "Whatever else you may believe, gentle members of the council, rest assured we are *not* lying about the threat at our borders. We truly *are* here to save Rodestat and consequently the rest of Cannamore."

The words might have been polite, but the tone wasn't. It was edged with the contempt I couldn't quite control.

"You're here for the goddamn sword and throne." Vin's tone was hoarse and spittle flew from his lips. "But it's not yours for the taking. No woman has ever ruled this land and no woman ever will."

I clenched my fists but resisted the urge to strike at him —to tighten the shackles that bound him and have the stone claimed him as fully as it had Sage. But that death was too easy—too quick.

I wanted him to suffer, as I had suffered.

And I wanted it done for the rest of his life, not a measly twelve years.

"You're right." I briefly paused at the stall's exit to catch my breath and met his gaze evenly. "I *am* here for the sword. The throne is just a bonus."

He spat at me. I didn't move. I didn't need to. The breeze that stirred ever so gently around me tossed it back. It splattered into his right eye and dripped slowly down his cheek.

I didn't bother restraining my smile as I pushed away from the stall's entry and walked toward the dais and the king. Power continued to pulse through the knife, its rhythm matching the thunder of my heart. Flames ran down its blade and dripped to the floor; at the touch of each drop, the veins within the stone came to life and golden fire spread before me, racing not only for the dais but also for the walls, the arches, and the ceiling. Repairing what I'd almost broken.

As a show of power it was hard to beat, even if it was coming at the cost of my own strength.

I slowly climbed the dais, concentrating on every step, refusing to show just how close to the edge I was.

Aside from the soft sound of my footsteps, the room was silent. All eyes were on me. I stopped beside the king and said, "Chamberlain Karland, will you please contact those outside and inform them to cease and desist. Tell them the situation is under control and they are to make no further attempts to get into the room until notified."

He hesitated, his gaze falling on the king before he nodded and moved away. "Lord Jedran," I added, "will you please ensure Karland *does* relay the correct message."

My uncle smiled and stepped away from the door he'd been bolstering to follow the chamberlain.

"Lords and ladies of the council," I continued, "for the last twelve years the king and my brother have participated in one of the greatest—and most dangerous—lies in Cannamore's history. It was my hand that drew the sword, not Vin's. In return for what they saw as treason on my part, my mother was murdered and I was placed in restraint bracelets and forced to obey my father's every order. And yet it wasn't me who paid the greatest price, but rather Cannamore and her people. In shedding the blood of one of the earth's own children, he lost his use of her, which meant we had no warning of the evil that was gathering beyond our borders."

"What evil?" The voice belonged to Holgrath, lord of De'Lorn Bylands and a man whose tastes ran to threesomes. "You speak lies and half-truths—"

"The Karva Pass fortress lies in ruins and half her garrison has been lost," Rutherglen said, anger evident. "Rodestat holds, but given our foe uses magic *and* the earth against us, I fear we'll fare no better than the fortress."

A murmur ran through the room. "If the fortress had fallen, we would have been inform—"

"As you were informed of our urgent request for reinforcements and—"

"Enough, Lord T'Annor," I said, softly but firmly.

Rutherglen glanced at me and bowed his head in acknowledgment.

I shifted my gaze to the last speaker. "Lady Harrison, the force that comes at us is the same foe that destroyed the Isle of Whyte and drove her people to Cannamore. The sword and the knife were created as a means of battling that foe, but both weapons can only be used by the true heir to the throne."

"Which is the king," she said staunchly. "I was a witness to him drawing the sword when he was little more than sixteen, Nyx, and—"

"You have *not* earned the right to use my name with such familiarity," I cut in. "And I do not deny the king's claim to the throne was legitimate. I am, however, stating that in murdering my mother—an earth mage herself—he has not only forsaken that right but has been abandoned by the earth."

"I find it hard to believe—"

"Oh, please *do* believe," Jedran cut in. "The earth is a gentle mistress, but she cannot abide the murder of one of her own by another. If you want evidence of his inability to control the earth, all you have to do is ask why he used guards to attack a Mauvaissian delegation or why neither he nor Vin did anything to counter Princess Nyx's use of the earth power."

Doubt lingered in her expression. "There could be any number of reasons—"

"Lady Harrison," I cut in, and raised my wrists. In the golden light, the silver bracelets gleamed harshly. "You know what these are, do you not?"

She cleared her throat. "From what the king said earlier, I believe they compel the wearer to do the bidding of whoever controls them."

"Indeed. Bracelets release."

"Don't you dare," the king growled. His skin had now lost much of its color; even his lips were pale. "Release me this instant and I'll grant you a swift—"

I flicked a finger upwards; the stone wrapped around his chest immediately flowed up and across the lower part of his face. He could still breathe through his nose, but he couldn't talk, and he certainly couldn't make any attempt to head butt me. I stepped forward and placed the bracelets on him. His eyes were little more than a sliver of gold, his chest heaved, and his fists clenched and unclenched. But there was no escape for him.

"King Rainer, you will step away from the throne and the sword when I release you, and you will make no sound nor will you attempt to attack me in any way." I paused, unable to help the edge of satisfaction in my voice as I added, "Or I will burn you every bit as badly as you have burned me. Understood?"

He couldn't move let alone nod, but there was murderous fury in his eyes.

"Earth," I added, "release the king."

As the stone encasing the king retreated, dizziness hit and the whole room briefly swam. I really had to finish this —and quickly—before the call of unconsciousness became too great.

The king stepped away from the throne. I wrapped my fingers around the hilt of the sword, felt the welcoming pulse that held a deeper, darker note, and pulled it free from the encasing stone. After checking it was indeed the real throne rather than the false one—which held an almost invisible slot in the seat's center to slide the blade in and out of—I raised the blade and shoved it home. Sparks flew as blade met throne, a shower of blue that glittered like icy stars in warm light of the hall.

"King Rainer, you have denied my accusations and continue to assert your right to this throne and sword. That being the case, you should have no problem once again drawing the sword from the throne."

"Don't dignify this farce by ceding to her orders," Vin shouted.

"He has no choice in this matter," I replied evenly. "Draw the sword, Rainer. Give proof to the council that you remain the legitimate ruler of these lands."

He fought the order. His muscles quivered and tensed and his eyes glittered with hate, but as the bracelets burned ever hotter and sweat trickled down his graying skin, he stepped forward, wrapped his hands around the hilt and heaved. The sword didn't move. He repeated the effort with an odd sort of desperation, to no avail. The earth had abandoned him, and so had the sword.

"Enough," I ordered. "Release the sword and step away from the throne."

He obeyed. He had no other choice, not if he wanted to avoid the pain that came with disobedience—and he'd witnessed its effects on me often enough not to want to go down that path.

"Earth, restrain the king again." The earth immediately obeyed—locking not only his body down but also looping loosely around his head and jaw, preventing him from opening it and thereby speaking. The fire in my head was now so fierce a weird sort of halo appeared on the outer edges of my vision; it was taking all my concentration to keep my knees locked and my body upright. I had minutes, not hours, before I collapsed. I took a deep breath that did nothing to ease the gathering tide of unconsciousness, then I ordered the bracelets to release and added, "Lord Donal, can you please gather them and place them on my brother?"

"With the greatest of pleasure," he said, even as Vin spat, "Don't you fucking *dare*."

As the wind picked up the bracelets and carried them across to Donal, I said, "Oh, I'll dare far worse than merely putting the bracelets on you, brother dearest."

"You're a fucking *trull*, and no one here will ever—"

Donal raised a hand and smacked him. Hard. As Vin's head snapped sideways and bloody spittle flew from his mouth, Donal said softly, "Princess Nyx has been a prisoner for twelve years, given no life beyond whatever was forced upon her by her captors. Which, in case you're not sure who's who in this drama, is you and the king. That she survived so many years of abuse *and* your attempts to kill her is something everyone in this room should admire even as they examine their own foul behavior. It's doubtful many here could or would have endured what she has."

I wanted to cheer him—loudly—but somehow restrained the urge. But I couldn't contain my smile or the happiness that surged through me. Fate and the god of war had certainly been on my side the day I'd been thrown into his cell.

Donal clipped the bracelets onto Vin's wrists—both his real and his mechanical. While I had no idea if his false limb would conduct the pain as well as regular flesh, he needed to be wearing both so that the magic could form a circuit and enforce commands.

"Vin, you are not to move or speak until I so command it. Earth, release him."

His eyes burned with hatred, but he neither moved nor

spoke as his stone shackles pulled back. Like my father, he'd witnessed the result of me going against commands often enough to know the inadvisability of attempting either.

"Vin, if you are indeed the true heir to the throne, you should have no trouble drawing the sword from the throne. I command you to do so."

He fought the order. His muscles twitched, his face twisted, and his hands clenched and unclenched. But as the restraint bracelets came to life, he was forced to walk up onto the dais to the throne. He gripped the hilt with two hands and heaved.

Once again, the sword didn't budge. A murmur ran through the room.

"Now tell the lords who were witness to you drawing this sword free eleven years ago the truth of that day."

"The sword was drawn from the heart of a false throne," he growled. "One that was designed with a near invisible slit within it."

"And who drew the sword from the real glass throne one year earlier?"

"You did. And I will kill—"

"Be silent, brother." I stepped past him, gripped the sword's hilt with one hand, and easily pulled it free. The murmuring got stronger.

I turned to the councilors again. "And there you have the truth of it. While neither of these men can now control the sword or the earth, *I* can. So the decision you face here today is whether you will follow the true heir or a king who no longer has any power in this land beyond that which *you* cede him and who will ultimately be responsible for the utter destruction of these lands."

"That's overstating the depth of the problem, is it not?" the lord of Guilderan said.

"If anything," Donal said, "Princess Nyx is guilty of *under*statement. The Westal Ranges has sent all available air mages to Rodestat, but even so, the wind continues to whisper of darkness and defeat if Cannamore does not join this battle."

Jedran stepped forward. "Lords, I'm speaking now not as the princess's uncle or a man whose wife has been held hostage via restraint bracelets these last twelve years." He made a motion toward the wall behind the throne. "Those words have governed how the rulers of this land have been chosen for nigh on a thousand years. Now that the truth has finally been revealed, we have no choice but to acknowledge it and pray that she forgives us rather than walk away and leave us to our fate. Because the threat to these lands—the darkness and destruction Lords T'Annor and O'Raen mention—is *very* real. The only hope we have of avoiding the same destruction that befell the Isle of Whyte are the two weapons Princess Nix now holds."

Once again, I felt like cheering. The councilors, however, were not so enthused. Perhaps it was the reminder of how badly they'd treated me over the years—or, more likely, concern over how it would affect my dealings with them in the future.

Which, if I was at all honest, was a very real concern.

But we had to survive before that became a problem.

"Lord, ladies, Rodestat could very well be under attack while we dither," I said. "You have two choices before you—accept the truth or not."

"And if we choose not?" Lady Harrison said mildly. "If we choose to reject your claim?"

I met her gaze evenly. "Then I will take this sword and do my best to save Rodestat. If I fall, then I wish you all luck, because neither the king nor Vin nor the might of

Cannamore's army will be able to save you. Not against a foe who have weapons that can eat through stone and metal and who can render the earth inert."

"And if you win?" she said.

I smiled. There was nothing pleasant in that smile. "Then I will be back to take what I have been long denied."

"So we basically have a choice between a peaceful takeover or a hostile one?"

"It's hardly a takeover when I am the rightful heir according to the rule of law these lands have followed for nigh on a thousand years, but... yes." I swept my gaze across the gathered councilors, but their faces were little more than a blur. My head felt as if it were on the verge of blowing apart. I needed to end this. *Now.* "Those who cede to the truth and my rule, stand with Lords Donal, Jedran, and Rutherglen. Those who do not, remain where you are."

For several seconds, no one moved. Then, gradually, two ladies and four lords walked over to stand with Donal as directed—which left two dissenters. Unsurprisingly, Lady Harrison was one of them.

"Lords and ladies of the council," I said, "given the urgency of the situation, I now request an immediate full council meeting to ratify my succession. If you'd please proceed into the chambers and—"

"And us?" Lady Harrison cut in. "You already have our disapproval and you dare not move against us, or it'll be considered a breach—"

"The treaty between Divona and both Chilbra and the De'Lorn Bylands was broken the second you both chose not to accept the legitimacy of my rule as according to both the Treaties Settlements Acts and the Crown Succession Act." I smiled benignly. "Your presence is still required in the council chamber, where you may record your objection to my succession. But afterward, I suggest you return home, dig the treaty out of the archives, and study it. And then consider the fact that you now face a long and lengthy rene-gotiation with someone who has not forgiven and does not forget."

Her face went pale. But she motioned toward the dais and said. "And what now happens to the king? What of your brother?"

"The king and my brother will be given the same luxu-rious surroundings that he afforded both Lord Donal and—"

I stopped abruptly. Though the king was still upright thanks to the stone that bound him, his eyes were closed and his lips held an unhealthy blue tinge.

And he wasn't breathing.

No, I thought. *No.*

He couldn't be dead. Not like this.

It was too damn swift, too damn easy.

And yet it was perhaps fitting that, in the end, he'd had the last laugh and deprived me of the one thing that had kept me going through the darkness the last twelve years.

The satisfaction of seeing him suffer.

Vin must have realized the same time as me what had happened, because he made a gargled, rage-filled sound and lunged at me. The bracelets flared to life but weren't fast enough to stop him. He hit me like a ton of stone and we went down in a tangle of arms and legs. He punched and kicked and bit, the force of his blows tempered but not stopped by the restraining magic of the bracelets and the protective nature of Marttia's vest. I avoided his blows as best I could and blocked the ones I couldn't, but I could barely see him even though his face only inches from mine. There was a roaring in my ears, my head felt ready to blow apart, and my limbs were weak and unresponsive.

The wind roared to life and ripped Vin off me. I tried to rise. Couldn't.

Felt the tremor of steps running toward me.

Felt the wind's whisper, filled with concern.

And collapsed into the welcome emptiness of unconsciousness.

FOURTEEN

The wheels of government moved with all the speed of an ice worm. While drawing the sword had proven my right to the throne, the Crown Succession Act required my succession to be formally acknowledged and written into legislation by the full sitting council. Which took far too long, even with the official crowning ceremony being delayed until *after* the Volker were dealt with.

If they were dealt with, that was. There was no guarantee that, even with the sword, we'd successfully stop their mages or repel the bipeds from our lands.

But those slowly turning wheels at least gave me time to recover my strength. Time to meet with not only the various departmental heads but also the chief of defense.

And time to blood the sword.

I knelt on the floor of my old bedroom and pressed the sword's point lightly against the stone. The earth pulsed in time with the beat of my heart and echoed warmly through the knife strapped to my side. But the sunlight streaming in through the window at my back did little to lift the chill from the sword's cold blue blade, and the runes that lay deep in its heart remained invisible. But they were never-theless etched into memory. *To defeat death and darkness, you must first accept it.*

If I bound this weapon to me, as I had the knife, I was all but signing my death warrant. Did I really want to give my life for these people? The people who'd used and abused me for twelve long years?

If I were at all honest, no, I did not.

But this wasn't about—or for—them. If I did this—if I made the commitment the runes in the sword seemed to demand—it would be for my aunt, uncle, and cousins. For all those in wider Cannamore who'd done nothing to deserve the death coming at them. And for Donal, so that he'd have time to find a woman worthy of bearing him many bonny children.

I took a deep breath and tried to ignore the tears that stung my eyes as I thought about what might have been, had we only been given time.

But we didn't have that time, and I needed to get this done rather than grieving for something that might never have amounted to anything more than a pleasurable way to pass a few months.

I placed my left hand on top of the right and then pressed the sword's point into the stone. Once it was deep enough to be held upright, I shifted my grip from the hilt to the blade then briefly closed my eyes. The earth offered encouragement, but the collective voices of mages past knew no more about this blade than what my aunt had found in the journals. Racinda's soul hadn't become one of them, and the truth of this sword was lost to us all.

I took another deep breath that did little to ease the trembling deep in my soul and then tightened my grip on the blade's sides. The sharp edges sliced into my skin as easily as it had the stone that now held it upright. Blood flowed, but it never reached the floor or the deeply embedded point. Instead, it was drawn *into* the sword, until the icy blue had been washed away by a dark-red hue. A heartbeat began, faint at first, but growing stronger as the bloody fire in the blade grew fiercer. Power surged—up through the earth, the sword, and into me.

It was a power unlike anything I'd ever felt before. It was the earth and yet not. It held light and hope, and yet ran with anger so deep and dark it frightened me to the core. I could feel the threads of the sword's creation—feel the wisdom and the energy of the woman who'd created both weapons. But I could also feel the antagonistic remoteness of the magic, and it was both vicious and foul. Darkness was as much a part of this blade as light and, in blooding it, I was drawing it into me.

Not into my heart but into my soul. It was a festering knot of barbarity just waiting to be unleashed, and it took every ounce of strength I had to maintain my grip on the blade. I didn't want this power—didn't want the sword or the darkness it had gifted me. And while I might have accepted the necessity to die, I didn't want to do so with my soul so stained. Not when there was a very real possibility that it would infect the earth's consciousness. It meant I'd be unable to become one with her on my death; meant that all that I was would be lost to both the earth and memory.

To defeat death and darkness, the earth whispered, *you must first accept it. There is no other way.*

Tears briefly stung my eyes. *So be it.*

The blade in my hand pulsed once, as if acknowledging my acceptance, and then the heat died, the power died, and the blade became a cool, icy blue again.

I shuddered and released her. The wounds on my palms

had been healed; all that remained were two thin scars and the knotted ball of darkness that sat like a weight deep inside.

I closed my eyes, fighting the fear threatening to overwhelm me. Not just because of this sword and that canker of evil, but also because by accepting both, I'd also accepted the necessity of stopping Donal.

He wouldn't let me face this alone and I simply couldn't let him die.

I took another deep, shuddering breath and walked across to the cabinet that held the fast-acting sleeping draughts. There'd been some nights—some dreams—that not even the earth's warm embrace could get me through.

And there'd certainly been more than a few nights when I'd used it to force sleep on others.

I found a pocket flask, poured a couple of the draughts into it, and then topped it up with water. After slipping it into my pocket, I walked back and drew the sword from the floor. A bloody-black fire ran briefly down its sides and a tremor ran through me. That fire very much reminded me of the hue that tainted the crystals atop the mage staffs.

Trepidation shuddered through me. I sheathed the sword and then slung the scabbard over my shoulder. It was the most practical way to carry the thing and it wasn't like I'd be drawing it in any sort of hurry. Not here in Divona, anyway.

The door opened as I approached, and Donal's gaze swept me briefly. "Everything okay?"

I smiled, though it felt tight. "Yeah."

His gaze narrowed. "I know you well enough now to see through that mask of yours. What's happened?"

"Nothing untoward. The power in the sword scares me, that's all." Which was the truth, as far as it went. I linked my arm through his and added, "I'm famished. Shall we go down to the royal kitchens and raid the pantries?"

"You're no longer a prisoner in this place, Princess." Though his tone was wry, concern lingered in his expression. "You can order whatever your heart desires and it will be brought to you no matter where you are."

Whatever my heart desires.... Four simple words that whispered through my being and made the wisps of regret pulse stronger. I did my best to ignore them. Now was not the time to chase satisfaction. Not in this place.

"It's the middle of the night and I'm not about to wake anyone. Besides, I'm not sure what I want."

At least when it came to food.

The desire that flared briefly in his eyes suggested he was well aware of what had been left unspoken. But all he said was, "Then let's go investigate. It would never do to have the queen starve in her own castle."

Especially not, I thought, when this was the first time in a long time said queen had felt *that* sort of hunger. But satisfying it would have to wait. Despite the fact that I now sat on the throne, the whisperings and rumors had not ceased. I guess it was foolish to even vaguely hope they would—not after twelve years of basically being viewed as the royal trull. Because of that, my behavior going forward would have to be the exact *opposite* of expectation. Passion and desire—the two things so very absent in my life up until this man had entered it—had to be approached with extreme caution lest it be seen as a validation of past opinion.

It was, I thought bleakly, just another reason to hate this place and everyone within it.

The next day, with my brother locked in the same foul cell that had been given to Donal and me, I named my uncle regent and ordered the military to fall out, leaving behind only a minimal force to defend Divona's walls should Rodestat fall. But I also ordered more air and earth witches to Divona—the latter to widen the Merrigold River to create a barrier the Volker couldn't easily jump and the former to raise the wrath of the skies and sweep away those who *did*.

The military moved out. The caterpillar haulers were given permission to go directly to Rodestat rather than follow the traditional route, but even so, it would take them two days to get there.

Donal, Rutherglen, and I raced ahead of the army in the Mauvaissian sprinter, with the Gigurri earth witches following us in one of the plush royal Divonian sprinters. The king had never been one to go without the very best, especially in his later years.

We arrived at Rodestat just as the setting sun set her walls ablaze. Initially, there was very little evidence of damage to the city, but as we moved through the long tunnel and deeper into her heart, the toll of the bipeds' acidy globules became more and more apparent. And yet, rather oddly, the arch that dominated the skyline appeared unscathed despite the fact it had to be an easy target, and the barracks and military zone close to the wall that divided Rodestat from both the canyon and the abandoned fortress also had little in the way of damage—and that suggested the Mauvaissians had found a way to at least neutralize some of the globules.

The sprinters had barely stopped when three red-cloaked guards approached with a request from Marttia that we meet—which made me smile. It would have been an order only days ago. I asked Bentli—the strongest of the five

Gigurri mages and my uncle's advisor—to come with us. It never hurt to have a second opinion when it came to the earth power, especially when my knowledge of it was so sparse.

As the remaining mages were led away, we were taken across to the arch's right side metal abutment then up the circular, surprisingly well-lit metal stairs until we reached the floor that held the war room.

Inside were Marttia, the commander, and the captain, as well as one other—a tall, slender woman with dark hair and the same sky-blue eyes as Donal.

"Neika," he said, pleasure in his voice, "it's lovely to see you again, although I do wish it was under better circumstances."

"You do have a habit of calling only in dire situations." Her voice was dry. She presented her cheek for his kiss and then gave me a somewhat frosty half bow—the Westal Ranges' dislike for their Divonian rulers coming to the fore in full, I suspected. "My queen."

"Please, call me Nyx, at least in the current situation." I introduced Bentli and then added, "What happens with the Volker?"

Amusement played lightly around Marttia's lips. "Is this the way your rule will proceed? All business, no time for pleasantries?"

"I'm all out of pleasantries after dealing with the other lords and ladies of the council." I took off the scabbarded sword and hooked it over the corner of a chair before sitting down. "So, situation?"

Marttia motioned to the commander, who immediately said, "Two of the other Skaran tribes currently harry the Volker rear defenses. It's giving us time to fortify ours."

"I gather you've found a way to counter the globules?" Donal asked.

Marx nodded. "Via a combination of wind, rain shields, and water cannons."

"We've not enough of the latter," Marttia said. "This end of the Kannel Mountains isn't prone to the wildfires that afflict the western edges. I've the smiths working around the clock to make more."

"I take it these cannons are the reason this arch and much of the military zone remain unscathed?" I said.

"Along with the air mages, yes."

"We're currently running a rotation of three shifts, two mages per shift," Neika said.

"With three running as overwatch?" Donal asked.

Neika nodded. "Myself, Rogan, and Teala."

"Ah, good." He must have felt my confusion over the term, because he glanced at me and said, "Overwatch is both the operational control and an additional source of energy should it be required."

I nodded. "Are the Volker continuing to shield their main force and their mages?"

"They're using the shield magic, but it's not protecting either of their encampments," Gallego said. "They've instead constructed two earth and stone domes. Their larger force remains at the border of the Wild Lands, with a minor encampment set up in the Gateway Canyon. They've shown no inclination to enter the fortress or drain the dam you created."

"We've had Blue Hawks out monitoring the situation," Marx added. "But other than the occasional clash with the Skaran, there's been little movement from either force."

"I take it you've tried bombarding the domes?" Donal said.

"Yes, but with little effect." Gallego looked at me. "Could you and your mages bring the entire thing down on top of them?"

"Given they're now well aware that they face at least one earth mage, it's likely they'll have drained the dome of life so it can't be used against them." I paused. "How big a force have the Skaran raised? Are they having any more success damaging the dome than we are?"

"There're at least three hundred Skaran massed at the destroyed settlement, and more are on their way. From what we've seen, their attacks so far have been little more than investigative probes."

"It's a shame there's no way to communicate with them and coordinate attacks. Between our two forces, we just might have some hope of stopping the bipeds."

Marttia snorted. "The Skaran consider us part of their food chain. Past attempts—which have been few, I admit—to come to some sort of treaty with them have ended with our emissaries being the main course at a Skaran banquet."

"The Westal Ranges also made an attempt, although it was long before we became a part of Cannamore. Let's just say if it wasn't for the wind, our people would have also ended on the menu." Amusement touched Donal's lips but didn't quite reach his eyes. "If there's no shield magic protecting either of their encampments, where is it?"

"It's currently moving into a section of the mountains apparently known as Dead Man's Gulf," Neika said.

"Are they tunneling?" I asked.

"No." Marttia glanced at me. "It would seem their tunneling was simply a means of concealing their presence from us for as long as possible."

Either that, or they were now saving the strength of

their mages for another task. "So why are they headed toward the Gulf?"

"It contains a narrow but deep fissure that splits the back half of the range, running from the broken edge of Hendlar's Peak into the flatlands," Marttia said. "If their forces reach it, they'll have a direct route into Mauvaissia."

"Or," added the commander, "they could bypass Rodestat altogether and march on to Divona."

I frowned. "If the Gulf allows easy access into Mauvaissia, why isn't it defended?"

"We have a watchtower at the Hendlar's Peak end," Marttia said, her tone curt. I hadn't meant the comment as criticism, but that was obviously how she'd taken it. "But the entire area has been decimated by multiple eruptions, and though the last happened over a hundred years ago, it remains as bleak and unforgiving as the Dead Lands. Even in the summer months, getting to both the Peak and the Gulf is difficult. The Skaran have never, in all the time Mauvaissia has held the area, ventured anywhere near that part of the Kannel Mountains. It's doubtful they even know the Gulf exists."

And yet the Volker apparently *did*. I doubted they'd forced the information from the earth's collective consciousness, if only because the biped mages didn't so much interact with the earth as use or drain it. But the Volker *did* live in an old volcano, and it was possible they were familiar with the Peak, if not the Gulf.

It was a thought that had foreboding pulsing through me. "Is the Peak active?"

"As I said, the last eruption was over a hundred years ago—"

"Which is not what I asked," I cut in. "Hasn't this entire region been beset by tremors recently?"

"Yes, but the source is the Cal-Alban volcano that dominates the eastern end of the Kannel Mountains. There's no indication Hedlar's Peak is also awakening—there's been no rise in the earth level in or around that peak, and no new steam vents."

If it was venting, then it wasn't exactly dormant. I leaned back in my chair and crossed my arms against the deepening sense of unease. "How big is the shield that's approaching the Gulf?"

"Probably no more than forty feet in length," Neika said.

"What sort of speed is it moving at?"

"Around one hundred miles a day, maybe a bit more."

"Which is extremely fast, even for those bastards," Donal commented. He glanced at me. "I take it you think it's something more than a recon team?"

"I think it's the mages in control of the black stone mage staffs and a protection detail."

"Why would they be heading at such speed for the Gulf?" Marttia said. "If they were intending to bypass Rodestat, wouldn't they be creating a tunnel so their warriors could move in safety, as they did through the dead lands?"

"How do we know they're not?" the commander said.

"We don't as yet," I said, "but I don't think they are. Nor do I think they're heading for the Gulf."

"Then what—" Donal paused, his expression darkening. "The Peak?"

I nodded. "Given they live in an old volcano, it's very possible they're aware of the two near here. Their regular mages are capable of making the earth molten, so it's not such a jump to think those in control of the old mage staffs could hasten an eruption."

"If their intention was to force an eruption," Marttia said, "why wouldn't they use a volcano that's already showing signs of activity?"

"Is the Cal-Alban volcano close enough to cause Rodestat major problems?"

She frowned. "No, but neither is the Peak."

"What if their goal isn't just the Peak or the Cal-Alban volcano?" Donal commented. "But rather the entire String of Fire?"

The String was a semicircular line of volcanic activity that stretched from Cal-Alban at the eastern edge of Mauvaissia through to the Grand Mount in De'lorn Bylands and onto Mount Neerim near Cannamore Bay.

"It's possible," Marttia said, "but the majority of the volcanoes that make up the string are either too far away to cause us any problems or were declared extinct long ago."

"Actually," Bentli said, "while a number of either active or extinct volcanoes do line the String, it's actually the nickname of a major fault line that runs from Og-dour Cove to Cannamore Bay."

The uneasiness that had been pulsing through me became full-blown fear. "And would it be possible for a mage to make use of that fault line?"

"One mage? No." Her gaze met mine, her expression grim. "But ten? Hell, yeah. And if they were able to force the divergence of the two plates—"

"Plates?" the commander said, with a frown.

Bentli hesitated and wrinkled her nose. "The outer shell of our world isn't solid, but rather divided into a number of sections—or plates, as they're more commonly known—that glide over the mantle, the rocky inner layer above the core. The position of these plates isn't fixed, although their actual movement year by year is minute. Cannamore consists of two such plates—the Marmara and Carale. Basically put, it's the pressure of these two pressing against each other that causes quakes and eruptions along what has become known as the String of Fire."

"And if the biped mages attack the string? Diverge these plates?" he asked.

"Then we face, at the very least, the destruction of *this* city and every other one that sits along the String, including a good portion of Divona."

"And at worse?" Marttia asked softly.

"Cannamore is torn apart along the fault line. Aside from the destruction of the cities, the low-lying nature of the Marmara plate around both the Sundar Flatlands and Chilba means much of the Divonian and Mauvaissian countryside would also end up under the sea."

"And in the process of all that, they'd decimate most of our military force," Donal commented grimly.

"Which is exactly what they did to the Isle of Whyte," I said.

"And the reason why the sword and knife were created," Bentli said. "The mages must be stopped. *You* have to stop them."

"I know." I looked at Neika. "Where is that shield currently located?"

She paused, her blue eyes briefly glowing as she communed with the air. "Twenty miles out from the Peak's base. It now appears to be stationary."

"Meaning they're either resting or they've reached their target. If it's the latter, it makes no sense," Marttia said. "That entire area is riddled with gullies and old lava tubes thanks to past eruptions, but it's a long way from the volcano itself."

"They don't need to get into the Peak's crater to activate

the String," Bentli said. "They simply have to position themselves over a point where the two plates meet."

I frowned. "If that's the case, why would they risk heading to the Peak? Why wouldn't they activate it from the Wild Lands, which they now control?"

Bentli shrugged. "Perhaps they thought it more likely we'd sense what they were doing."

"It would at least explain why their main force waits near the Quaih River," Donal said, expression grim. "It's far enough away to avoid the utter destruction that will afflict this entire region."

I rubbed a hand across my eyes. "The minute we attack the mages, their main force is going to come after us. We need to ensure that doesn't happen, as I have no idea how the sword will work or even if it *can* destroy the mages."

Marttia frowned. "But wasn't that the reason behind the sword's creation—to stop the Volker?"

"Only the black stone staffs, not them," Bentli said. "But Racinda didn't leave a whole lot of information about either the sword or the knife, and they've never been tested."

"Can't the collective consciousness fill in the blanks?"

"If Racinda's soul had joined them on death, yes," Bentli said, "but it didn't, so the consciousness can only give us what information those who attended her during the making of both weapons can supply—which is very little indeed and provides no greater clarity as to their use or how they function as a unit."

"Then let's pray to whatever gods you believe in that the damn things *do* work." Marttia frowned. "For any attack on their warriors to be successful, we'll first need to deal with the domes that protect them."

"It'll take all ten remaining mage staffs to activate the

String," Bentli said, "which means they've probably left their stone domes unprotected—"

"I wouldn't bank on that," I said. "They still have their blood magic, and we don't know enough about its use to say whether or not it could be used to bolster the earth."

"Yes, but their blood magic doesn't kill or mute the earth's power," she said.

"There's one way we can find out—ask the earth."

She immediately rose, but I motioned her back down and added, "I don't need to be in direct contact with her, Bentli."

I let my hand rest on the knife's hilt. The response was immediate. *Your wish?*

Has the earth and stone used to create the domes over the biped forces been rendered inert?

Yes. But the earth on which it rests has not.

I released the knife and repeated the earth's comment. Anticipation touched Bentli's lips. "So while we can't break the dome, we *can* break the earth that supports it and possibly even bring the thing down on top of them all."

"Even if that doesn't succeed," the commander said, "you can at least create multiple tunnels into the dome through which we can blast the bastards."

"We'll need to attack both domes at the same time, though. Otherwise, we risk the bipeds reinforcing the larger one through blood magic." Marttia glanced at Bentli. "Will five of you be enough?"

Bentli nodded. "Two of us should be able to deal with the smaller Gateway dome. That leaves three for the larger one."

"If we can provide access points into the far side of that dome," Marttia said, "the Skaran should do all the distracting we'd need."

"But their presence also makes any attack on that dome doubly dangerous," I said.

"Not if we're transported to and from by air mages." Bentli glanced at Neika. "That is possible, is it not?"

"It would take a number of us to transport three people, but yes, it's possible."

"We can at least use the old access tunnels to attack the Gateway dome," the commander said. "I gather it wouldn't take much energy to open the exit back up?"

"No, it shouldn't." I was actually surprised the Volker hadn't tried to do so, given they had to be aware the mountain was riddled with caves and tunnels. But maybe their mages were too intent on chasing their ultimate prize—the destruction of not just one city, but many.

Marttia's gaze met mine. "How soon do you want to move?"

Never. I took a deep breath and released it slowly. "The longer we leave it, the more time they have to set up." I glanced at the clock. "I'll need—"

"*We'll* need," Donal cut in. "There's no way you're going up there alone, Princess."

I couldn't help the slight smile that tugged my lips. I'd expected such a response—prepared for it.

"Actually," Marttia said, tone dry, "she's your queen, not your princess."

He glanced at her. "She'll always be my princess, no matter what her title."

Warmth surged through me, but with it came a fierce stab of anger. After waiting so long to have the freedom to choose, it was a bitter pill indeed to know it was death rather than life or love that now lay ahead of me.

"Neither of you should be going out there alone," Neika said, her tone curt. "Someone needs to watch your back,

Donal, even as you're watching hers. This is far too important to be taking any sort of risks."

"I agree," Marttia said. "We have no idea how many warriors accompany the mages, but given the size of the domes, there's likely to be quite a number."

"Which the wind can haul a very great distance away with a flick of my wrist," Donal said. "I'd rather not risk—"

"The choice isn't yours." I said it softly but firmly. "If something goes wrong out there, we need a plan B. Neika can provide that."

Would provide that. Using the sword might be my end, but I wasn't about to let it be his.

His gaze narrowed, but he didn't say anything. I rather suspected that would *not* be the case once we were alone—which just meant I had to ensure we weren't alone.

"Now that *that's* sorted," Marttia said, "Commander, how long will you need to ready for an attack?"

"Realistically, an hour, as we'll need to dismantle the pulse cannons to carry them through the tunnels, then reassemble them."

Marttia nodded and glanced at me. "What sort of provisions will you need?"

"Speed and silence will be the key for us, but I don't like the thought of going in without some form of physical backup." I hesitated. "We'll need pulse rifles and pomegranates, at the very least. And I'll need to eat before we go anywhere."

"Hargon will escort you across to the royal dining room. I'll have something ordered—"

"The mess hall—"

"Will be packed and noisy at this hour." Marttia glanced at the time and rose. "We'll attack the domes at twenty forty-five. The countdown has begun, people. Let's get a move on."

———

I didn't go to Marttia's private dining room; I instead asked Hargon to take me across to the mess hall. Aside from the desire to avoid a confrontation with Donal, if this was going to be the last night of my life, then I wanted to spend it in the company of others. Wanted to fill my plate with meats and bread, fight for a seat in a corner somewhere, and listen to raucous laughter and bawdy jokes. Wanted to draw in the determination to enjoy from those who'd seen too much death and devastation over the last few days. Wanted something—anything—to distract me from the gathering tide of fear and sadness.

"You're very quiet."

Though it was softly said, I heard it clearly thanks to the gently stirring air.

"Sorry. I'm just afraid."

Afraid of dying.

Afraid of *not* dying. Of the darkness that stained both the sword and my soul consuming me, as it had the mages who'd made the staffs.

Donal placed his fingers over mine and squeezed gently. Strength flowed from his touch. Strength and caring.

"We started this together, and we'll finish it the same way," he said. "I won't let anything happen to you, Nyx."

"I know."

Just as I knew he'd give his life to save mine, I could do no less.

His gaze was a weight I felt deep inside. I didn't return

it. I didn't dare. Not until I had the river of emotion running through me under control.

A few minutes later, I spotted Rutherglen winding his way through the hall. He stopped the other side of the table and handed us each a halo. "The Gateway attack team should be in position in ten minutes, and the main dome team will leave at the same time as you. When you're in position, give us the go and we'll attack."

I nodded and hooked the halo over my ear.

"Marttia also asks if you wear the vest she gave you."

I smiled. "The only time I've taken it off is to shower."

"Good." He glanced at Donal. "Keep her safe, high-lander, or face the displeasure of Mauvaissia."

With that, he turned and walked away.

"I think Rutherglen likes you," Donal said, amusement evident.

"As much as he likes anyone." I pushed upright and slung the sword over my shoulder. "Shall we head out to the courtyard and wait for Neika?"

"She's already there." He touched a hand to my spine, lightly guiding me through the crowd. "She's nothing if not prompt."

It was said with a note of almost tolerant amusement that had questions rising, but I didn't give them voice. It wasn't like I had the right or the time for such things.

We clattered down the stairs and made our way across the courtyard to where Neika waited. The captain and several soldiers were approaching from the opposite direction.

"Nyx, Donal," he greeted. "Good luck out there this evening."

"Thanks, Cap."

He motioned to the two men with him, who immediately handed us packs, rifles, and thick coats. "There's water but no rations. I figured—"

"We get in and get out fast, or we get dead," Donal finished for him. He donned his coat and then took both packs, slinging one over his shoulder and holding the other while I unslung the sword and donned my coat. "And I can assure you, Cap, I don't plan on doing the latter."

"Excellent." Amusement touched Marx's lips, but faded when his gaze touched mine. "You're a good soldier, Nyx, and I think you're going to be an even better queen. It will be an honor to serve under you."

Only if I survive.... "Thanks, Cap."

He nodded and stepped away. I glanced at Donal. He immediately caught my hand and tugged me close. As the wind stirred around us, he glanced at Neika and said, "You lead the way. We'll follow."

A heartbeat later, we were high in the air and being swept over craggy canyons, barren slopes and desolate snow-topped mountain peaks. If the place looked this inhospitable from up high, it was going to be damn horrendous down on the ground.

As one peak began to dominate the skyline, our speed slowed and we started to drop. The broken nature of the area became more evident as we neared the ground, with boulders, weirdly shaped lava tree molds, and long straps of crisscrossing chasms making it seem as if the entire area was some giant's long-abandoned playground.

Black dust plumed around us as we were placed on the ground. The night was crystal clear but the air close to freezing; my breath frosted and my nose almost immediately began to run.

I stepped back from Donal then knelt and placed my fingers into the ashy soil. While I no longer needed direct contact with the earth to either use her or converse with her consciousness, something within warned against using the knife any more than necessary. Perhaps it was nothing more than the fear that in doing so, I'd strengthen the bond between knife, sword, and that darkness, which in turn would strengthen its hold on me.

I might have accepted the necessity of dying to save those I loved, but there was still some part of me holding onto hope.

Energy stirred under my fingertips, a pulse that was fierce and angry. But there was no thread of darkness, no hint that the Volker mages had yet planted their staffs into the String's heart in an attempt to shatter Cannamore's. We still had time to stop them.

Only if you hurry, came the earth's warning. *They head for an active vent near the beginning of this lava tube. Once they reach that, they will be able to access the String.*

How far ahead of us are they?

Only a mile.

Which, even as fast as the bipeds moved, wasn't much of a lead. *How many in total are there?*

Twenty.

So not just the mages but ten guards as well. I swore softly and rose.

"Problem?" Donal asked instantly.

"The mages are a mile deep in the mountain."

"Which means nothing when we have the wind behind us," he replied. "But we'll first have to deal with the shield and whatever Volker it holds."

"How far ahead is it?"

"It's over the next rise." Neika glanced at Donal. "How do you want to play this?"

"We can't play it any way until the princess peels open the shield. Follow me."

We began to climb the long slope, jumping the smaller chasms and going around the wider ones. As the boulders grew smaller, the lava trees became more prevalent until we were walking through a petrified forest. But there was no sound in this place other than the eerie cry of the wind as she wandered through the various shapes and hallows. If life *did* exist up here, then it was well and truly silent.

As we neared the crest, the wind grew stronger, tugging at Donal's hair as she whispered her secrets in his ear. He immediately stopped. "The shield's edge lies just over this slope. There's no sign of guards around its exterior, but I daresay there'll be plenty within."

I nodded. "I'll open the shield up, you and Neika rip them out."

"Be careful."

My smile flashed, though it felt tight. "Always."

I dropped and crab crawled the few remaining feet to the top of the slope. Dust stirred around me, tickling my nose as it spun into the air. The earth's heat pulsed through my clothes—a steady beat that offered courage, strength, and information. Seven bipeds stood within the confines of the shield.

I moved down the slope, avoiding the sharper stones and slipping around the cracks and crevices that spread like skeletal fingers all around me. The knife flared to life as I neared the shield, her golden glow quickly turning red as I stopped and pressed her forward. My arm was almost straight when her point hit the shield. After a deep breath, I swept the knife in a large arc, creating a doorway through the invisible shield. The air immediately rushed past me, its force such that I was almost sucked in after it. But it very quickly reversed and, a heartbeat later, seven bipeds shot so high into the air that I briefly lost sight of them. They quickly reappeared, arrowing down with such speed that they were little more than gray blurs against the starlit skies. The combined power of two air mages had them hitting the ground so hard their bodies split open, their innards splattering everywhere. Thankfully, the swirling wind kept the goo well away from my position, but even so, my stomach stirred at the sight.

I swallowed heavily and peered inside the dome as Donal and Neika scrambled down the hill. The lava tube's entrance was a jagged semicircular hole that broke through the sharply rising ground on the far side of the dome. A curtain of lifeless-looking creeper grass hung over the entrance, and there were boulders and dirt strewn down the slope on either side—the bipeds had obviously cleared them away to get inside.

Donal stopped beside me. "At least the tube looks to be a decent size."

"It'd have to be, considering the height of the bipeds."

He stepped through the knife-created entrance. As Neika followed, my heart began to race. If I was going to stop Donal, I had to do it now—here—before we got into the mountain and he switched to full alert.

I stepped through the shield opening, then pulled the knife away and sheathed it. Then I dug out the draught-laced flask of water from my pocket and unstopped it. After swishing the water around enough to wet the lip and collar, I hurried forward.

"Water?" I said, offering him the flask.

He took it without question and had a drink. It wasn't long or deep, but it didn't need to be. Not when I'd double-dosed the water.

"Thanks." He handed it back, his gaze on the tube ahead. "If the entrance is anything to go by, the lava tube is a fairly wide one. Why don't we just send the wind in to grab the mages and smash them as soundly as we smashed their guards?"

I stoppered the flask and tucked it back into my pocket. He'd be asleep in a couple of minutes. All I had to do then was convince Neika to return to Rodestat with him.

"The remaining staffs have to be embedded in the earth and in use for me to destroy them with the sword," I said.

Neika raised an eyebrow. "So why not just destroy the mages? The staffs aren't dangerous in and of themselves, are they?"

"No, but any earth mage alive today is capable of using them," I replied. "And remember, the twelve greatest earth mages ever born fell to the evil that now claims those staffs. Do you really think it wise to leave such weapons active in a day and age where the mage bloodlines are fading?"

"No." She studied me for a second, then shook her head. "You are very much *not* what I expected, Nyx."

My smile held little amusement. "I am not my father, Neika, and I'm certainly not what he tried to make me."

"That much is already evident."

Donal walked up to the tube's entrance. I followed, listening to the whispers of the earth. A mile and a half now separated us from the mages. I had to move, and quickly, if I wanted to be close enough to stop them.

Donal unslung his pack, then pulled out a flash stick and activated it. Warm light flared from its length and washed into the darkness beyond the entrance. "There's a steep, rubble-filled slope about thirty feet long, but it levels out into a wide, smooth tube. We should be able to move fairly quickly through it."

"But we can't use the wind to do so." I stopped beside him, my body practically humming with tension.

His quick frown suggested he could sense it, though I doubted he understood the true reason. Not yet.

"Why not?"

I waved a hand toward the lava tube cave. "The air in there is heated and still. If we grab a lift via the wind, they're going to feel us coming."

"We can still use the wind to go at least part of the way," Neika said. "Speed is of the essence and it can get us into that mountain far faster than feet."

"I agree," Donal said, "so let's all stop talking and get moving."

But his words came out slurred and alarm spread through his expression as his knees buckled. He lashed out with one hand, gripping the nearby tube wall fiercely to keep upright.

"What's wrong?" Neika asked, an edge in her voice.

"Nothing's wrong." My voice was calm, even if I was feeling anything but.

Anger flared deep in Donal's eyes. Anger and fear. He knew what I'd done. Knew why.

"I'm sorry, Donal—"

"You can't," he cut in. He was fighting to keep upright, to keep his eyes open now. "Not alone."

"The sword was created out of the ashes of two mage staffs stained by an evil that demands blood in exchange for power," I said. "To use it, I not only have to accept that evil but also death."

"No," he said, and reached for me.

I stepped back quickly. He would have fallen had not Neika quickly propped him upright. "Damn it, Nyx," she said, "you can't do this—"

I couldn't tear my gaze from Donal's. From the anger and anguish that moved fluidly across his face. "I can and I have."

"There has to be another way—"

"There isn't. I wish it were otherwise, believe me." Tears stung my eyes. "But my death cannot be yours. It *will* not be yours."

"This is not what the wind promised," he said. "This is not how it has to end."

"The wind cannot always see the future—you once said that to me."

"Yes, but—"

"There are no *buts*. There is no other way. Live your life as you were meant to, Donal. Go find that woman worthy of bearing you many bonny babes."

He opened his mouth, but no sound came out. His eyes rolled back into his lids and his body slumped in Neika's arms.

"Take him back to Rodestat," I ordered. "Under no circumstances is anyone else to come after me. It's very likely the force I have to use to destroy the mage staffs will awaken this volcano."

"Without my help, you may not get far enough into the volcano to stop them."

"And with it, I may fail. They know we have mages capable of controlling the weather. They'll sense the change in the air and know we are coming."

"You can't be certain of that—"

"I can, and I am," I cut in softly, "but I'm a daughter of kings, and one who has Sifft blood in her veins. I can run— fast. I'll catch them, trust me on that."

Disbelief crossed her expression. "I can't just—"

"I'm your queen, Neika, and this is an order. Leave." I walked across to the shield and opened it up. "*Now*."

She hesitated and then nodded. A heartbeat later, the wind whipped up around the two of them, throwing dust and stone chips into the air. I raised a hand up to protect my face.

Then that force died and they were gone.

A sob rose up my throat, but I bit my lip against it. I had a bad feeling that if I unleashed *that* particular dam, there'd be no stopping it.

The god of war had chosen this path for me long ago. This was what I'd been born to do—why he'd marked me as his.

To win a war no one else could.

To stop the utter destruction of my homeland.

If in the process I saved the life of a man I might well love, then I'd consider *that* a personal win.

I unslung the sword and rifle and stripped off the coat. It might be cold here out in the open, but the gentle airflow coming from inside the lava tube held the distant promise of heat. I had no doubt it would increase the closer I got to the active vent. I slung the sword back over my shoulder but then hesitated as my gaze fell onto the backpack. If I failed to destroy them with the sword and knife, then I could at least use the pomegranates to bring the whole damn mountain down on top of us all.

I slung the pack over my other shoulder and—with another deep breath that did little to bolster my courage or cage the fear—walked across to the tube and stepped inside. I slid more than walked down the steep hill and, with every step, a gathering force of small stones and dust bounced ahead of me. The noise echoed through the chamber, and I could only hope the Volker were now far enough ahead not to hear it.

I reached the bottom of the tube unhurt and upright, but the earth now pulsed with urgency. I swore and broke into a run, my steps echoing softly on the tube's hard black base. There was no light in this place, but I didn't really need it once my eyes had adjusted.

Though the air remained relatively cold, sweat slicked my body—fear as much as exertion, I suspected. While the floor was fairly smooth in this portion of the tube, lavacicles hung from the ceiling like stalactites and the walls were ledged and ropey-looking. It was all rather surreal and, at any other time, would have been quite awe-inspiring.

But I had no time for wonder. No time to do anything more than run as hard and as fast as I could.

The tube grew rougher, narrower. I sped on, brushing past jagged edges of rock and leaping over volcanic clumps that had fallen from the ceiling, leaving gaping holes through which water seeped. Up ahead, a black wall loomed. I slid to a halt and scanned the immediate area, knowing there had to be a way around the blockage given that the Volker weren't anywhere near. Even as the earth whispered her secrets, I spotted it—a thin slash in the wall to my right.

I unhooked the sword and backpack, then squeezed in sideways. It was a tight fit—the tunnel's ceiling was barely inches above my head and my breasts were pressed hard against the wall. Jagged edges of stone tore at my shirt as I forced my way through and would have done the same to my skin if not for Marttia's vest.

Of course, I could have very easily fixed that just by asking the earth to retreat. But doing so would not only alert the mages to my presence but also pull on my strength.

Right now, I couldn't afford either, not when it would undoubtedly take everything I had to destroy the staffs.

The air grew hotter and sweat dripped from my chin and my hair. I peered into the deeper darkness, hoping to see an end to this thing, but there was nothing visible other than a gentle curve away to the right. As I approached it, the walls grew even rougher and the top of the tunnel closer and more treacherous. A jagged piece of stone scraped my forehead, although I couldn't tell if it was deep enough to draw blood thanks to the river of sweat already flowing down my face. I cursed softly and dropped down to all fours, shoving the sword and pack ahead of me as I alternated between crawling and thrusting sideways through the increasingly narrow space. How the bipeds had gotten through here without leaving behind a river of skin and blood, I had no idea.

But then, maybe they hadn't had to. Maybe they'd simply done what I was afraid to, and opened this tunnel up long enough to slip through without hassle. Or maybe they were behind the near impassible nature of the damn thing.

The deeper darkness finally began to lighten, and the thick, heated air stirred, an indication that somewhere up ahead there was an end to this narrow nightmare. Fresh energy spurted through me, and I pushed on quickly. But just as the tunnel started to widen, a tremor ran through the earth and dust and debris began to fall.

That tremor wasn't born of natural causes. It had come from a biped burying the first of the staffs into the ground.

Time was almost out.

I swore again and pushed through the tunnel, tearing clothes and skin and not caring.

Another tremor ran through the earth. Cracks appeared in the tunnel walls, slithering through the darkness far faster than me. Rocks rained down with bruising efficiency and I bit my lip against the desire to scream in frustration and pain.

A third tremor. A third staff planted into the ground.

The floor cracked underneath me. I scrambled on, knowing by the ever-growing lightness in the air that the end of the tunnel was close. The gentle sweep straightened and, up ahead, a strange green luminescence appeared. For one heart-stopping moment, I thought I was staring at the eyes of some gigantic animal. Then other glowing orbs appeared, some of them round, some of them long slashes of brightness. Not a life form but rather some sort of plant that had found a way to survive in the damp darkness of this place.

A fourth tremor ran through the ground, and this time, the tunnel's floor gave way. I dropped like a stone, bounced off something solid, and then slid down a long, steep slope for far too many seconds—only to crash with breath-stealing force into a large boulder. Unconsciousness briefly threatened, but I somehow fought it back and threw my hands over my head to protect it against the debris still bouncing down the slope after me.

A fifth tremor.

This time it was accompanied by the first surge of power—but it wasn't *just* earth power. It was magic. *Blood* magic.

I cursed and pushed upright, shedding rocks and dirt like water. Realizing I no longer had the sword and backpack, I looked around frantically and spotted a glimmer of blue ice half buried in debris some twenty feet away. Not far to its left was the edge of a strap. I raced over, drew the sword free, hauled the pack from under the mound of rubble, and then kept on running. Almost every part of my body was protesting, and there were bloody scrapes all over my legs and arms. But they didn't matter. Nothing mattered. Nothing except getting into position before the last staff was plunged into the earth.

The cavern into which I'd fallen was a huge, dome-like structure filled with not only glowing moss, but also stalactites and stalagmites. At the other end, at the top of a roughly hewn staircase that had been created by the Volker rather than time or volcanic eruption, was another tunnel entrance.

Another mage staff went into the ground, and this time the tremor was more violent. The cavern's vast dome cracked and stalactites crashed down and shattered, sending razor-sharp splinters spinning through the air.

But I was close to them now. So close.

The knowledge sent a fresh spurt of energy through my limbs. I ran through the mini forest of stalagmites, my footsteps lost to the vastness of the cavern, the trembling of the earth, and the destruction it was causing. The steps were awkwardly spaced, built for Volker ease of use rather than mine, each one taking two steps rather than one. By the time I reached the top, another mage staff had been buried in the ground, my lungs were burning, and my legs were threatening to give

The eighth mage staff went into the earth. The tremor this time was so violent it threw me sideways. I somehow caught my balance and raced into the tunnel, the earth's urgency lending my feet wings.

The ninth staff connected. Cracks appeared all around me, and the earth was now heaving.

At the far end of the long and narrow tunnel was a distant dot of dark, dark red. It was the glow coming from the stones that sat on top of the nine earth-connected mage staffs.

I wasn't going to get there in time to stop the tenth.

I knew it. The earth knew it.

I skidded to a halt, dropped the pack, and swung the sword off my shoulder. I tossed the sheath aside, then dropped to my knees, ignoring the pain that shuddered up my spine as I raised the sword high. The earth pulsed under me, through me, and then into the sword. Light flared deep in its heart, a bloody color that matched the distant glow up ahead.

I closed my eyes and shed awareness of everything except the earth and the power that surged all around me.

Not earth power.

Magic.

It was now so fierce it felt like a swarm of biting, stinging gnats. But in that awareness, there was also knowledge. I waited, my muscles twitching and jumping under the increasing weight of magic, until it felt as if I was being flayed alive.

As it reached a crescendo, earth and instinct screamed, *Now!*

Protect me, I said, then plunged the sword down with as much strength as I could muster, burying her deep into the ground. Power exploded, a force so strong that it was only my fierce grip on the hilt that kept me upright. A shockwave that was both energy and magic rolled outward from the sword's blade, causing the walls and earth to roll with even fiercer intensity as the wave raced toward the bloody glow at the far end.

The runes in the blade came to life, the glow so intense I could see them through my closed eyelids. As shuddering in the tunnel increased and stone began to rain all around me, my hands were forced down the hilt, over the guard, and onto the blade.

There must be blood to combat blood, a soft feminine voice whispered. Whether it was the earth or my imagination, I had no idea—and no time to wonder.

My blood was being drawn deep into the sword's pulsing heart and, as before, it unleashed a dark power. This time it came not just from the sword, but also from the ten staffs. The stain that had lodged deep within my soul rose swiftly to accept it.

There would be no coming back from this. There couldn't be.

You must accept rather than fight it. There is no other way, that voice said. *No other choice.*

I did. And in that moment, the link between the sword and the other staffs was forged.

The circle of evil was complete.

This sword was now part of the very darkness it had been designed to counter. Racinda might have escaped the final fate of the twelve mages, but she'd nevertheless succumbed to the evil within the mage staffs, and transferred it to the weapon in my hand.

No.

But that voice was lost to darkness and power that swept all around me. It was all I could see, all I could feel, within and without. It was a vortex that sucked me deeper and deeper, swamping thought and fight, filling the void— filling me—with its barbaric viciousness. All I wanted was to destroy and dominate—to wrench apart the world that existed and create a new one of fire, heat, and anger—a world where only those acclimatized to such things could ever exist. It was what I was born to do, after all. Had I not been told that all my life? I was marked by the god of war; darkness and destruction was my destiny.

Only if you wish it to be. Fight.

Another voice—alien and yet oddly comforting in this world of dark destruction—overran the advice. It was a clarion call to power—power fueled by blood sacrifice and by earth. The ground heaved and screamed as one alien voice became two, then three, then four.

Fight, that other voice demanded, even as the left side of my body began to burn.

Four voices became five, then six. Their song of darkness dragged me deeper, swamping me, making it impossible to think, to breathe.

You are my blood, and you are stronger than this darkness. Fight.

The burning in my side became a light. A fierce white light that began to pierce the utter darkness surrounding me.

Six voices became seven.

If you let this darkness win, you will be responsible for the destruction of everything you care for.

Donal's image rose.

And with it, some clarity.

I *wasn't* this darkness. I wasn't what my father and brother had for so long forced on me or made me believe.

The god of war was one of choice—life or death.

I chose life. For others, even if that was now impossible for me.

Draw in the earth's destructive power. Force it through the connection.

The sword's light grew brighter. I grabbed it, held it close, using it as a shield against the vortex of evil, shattering some but not all of its talons. I reached through that light to connect with the earth on a level that was free of taint. She answered instantly, swept through me with such fierceness that it felt as if flesh, blood, and bone were torn away, and all that was left was soul and consciousness.

That force leapt from me to the sword and swept on, funneling through each and every one of the connected staffs.

They exploded, the force such that it ripped my hands from the sword and sent me tumbling backward.

Where I drifted for who knew how long, caught between life and death as the world around me came apart.

Survive, a voice whispered.

Not the same voice. Another. It rode in on the breeze that stirred past my face and played with my hair.

Move, it added. Fiercely. Angrily.

"I can't." It was little more than a croak, but the wind nevertheless heard.

You can.

"Death is my fate."

Death is not. The wind doesn't lie.

"But the runes—"

Listen to me, Princess, you're alive, and you'll damn well remain that way. Get up. Get up now.

Something stirred in me. Hope. Determination.

"Donal?"

Yes. Now get up and run. We can't yet pull you free.

"Why?"

Now is not the time for questions. Just move it.

I forced my eyes open. Blue-white light washed through the darkness, highlighting the slab of stone above. Underneath me, the earth was still, despite the destruction happening beyond my small haven. The earth had protected me, just as I'd asked.

You are not safe yet, she said. *The explosion that destroyed the staffs also woke the volcano.*

The mages?

Are in as many pieces as the weapons they wielded.

And yet I'd somehow survived. A miracle? Or perhaps a parting gift from the woman who'd created both sword and knife—a woman whose soul *inhabited* the sword, and who'd guided me through its darkness.

I rolled onto my stomach and then pushed up onto hands and feet, where I remained for altogether too many seconds, waiting for my vision to stop spinning. Every muscle and bone in my body ached, and sweat dripped from my face and slicked my body. Sweat and blood.

I thrust a hand against the wall and slowly pushed upright. Saw that the dome that protected me only had three sides—the tunnel that led back to the glowing moss cave remained open. Then I became aware of something else—the weight of footsteps against the earth.

I might have destroyed both the staffs and the mages, but three biped warriors had survived and were now coming at me.

I swore and carefully pulled the sword free from the ground. Flames rolled briefly down her sharp sides, but they were golden rather than the bloody red-black of before. The darkness had left its core.

Just as, I realized, it had left me.

To defeat death and darkness, that feminine voice whispered, *you must first accept it.*

I'd accepted, and because of that, survived.

But if I didn't get moving, that survival would be all too brief.

I pushed away from the wall and staggered more than strode down the tunnel. The ground continued to convulse, and the air was thick and heated. Steam. The threatening eruption must have blown open a new vent somewhere nearby. I wished there was something I could do to stop the eruption, but I doubted that would have been possible even if I'd been at full strength, let alone when I barely had enough to keep moving.

The ground rolled, sending me staggering sideways. Big cracks chased me through the darkness, growing wider as rocks and debris rained down on top of me. There was nothing I could do. Nothing except run and hope.

As I neared the end of the tunnel, the wind hit my back and sent me flying. I fell hard and skidded along the ground's rough surface, skinning chin and knees. Saw a yellow-green globule fly inches above my head and splatter against the nearby wall.

The Volker were close.

Far too close.

I swore, pushed upright, and fought the urge to ask the earth to ensnare them. My heart was racing, my head was on fire, and my strength was as uncertain and unstable as this entire area. If I wanted to run—to survive—the earth had to be a last resort. A last stand. Even if I used the sword as a conduit, the earth would still pull on my strength. In this state, that would be deadly.

Another globule splattered the wall to my left. As the stone dripped to the floor, I spotted something sticking out of the debris directly ahead. After a moment, I realized what it was—the backpack. Hope surged. I swept the pack up and opened it even as I continued to stagger forward. After grabbing one of the pomegranates, I set it for a minute, then tossed it over my shoulder and ran with every ounce of speed I could muster for the tunnel's exit. I'd barely reached it when there was a huge whoomp. A second later, I was hit by a blast of air and debris and sent tumbling —skidding—across the platform. Saw the ledge approaching way too fast, realized I was somehow still holding the sword and stuck the point into the stone. I came to an abrupt halt with my legs dangling over the long drop.

Felt the approaching thunder of footsteps.

A biped had survived the blast.

I swore and pushed upright, then caught a glimpse of yellow-green and threw myself sideways. I hit the ground hard and rolled back onto my feet, the sword still gripped in hands that shook. The Volker came out of the tunnel and launched at me. I dropped low and thrust the sword up as it soared over the top of me. The blade's sharp tip sliced through armor and skin with ease, showering me with stinking blood and gore. A scream rent the air, a sound all but lost to the growing cacophony of destruction that surrounded us. The Volker hit the ground, swung around, and unleashed a hellfire of greeny-gold.

I did the only thing I could do.

I threw myself over the ledge.

The biped's scream followed me down, but he didn't fire. Instead, he leapt after me.

I'd forgotten just how well they could clamber up and down mountainsides.

I shoved the sword into the ledge's wall and came to an abrupt halt, hitting the wall hard enough to force a grunt. I sucked in air, thrust my left foot into a fissure to give me stability, hooked the crook of my arm around the sword's hilt, and then drew the knife. Air stirred. I glanced up to see the Volker's claws slashing toward my face. I raised the knife, blocked the blow with the blade. Flesh was no impediment for a weapon that could cut stone and the biped's hand tumbled past me.

But he wasn't yet finished. He dug his remaining claws into the wall and lashed out with his feet. Again, I countered the blow with the blade, but he somehow twisted in midair; one foot connected with the side of my head and smashed it back against the wall. As stars danced, unconsciousness loomed, and with the realization that death would be my fate if I didn't finish this biped, I finally reached for the earth.

Smother him.

She did. Quickly.

For several seconds, I didn't move. Couldn't move. My head felt like it was splitting apart and consciousness was a heartbeat away from giving up.

But I'd come this far. I had to at least try to get out of this place.

Steps, the earth whispered. *Use them.*

I looked left and realized that the mages' stone steps had been thrust sideways by one of the tremors and were now within reach. I shoved the knife into the wall, shifted my grip and balance to it, and then drew the sword out and repeated the process until I reached the steps. I stumbled down them and finally reached the cavern floor. Elation surged, but it was short-lived. The tunnel I'd used to access this area had collapsed. The only sign it had ever existed was the pile of stone that had tumbled down the slope with me.

Despair surged but quickly died under the rush of determination. One exit might have closed, but there'd have to be others, given this entire region was riddled with tubes and crevices.

I ran on, but keeping any sort of pace was becoming more and more difficult. Not only because my strength was waning as fast as the thick, sticky moisture pouring down the left side of my face, but because the earth's violence was shattering stalactites and sending them hurtling to the ground. I had no idea how close the volcano was to eruption and no desire to find out. I had to get out of here. Had to.

As the rain of stalactites increased, the air stirred around me, a gentle caress that promised safety. But my legs were trembling, my head booming, and my vision was fading in and out. Only utter stubbornness was keeping me going, and even that would only last so long.

Then I heard it. A thunderous boom shook the air and the earth. It knocked me off my feet and sent me crashing down onto all fours. I tried to push up, only to be knocked down again. Felt the ground around me shudder and shake violently. Smelled ash and heat and death.

Heard another huge boom, this time from up ahead. Saw a huge chunk of ceiling splinter and fall. Saw the distant flags of pink and yellow glowing in skies still held by night.

Safety. So near and yet so far.

Not far, the wind whispered. She wrapped around me, cocooned me, then lifted me up and carried me away from destruction and death.

Against all the odds, I survived.

Tears once again stung my eyes, and this time I let them fall.

FIFTEEN

I woke to the all too familiar feeling of being watched. A smile twitched my lips, but I didn't immediately open my eyes. Aside from the steady beeping coming from my left—one that matched the beat of my heart—the room was silent. But people moved through the corridors beyond, their laughter and conversation filling the air with noise and happiness. There was no tension evident, no hint of danger or fear, which suggested the Volker were no longer a threat.

Aside from the lingering pain in my head and an odd tightness near my left ear and cheek, I felt better—stronger —than I had in ages. I wasn't wrapped in bandages, my limbs were free of pain, and my fingers and toes all responded. All of which was something of a miracle—especially considering I'd been so certain death would be my fate, not life.

Donal was sitting in a chair to my right, his feet propped up on the end of the bed. There were circles under his eyes and a heavy air of tiredness surrounding him. The smile that tugged his lips when my gaze met his was warm, but it fled all too quickly.

"About time you woke," he said, his voice neutral. "I was beginning to think you intended to sleep the entire week away. How do you feel, your majesty?"

"Other than a lingering headache, everything seems to be in working order." His sudden formality—distance, even —had uncertainty surging. I'd expected a certain amount of anger, but not this. "How long have I been out?"

"Six days, three hours, and seventeen minutes. Not that I was clock-watching or anything."

I snorted softly and pushed upright, being careful not to disturb the IVs in my arm. "I take it we're still in Rodestat?"

He nodded. "The medics didn't want you moved anywhere until you'd gained consciousness."

Suggesting they'd thought it possible I might not. "What's happened with the Volker?"

"The Gigurri mages undermined their domes as planned. The bipeds who survived our attack and that of the Skaran are on the run back to their volcano."

"Did we take much in the way of casualties?"

"Plenty, but that's to be expected in any war."

His replies remained perfunctory. I hesitated, and then said softly, "I'm sorry, Donal, but it was necessary—"

"No," he cut in, "it wasn't. You should have trusted me, Princess."

"I did—I *do*. But the runes in the sword spoke of death, and I couldn't bear the thought of taking you down with me."

"That choice was mine to make, not yours."

"I know. I just—" I hesitated again. There was nothing to be read in either his expression or his body language. Whatever he might be feeling, it was well and truly locked down. And that scared me. Seriously scared me. I took a deep breath and released it slowly. "I know I betrayed your trust, but you have to believe I did it for the right reasons."

He raised an eyebrow. "If death by your side was to be my fate, then I would have accepted it gladly."

"But I *couldn't*," I bit back fiercely. "I wanted you to live. I *needed* you to live."

"Why?"

I opened my mouth to reply, then closed it again. Uncertainty stirred through me. Uncertainty and fear. I'd spent so damn long guarding my emotions that it was now hard to release my grip, to set them free.

"Answer the question, Princess."

"Because I wanted you to find what would never be mine."

"And what might that be?"

"Happiness," I muttered. "Love."

That eyebrow rose again. "And how do you know these things would not have been yours?"

Not have been... three words that gripped my throat tight and made it difficult to breathe. Three words that suggested they could have been mine but now weren't.

I swallowed heavily and somehow said, "I did what I believed was right, Donal. Death—"

"Didn't take you, thanks to the timely intervention of the wind."

"*And* the eruption that opened a gigantic hole in the roof and gave you and the wind full access into the cavern." I hesitated. "Did that eruption cause wider damage?"

"No—the mages contained it to the Gulf region."

"At least that's something."

"Yes. And you've yet to fully answer my question."

I stared at him, aware of the gulf growing between us and uncertain how to bridge it. After twelve years of having hopes and dreams crushed, it was hard to step beyond the shelter of self-preservation. Hard to admit my emotions when what I felt was far too new and raw.

"I'm not sure what you want, Donal, but—"

"That," he cut in heavily, "is not the problem here."

I frowned. "I'm not sure what you're expecting given we—"

"All I've ever expected is honesty, Princess. In words, deeds, and emotions. If you can't commit to that, then I can't be here."

He dropped his feet to the floor and rose. Fear clutched at my heart and yet at the same time kept the words I knew he was seeking locked deep inside.

"When you find the answer to my question, you know where to find me."

He leaned over the bed and kissed me. It was so gentle —little more than a brush of lips against lips—and yet it was filled with so much passion and hope that tears stung my eyes.

Then he pulled away, turned around, and walked out of the room. He didn't look back, didn't say goodbye. And, like the fool the king had made me out to be for the last twelve years, I let him go.

I stood in front of the full-length mirror and stared at all my scars. Scars that were new—like the one that ran from my left ear to my cheek, where it met the scar my brother had given me long ago—and scars that were old but nevertheless lifelong reminders of my twelve-year battle to survive.

Then there were the scars nobody could see. Scars that still held sway over my thoughts and actions, even today.

Six months had passed since Donal had walked away. Six months with no contact between us, where I'd vacillated between anger over what he'd said and done, and frustration over what I *hadn't*.

Six months in which—with Jedran and my aunt by my side acting as advisors and guides—I navigated my way through the intricacies of ruling, confirming old alliances and forging new ones with both Chilbra and the De'Lorn Bylands—treaties that were far fairer than either really deserved. I'd also upheld the promise I'd made to Donal at the very start of our journey and written the Home Rule Act into law, giving not only the Westal Ranges the freedom of total self-government while still remaining a part of greater Cannamore but also Mauvaissia.

Donal's father and brother had come to witness the passing of that act, but he'd been conspicuously absent.

It had hurt.

Deeply.

But this time, I could blame no one but myself for that hurt. And there was nothing—absolutely nothing—I could do about it now.

It shouldn't have mattered—not when the dreams that had kept me alive for so long had all come true. I'd taken the sword, claimed the throne, and all of Cannamore was now mine to rule.

But I wasn't happy. Would *never* be happy. Not in this place. Not when the scabs of past indignities and abuse were constantly being torn open by an unguarded sneer or ill-considered comment. Oh, they were all very correct in my presence, but old habits quickly reasserted themselves when they thought I was beyond sight and hearing.

Footsteps approached. I took a deep breath, marshaled

my emotions, and then turned around and held up my hands. "I know, I know, I'm not ready and I should be."

The woman who came into the room was my height, with red-brown skin, darker brown hair, and eyes as green as freshly grown grass. She was also the image of my mother and, even after six months of being in her presence almost daily, grief still rose whenever I saw her. But while I'd lost a mother, she'd lost a sister, and both us had been imprisoned by the will and word of a madman. More than anyone else in this place, she understood what I'd gone through. What I'd suffered.

"Punctuality is a politeness many here don't deserve." She scanned me critically. "If you lose any more weight, you'll be nothing but bone."

"I *am* eating, but it's—"

"Difficult to keep anything down when you're forced to deal with idiots on a daily basis. I know."

A smile twitched my lips. "To put it politely, yes."

She stopped in front of me and pressed her hands to my cheeks. Her skin was warm against mine, her bright gaze understanding, and her wrists free of silver. The bracelets had released the moment my father had died.

"If you're not happy here, Nyx, then do something about it."

"I can't—"

"You can. You *must*." She said it gently but firmly. "You owe these people nothing. You owe the *crown* nothing— certainly not after all you've been through and all you've done. If your heart lies elsewhere, then don't linger here; otherwise, bitterness and hatred will corrupt your soul as thoroughly as it did your father and brother."

"But Mom—"

"Would have, above all else, wanted you to be happy.

Don't go through this coronation if you don't want to sit on the throne for the next sixty or seventy years."

"Tonight's nothing more than a formality. If I was going to back out, I should have done it long ago."

"You're the queen of greater Cannamore. You can do whatever the hell you want."

Amusement bubbled through me. "I wish it was that easy—"

"It *is*."

"I have no successor to claim the sword, and no one I trust beyond you and Jedran. I wouldn't wish this rabble on either of you—not on a full-time basis."

"The fair lords and ladies of the council have a much greater respect for the earth and those who wield her now that the stories of what happened in Mauvaissia and the Karva Pass are circling. Your legend grows."

I snorted. "And yet most here still consider me little more than a common trull—a half-wit who nevertheless needs to be claimed so that they might rule in my stead."

"Those with any sense certainly do *not* think that."

"I'm not sure there are many within the court who could be described as sensible."

"That is, unfortunately, more true than not." A smile touched her lips but failed to touch the seriousness in her eyes. "Jedran wouldn't have accepted the position of regent if he wasn't prepared to rule in your stead should it become necessary."

"Yes, but Gigurri—"

"Yuri has been doing a splendid job in the six months we've been here. She'll be fine."

I tried to make another protest, but she raised a finger, halting my words before they ever passed my lips.

"For the last twelve years, you've lived your life at the

whim of others. Don't let your future be held hostage by duty and expectation if this isn't what you want."

A somewhat bitter smile twisted my lips. "The problem being, if I walk away from this, I have nothing."

"You have us. You have Gigurri. You can live out your life there in whichever way you want. Or you can travel—visit lands near or far. You can set up home in some remote backwater or visit grand palaces on distant shores. The choice is finally yours, Nyx dearest. Don't waste it here if it's not what you want."

"What I want—" I stopped. What I wanted had walked away, and I wasn't entirely sure it had ever been a true possibility anyway.

I took a deep breath and released it slowly. "I'll think about it."

"Good. In the meantime, you'd better get dressed, or the coronation will run into the feasting and the kitchens will be complaining about the impoliteness of queens and food spoilage."

I laughed softly and got dressed. An hour later, I was kneeling in front of the glass throne. Cannamore's finest was gathered behind me, the sword lay gleaming in front of me, and the ceremony was almost at its end. I'd been blessed by the prelate and undertaken the coronation oath. All that was left was the placement of the crown on my head.

I crown I *didn't* want.

I closed my eyes, took a deep breath, and then said, "Stop."

The prelate leaned closer and whispered, "Your majesty, is there something wrong?"

I didn't immediately answer; instead, I pushed to my feet and swung around. Looked at the gathered lords and ladies, some of whom I knew far more intimately than I'd ever wanted or desired. Saw the disdain that many couldn't quite hide.

Saw, too, my brother, a picture of utter misery, and his new mistress—Marttia, who was pregnant with his child. A child she hoped would one day claim *this* throne rather than her own.

Saw Jedran and Helena. Saw the encouragement and understanding in their eyes.

I took another deep breath and said, "Yes, there most certainly *is* a problem."

"Your majesty," the prelate began, but I raised a hand, silencing him.

"The problem, lords and ladies of the court, is not only the fact that I've spent twelve years being forced to cater to your every whim, but for the last six months have had to contain not only my utter hatred but the deep desire to raise the earth and smother the smug contempt from your ugly faces. I've forced myself to act as a queen should, to be fair in all my dealings with you when all I wanted was revenge. But I don't want to spend a lifetime doing that. I don't want to be a part of any more of your false courtship overtures when we all know that what you really want is the throne I hold. So, let me give you all that chance without my body being part of the so-called bargain."

I bent, swept the sword up, and then took two steps forward and thrust her into the glass throne—the real one, not the false. Sparks flew, gold and red stars that twinkled brightly in the white magnificence of the hall.

"Whomsoever draws that sword from the throne shall rule all Cannamore." I turned to face them again. "Until that point, however, my uncle, as regent, will rule in my place. And be warned, lords and ladies, if any of you take action against him or make an attempt to remove him *unless* by right of drawing the sword, I *will* return and take my vengeance."

With that, I picked up my skirts, walked down the platform's steps, and left the hall.

A day later, after goodbyes to Jedran, Helena, and Marttia, I left Divona. And felt as if a great weight had been lifted from my shoulders. For the first time in six months, it felt like I could breathe again.

With a silly grin on my face, I programmed my destination into the unmarked sprinter. It'd take me five days to reach the Blackwater Gateway—the entrance into the Westal Ranges. I had absolutely no idea what sort of reception might await me there, but I had to at least try.

I skirted most of the major cities along the way, preferring to stop in smaller towns where it was unlikely I'd be recognized. It was nice to be treated as an ordinary person, to sit in old taverns in utter anonymity and just enjoy the company and food.

As I neared Seilia, the conversation Donal and Merlyn had had about Faloria, man parts, and lots and lots of booze had me heading toward the capital rather than a much quieter location. It wasn't hard to find such a bar and, after grabbing a large tankard of ale and a platter of meats and breads, I settled down to enjoy the fun. Who knew watching grown men attempting to shoot their load the greatest distance could provide so much hilarity?

A shadow fell over my table midway through proceedings, and an all too familiar voice said, "This is not the sort of establishment in which one expects to find a princess."

My gaze leapt to Donal's. He hadn't physically changed, though I guess that wasn't so surprising given it *had* only been six months since I'd last seen him. He was still a big, powerful man with shaggy brown hair that remained tamed by my somewhat battered silver clasp and a beard that had yet to become fully acquainted with the end of a razor. What had changed—at least from our last restrained and awkward meeting in the hospital room—was his demeanor. His eyes shone and his emotions were very clear—very evident—in his expression and his bright blue eyes.

Any fear I'd held about my reception vanished, and it was all I could do to remain seated, to not get up, throw myself into his arms, and let myself drown in all that desire and love.

But if he wanted to play word games, I was more than happy to do so.

He was here. For me. I knew that. He knew that. Nothing else needed to be said, although it would be.

"That would be queen, if you don't mind," I said, somehow keeping my tone dry. "And isn't this a little far from your usual haunts, highlander?"

"Indeed it is." He pulled up the chair and sat down opposite me. "But I'd heard a runaway queen was in the area, seeking entertainment, and I decided she deserved nothing but the best."

I raised an eyebrow. "I've seen the competition and viewed the goods that would challenge the current participants. I'm not entirely sure the latter qualifies as the best."

"Oh, that cuts, Princess. Deeply."

I grinned. "Of course, to be sure, I'd have to test said goods more thoroughly."

He leaned back in the chair and regarded me steadily. "And is that what you've decided you want? A longer test run?"

"That depends."

"On what?"

"On why the owner of said goods walked the fuck out of my life without ever telling me what he truly wanted or what he felt."

"Ah," he said, amusement evident. "I'm surprised you can't guess."

"If I'd been able to guess, I wouldn't have spent the last six months tying myself in knots over it."

His eyebrows rose and the emotion in his eyes grew stronger. "Does this mean you might care for me?"

"Just answer the damn question, highlander."

He laughed, then leaned forward and caught my hands in his. "Walking out of that room was the hardest thing I've ever had to do in my entire life, but it was very, *very* necessary."

I frowned even as I twined my fingers through his. It was such a little motion, but one that somehow made me feel whole. Complete. "Why?"

"Because for twelve years you'd been forced to obey the rule and desires of others." The amusement fell from his expression—all that remained was compassion. Understanding. *Love.* "I might have released you from the physical shackles, but your thoughts and feelings very much remained locked behind a barrier. Bluntly stating what I wanted would have sent you running."

"Ah," I murmured, a little in awe of just how deeply this man understood me, "so these 'wants' you speak of—what are they, exactly?"

"Are you sure you're ready to hear them?"

"Yes."

"Utterly sure?"

"I will be tempted to violence if you don't get on with it."

He grinned. "I believe it was another such threat—the

offer to kick me in the balls if I so much as took a step in your direction—that made me realize I might have just met my perfect woman."

I lifted a foot and pressed it between his legs. "I will carry through with that threat, you know."

He laughed. "My 'wants' involve you, me, a big old bed—"

"*Only* a bed?" I cut in. "I'm disappointed, highlander."

"Hush, woman, and let me finish."

"Only if you promise not to go on too long. The entertainment is about to start."

He gave me a deadpan look, but his eyes shone. "As I was saying before I was so rudely interrupted, a big old bed and lots and lots of sex. There would also be marriage, and children—lots of them. I want girls with their mother's fierceness and boys with her strength. I want to watch them grow up, grow strong, and go out into the world as happy, whole adults who will conquer said world with you. But most of all, I simply want to spend the rest of my life with you."

"That," I said evenly, "sounds like a plan."

He blinked, and then let out such a fierce whoop that it overran all other sound and had heads turning to see what was going on.

He jumped up, dragged me up into his arms, and kissed me with all the passion I could ever desire.

"So," he said eventually, "how shall we celebrate this momentous occasion? Shall I order a bottle of the establishment's finest?"

"I've tasted this establishment's finest. Trust me, it's unworthy. I have, however, acquired a chamber in a fine establishment only ten minutes down the road. We could retire there and celebrate in private."

434

He raised his eyebrows. "You don't want to stay and watch the entertainment here?"

"I haven't had sex in six months. I very much need to have my wicked way with you."

"Princess," he murmured, his lips brushing mine, "you can have your wicked way with me any time you desire."

I smiled. I'd spent twelve years believing a sword and a throne would be my salvation.

It was rather ironic that it had instead come in the form a Wildman.

A man I loved—and who loved me—with a fierceness I'd never thought possible.

"I'll hold you to that promise, highlander."

"I look forward to it. Shall we go?"

I nodded and held out my hand. He wrapped his fingers around mine, and as one, we walked out of the tavern to my chamber, where we did indeed celebrate long into the night.

It was a pretty perfect start for what was to be the rest of my life.

ABOUT THE AUTHOR

Keri Arthur, author of the New York Times bestselling Riley Jenson Guardian series, has now written more than thirty-nine novels. She's received several nominations in the Best Contemporary Paranormal category of the Romantic Times Reviewers Choice Awards and has won RT's Career Achievement Award for urban fantasy. She lives with her daughter in Melbourne, Australia.

for more information:
www.keriarthur.com
kez@keriarthur.com

ALSO BY KERI ARTHUR

Kingdoms of Earth & Air
Unlit (May 2018)
Cursed (Nov 2018)

Lizzie Grace series
Blood Kissed (May 2017)
Hell's Bell (Feb 2018)
Hunter Hunted (Aug 2018)
Demon's Dance (Feb 2019)

The Outcast series
City of Light (Jan 2016)
Winter Halo (Nov 2016)
The Black Tide (Dec 2017)

Souls of Fire series
Fireborn (July 2014)
Wicked Embers (July 2015)
Flameout (July 2016)
Ashes Reborn (Sept 2017)

Dark Angels series
Darkness Unbound (Sept 27th 2011)

Darkness Rising (Oct 26th 2011)

Darkness Devours (July 5th 2012)

Darkness Hunts (Nov 6th 2012)

Darkness Unmasked (June 4 2013)

Darkness Splintered (Nov 2013)

Darkness Falls (Dec 2014)

Riley Jenson Guardian Series

Full Moon Rising (Dec 2006)

Kissing Sin (Jan 2007)

Tempting Evil (Feb 2007)

Dangerous Games (March 2007)

Embraced by Darkness (July 2007)

The Darkest Kiss (April 2008)

Deadly Desire (March 2009)

Bound to Shadows (Oct 2009)

Moon Sworn (May 2010)

Myth and Magic series

Destiny Kills (Oct 2008)

Mercy Burns (March 2011)

Nikki & Micheal series

Dancing with the Devil (March 2001 / Aug 2013)

Hearts in Darkness Dec (2001/ Sept 2013)

Chasing the Shadows Nov (2002/Oct 2013)

Kiss the Night Goodbye (March 2004/Nov 2013)

Damask Circle series
Circle of Fire (Aug 2010 / Feb 2014)
Circle of Death (July 2002/March 2014)
Circle of Desire (July 2003/April 2014)

Ripple Creek series
Beneath a Rising Moon (June 2003/July 2012)
Beneath a Darkening Moon (Dec 2004/Oct 2012)

Spook Squad series
Memory Zero (June 2004/26 Aug 2014)
Generation 18 (Sept 2004/30 Sept 2014)
Penumbra (Nov 2005/29 Oct 2014)

Stand Alone Novels
Who Needs Enemies (E-book only, Sept 1 2013)

Novella
Lifemate Connections (March 2007)

Anthology Short Stories
The Mammoth Book of Vampire Romance (2008)
Wolfbane and Mistletoe--2008
Hotter than Hell--2008

CPSIA information can be obtained
at www.ICGtesting.com
Printed in the USA
LVHW050039230520
656338LV00001B/52